THE
PENGUIN BOOK
of the

CONTEMPORARY BRITISH SHORT STORY

―――

Selected and Introduced by
PHILIP HENSHER

PENGUIN BOOKS

PENGUIN CLASSICS

UK | USA | Canada | Ireland | Australia
India | New Zealand | South Africa

Penguin Books is part of the Penguin Random House group of companies
whose addresses can be found at global.penguinrandomhouse.com.

This collection first published in Penguin Classics 2018
001

Introduction and selection copyright © Philip Hensher, 2018
The acknowledgements on pp. 408–10 constitute an extension of this copyright page

The moral right of the editor has been asserted

Set in 11.25/14.75 pt Adobe Caslon Pro
Typeset by Jouve (UK), Milton Keynes
Printed and bound in Great Britain by Clays Ltd, Elcograf S.p.A.

A CIP catalogue record for this book is available from the British Library

ISBN: 978-0-241-34746-1

The Penguin Book of the Contemporary British Short Story

Contents

Contents

MEN

WOMEN

Contents

WAR & POLITICS

CATASTROPHIC WORLDS

ENVOI

Introduction

Two years ago, I edited *The Penguin Book of the British Short Story*, an anthology that sought to show the history of the short story in this country since 1700 or so. Although the anthology had been commissioned on a very generous scale, and although it contained ninety writers, it necessarily omitted some well-known names. In my view, there was a special case for exploring contemporary short-story writers in more detail. This is an attempt to survey the best British short-story writers of the last twenty years, and to suggest what the short story still does well. The British short story is still producing masterpieces. The sad fact is that the mechanisms for bringing those masterpieces to a reading public have become grossly defective.

Writers are inventive, responsive people, and literary genres have a habit of changing shape as circumstances change. The short story emerged from a miscellaneous bundle of small-scale prose forms sometime in the nineteenth century: it flourished with most splendour in the period of magazines between the introduction of universal education and the rise of the cinema; it went on being supported by publishers' faith in the single-author collection and a steadily shrinking number of magazines at least to the end of the twentieth century. Since then, circumstances have changed somewhat. In putting together this anthology of British short stories written and published in the last twenty years, I was struck by the energy with which writers have managed to make their work happen. Looking at it from one point of view, circumstances have made the writing of short stories more difficult. But nobody ever said it was going to be easy.

It is important to decide what 'contemporary' might mean. At many moments in the past, this decision would have been challenging. In 2018, I found the answer quite obvious. This anthology of contemporary British short stories takes the year 1997 as its starting point, for five reasons. The first two are moments in British history. The election of Tony Blair's government on 2 May 1997, in a colossal landslide, was widely experienced as a change in the national mood; Blair's Labour Party had spent eighteen years in opposition. The second apparently decisive event of that year was the violent death of Diana, Princess of Wales, and the days of wild national mourning that followed. Both events were experienced by those who lived through them as revealing huge changes in the nation's psyche and manners – apparently more open and kindly, at ease with a higher emotional temperature and the proximity of others.

We can debate endlessly what effect such occasions had on literature in general, or on the specific genre of the short story. Another two events around that time may be more precisely quantified. The first was an assault on the cost of literature, with the declaration of the Restrictive Practices Court in March 1997 that the Net Book Agreement was against the public interest and therefore illegal. The Net Book Agreement had been in existence since 1900, and allowed publishers to set the prices of their books. With the removal of the Net Book Agreement, the price of books plummeted, and never recovered. (My second novel, published in 1996, was priced by the publisher at £17.99; my tenth novel, published in 2018, was priced at £14.99 before any discounting.)

The fourth change of mood must be the most far-reaching. I would say that around 1997, the Internet and the mobile telephone established themselves as necessities in the lives of a Western democracy like Britain. I had a mobile phone and an email account at work in 1995, and wrote a short story about the Internet in 1996. The Internet, it now seems plain, has changed everything. Plenty of pundits believe that habitual use of the Internet changes ways of thinking. It seems plausible. In the spring of 2017, I switched off all devices for a fortnight; the pleasure in reading I rediscovered was very marked, and the classics sprang to life again. Such a change in thinking, and the style in which we are likely to encounter writing, must engender a substantial change in expression. It is one of the aims of this anthology to reintroduce the reader to the practitioners of extravagant, colourful, comedic, outward-facing writing; which, it sometimes seems to me, our Internet habits have replaced with an ineffective, affectless, colourless, solipsistic style that nobody much likes anyway.

The fifth event was a more symbolic one, a quiet ending. The predecessor to this anthology, *The Penguin Book of the British Short Story*, came out in 2016. After reading for two years to prepare for that, I came to the firm conclusion that the greatest of all British short-story writers was V. S. Pritchett. Pritchett died on 20 March 1997, revered and respected, but less of a living influence than he might be. Pritchett's virtues – a freshness of human observation, the unique phrase, the love of crowded narratives and the ability to write across a social range – ought to be as vital today as they ever were. But there is no doubt that Pritchett's death, and the death of his influence, marks the end of a chapter.

3

The ways in which literature might reach a reader are changing. Some traditional means of short-story publication have more or less disappeared. Very few periodicals can, or will, pay for a short story. Other means, however, have arisen and may offer new opportunities. It is possible for a short-story writer, even a totally untried one, to publish a single short story as an e-book. If a work of literature exists only in virtual form, there is no reason why an author should not explore the possibilities of million-word novels, or stand-alone short stories twenty words long. The tyranny that tied short fiction to periodical publication, or to appear in a collection or an anthology, has been overthrown. An author may try to establish the market value of his own work; and if that value is zero, he may still publish his work for no charge, and find readers. Possibilities for short fiction are still being discovered.

The decline of magazine publication should not particularly matter. A writer can, after all, find a paying readership without much trouble. This excellent opportunity has not been taken up. Writers always need a readership, and not just a sponsor of donations. The curious fact is that the literary ecology is now well structured to allow writers of short stories to reach a public. Three things would greatly help the connection between readers and writers. First, newspapers could very easily incorporate a weekly short story in their online versions. They might become as standard a part of a newspaper's structure as, say, the celebrity interview, and rather more rewarding. Second, mainstream publishers should start to think of the possibilities of publishing single short stories in digital form, charging accordingly. The potential of a popular writer such as Mark Haddon, interested in writing short fiction, is certainly not harnessed by the whims of commissioning editors. His publisher should think it possible to put out a short story whenever he writes one at 99p a pop. Third, when collections, or indeed anthologies like this one, are published by mainstream publishers, it should be possible for interested readers to buy (some) single stories from the collection, in exactly the same way that it is possible either to purchase an entire album of a music artiste, or the recording of a whole opera, or, if one's interest is more casual, just to pay 99p for the 'Liebestod' or a particular dance track. These steps might serve to re-establish a relationship between an author and his or her readers that is currently rather attenuated. He or she could instantly see which stories readers liked best. This relationship has been maintained by genre writers, and by the army of self-published writers; it could usefully be reintroduced to all writers of short fiction.

What currently structures public attention towards short fiction, alas, is the literary competition. Literary competitions are, in my view, mostly harmless if they form part of a healthy ecology. There ought to be a number of ways in which a work of fiction is recommended to the market, of which competitions are only one. The problem is simply that there is no market, and the only readership many short-story writers seem to envisage is that of the members of a judging panel. The idea that one might write a story to interest a wider readership, and that a prize's only function is to draw the attention of that wider readership to an excellent piece of writing, seems beyond the comprehension of writers and the organizers of prizes. A story is written to satisfy the strictures of a judging panel; the panel awards a prize and a cheque; nobody else reads the story, or is intended to. Readers have been replaced by patrons who are not even risking their own money, and the results are unappealing. Just as medieval princes paid monks to pray on their behalf, having better things to do, so we pay provincial dons and actors between engagements to sit and read a hundred humourless two-handers about war crimes in Taiwan before declaring one of them to be worthy of the cheque, though not of readers. In my view, short-story competitions have actually destroyed the readership of short stories, by elevating and promoting a style of writing which, demonstrably, nobody wants to read.

Quite a lot of the reading for this book was wasted looking at short stories that had been shortlisted for, or had even won, some very well-funded prizes. Very few of these had any literary merit. I quickly came to the conclusion that the judges had no means of assessing literary merit other than the gravity of a subject and what they knew about an author, usually his or her sex. Sometimes a prize jury would state the usual banality about a short story being a form in which not a single word was wasted, before handing the cheque over for a story containing the sentence 'I think to myself, again, what does it matter?'

Literary quality is ultimately subjective; there may even be people who believe the expression 'She thought to herself' the height of meaningfully concise writing. There is no dispute, however, over the fact that short-story prizes do precisely nothing to recommend a writer to a readership. The rather melancholy case here is a writer called Jonathan Tel. Mr Tel has done very well indeed with prize juries. Short stories of his have won the Commonwealth Prize, the V. S. Pritchett Prize, and the best-publicized of all short-story prizes, the *Sunday Times* Prize, which hands over £30,000. Everything that short-story competitions could do for a writer has been done for Mr Tel. He has published two short-story collections, in 2002 and 2009. At the end of November 2017, after his name had been brought to the British public in such magnificent style and the public had had the opportunity to react, I thought I would look at the sales figures of his two books. According to BookScan, in fifteen and eight years respectively since their publication, his two collections have sold seventeen copies each.

An alternative method of measuring success appeared as I was preparing this anthology, from another culture. The *New Yorker*, which has gone on promoting and publishing short stories, published a short story called 'Cat Person' by an unknown writer, Kristen Roupenian. They liked it, and they thought that it was likely to interest their readers. It was about a subject very much on the communal mind and in the news, sexual consent, and gave an account of a sad and uncertain wooing. The story, despite its author's lack of previous reputation, made an enormous and immediate impact on readers, who were quickly to be found discussing it in all sorts of forums. The publication of 'Cat Person' exactly repeated one of the most celebrated reader responses of the twentieth century, when in June 1948 the *New Yorker* published Shirley Jackson's 'The Lottery'. The magazine, in publishing Roupenian's story, had acutely judged the interests and tastes of its readers. Publishers quickly moved in, and in the days after the publication of 'Cat Person' it was reported that Roupenian had been offered over a million dollars for a short-story collection. The episode demonstrates that there is, after all, a free, interested and engaged public for short fiction. It is a great shame that the effective mechanism for bringing a talented new author of short fiction to a wide and engaged readership through periodical publication hardly exists any longer in the UK.

4

The publication of short fiction in the UK is steadily shifting towards the publication of collections. It is certainly true that most readers will encounter short stories within collections rather than, as in the past, in magazine publication. It is also shifting towards hybrid forms between the novel and the short-story collection. It has long been established among writers that a publisher will look more favourably on collections of short fiction if they have a clear single setting, such as James Joyce's *Dubliners* or Jon McGregor's *This Isn't the Sort of Thing That Happens to Someone Like You*, or a single theme, as in Helen Simpson's collections. In recent decades, a hybrid form has become more common, in which a collection of connected but distinct narratives may be justly regarded as either a short-story collection or a novel. Some of the best short fiction in recent years will be found embedded in works of this kind, including several books by Rachel Cusk, Tim Winton's *Turning* and David Mitchell's *Cloud Atlas*. After some reflection, I thought it would in most cases be wrong to fillet a longer work to extricate a short story; Cusk's connected narratives are so beautifully balanced that anyone who knew the whole work could only regard an extract as a bleeding chunk. Some of the short stories in this anthology, nevertheless, have implications that are only fully explored in their original context; Kazuo Ishiguro's story, from a collection of refined echoes and repetitions, is an example. The one indubitable bleeding chunk I took is David Szalay's story, the second chapter of a marvellous novel, *All That Man Is*. The chapter is an entirely self-contained story, and a beautifully classical short story at that. There is no doubt, however, that it is also a chapter of a novel, one of a steadily advancing narrative line. Its inclusion here should suggest that there is no need to decide in every case what, precisely, a work of literature is. The debate about whether a book is a novel or a collection of stories may, in time, come to resemble the question of whether the *Faerie Queene* is an epic or a romance, and be just as irrelevant to most readers.

The form is becoming hybrid in other ways unanticipated by previous generations. The very short short story, of a matter of a few words, had for years been a parlour game, such as the 100-word short-story form known for some reason as a 'drabble'. More recently it had become the academic creative writing exercise known as 'flash fiction'. Although neither of these was really intended to acquire an audience, the scale of academic creative writing in universities undoubtedly created a substantial readership who had an interest in the very short short story. There is no British writer in the form to match the American Lydia Davis as yet: I was rather tempted to include one of James Robertson's one-a-day stories from *365*, but a single example looked exceedingly odd in context. Hybridity may be approaching from another direction. In 2017, the Welsh author Cynan Jones was awarded the BBC National Short Story Award for a piece of writing called 'The Edge of the Shoal', described by one of the judges as 'as perfect a short story as I've ever read'. The story, however, was an abridged version – not an extract, but a complete abridgement – of Jones's previously published novel *Cove*. Neither the award, nor the judges, nor the author, made any acknowledgement of the status of the winning entry as an abridged novel rather than a conventional short story. Might it be that the long and unrespectable history of the abridged novel might be entering into the genre of the short story? Can we expect a prestissimo, 6,000-word version of a Robert Harris thriller to be rewarded with prizes and acclaim in the same way that Jones's 'short story' was? This kind of hybridity might well lead to an increase in energy in the form in general.

5

The anthology is arranged under six general themes, quite widely interpreted. The first theme I chose is love. The examination of love is as old as literature, and is constantly rediscovered and made new by writers. A. L. Kennedy's transfixing story focuses on the roads taken and not taken in an illicit relationship; it branches and divides in ways not like anything seen before. One of the best new strains of recent British literature has been the prominence of lesbian writers, and Jackie Kay's 'Physics and Chemistry' is conscious of exploring a marriage which is discovering all sorts of conventions for itself, and telling a story which, like all marriages, is very familiar and completely unique. Love is not just romantic love, of course: what being a parent means – taking charge of a helpless child – enriches the sad, wise and inspiring stories of Tessa Hadley and Jane Gardam. The triumph of a love that is voluntary and not obligatory at the climax of Hadley's 'Funny Little Snake' is as concrete and exhilarating as Charles Dickens's Betsey Trotwood evicting Jane Murdstone in the words 'Let me see you ride a donkey over *my* green again, and as sure as you have a head upon your shoulders, I'll knock your bonnet off.' Love is important in life because it usually introduces us to the notion that other people have other ideas about their happiness. It becomes important in literature because literature cannot do without conflicting identities, and irreconcilable differences. The revelations of difference and disappointment in the Ishiguro and Graham Swift stories are not statements of disillusionment in romantic love; they are sad celebrations of how different and surprising people always are, and how love and surrender, even for a time, are precious overcomings of a fundamental truth.

A self-consciousness about story was a very common preoccupation in the stories I considered. I wondered whether the increasing difficulty writers faced in publishing individual short stories was a concern that had tried to elevate itself above the self-interested and into expressions of doubt about literary principles. Was it worth writing any of this at all? Let us respond with a short story beginning with the italicized word *Listen*. Like any fashionable theme, it has quickly allowed its own conventions to harden. One absurdly prevalent mode is the single character monologue written in the second-person present tense, something that has become completely conventional while hardly ever appealing to a paying customer. I thought I did not need to trouble about the many stories set in creative-writing classes, the ones that recapitulated the overture to *If on a Winter's Night a Traveller*, or the many that incorporated a novelist as the main character. These seemed fairly deadly to me. They were, overwhelmingly, an imitation of rebellion and subversion that was actually a sort of panicked huddling together, for warmth. But there was a good strain of original and quirky minds who had really thought about what a story was doing, conjuring up a possible world in one word after another. Ali Smith's wonderful story makes you feel the act of creation, spinning a reality with what seems like great fragility, and ultimately is of great solidity. The ongoing presence of the Gothic is a joy: both Neil Gaiman and China Miéville seem to draw on classics of the genre, Robert Aickman and M. R. James. Miéville's approach is an unforgettable reflection on the transmission of ideas, and ultimately of what a memorable story might be doing to us. I wondered, a year after I first read it, about the sinister truth that I could still remember the deadly word, and might one day, I hope not with malign intent, mention it to another person. Martin Amis's story is not, perhaps, a story; he presents it as a fragment of a fictional project, like Waugh's *Work Suspended*. (A work rightly included in Waugh's collected stories.) It is a superb examination of propriety and comedy, of what we might feel is the rightful ground of literature and the ways in which the commissars of public utterance have produced rules about words and literary forms. It is one of the most thought-provoking statements about what may be said about Islamist terror, and it comes (of course) in the form of fiction. Finally in this group an underrated but brilliant writer, Peter Hobbs, and a glorious piece of what-the-heck pastiche and playfulness and one-thing-after-another. It reminded me of the pleasures a story can offer, even one that makes no sense at all.

At previous times, short fiction was a useful way for the best and most responsive writers of the time to comment on current events. I noted in the introduction to my previous Penguin anthology how the first short stories about the outbreak of war appeared within days of the real thing. That possibility has largely been removed. I had the unusual experience recently of having a short story commissioned and accepted by a newspaper, and then being told that it could not be run because it contained a reference to a historic terrorist attack, and another had just taken place in real life. A previous age might have thought that this was a good moment to start talking. Without a relationship to real current events, the nearest comparable area of energy is in a much-discussed subject, the nature of gender, and what men and women are supposed to be. The eruption of splendid energy and comedy in the stories by Thomas Morris and David Szalay came as a great relief among acres of humourless writing. Comedy is one of the British short story's historical excellences, and one which the competition culture has effectively repressed – no one ambitious would expect a prize jury to reward a funny story, even ones as thoughtful and resonant as these. There has been a surprising decline in the number of good gay male short-story writers, considering how important they were during the whole twentieth century, but both Morris and Irvine Welsh (themselves heterosexual) take on the subject of gay sexuality and show how violently traumatic it remains for outsiders to contemplate. Masculine tenderness in an unexpected setting was beautifully new: David Rose's story had a real freshness and honesty.

Some viewpoints would now insist that the short story is actually a woman's form. Some commentators on my previous anthology expressed astonishment that I had not been able to achieve equality in the representation of the sexes, without being able to suggest many of the names of eighteenth- and nineteenth-century women writers who had been wilfully omitted. As in the previous anthology, parity of achievement in publication is reflected in the representation of the sexes – in the previous anthology, from 1950 onwards, and here throughout. Writing about women's roles has acquired a conventionality, too, but there is a good deal of surprising energy. Rose Tremain unpicks the ideas of the ways women might be permitted to behave in a historical context with a good deal of pleasure; the pursuit of possibilities is core territory for the short story, as well as for the ways women might think about their liberation. Education has an important presence in Lucy Caldwell's marvellous and, for once, funny story, full of local detail. Helen Simpson has made a particular sort of moneyed London domesticity her subject, which chimes exactly with her readership. Here thoughts of death start to change things, and an unpredictability of tone I found very alluring. That unpredictability of tone may be a feminine virtue: it certainly animates Helen Oyeyemi's splendid story, in which we hardly know what to think of anything that happens, or anyone involved. Leone Ross was one of my most enjoyable discoveries: when too many writers seem to come from the same sort of background and share the same ways of looking at the world, Ross had a wonderfully overripe vision of physical pleasures, revenge, excess, restaurants and indulgence. Here was a writer that Angela Carter would have enjoyed.

Some of the most powerful and complex writers were drawn, it was clear, to an unfashionable subject, political activity. Gerard Woodward's transfixing story makes us understand what political violence and power really mean: it has a simple but unbeatable strategy, of retelling a political coup – perhaps the last days of the Ceaușescus – in an English context, with English names. He is one of the most unfailingly empathetic of English writers – a quality which does not exclude judgement – and here we have the dizzying sensation of being invited to share that capacity for empathy. Will Self's 'The Rock of Crack as Big as the Ritz' is an extraordinarily wild invention, but underpinning everything is the destruction wrought by public violence: the experience of war is not an ornamental decision here. Zadie Smith is building a body of work that will prove her one of the best of short-story writers. This one, first published like much of her fiction in the *New Yorker*, reaches out to a fraying part of the world, where dignity and status have to be insisted on: there is a fruitful echo of one of the greatest moments of recent British fiction, the central narrative of V. S. Naipaul's *In a Free State*. James Kelman's disenfranchised and difficult voice can be a matter of abrupt assault: it perfectly forms a violent utterance about people coming together, or not together, in rage or perhaps protest, of being accepted and being pulled along. It is unspecific, and yet possesses a tremendous sense of range and possibility. More politics – by which I don't mean more overt political commitment to the approved positions of the lumpenintelligentsia – would be very good for the state of the British short story.

Disaster, and the horrors of the world, haunt these writers. I suppose many of them live in a vulnerable professional state – if you are a writer under forty, you are not very likely to be able to afford to buy anywhere to live in the UK, for instance. Immediate and personal concerns may in some cases be artistically transformed into more apocalyptic accounts of climate change or brutal catastrophe. Or it may just be a general sense of things going wrong in general, which much of this generation of writers has had since the financial collapse of 2008. Lucy Wood is an intensely local writer, but this Ionesco-like fable of crap filling up, of the compulsions and duties and obligations of old age, is not just Cornish in its power. Like a particular sort of the best writing, its pages almost stink. Hilary Mantel's catastrophe is at once historic, brutally paternalistic, and individual: she knows how long-ago obliteration marks people in their every living moment. Eley Williams is a writer of almost excessive intimacy – she has spoken in interviews about her sense that the short story dwells on a single character in reflection. I quite disagree with this, but the exquisite nature of her handling is always apparent, most effective when applied to brutal, if small-scale violence, and at its best when it starts, against its writer's best intentions, to engage with rich social interaction. Sarah Hall is an expert writer whose expertise has been clearly formed by a serious engagement with creative writing courses. This story is perhaps the most conventional in the book, in contemporary terms: it engages with climate change, and it forms an obvious variation on one of the most commonly taught short stories in British creative writing classes, Eudora Welty's 'A Worn Path'. But the story possesses its own energy, and the imagining of a world of wind is exact and evocative. There are plenty of bad writers in Hall's vein: she is a very good writer, working within publicly accepted conventions. Nobody could describe Mark Haddon as a conventional writer. His best writing has drawn large audiences by its startling newness of form. This magnificent story is a ruthless *machine à raconter*. Once the procedure is set in motion, nothing will or may intervene. It reminded me of one of the greatest of such *machines*, Tolstoy's 'How Much Land Does a Man Need?'.

I wanted to finish the anthology with one of the writers I most regretted having to leave out of my previous anthology, Helen Dunmore. Helen Dunmore, who died in June 2017, was a rare writer who constantly looked outwards, and who wrote at a very high level in long and short fiction and poetry: everything she wrote had a respect for the form's possibilities, and an unmistakable mark of her own personality. She was a generous writer who was interested in a good deal that was unconnected to her own existence, and this final superb story, looking out into a Europe floating between existences and utterly specific, seemed a good place to end. Britain, as I write, seems determined to turn its back and look inwards. This last story, like *Beowulf,* the first work of English literature, does what our literature has always done, and looks abroad, looks at foreigners, looks at the dissimilar and the other, looks hard at other people and not just at ourselves. If there is a way forward for short fiction in Britain or anywhere else, it must be here.

Philip Hensher,
2018

LOVE

A. L. KENNEDY

Spared

Things could go wrong with one letter, he knew that now. Just one.

'Actually, I moved here ten years ago.'

He had found it so terribly, pleasantly effortless to say, 'Actually, I moved here ten years ago.'

There had only been a little thickness about the *m*, a tiny falter there that might have suggested a stammer, or a moment's pause to let him total up those years. Nobody listening, surely, would have guessed his intended sentence had been, 'Actually, I'm married.' In the course of one consonant everything had changed.

He'd been standing in the cheese queue. His bright idea: to visit the cheese shop, the specialist. Even though such places annoyed him and made him think there was too much money in the world being spent in far too many stupid ways, he had gone to the purveyors of nothing but cheese and things cheese-related to buy something nice for Christmas, a treat. Of course, thirty other people had been taken with the same idea and were lined right through and out of the shop and then along the pavement, all variously huddled and leaning away from the intermittent press of sleety rain. There was an awning, but it didn't help. And, at that point, he should simply have gone home, but for no particular reason, he did not.

Instead, he stood and turned up his collar and peered, like everyone else, into the cheese-shop window where the cheesemongers, busy and vaguely smug, trotted about in white wellingtons, white jackets, white hats. The facts that he personally didn't much like cheese, that his gloves were back, safe and warm, in the car, and that any wait here now would be quite ludicrously dismal – none of these disturbed him. On the contrary, they seemed perversely satisfying: a rare chance to perform an unpleasant task that was wholly of his own choosing.

His satisfaction had, quite reasonably, produced a happy kind of pressure in his chest which had caused him to turn and say, really to no one, 'They look like dentists, don't they?' and then to smile.

'Yes, dentists. Or maybe vets. Cheese vets.'

And he'd been mildly aware of a girl in the shop window smoothly drawing down a wire and opening up the white heart of something or other with one slice, but mainly there'd been this woman standing behind him in the queue, this woman he had never met, and then there'd been this thought which had said very softly but unmistakably, *My God, she has a wonderful voice.* This thought which had seemed just as confident and hungry as he'd always meant and never quite managed to be.

Although, truthfully, what it said wasn't really right – she had a perfect voice.

He could almost hear her now, if he concentrated: lying awake – as usual awake – and grinning like a night light, because he could imagine the flavour of her *maybe* and her *yes.*

His right arm, the one that was furthest from Karen in their bed, the one that was his least matrimonial arm, was crooked up to let his wrist settle in nicely under his head and make him, at least, a comfortable insomniac. He was trying to breathe as if he wasn't conscious, wasn't turning helplessly inside his kicking mind, wasn't opening and closing his eyes between one type of blank and another to see which was best as a background for the image of a woman who wasn't Karen, who wasn't in any way his wife.

Dark coat, mainly dark with water, but also sensible and warm – his mind now slipped away to thoughts of silky linings, but he pulled it back – a golden-coloured scarf that covered up her chin – he did like that – and then one of those horrible hill-walker's fleecy hats which, in this case, looked fantastic because it was hers, she was wearing it.

He had been immediately, impossibly, mortally charmed. The truth of this made a brief swell in his breathing, followed by a sigh.

'Greg, *please.*' By which Karen didn't mean, 'Greg, *please* torment me with your luscious manhood now and for the rest of the night until I speak in tongues.' She meant – half asleep, but still determined, she always was determined – 'Greg, *please* either fall asleep now or go to the spare room

4

and give me peace, because I've got to get up for work tomorrow morning, just as early as you do.'

So, like a dutiful and undisturbing partner, he slid out of bed on to one braced arm, one knee, and then staggered softly up into a standing position and took himself away. This had happened before the cheese queue, this type of midnight banishment: Greg hadn't really slept well in months. The muffling of the pillow at his ears could very easily make him picture coffins and drowsiness often produced a sensation of morbid, jerked descent, as if into a curiously sticky grave. He suffered from nocturnal sweats.

By the time he had joked to Karen over breakfast that fixing up a variation on a Victorian casket alarm might keep him calmer, she hadn't found his difficulties funny. He had tried, although he was extremely tired, to be more playful, to expand the idea, suggesting that he really should tie one finger with thread in the hope that his subconscious might believe itself safely connected to the brand of handy little bell designed, in a more cautious age, to prevent premature burial.

'You should try the pills again – break the cycle.'

'The pills made me sleep in the daytime. I can't keep being discovered in the office with my head on the desk, people will end up thinking I have a life.' This said in a self-deprecating and not vicious way, but all the same.

'You *do* have a life. It just seems incompatible with mine.' *This* said in a way that was a little light-hearted, but with eyes that fixed him for a threatening moment before she went to turn over the toast. 'We should get a toaster.'

'I'll get one.'

'You'll forget, you always forget.'

'I'll get one. Tomorrow: I can't today.'

'Mm hm.'

Greg loathed the way she did that; closing everything off with her favourite passive/aggressive little noise, the agreement that didn't agree – *Mm hm.*

'Mm hm.'

In other times, though, in other places, it was a good sound to make. In that other time, that other place, it had been the best, 'Mm hm. They could be vets, couldn't they . . . Yes.'

He settled his limbs out in the chill of the spare bed and recalled the horrifying pause when the conversation might have faltered, stopped, and left him to the queue, let his head go sliding under, back into the fetid sump that held his nights and days. He'd known, in a way that made his ears ache, that he hated his shoes, his not waterproof shoes, and that his latest haircut had been shoddy and would look especially dreadful when it was wet and that naked drips of rain were clinging just exactly where they shouldn't on his face: like unwanted ear-rings, tears, snot: but he'd kept himself steady, he'd raised his chin – broken his very personal, gloomy surface – and stolen a breath. And, blinking into her face, he'd understood that this whole situation might possibly, conceivably, turn out fine. He might come to be as he'd like to be, without breakages or loss, because she was smiling, smiling only at him.

Greg's hands scrambled for his pockets and a fraying tissue that rapidly transformed itself into a greyish wad, 'Christ, what a day', and he mopped his face while praying sincerely that he wouldn't sound so cretinous the next time he opened his mouth.

'Yes, but it'll be worth it.'

And he did realize she was talking about the cheese, saying simply that the bloody cheese would be worth the wait, but still he felt himself swallow, needed to hold one hand in the other and couldn't help stumbling back with, 'Yes. It will. I hope. No, it will. Naturally. Yes', before coughing out a remarkably ugly and – in God's name – unmistakably equine, laugh.

'I don't suppose any of us come here normally – it's just Christmas, isn't it?'

So is she celebrating Christmas for herself, or for somebody else who is with her, who is allowed to touch her face?

'It can't be absolutely *just* Christmas . . .' *Don't contradict her – what the fuck are you doing?* 'I mean, I mean . . .' *Do you **want** her to be pissed off?* 'They must get *some* customers, sometimes – they stay open . . .' *Oh, that was scintillating, wasn't it? Well fucking done.*

'Maybe they're only a front for the CIA.'

God, thank you, God. 'Now that you mention it, I did see them shoot this shoplifter once . . .'

'Execution-style with a silenced gun?'

'Absolutely. Extremely professional.'

'Oh, well then, that's that. Definitely CIA. Or MI5.'

I want to lick her. Now. The rain from her eyes. Just to lick. 'Do you think we should still let them have our money?'

'Yes. But only if they give us cheese.'

They were properly established then, talking: about the absurdities of Christmas, about tropical holidays neither of them would take, about the concept of cheese which – if you thought of it – was a strange one.

'I mean – cheese – you couldn't have come up with that by accident.' He felt warmer, he felt taller, he felt fate snuggling round him with a good, good plan. 'Cheese.' His tongue moved in his mouth especially deftly, as if each word were more than usually intended. 'But who would have thought to try and make it – who would have known *how*?'

'I know, it's like bread dough with yeast, or meringues – especially meringues. Who on earth could have guessed *that* would happen to an egg white if you pummelled it enough?'

'I think the correct term is *beat*.' While he thought, 'But pummel would do, I'm sure', he could really do nothing *but* think, 'There must have been a Lost Meringue Age'; that egg white looked so much like spunk, *was* so much like spunk.

Spunk. There was nowhere his mind wasn't willing to go and he was so happy to follow it nearly scared him.

I wonder what she sounds like when she comes.

'The Meringue Age.' She patted his forearm quickly, approvingly. 'Of course, the Lost Meringue Age. An era of peace and random food experiments.'

I will know what she sounds like when she comes. I will be there and I will hear her and I will see. I have to.

But no harm done, only thinking.

His eyelids had closed and he couldn't quite coax them back apart. *Under her knee, in that curve, there would be sweat. And in between –*

'Your accent, by the way . . . If you don't mind my asking, where are you from?'

Greg finally eased his eyes open: peeled up a muzzled guess at the shape of her thighs, of her arse, laid naked for his hand: and he saw her face. She met his gaze, seemed to take it from him whole, while he tried to organize a sentence, 'Oh, I . . . My accent? Well, I used to live in England.'

'Ah, English – as I suspected. And you haven't been here long?'

A brief knot of conscience and impatience lashed open at the base of his brain and, before he could stop himself, he'd told her, 'Actually, I *moved* here ten years ago,' which wasn't exactly a lie.

After which, there had been no stopping, no space in his will for even a pause. By the time they'd made it inside the shop, he'd known it was safe to play, make a little rehearsal, and pretend that he was shopping with a girlfriend, a sexual partner, a woman who would never look revolted if he asked her to suck his cock, who would never clatter him with her molars in little bounces of mute revenge and then swallow what he surrendered as if it were only cruel and unusual and not a part of him.

Shopping with Karen was hardly exciting, either: it was like shopping with himself only slower and more expensive. It was one of the things they did together which had, at no time, ever been any fun. That day in the queue had been different, though, that day when he'd gone shopping with somebody new.

'This is silly.'

'What is?' She'd been almost, almost leaning against him while the cheesemonger cut two pieces each of their choices – one to keep and one to swap, which was what they'd decided. 'What's silly?'

Greg had dipped his head and spoken close, close as a kiss beside her ear, because this was appropriate under the circumstances and because he'd hoped that she might like it. 'That we've talked for ages – about half an hour – and now we're buying cheese together . . .'

'Which is a very personal thing.' She was joking and not joking – he liked that. He loved that.

This is the way you seduce someone, isn't it. Who could have guessed I'd remember how. And this is the time to do it, maybe the last chance to try.

'Yes. Extremely personal.' And now Greg wasn't joking at all. 'But we don't know each other's names. That can't be right.' He angled near again, made this soft, 'Can it?'

'Amanda.'

'Really? That's great.' Because he'd been rushed by the lunatic fear that she might be called Karen, or something like Karen. 'Wonderful.' Not that anything *was* like Karen.

'Why?'

'Oh . . . I don't know – it suits you. That kind of idea. I'm Greg.' *Say my name.* 'So now we know each other, that's good.' *Say my name.*

'Greg. OK. Great.'

Say my name when I'm in you and I probably will weep.

Amanda was waiting for a quarter pound of olives – he didn't like olives, but she was free to – when he asked her, 'Look, I don't know your phone number, either, do I?' Which was speeding the process more than he ought, but he'd have to go home soon: he was practically late now, Saturday's dinner already suppurating in the microwave, no doubt. 'It's just that I would like to take you and have a coffee –'

'To take me *and* have a coffee?'

'Well . . .' He watched her mouth. 'Yes. I like coffee. Only I can't do it now, I have to . . . go out tonight with . . . no one.' Good mouth. Wonderful mouth. 'But I have to . . . go out and so . . . If I had your number, I could phone. It's the gentleman who phones, isn't? I have got that right?'

Greg hadn't intended this to make her laugh, but believed it to be a splendid thing when she did. 'The *gentleman*? So you're a gentleman?'

He checked her eyes. 'At times.'

She paused for precisely long enough to please him very much. 'OK.'

Amanda had offered a pen but no paper and all of the cheese wrappings, they'd discovered, were greased and wouldn't take ink, so he'd rolled up his sleeve, delighted, and let her write her number on the inside of his wrist.

He'd kept the secret on him all that evening: had taken it, and never mind the risk, with him into bed. The tickle of her nib had set his skin ringing for hours until he had to pad off, voluntarily, into the other room and stretch out on top of the covers, stiffer than he'd been in years. And for almost fifteen minutes he'd only tensed, spread like a starfish, and concentrated on reclaiming the scent of her hair. Then, locked silently in the bathroom, he'd come twice: the first time through a kind of wrenching haze, the second more melancholy, empty. By the time he'd got back and into bed, he'd been completely lonely. He'd dreamed briefly of an undefined apocalypse and gasped back awake with the idea of kissing her throat.

Greg couldn't be here now without a trace of that night pressing through, as if she'd really joined him somehow and this had become their bed. As if his loneliness had been sweated into fragments in this room and not another.

'I want to see everything.'

'What?'

9

After he'd had coffee with Amanda, and then after they'd met for lunch, he'd chiselled out one complete evening, to have for his own. They'd eaten dinner in Amanda's flat, his imagination ceaselessly bolting and clambering, and then she'd gone through to the kitchen to fetch their dessert.

'I said I want to see everything.'

He'd been rolling an olive gently between his forefinger and thumb, hoping that if he made the bloody thing seem vaguely horny he might fancy eating it. He'd only been able to kiss Amanda once, a little, since he'd arrived and perhaps this was all there would be now: perhaps women, once they knew him, didn't find him attractive, perhaps he'd got too old: he couldn't tell and it was all just worrying. But this was when she'd called, 'I don't want us to put the lights out.' She appeared in the doorway and paused, holding out two plates of lemon cake. 'I don't want us to close our eyes, or run and hide under the duvet, as if it wasn't really happening. I want to see everything.'

'Oh.' He would have swallowed, but had no spit. And he didn't want any cake.

'Was that the wrong way to say it? I didn't mean to be –'

'I want to see everything, too.' This not the kind of stuff that he would ordinarily admit. 'I've wanted to . . .' Perhaps because there was, ordinarily, no point.

'You've wanted to what?' She put the plates down on the table as he turned in his chair to face her. He watched her walk towards him, only halting when her knees were touching his. 'I don't mind. I don't *think* I'll mind – what?'

With the crook of one finger he stroked her stomach through her blouse, easing down, aware of a nice, taut heat, 'I just wasn't sure . . .' and he understood why she hadn't touched him at all this evening, 'I didn't know how to put it . . .' She'd known that if she started she wouldn't stop. He hoped that was it. Or maybe she'd known that, if she started, *he* wouldn't stop. 'You wouldn't be offended if I told you that I wanted to fuck you the first time we met.' She laced both her hands at the back of his head while he looked up and his mouth made declarations he'd never expected, 'Now that . . . we've properly introduced ourselves and I like you and I think I love you, probably, I do want to make love to you, but I still want to fuck you. I want both.'

Amanda nuzzled the top of his head. 'All right.'

'You mean that's all right?' He was whispering, in case he made this go away.

'That's what I said. Yes. That's all right. Do you want your cake first?'

'No, I don't. I really don't, definitely. No. I do not.'

'You don't like lemon cake?'

'Amanda, *please*.'

They didn't have long enough, really, not as long as he'd have liked.

I'd have liked a week. Seven days, with little breaks for nourishment, that would have been what I needed to get myself used to it, to her. I mean somebody, a woman, who would . . .

His mind pitched back into the catalogue of daring things he'd wanted to try. With Amanda they were taken for granted, done. In fact, she had opinions on each one, along with small habits about their execution. Every time he tried to shock her, she shocked him back, stripped and splayed his favourite imaginings with her clinical enjoyment, her reality. All this, when he couldn't help wincing defensively the first time that she simply sucked him, even though she did so in a way he could not have anticipated that anyone ever would, with such a beautiful, soulless determination. She didn't hurt him, was only impeccably, firmly smooth, the close of her putting a tourniquet on the last of his sanity.

Very quickly, Amanda had worked him adrift from anyone he could have thought he'd like to be. Greg remembered pulling back the curtain of her shower and seeing them both together, caught in the sweat of her bathroom mirror, his face staring back at him from a soaped configuration of shuddering pinks, his eyes unmistakably afraid.

He'd made it home by two and had ducked directly into the spare room, feeling beautifully bruised and scandalized. Still awake, he'd seen the dawn crawl across the ceiling and was almost surprised: a part of him had imagined the day would start differently now, or just not happen any more, everything necessary being over. A chill of anticipation jumped in his chest and perhaps this was the fear of discovery, of being forced to stop, or perhaps this was the fear of successful concealment and having to carry on. He didn't feel right, that was all – he didn't truly feel what he'd call right.

'Hung over?'

Naturally, at breakfast, he'd imagined that Karen would guess just what he'd done. She didn't.

'No, I think I'm getting flu.' This was a gift and he meant it to be, the kind of lie that she enjoyed dissecting.

'You weren't in before one, I'm sure of that – this would be the 'flu to do with being up all night? Is this going to be a habit?'

I could get used to this, yes. It's nothing I should be scared of.

'No, it won't be a habit. The people from Sales – you know what they're like. I have to keep them happy, now and then.'

It's only, currently, unfamiliar. I will get my second wind.

'Well, I'm glad you're keeping someone happy.'

Greg, producing a suitably hangdog frown, had felt it curdle slowly when he glanced at Karen and found that she was smiling. She had decided to be teasing, but sympathetic. He couldn't begin to guess why and, frankly, didn't want to: he'd been too busy indulging a good, low beat of preparative thinking.

I can't plausibly get another evening soon enough. We could fuck on a Saturday, though, on a Saturday afternoon.

His wife had made him take a Beechams' powder and kissed him on the lips before he left for work. He had not felt remotely guilty, only slightly peculiar, as if he were moving in a pre-directed path, one that gripped him, gleeful, that left him raw and luminous, under the skin.

Greg had almost the same feeling now, a similar chafing of weighted expectancy. Although there was also the rash: that did have to be considered, a nervous thing he hadn't suffered from in years. In the fold of each elbow and on each shin he'd grown an irritable patch of crimson pinpricks. The doctor had given him ointment and, no doubt, the trouble would pass and Greg hadn't needed to hear it was stress-related. Sometimes, he'd stare at one patch or another and wonder if it might not cohere some morning, arranging itself to spell out Amanda's name. Or something worse, some message he didn't want to bear.

The digital red of his alarm clock showed 05:42 and he'd set it for six, but he might as well start, get up. Karen wouldn't surface before seven and by then he should really have everything done.

He didn't shave because it wasn't necessary, applied his ointment as directed on the tube, dressed quickly in a shirt and jeans and then took his bag from the bottom of the wardrobe. There wasn't much in it: a paperback, toothbrush and paste, another shirt, a pair of underpants and a Gideon's bible he'd stolen from a hotel recently. In the kitchen he added a packet of chocolate digestives and two apples, as if it really mattered what he took. When he'd been a promising youth of good moral fibre and hill-walking for his Duke of Edinburgh Awards, he'd always made sure to pack chocolate digestives and apples in his regulation haversack and he'd always come to no harm. Which was an adequate reason for taking them with him today – they might bring him safety, which was much more important than luck.

It was only half past six when he washed up his coffee cup and realized that he could go, because there was nothing else left for him to do. So he folded his raincoat over his arm, eased out of the back door and closed it, quiet behind him. A street away, he'd parked the car so that Karen wouldn't hear him when he started up the engine and drove off.

In an hour he was well clear of the city and rolling between dark stands of conifer. The daybreak had been smothered almost immediately in cloud and by ten it was raining hard, the peck of water overhead making his car seem cosy and sound. He turned on the radio and bounced across the frequencies, neither more nor less happy with any of them, but finally staying with one which conducted its business solely in Gaelic. This morning he wanted information that he could not understand, news that brought no disturbance, that didn't concern him. Every now and then a crow would fling itself into a sinking flight across the road, only to perch in a wet hump once it reached the sombre plush of the opposing trees.

When Greg noticed he was hungry he stopped in a small, rain-shuttered town and ate lunch in a gift shop café. The food was dreadful: oily tea, a mournful cheese sandwich, a forbidding raisin scone: but he didn't mind it, the nature of these things was the nature of these things and needn't be argued with, not any more. He loitered in amongst the available gifts along with a brace of sodden tourists and, inevitably, three hill-walkers. He bought the most pointless things he could find, then beamed while the assistant duly bagged a ceramic stag's head, a video tape of pipe bands and a pink Pringle golfing sweater.

'Is this for you?'

'Hm?'

'This is an extra large. A medium is quite big . . .' She eyed him appraisingly.

'That's fine. I'm not going to wear it.' He grinned in what he hoped was an unbalanced way and eyed her in return. She didn't flinch.

Back in the car with his prizes, he pushed north, this time without turning on the radio.

The thing about this is, I can't be sure I'm right. In fact, I can be almost certain that I'm not.

*But if I **am** right.*

If I am right, I should be like this when it happens – with myself alone, contented. As close to contented as I get.

The idea must have nested in him for a while, only showing itself in needling little pieces, opening and spiralling out into his undefended sleep: here the taste of ash and there the sense of an absent sky. It finally, completely demanded his attention during his third time with Amanda – their hotel début. As far as Karen was concerned, he was leaving Glasgow fairly early one Saturday morning and driving to Edinburgh in order to meet a friend and get a cheap computer. The computer in question was already sitting in his office, bought with cash from a man in Sales. In reality, lovely reality, he was driving to Edinburgh fairly early one Saturday morning with Amanda and the intention of spending several hours in a hotel bed, or thereabouts. She would then take the train home, believing that he had a business dinner to attend, followed by a highly boring, all-Sunday conference. He would wait half an hour or so, check out with an excuse he'd never fully fixed on and go home once he'd picked up the computer. This was all rather complicated, but meant that he would have roughly five hours free for sex. Not counting whatever she did while he was driving.

As it turned out, she was an unexpectedly docile passenger.

'I don't like to distract you while you're driving.'

'Distract away.'

'I want all of your mind on what we're doing when we do it. I can wait.'

So he had to, but as soon as they'd booked in and made it as far as the lift she compensated him for his patience.

'I'm not wearing any. Look.'

'Jesus Christ, what if it . . . if someone comes in?' Although, as soon as he'd said it, he didn't care. 'Fuck, that's gorgeous.'

'I know.'

His plan for the day only foundered, that waiting idea only slipped its claws inside, when he looked down at Amanda, bent over the chair, the pale flesh of her back cool under his palms. She felt so ideal against him and her spine made such an adorably undulating arch and there was absolutely no way she could turn her head to face him and meet his eyes, so that was when he told her, 'Actually, I'm married.'

Karen slowed their pace, but didn't stop, 'I know', seemed to ask him to go deeper.

And he did so; bewildered, but rather more turned on than he had been all afternoon. 'You *know*? How?' Rather more turned on than he could bear.

'You wear clothes you've picked to please someone else. They're not you, or not the whole of you.'

He was going to come soon, if he wasn't careful. 'And?' She was making it hard to be careful.

'We're fucking in a hotel room on a Saturday afternoon.'

Which did it, which just did it, and left him faintly rocking, laid forward over her back, only gradually aware of a rolling sweat. 'You don't mind?' His mouth seemed awfully gritty, odd.

'I'm here, aren't I?'

'But you won't . . .' It was tricky to speak.

'This is what I want.'

'God.' Words bouncing numbly in his skull, 'I love you.'

'You're very sweet.'

Then Greg had rested across the bedspread with Amanda drowsily beside him and fitted to his shape remarkably. They had another two hours left and then she would set off home, but now he felt unnaturally sleepy and had begun to slip adrift when something seemed to hit him inside his head. An audible colour. A twist of light.

No. Not now. No.

That feeling of nearing extinction, the threat of heat under each of his lurching and unsatisfying dreams, the horrible conviction that he might reach out, unconscious, and touch the end of everything – here it was, with him, nakedly clear.

But that would be ridiculous.

Still, the moment slapped him awake, put a spasm in his neck.

'What's the matter?' The voice of Amanda. 'Greg?' The woman who'd sprung the terminal lock, who'd shut him up alone with this.

'Nothing. I dreamed. Nothing.'

'Do you want to start again, then? Hm?' The woman who could lick and tug and buck him away from it. 'My greedy boy?' And now she'd have to, she owed him that.

So, although he didn't want to, not right then, although he actually needed to hug her, to hug someone, to be only held, 'Oh . . . Yes,' he made himself begin, 'Why not?' because she would let him do that, 'Yes.' Because it was something to do. 'Yes. Let's start again.'

The end of days. Dear Lord, it's coming, the End of Days.

He'd pushed them both hard, harder than he liked, then decided to steal the bible as they were leaving.

'What on earth do you want that for?'

And he hadn't been able to tell her that this was foolish, but nevertheless, he would just feel safer if they had it with them in the car.

There are so many dates for the End of the World: you read about them in the paper when they've already gone and you hadn't been remotely aware, would have got no warning if they'd been right . . .

Nobody would know for sure. They couldn't. I couldn't.

Despite this, he'd dropped off Amanda, uplifted the computer and delivered it – and himself – home, with his head reeling round and round the list of every animal he thought he could remember that was said to sense coming earthquakes, or was forewarned of calamities.

And some people get this feeling when close relatives have died. And twins . . .

It was silly, though, to expect he'd be the only one, the only human to be aware of something this monumental. It was ridiculous. Ever since the day in the hotel he'd tried to think that.

And he did now, almost wholeheartedly, believe that his repeated premonitions and that single afternoon's burst of certainty did no more than prove he had a highly masochistic type of arrogance. This drive he was taking up north, it was primarily therapeutic. It really wasn't so very much to do with the end of the world. He was going away to relax – and his rash hadn't bothered him a bit since he'd started out – that was proof that he'd needed a break and here he was having it. From the coming midnight until the next, he'd decided that he would stay up here by himself, but it would be much more for a necessary rest than because he expected the close of recorded time.

I didn't believe the Millennium would trigger it, that would have been too neat. I wasn't anxious, then. Only averagely anxious, anyway. The way a person in my position would be anxious.

It was over eight months, now, that he'd known Amanda and more than seven since they'd started to have sex. They'd settled into a pattern, her variation on normality.

'I don't need that. I've told you, I have what I want.'

He'd tried to give her presents, 'It's only a scarf . . . You don't have anything from me.'

'Yes, I do.' She started to unbuckle his belt.

'You wouldn't like to talk? Anticipation . . .' Sometimes, when she touched him, he thought it might happen again: the outbreak of emptiness, of ending. 'We could go and have coffee and then . . .'

'We've done that.'

'We've done this.'

'But this is much more interesting. I don't suppose you've ever sodomized anyone.'

'Ever . . . ? Uh, no.' She would always do that, nudge through his fear and his better nature with something impossible to resist. 'Do you think I will soon?' She made him forget himself.

'Yes, I do.'

'Well, then . . .' He wanted to forget himself. 'That's good.'

The memory of it, of seeing her like that, made a touch of blood head south, plumbing his depths. Although it hadn't been something he'd enjoyed, so much as something he couldn't help wanting to do again. There was a great deal he couldn't help wanting to do again.

He turned the radio back on and retuned until he found some music, turned it up loud. A few miles further and Greg came to a section of road that was heavy with standing water. Careless for his engine, he drove at each pool directly and made plume after plume cape across his windscreen, each liquid impact scrabbling under his bodywork. He felt more peaceful afterwards and was calmed even more by the flat of the glen floor around him, the slow spin of mountains, parting and meeting before and behind.

Because there was a minute chance that it might be his last, he pulled off the road to watch what starts and licks of light the sunset could force through the cloud. He left the car and walked through the coarse, drizzly grass and into the whip and bounce of heather. He lay down as the valley dimmed to shadow and the rain fell on his face and he set himself aside from Amanda and Karen, from the misery of excitements, the bitter comforts, the whole thing. A curlew called and then there was a great peace. He fell into an utterly painless sleep.

What woke him was the cold. Greg was shivering before he was fully conscious. The ground around still smelt of summer, but the slight breeze was stern and he was soaked – all but the middle of his back. He got to his feet in a confusion of stiffness and chill and was immediately terrified by the total dark, couldn't see his watch, couldn't tell if he'd moved past midnight, if this was it. Then he tripped on a high sprawl of roots and fell where he could see his headlamps, still mercifully there and bright in a way which implied he hadn't fucked the battery by leaving them to burn.

I didn't want this to be over, not everything. I hate it, but I didn't want it to have gone away. Or maybe I didn't want it to leave me behind.

Safely in the car, he started up the engine without a hitch, changed his shirt and was forced to put on the pink sweater, just to get warm. Its sleeves were long enough to act as mittens, which was a mercy.

I didn't want it to leave me behind.

Gently, he circled and jolted down into the road, got under way again, his watch showing just past two in the morning, which meant he hadn't paid attention as well as he might. This could be the big day, could be coiled right down around the start of the big moment. Any second now. Already, The End could have taken him unawares. He could have missed it and never known.

But I'm wrong. Nothing's going to happen. Nothing's going to leave me and I really ought to be certain of that. I've got no proper cause for doubt.

I'm wrong and by midnight tomorrow, I'll know that I'm wrong.

That should make me happy.

By midnight tomorrow, that's how I should be.

Happy.

That's how I should be.

TESSA HADLEY

Funny Little Snake

The child was nine years old and couldn't fasten her own buttons. Valerie knelt in front of her on the carpet in the spare room as Robyn held out first one cuff and then the other without a word, then turned around to present the back of her dress, where a long row of spherical chocolate-brown buttons was unfastened over a grubby white petticoat edged with lace. Her tiny, bony shoulder blades flickered with repressed movement. And although every night since Robyn had arrived, a week ago, Valerie had encouraged her into a bath foamed up with bubbles, she still smelled of something furtive – musty spice from the back of a cupboard. The smell had to be in her dress, which Valerie didn't dare wash because it looked as though it had to be dry-cleaned, or in her lank, liquorice-coloured hair, which was pulled back from her forehead under an even grubbier stretch Alice band. Trust Robyn's mother to have a child who couldn't do up buttons, and then put her in a fancy plaid dress with hundreds of them, and frogging and leg-of-mutton sleeves, like a Victorian orphan, instead of ordinary slacks and a T-shirt so that she could play. The mother went around, apparently, in long dresses and bare feet, and had her picture painted by artists. Robyn at least had tights and plimsolls with elastic tops – though her green coat was too thin for the winter weather.

Valerie had tried to talk to her stepdaughter. It was the first time they'd met, and she'd braced herself for resentment, the child's mind poisoned against her. Robyn was miniature, a doll – with a plain, pale, wide face, her temples blue-naked where her hair was strained back, her wide-open grey eyes affronted and evasive and set too far apart. She wasn't naughty, and she wasn't actually silent – that would have been a form of stubbornness to combat, to coax and manoeuvre around. She was a nullity, an absence, answering yes and no obediently if she was questioned, in that languid drawl that always caught Valerie on the raw – though she knew the accent wasn't the child's fault, only what she'd learned. Robyn even said please and thank you, and she told Valerie the name of her teacher, but when Valerie asked whether she liked the teacher her eyes slipped uneasily away from her stepmother's and she shrugged, as if such an idea as liking or not liking hadn't occurred to her. The only dislikes she was definite about had to do with eating. When Valerie put fish pie on Robyn's plate the first night, she shot her a direct look of such piercing desperation that Valerie, who was a good, wholesome cook and had been going to insist, asked her kindly what she ate at home. Eggs? Cottage pie? Baked beans?

Honestly, the girl hardly seemed to know the names of things. Toast was all she could think of. Definitely not eggs: a vehement head shake. Toast, and – after long consideration, then murmuring hesitantly, tonelessly – tomato soup, cornflakes, butterscotch Instant Whip. It was lucky that Gil wasn't witness to all this compromise, because he would have thought Valerie was spoiling his daughter. He and Valerie ate together later, after Robyn was in bed. Gil might have been a left-winger in his politics, but he was old-fashioned in his values at home. He despised, for instance, the little box of a house the university had given them, and wanted to move into one of the rambling old mansions on the road behind his office. He thought they had more style, with their peeling paint and big gardens overgrown with trees.

Valerie didn't tell him how much she enjoyed all the conveniences of their modern home – the clean, light rooms, the central heating, the electric tin opener fitted onto the kitchen wall. And she was intrigued, because Gil was old-fashioned, by his having chosen for his first wife a woman who went barefoot and lived like a hippie in her big Chelsea flat. Perhaps Marise had been so beautiful once that Gil couldn't resist her. Valerie was twenty-four; she didn't think Marise could still be beautiful at forty. Now, anyway, he referred to her as the Rattrap, and the Beak, and the Bitch from Hell, and said that she would fuck anyone. When Valerie first married him, she hadn't believed that a professor could know such words. She'd known them herself, of course, but that was different – she wasn't educated.

*

20

On the phone with his ex-wife, Gil had made a lot of fuss about having his daughter to visit, as a stubborn point of pride, and then had driven all the way down to London to fetch her. But, since getting back, he'd spent every day at his office at the university, even though it wasn't term time, saying that he needed absolute concentration to work on the book he was writing. Robyn didn't seem to miss him. She looked bemused when Valerie called him her daddy, as if she hardly recognized him by that name; she'd been only three or four when he'd moved out. Valerie didn't ask Gil what he'd talked about with his daughter on the long car journey: perhaps they'd driven the whole way in silence. Or perhaps he'd questioned Robyn about her mother, or ranted on about her, or talked about his work. Sometimes in the evenings he talked to Valerie for hours about university politics or other historians he envied or resented – or even about the Civil War or the Long Parliament or the idea of the state – without noticing that she wasn't listening, that she was thinking about new curtains or counting the stitches in her knitting. He might have found fatherhood easier, Valerie thought, if his daughter had been pretty. Moodily, after Robyn had gone to bed, Gil wondered aloud whether she was even his. 'Who knows, with the Great Whore of Marylebone putting it about like there's no tomorrow? The child's half feral. She doesn't look anything like me. Is she normal? Do they even send her to school? I think she's back-ward. A little bit simple, stunted. No surprise, growing up in that sink of iniquity. God only knows what she's seen.'

Valerie was getting to know how he used exaggerated expressions like 'sink of iniquity', whose sense she didn't know but could guess at, as if he were partly making fun of his own disapproval, while at the same time he furiously meant it. He stayed one step ahead of any fixed position, so that no one could catch him out in it. But Robyn looked more like him than he realized, although she was smooth and bland with childhood and he was hoary and sagging from fifty years' experience. He had the same pale skin, and the same startled hare's eyes swimming in and out of focus behind his big black-framed glasses. Sometimes, when Gil laughed, you could see how he might have been a different man if he hadn't chosen to be this professor with his stooping bulk and crumpled, shapeless suits, his braying, brilliant talk. Without glasses, his face was naked and keen and boyish, with a boy's shame, as if the nakedness must be smothered like a secret.

Gil's widowed mother had owned a small newsagent's. He'd got himself to university and then onward into success and even fame – he'd been on television often – through his own sheer cleverness and effort. Not that he tried to hide his class origins: on the contrary, he'd honed them into a weapon to use against his colleagues and friends. But he always repeated the same few anecdotes from his childhood, well rounded and glossy from use: the brew-house in the back yard, where the women gossiped and did their washing; the bread-and-drippings suppers; a neighbour cutting his throat in the shared toilet; his mother polishing the front step with Cardinal Red. He didn't talk about his mother in private, and when Valerie once asked him how she'd died he wouldn't tell her anything except – gruffly barking it, to frighten her off and mock her fear at the same time – that it was cancer. She guessed that he'd probably been close to his mother, and then grown up to be embarrassed by her, and hated himself for neglecting her, but couldn't admit to any of this because he was always announcing publicly how much he loathed sentimentality and guilt. Valerie had been attracted to him in the first place because he made fun of everything; nothing was sacred.

She didn't really want the child around. But Robyn was part of the price she paid for having been singled out by the professor among the girls in the faculty office at King's College London, having married him and moved with him to begin a new life in the North. There had been some quarrel or other with King's; he had enemies there.

As the week wore on, she grew sick of the sound of her own voice jollying Robyn along. The girl hadn't even brought any toys with her, to occupy her time. After a while, Valerie noticed that, when no one was looking, she played with two weird little figures, scraps of cloth tied into shapes with wool, one in each hand, doing the voices almost inaudibly. One voice was coaxing and hopeful, the other one reluctant. 'Put on your special gloves,' one of them said. 'But I don't like the blue colour,' said the other. 'These ones have special powers,' the first voice persisted. 'Try them out.'

Valerie asked Robyn if these were her dollies. Shocked out of her fantasy, she hid the scraps behind her back. 'Not really,' she said.

'What are their names?'

'They don't have names.'

'We could get out my sewing machine and make clothes for them.'
Robyn shook her head, alarmed. 'They don't need clothes.'

Selena had made them for her, she told Valerie, who worked out that
Selena must have been their cleaner. 'She doesn't come any more,' Robyn
added, though not as if she minded particularly. 'We sacked her. She
stole things.'

When Valerie tied her into an apron and stood her on a chair to
make scones, Robyn's fingers went burrowing into the flour as if they were
independent of her, mashing the butter into lumps in her hot palms.
'Like this,' Valerie said, showing her how to lift the flour as she rubbed,
for lightness. Playfully, she grabbed at Robyn's fingers under the surface
of the flour, but Robyn snatched them back, dismayed, and wouldn't try
the scones when they were baked. Valerie ended up eating them, although
she was trying to watch her weight, sticking to Ryvita and cottage cheese
for lunch. She didn't want to run to fat, like her mother. She thought Gil
refused to visit her mother partly because he worried about how Valerie
might look one day, when she wasn't soft and fresh and blonde any more.

Robyn had hardly brought enough clothes to last the week – besides
the dress with the buttons, there was only a grey skirt that looked like a
school uniform, a ribbed nylon jumper, one spare pair of knickers, odd
socks, and a full-length nightdress made of red wool flannel, like something out of a storybook. The nightdress smelled of wee and Valerie
thought it must be itchy; she took Robyn shopping for sensible pyjamas
and then they had tea at the cafeteria in British Home Stores, which had
been Valerie's treat when she was Robyn's age. Robyn didn't want a meringue but asked if she was allowed to hold her new pyjamas, then sat with
the cellophane package in her lap and an expression of conscious importance. The pyjamas were white, decorated with yellow-and-blue yachts and
anchors. 'Can I keep them?' she asked tentatively, after a long, dull silence.
Valerie had grown tired of chatting away inanely to no one.

She had been going to suggest that Robyn leave the pyjamas behind,
for the next time she visited, but she didn't really care. Every child ought
to want something; it was only healthy. And, packed into Robyn's suitcase
along with the rest of her clothes – all freshly washed, apart from the
dress, and pressed, even the socks, with Valerie's steam iron – the pyjamas
would be like a message, a coded reproach, for that mother in Chelsea.

She imagined Marise unpacking them in some room of flowery frivolity she couldn't clearly visualize and feeling a pang for the insufficiency of her own maternal care. Valerie knew, though, that her parade of competence and righteous indignation was a lie, really. Because the truth was that she couldn't wait for Robyn to go home. She longed to be free of that dogged, unresponsive little figure following her everywhere around the house.

Gil was supposed to be driving Robyn back down to London on Wednesday. On Tuesday evening, when he came home early, Valerie knew right away that something was up. He stood behind her while she was preparing meat loaf at the kitchen counter, nuzzling under her ear and stroking her breast with one hand, determinedly jiggling the ice cubes in his Scotch with the other. He always poured himself a generous Scotch as soon as he came in: she'd learned not to comment. 'You're so good to me,' he said pleadingly, his voice muffled in her neck. 'I don't deserve it.'

'Oh dear, what's Mr Naughty's little game now?' Valerie was long-suffering, faintly amused, swiping onions from her chopping board into a bowl with the side of her knife. 'What's he sniffing after? He wants something.'

'He knows he's so selfish. Causes her no end of trouble.'

These were two of the roles they acted out sometimes: Valerie brusquely competent and in charge, Gil wheedling and needy. There was a truth behind their performances, as well as pretence. Gil groaned apologetically. A problem had come up at work tomorrow, a special guest coming to dinner at High Table, someone he needed to meet because he had influence and the whole game was a bloody conspiracy. He'd never be able to get back from London in time. And Thursday was no good, either – faculty meeting; Friday he was giving a talk in Manchester. They could keep Robyn until Saturday, but the She-Bitch would never let him hear the end of it. He wanted Valerie to take her home tomorrow on the train. Valerie could stay over with her mother in Acton, couldn't she? Come back the following day?

Valerie had counted on being free in the morning, getting the house back to normal, having her thoughts to herself again, catching a bus into town perhaps, shopping. She was gasping for her solitude like a lungful of clean air. Biting her lower lip to keep herself from blurting out a protest, she kneaded onions into the minced meat; the recipe came from a magazine – it was seasoned with allspice and tomato ketchup. Certainly she didn't fancy three extra days with the kid moping around. She thought, with a flush of outrage, that Gil was truly selfish, never taking her needs into consideration. On the other hand, important men had to be selfish in order to get ahead. She understood that – she wouldn't have wanted a softer man who wasn't respected. She could squeeze concessions out of him anyway, in return for this favour. Perhaps she'd ring up one of her old girlfriends, meet for coffee in Oxford Street, or even for a gin in a pub, for old times' sake. She could buy herself something new to wear; she had saved up some money that Gil didn't know about, out of the housekeeping.

Theatrically, she sighed. 'It's very inconvenient. I was going to go into Jones's, to make inquiries about these curtains for the sitting room.'

He didn't even correct her and tell her to call it the drawing room.

'He's sorry, he's really sorry. It isn't fair, he knows it. But it could be a little holiday for you. You could just put Robyn into a cab at the station, give the driver the address, let her mother pay. Why shouldn't she? She's got money.'

Valerie was startled that he could even think she'd do that. The child could hardly get herself dressed in the mornings; she certainly wasn't fit to be knocking halfway around London by herself, quarrelling with cab-drivers. And, anyway, if Valerie really was going all the way to London, she might as well have a glimpse of where her stepdaughter lived. She was afraid of Marise, but curious about her, too.

Outside the front door in Chelsea, Valerie stood holding Robyn's suitcase in one leather-gloved hand and her own overnight bag in the other. The house was grand and dilapidated, set back from the street in an overgrown garden, with a flight of stone steps rising to a scruffy pillared portico, a broad door painted black. Names in faded, rain-stained ink were drawing-pinned beside a row of bells; they'd already rung twice, and Valerie's feet were like ice. The afternoon light was thickening gloomily under the evergreens. Robyn stood uncomplaining in her thin coat, although from time to time on their journey Valerie had seen her quake with the cold as if it had probed her, bypassing her conscious mind, like a jolt of electricity. The heating had been faulty on the train. While Valerie read her magazines and Robyn worked dutifully through one page after another in her colouring book, the washed-out, numb winter landscape had borne cruelly in on them from beyond the train window: miles of bleached, tufted dun grasses, purple-black tangled labyrinths of bramble, clumps of dark reeds frozen in a ditch. Valerie had been relieved when they got into the dirty old city at last. She hadn't taken to the North, though she was trying.

Staring up at the front door, Robyn had her usual stolidly neutral look, buffered against expectation; she hardly seemed excited by the prospect of seeing her mother again. And, when the door eventually swung open, a young man about Valerie's age – with long fair hair and a flaunting angel face, dark-stubbled jaw, dead cigarette stuck to the wet of his sagging lip – looked out at them without any recognition. 'Oh, hullo?' he said.

With his peering, dozy eyes, he seemed to have only just got out of bed, or to be about to slop back into it. He was bursting out of his tight clothes: a shrunken T-shirt exposed a long hollow of skinny brown belly and a slick line of dark hairs, leading down inside pink satin hipster trousers. His feet were bare and sprouted with more hair, and he smelled like a zoo animal, of something sour and choking. Realization dawned when he noticed Robyn. 'Hullo!' he said, as if it were funny. 'You're the little girl.'

'Is Mrs Hope at home?' Valerie asked stiffly.

He scratched his chest under the T-shirt and his smile slid back to dwell on her, making her conscious of her breasts, although he only quickly flicked his glance across them. 'Yeah, somewhere.'

A woman came clattering downstairs behind him and loomed across his shoulder; she was taller than he was, statuesque, her glittering eyes black with makeup, and diamonds glinting in the piled-up mass of her dark hair, in the middle of the afternoon. Though, of course, the diamonds were paste – it was all a joke, a pantomime sendup. Valerie wasn't such a fool, she got hold of that. Still, Marise was spectacular in a long, low-cut white dress and white patent-leather boots: she had an exaggerated, coarse beauty, like a film star blurred from being too much seen.

'Oh, Christ, is it today? Shit! Is that the kid?' Marise wailed, pushing past the young man, her devouring eyes snatching off an impression of Valerie in one scouring instant and dismissing it. 'I forgot all about it. It can't be Wednesday already! Welcome home, honeypot. Give Mummy a million, million kisses. Give Jamie kisses. This is Jamie. Say hello. Isn't he sweet? Don't you remember him? He's in a band.'

Robyn said hello, gazing at Jamie without much interest and not moving to kiss anyone. Her mother pounced in a cloud of perfume and carried her inside, calling back over her shoulder to Valerie in her husky voice, mistaking her for some kind of paid nanny, or pretending to. 'Awfully kind of you. Are those her things? Do you want to drop her bags here in the hall? James can carry them up later. Do you have a cab? Or he can get you one. Oof, what a big, heavy girl you're getting to be, Robby-bobby. Can you climb up on your own?'

The hall was dim and high, lit by a feeble unshaded bulb; when determinedly Valerie followed after them, her heels echoed on black and white marble tiles. 'Hello, Mrs H.,' she sang out in her brightest telephone voice. 'I'm the new Mrs H. How nice to meet you.'

Marise looked down at her from the curve of the staircase, where she was stooping over Robyn, setting her down. 'Oh, I thought you might be. I thought he might have chosen someone like you.'

'I'm hoping you're going to offer us a cup of tea,' Valerie went on cheerfully. Of course Marise had known that she was bringing Robyn – Gil had telephoned last night to tell her. 'Only we're frozen stiff, the pair of us! The heating on the train wasn't working.'

'Do you take milk?' Marise wondered. 'Because I don't know if we have any milk.'

'So long as it's hot!'

She submitted graciously when Jamie offered to take both bags, then was aware of his following her up the stairs, appraising her from behind, and thought that Marise was aware of it, too. A door on the first floor, with a pillared surround and a pediment, stood open. You could see how it had once opened onto the best rooms at the heart of the house: now it had its own Yale lock and was painted purple and orange. The lower panels were dented and splintered as if someone had tried to kick through them. In the enormous room beyond, there was a marble fireplace and a candelabra and floor-length windows hung with tattered yellow brocade drapes;

the glass in a vast gilt mirror was so foxed that it didn't double the perspective but closed it in, like a black fog. Valerie understood that, like the diamonds in Marise's hair, this wasn't really decaying aristocratic grandeur but an arty imitation of it. Marise led the way past a glass dome as tall as a man, filled with stuffed, faded hummingbirds and a staring, dappled fairground horse, its flaring nostrils painted crimson; Robyn flinched from the horse as if from an old enemy.

In the next room, which was smaller, a log fire burned in a blackened grate beside a leather sofa, its cushions cracked and pale with wear. Jamie dropped the bags against a wall. Robyn and Valerie, shivering in their coats, hung over the white ash in the grate as if it might be lifesaving, while Marise hunted for milk in what must have been the kitchen next door, though it sounded cavernous. Jamie crouched to put on more logs, reaching his face towards the flame to reignite his rollie. The milk was off, Marise announced. There was a tin of tomato juice; wouldn't everyone prefer Bloody Marys? Valerie said that might be just the thing, but knew she must pace herself and not let the drink put her at any disadvantage.

The Bloody Marys when they came were strong, made with lots of Tabasco and ice and lemon and a stuffed olive on a stick: Marise said they were wonderfully nourishing, she lived on them. She even brought one – made without vodka, or only the tiniest teaspoonful – for Robyn, along with a packet of salted crisps, and she kissed her, pretending to gobble her up. Robyn submitted to the assault. 'You're lucky, I saved those for you specially. I know that little girls are hungry bears. Because Jamie's a hungry bear, too – he eats everything. I'll have to hide the food away, won't I, if we want to keep any of it for you? Are you still my hungry bear, Bobbin?'

Robyn went unexpectedly then into a bear performance, hunching her shoulders, crossing her eyes, snuffling and panting, scrabbling in the air with her hands curled up like paws, her face a blunt little snout, showing pointed teeth. They must have played this game before; Marise watched her daughter with distaste and pity, austerely handsome as a carved ship's figurehead. For a moment, Robyn really was a scruffy, dull-furred, small brown bear, dancing joylessly to order. Valerie wouldn't have guessed that the child had it in her, to enter so completely into a life other than her own. 'Nice old bear,' she said encouragingly.

'That's quite enough of that, Bobby,' Marise said. 'Most unsettling. Now, why don't you go and play, darling? Take your crisps away before the Jamie-bear gets them.'

Robyn returned into her ordinary self, faintly pink in the face. 'Shall I show Auntie Valerie my bedroom?'

Marise's expression ripened scandalously. She stared wide-eyed between Robyn and Valerie. ' "Auntie Valerie"! What's this? Valerie isn't your real auntie, you know. Didn't anyone explain to you?'

'We thought it was the best thing for her to call me, considering,' Valerie said.

'Well, I'm relieved you didn't go in for "Mummy". Or "Dearest Mamma", or "Mom".'

Flustered, Robyn shot a guilty look at Valerie. 'I do know she's my stepmother, really.'

'That's better. Your *wicked* stepmother, don't forget.' Marise winked broadly at Valerie. 'Now, off you go. She doesn't want to see your bedroom.'

They heard her trail through the kitchen, open another door on the far side, close it again behind her. The fire blazed up. Jamie began picking out something on his guitar, while Marise rescued his rollie from the ashtray and fell with it onto the opposite end of the sofa. Valerie guessed that they were smoking pot – that was what the zoo smell was. And she thought that she ought to leave. There was nothing for her here – she had made her point by coming inside. 'So, Valerie,' Marise said musingly. 'How did you get on with my dear daughter? Funny little snake, isn't she? I hope Gilbert enjoyed spending every moment with her, after all those protestations of how he's such a devoted father. Was she a good girl?'

'Awfully good. We didn't have a squeak of trouble.'

'I mean, isn't she just a piece of Gilbert? Except not clever, of course. Poor little mite, with his looks and my brains.'

Outside, the last of the afternoon light was being blotted out, and although wind buffeted the loose old windowpanes, no one stirred to draw the curtains or switch on the lamps. Valerie wanted to go, but the drink was stronger than she was used to, and the heat from the fire seemed to press her down in the sofa. Also, she feared returning through the next room, past the stuffed birds and that horse. She was imagining how her husband might have been impressed and excited once by this careless, shameless, disordered household. If you owned so much, you could afford to trample it underfoot in a grand gesture, turning everything into a game.

'I do adore clever men,' Marise went on. 'I was so in love with Gilbert's intelligence, absolutely crazy about him at first. I could sit listening to him for hours on end, telling me all about history and ideas and art. Because, you know, I'm just an absolute idiot. I was kicked out of school when I was fourteen – the nuns hated me. Valerie, truly, I can hardly read and write. Whereas I expect you can do typing and shorthand, you clever girl. So I'd just kneel there at Gilbert's feet, gazing up at him while he talked. You know, just talking, talking, droning on and on. So pleased with himself. Don't men just love that?'

'Do they? I wouldn't know.'

'But they do, they love it when we're kneeling at their feet. Jamie thinks that's hilarious, don't you, Jamie? Because now I'm worshipping him instead, he thinks. Worshipping his guitar.'

'My talent,' Jamie chastely suggested. Marise shuffled down in the sofa to poke her white boot at him, prodding at his hands and blocking the strings so that he couldn't play until he ducked the neck of his guitar out of her way. His exasperated look slid past her teasing and onto Valerie, where it rested. Marise subsided with a sigh.

'So Gilbert's sitting there steering along in the little cockpit of his own cleverness, believing himself so shining, such a wonder! And then suddenly one day I couldn't stand it! I thought, But the whole *world*, the whole of real life, is spread out underneath him. And he's up there all alone in his own clever head. Don't you know what I mean?'

'I've never taken much interest in Gil's work,' Valerie said primly. 'Though I'm aware how highly it's regarded. I've got my own interests.'

'Oh, have you? Good for you! Because I've never really had any interests to speak of. I've counted on the men in my life to supply those. Gilbert was certainly interesting. Did you know that he beat me? Yes, really. To a pulp, my dear.'

What melodrama! Valerie laughed out loud. She didn't believe it. Or perhaps she did. When Marise, mocking, blew out a veil of smoke, she had a glimpse for a moment of Gil's malevolent Bitch from Hell, the strong-jawed dark sorceress who might incite a man to violence. Poor

Gilbert. And it was true that his rages had been a revelation when they were first married. In the university office, all the women had petted him and were in awe of his mystique: he had seemed thoughtful, forgetful, bumbling, dryly humorous, and high-minded. She stood up, trying to shake off the influence of the Bloody Mary. Her mother would be expecting her, she said. 'And I don't know what your plans are for Robyn's tea. But I made us cheese sandwiches for the train, so she's had a decent lunch, at least, and an apple and a Mars bar.'

Marise was amused. 'I don't have any plans for Robyn's tea. I've never really made those kinds of plans.'

She stretched out, luxuriating into the extra space on the sofa, putting her boots up. Valerie meant to go looking for Robyn then, to say goodbye, but the sight of chaos in the kitchen brought her up short: dishes piled in an old sink, gas cooker filthy with grease, torn slices of bread and stained tea towels and orange peels lying on the linoleum floor where they'd been dropped. The table was still laid with plates on which some dark meat stew or sauce was congealing. She went to pick up her bag instead. 'Give her my love,' she said.

No one offered to show Valerie out. Heroically, like a girl in a film, she made her way alone through the next-door room, where the pale horse gleamed sinisterly; she jumped when something moved, thinking it was a flutter of stuffed birds, but it was only her own reflection in the foxed mirror. On the stairs, she remembered that she shouldn't have called it 'tea'. Gil was always reminding her to say 'dinner' or 'supper'. And once she was outside, on the path in the wind, Valerie looked back, searching along the first-floor windows of the house for any sign of the child looking out. But it was impossible to see – the glass was reflecting a last smouldering streak of sunset, dark as a livid coal smashed open.

That night it snowed. Valerie woke up in the morning in her old bedroom at her mother's and knew it before she even looked outside: a purer, weightless light bloomed on the wallpaper, and the crowded muddle of gloomy furniture inherited from her grandmother seemed washed clean and self-explanatory. She opened the curtains and lay looking out at the snow falling, exhilarated as if she were back in her childhood. Her mother had the wireless on downstairs.

'Trains aren't running,' she said gloatingly when Valerie came down. She was sitting smoking at the table in her housecoat, in the heat of the gas fire. 'So I suppose you'll have to stay over another night.'

'Oh, I don't know, Mum. I've got things to do at home.'

The snow made her restless; she didn't want to be shut up with her mother all day with nothing to talk about. She found a pair of zip-up sheepskin boots at the back of a cupboard and ventured out to the phone box. Snow was blowing across the narrow street in wafting veils, and the quiet was like a sudden deafness; breaking into the crusted surface, her boots creaked. No one had come out to shovel yet, so nothing was spoiled. Every horizontal ledge and edge and rim was delicately capped; the phone box was smothered in snow, the light blue-grey inside it. She called Gil and pushed her money in, told him she was going to go to the station, find out what was happening. He said that there was snow in the North, too. He wouldn't go to the faculty meeting today; he'd work on his book at home. 'Please try to get here any way you can,' he said in a low, urgent voice. 'He misses you.'

'I have to go,' she said. 'There's quite a queue outside.'

But there wasn't; there was only silence and the shifting vacancy. The footprints she'd made on her way there were filling up already.

'I don't know why you're so eager to get back to him,' her mother grumbled. But Valerie wasn't really thinking about Gil: it was the strangeness of the snow she liked, and the disruption it caused. It took her almost an hour and a half to get to King's Cross – the Underground was working, but it was slow. When she surfaced, it had stopped snowing, at least for the moment, but there still weren't any trains. A porter said she should try again later that afternoon; it was his guess that if the weather held they might be able to reopen some of the major routes. Valerie didn't want to linger in King's Cross. She put her bag in left luggage, then thought of going shopping – they'd surely have cleared Oxford Street. But she took the Piccadilly line instead, as far as South Ken. By the time she arrived at the Chelsea house, it was gone two o'clock.

The house was almost unrecognizable at first, transformed in the snow. It seemed exposed and taller and more formidable, more mysteriously separated from its neighbours, standing apart in dense shrubbery, which was half obliterated under its burden of white. Valerie didn't even know why she'd come back. Perhaps she'd had some idea that if she saw Marise today she'd be able to behave with more sophistication, say what she really thought. As she arrived at the corner, she glanced up at the side windows on the first floor. And there was Robyn looking out – in the wrong direction at first, so that she didn't see Valerie. She seemed to be crouched on the windowsill, slumped against the glass. It was unmistakably her, because although it was past lunchtime she was still dressed in the new white pyjamas.

Valerie stopped short in her tramping. Her boots were wet through. Had she seriously entertained the idea of ringing the doorbell and being invited inside again, without any reasonable pretext, into that place where she most definitely wasn't wanted? The next moment it was too late: Robyn had seen her. The child's whole body responded in a violent spasm of astonishment, almost as if she'd been looking out for Valerie, yet not actually expecting her to appear. In the whole week of her visit, she hadn't reacted so forcefully to anything. She leaped up on the windowsill, waving frantically, so that she was pressed full length against the glass. Remembering how those windows had rattled the night before, Valerie signalled to her to get down, motioning with her gloved hand and mouthing. Robyn couldn't hear her but gazed in an intensity of effort at comprehension. Valerie signalled again: Get down, be careful. Robyn shrugged, then gestured eagerly down to the front door, miming opening something. Valerie saw that she didn't have a choice. Nodding and pointing, she agreed that she was on her way around to the front. No one had trodden yet in the snow along the path, but she was lucky, the front entrance had been left open – deliberately, perhaps, because, as she stepped into the hall, a man called down, low-voiced and urgent, from the top landing, 'John, is that you?'

Apologizing into the dimness for not being John, Valerie hurried upstairs to where Robyn was fumbling with the latches on the other side of the purple-and-orange door. Then she heard Jamie. 'Hullo! Now what are you up to? Is someone out there?'

When the door swung back, Valerie saw that – alarmingly – Jamie was in his underpants. He was bemused rather than hostile. 'What are you doing here?'

She invented hastily, hot-faced, avoiding looking at his near-nakedness. 'Robyn forgot something. I came to give it to her.'

'I want to show her my toys,' Robyn said.

He hesitated. 'Her mother's lying down – she's got a headache. But you might as well come in. There's no one else for her to play with.'

Robyn pulled Valerie by the hand through a door that led straight into the kitchen; someone had cleared up the plates of stew, but without scraping them – they were stacked beside the sink. The only sign of breakfast was an open packet of cornflakes on the table, and a bowl and spoon. In Robyn's bedroom, across a short passageway, there really were nice toys, better than anything Valerie had ever possessed: a doll's house, a doll's cradle with white muslin drapes, a wooden Noah's Ark whose roof lifted off. The room was cold and cheerless, though, and there were no sheets on the bare mattress, only a dirty yellow nylon sleeping bag. No one had unpacked Robyn's suitcase – everything was still folded inside; she must have opened it herself to get out her pyjamas. There was a chest with its drawers hanging open, and most of Robyn's clothes seemed to be overflowing from supermarket carrier bags piled against the walls.

'I knew you'd come back,' Robyn said earnestly, not letting go of Valerie's hand.

Valerie opened her mouth to explain that it was only because she'd missed her train in all this weather, then she changed her mind. 'We weren't expecting snow, were we?' she said brightly.

'Have you come to get me? Are you taking me to your house again?'

She explained that she'd only come to say goodbye.

'No, please don't say goodbye! Auntie Valerie, don't go.'

'I'm sure you'll be coming to stay with us again soon.'

The child flung herself convulsively at Valerie, punishing her passionately, butting with her head. 'Not soon! Now! I want to come now!'

Valerie liked Robyn better with her face screwed into an ugly fury, kicking out with her feet, the placid brushstrokes of her brows distorted to exclamation marks. Holding her off by her shoulders, she felt the after-tremor of the child's violence.

'Do you really want to come home with me?'

'Really, really,' Robyn pleaded.

'But what about your mummy?'

'She won't mind! We can get out without her noticing.'

'Oh, I think we'll need to talk to her. But let's pack first. And you have to get dressed – if you're really sure, that is. We need to go back to the station to see if the trains are running.' Valerie looked around with a new purposefulness, assessing quickly. 'Where's your coat? Do you need the bathroom?'

Robyn sat abruptly on the floor to take off her pyjamas, and Valerie tipped out the contents of the suitcase, began repacking it with a few things that looked useful – underwear and wool jumpers and shoes. The toothbrush was still in its sponge bag. Then they heard voices, and a chair knocked over in the kitchen, and, before Valerie could prepare what she ought to say, Marise came stalking into the bedroom, with Jamie behind her. At least he'd put on trousers. 'How remarkable!' Marise exclaimed. 'What do you think you're doing, Valerie? Are you kidnapping my child?' Wrapped in a gold silk kimono embroidered with dragons, the sooty remnants of yesterday's makeup under her eyes, she looked as formidable as a tragic character in a play.

'Don't be ridiculous,' Valerie coolly said. 'I'm not kidnapping her. I was about to come and find you, to ask whether she could come back with us for another week or so. And I've got a perfect right, anyway. She says that she'd prefer to be at her father's.'

'I'm calling the police.'

'I wouldn't if I were you. You haven't got a leg to stand on. It's criminal neglect. Look at this room! There aren't even sheets on her bed.'

'She prefers a sleeping bag. Ask her!'

Frozen in the act of undressing, Robyn turned her face, blank with dismay, back and forth between the two women.

'And I'd like to know what she's eaten since she came home. There isn't any milk in the house, is there? It's two-thirty in the afternoon and all the child has had since lunchtime yesterday is dry cornflakes.'

'You know nothing about motherhood, nothing!' Marise shrieked. 'Robyn won't touch milk – she hates it. She's been fussy from the day she was born. And she's a spy, she's a little spy! Telling tales about me. How dare she? She's a vicious, ungrateful little snake and you've encouraged her in it. I knew this would happen. I should never have let Gilbert take her in the first place. I knew he'd only be stirring her up against me.

Where's he been all these years, with his so-called feelings for his daughter, I'd like to know? Jamie, get this cheap kidnapping whore out of here, won't you? No, I like whores. She's much worse, she's a *typist*.'

Valerie said that she didn't need Jamie to take her anywhere, and that, if they were slinging names about, she knew what Marise was. Minutes later, she was standing outside in the garden, stopping to catch her breath beside the gate, where the dustbins were set back from the path behind a screen of pines. She was smitten with the cold and trembling, penitent and ashamed. She shouldn't have interfered; she was out of her depth. It was true that she didn't know anything about motherhood. Hadn't she encouraged Robyn, just as Marise said, trying to make the child like her? And without genuinely liking in return. Now she had abandoned her to her mother's revenge, which might be awful. Then the front door opened and Jamie was coming down the path, with a curious gloating look on his face: under his arms, against his bare chest, he was carrying the dirty yellow sleeping bag that had been on Robyn's bed. Hustling Valerie back among the pines, out of sight of the windows, he dumped the bag at her feet. 'Off you go,' he said significantly, as if he and Valerie were caught up in some game together. 'Her mother's lying down again. Take it and get out of here.'

It took her a moment or two to understand. In the meantime, he'd returned inside the house and closed the door. There was a mewing from the bag, she fumbled to unroll it, and Robyn struggled out from inside and wrapped her arms, with a fierce sigh of submission, around Valerie's knees. But she was in her white pyjamas, barefoot, in the snow! How could they make their way through the streets with Robyn dressed like that? A window opened above them and Jamie lobbed out something, which landed with a soft thud on the path: one of the carrier bags from Robyn's room, packed with a miscellany of clothes – and he'd thought to add the pair of plimsolls. Then he closed the window and disappeared. There was no coat in the bag, but never mind. In panicking haste, Valerie helped Robyn put on layers of clothes over her pyjamas: socks, cord trousers, plimsolls, jumper.

'I thought he was going to eat me,' Robyn said.

'Don't be silly,' Valerie said firmly. She kicked the sleeping bag away out of sight, among the hedge roots.

'Are we escaping?'

'We're having an adventure.'

And they set out, ducking into the street, hurrying along beside the hedge. By a lucky chance, as soon as they got to the main road there was a taxi nosing through the slush. 'How much to King's Cross?' Valerie asked. She had all the money she'd been saving up to spend on a new dress. She'd have to buy Robyn a train ticket, too. Then she asked the taxi to stop at a post office, where she went inside to send a telegram. She couldn't telephone Gil; she knew he'd forbid her to bring the child back again. But she couldn't arrive with Robyn without warning him. 'Returning with daughter,' she wrote out on the form. 'No fit home for her.' She counted out the shillings from her purse.

Back in the taxi, making conversation, she asked Robyn where her dollies were. Robyn was stricken – she'd left them behind, under her pillow. It was dusk in the streets already: as they drove on, the coloured lights from the shops wheeled slowly across their faces, revealing them as strangers to each other. Valerie was thinking that she might need to summon all this effort of ingenuity one day for some escape of her own, dimly imagined, and that taking on the child made her less free. Robyn sat forward on the seat, tensed with her loss. Awkwardly, Valerie put an arm around her, to reassure her. She said not to worry, they would make new dolls, and better ones. Just for the moment, though, the child was inconsolable.

KAZUO ISHIGURO

Come Rain or Come Shine

Like me, Emily loved old American Broadway songs. She'd go more for the up-tempo numbers, like Irving Berlin's 'Cheek to Cheek' and Cole Porter's 'Begin the Beguine', while I'd lean towards the bitter-sweet ballads – 'Here's That Rainy Day' or 'It Never Entered My Mind'. But there was a big overlap, and anyway, back then, on a university campus in the south of England, it was a near-miracle to find anyone else who shared such passions. Today, a young person's likely to listen to any sort of music. My nephew, who starts university this autumn, is going through his Argentinian tango phase. He also likes Edith Piaf as well as any number of the latest indie bands. But in our day tastes weren't nearly so diverse. My fellow students fell into two broad camps: the hippie types with their long hair and flowing garments who liked 'progressive rock', and the neat, tweedy ones who considered anything other than classical music a horrible din. Occasionally you'd bump into someone who professed to be into jazz, but this would always turn out to be of the so-called crossover kind – endless improvisations with no respect for the beautifully crafted songs used as their starting points.

So it was a relief to discover someone else, and a girl at that, who appreciated the Great American Songbook. Like me, Emily collected LPs with sensitive, straightforward vocal interpretations of the standards – you could often find such records going cheap in junk shops, discarded by our parents' generation. She favoured Sarah Vaughan and Chet Baker. I preferred Julie London and Peggy Lee. Neither of us was big on Sinatra or Ella Fitzgerald.

In that first year, Emily lived in college, and she had in her room a portable record player, a type that was quite common then. It looked like a large hat box, with pale-blue leatherette surfaces and a single built-in speaker. Only when you raised its lid would you see the turntable sitting inside. It gave out a pretty primitive sound by today's standards, but I remember us crouching around it happily for hours, taking off one track, carefully lowering the needle down onto another. We loved playing different versions of the same song, then arguing about the lyrics, or about the singer's interpretations. Was that line really supposed to be sung so ironically? Was it better to sing 'Georgia on My Mind' as though Georgia was a woman or the place in America? We were especially pleased when we found a recording – like Ray Charles singing 'Come Rain or Come Shine' – where the words themselves were happy, but the interpretation was pure heartbreak.

Emily's love of these records was obviously so deep that I'd be taken aback each time I stumbled on her talking to other students about some pretentious rock band or vacuous Californian singer-songwriter. At times, she'd start arguing about a 'concept' album in much the way she and I would discuss Gershwin or Harold Arlen, and then I'd have to bite my lip not to show my irritation.

Back then, Emily was slim and beautiful, and if she hadn't settled on Charlie so early in her university career, I'm sure she'd have had a whole bunch of men competing for her. But she was never flirty or tarty, so once she was with Charlie, the other suitors backed off.

'That's the only reason I keep Charlie around,' she told me once, with a dead straight face, then burst out laughing when I looked shocked. 'Just a joke, silly. Charlie is my darling, my darling, my darling.'

Charlie was my best friend at university. During that first year, we hung around together the whole time and that was how I'd come to know Emily. In the second year, Charlie and Emily got a house-share down in town, and though I was a frequent visitor, those discussions with Emily around her record player became a thing of the past. For a start, whenever I called round to the house, there were several other students sitting around, laughing and talking, and there was now a fancy stereo system churning out rock music you had to shout over.

Charlie and I have remained close friends through the years. We may not see each other as much as we once did, but that's mainly down to distances. I've spent years here in Spain, as well as in Italy and Portugal, while Charlie's always based himself in London. Now if that makes it sound like I'm the jet-setter and he's the stay-at-home, that would be funny. Because in fact Charlie's the one who's always flying off – to Texas, Tokyo, New York – to his high-powered meetings, while I've been stuck in the same humid buildings year after year, setting spelling tests or conducting the same conversations in slowed-down English. My-name-is-Ray. What-is-your-name? Do-you-have-children?

When I first took up English teaching after university, it seemed a good enough life – much like an extension of university. Language schools were mushrooming all over Europe, and if the teaching was tedious and the hours exploitative, at that age you don't care too much. You spend a lot of time in bars, friends are easy to make, and there's a feeling you're part of a large network extending around the entire globe. You meet people fresh from their spells in Peru or Thailand, and this gets you thinking that if you wanted to, you could drift around the world indefinitely, using your contacts to get a job in any faraway corner you fancied. And always you'd be part of this cosy, extended family of itinerant teachers, swapping stories over drinks about former colleagues, psychotic school directors, eccentric British Council officers.

In the late '80s, there was talk of making a lot of money teaching in Japan, and I made serious plans to go, but it never worked out. I thought about Brazil too, even read a few books about the culture and sent off for application forms. But somehow I never got away that far. Southern Italy, Portugal for a short spell, back here to Spain. Then before you know it, you're forty-seven years old, and the people you started out with have long ago been replaced by a generation who gossip about different things, take different drugs and listen to different music.

Meanwhile, Charlie and Emily had married and settled down in London. Charlie told me once, when they had children I'd be godfather to one of them. But that never happened. What I mean is, a child never came along, and now I suppose it's too late. I have to admit, I've always felt slightly let down about this. Perhaps I always imagined that being godfather to one of their children would provide an official link, however tenuous, between their lives in England and mine out here.

Anyway, at the start of this summer, I went to London to stay with them. It had been arranged well in advance, and when I'd phoned to check a couple of days beforehand, Charlie had said they were both 'superbly well'. That's why I'd no reason to expect anything other than pampering and relaxation after a few months that hadn't exactly been the best in my life.

In fact, as I emerged out of their local Underground that sunny day, my thoughts were on the possible refinements that might have been added to 'my' bedroom since the previous visit. Over the years, there's almost always been something or other. One time it was some gleaming electronic gadget standing in the corner; another time the whole place had been redecorated. In any case, almost as a point of principle, the room would be prepared for me the way a posh hotel would go about things: towels laid out, a bedside tin of biscuits, a selection of CDs on the dressing table. A few years ago, Charlie had led me in and with nonchalant pride started flicking switches, causing all sorts of subtly hidden lights to go on and off: behind the headboard, above the wardrobe and so on. Another switch had triggered a growling hum and blinds had begun to descend over the two windows.

'Look, Charlie, why do I need blinds?' I'd asked that time. 'I want to see out when I wake up. Just the curtains will do fine.'

'These blinds are Swiss,' he'd said, as though this were explanation enough.

But this time Charlie led me up the stairs mumbling to himself, and as we got to my room, I realized he was making excuses. And then I saw the room as I'd never seen it before. The bed was bare, the mattress on it mottled and askew. On the floor were piles of magazines and paperbacks, bundles of old clothes, a hockey stick and a loudspeaker fallen on its side. I paused at the threshold and stared at it while Charlie cleared a space to put down my bag.

'You look like you're about to demand to see the manager,' he said, bitterly.

'No, no. It's just that it's unusual to see it this way.'

'It's a mess, I know. A mess.' He sat down on the mattress and sighed. 'I thought the cleaning girls would have sorted all this. But of course they haven't. God knows why not.'

He seemed very dejected, but then he suddenly sprang to his feet again.

'Look, let's go out for some lunch. I'll leave a note for Emily. We can have a long leisurely lunch and by the time we come back, your room – the whole flat – will be sorted out.'

'But we can't ask Emily to tidy everything.'

'Oh, she won't do it herself. She'll get on to the cleaners. She knows how to harass them. Me, I don't even have their number. Lunch, let's have lunch. Three courses, bottle of wine, everything.'

What Charlie called their flat was in fact the top two floors of a four-storey terrace in a well-to-do but busy street. We came out of the front door straight into a throng of people and traffic. I followed Charlie past shops and offices to a smart little Italian restaurant. We didn't have a reservation, but the waiters greeted Charlie like a friend and led us to a table. Looking around I saw the place was full of business types in suits and ties, and I was glad Charlie looked as scruffy as I did. He must have guessed my thoughts, because as we sat down he said:

'Oh, you're so home counties, Ray. Anyway, it's all changed now. You've been out of the country too long.' Then in an alarmingly loud voice: '*We* look like the ones who've made it. Everyone else here looks like middle management.' Then he leant towards me and said more quietly: 'Look, we've got to talk. I need you to do me a favour.'

I couldn't remember the last time Charlie had asked my help for any-thing, but I managed a casual nod and waited. He played with his menu for a few seconds, then put it down.

'The truth is, Emily and I have been going through a bit of a sticky patch. In fact, just recently, we've been avoiding one another altogether. That's why she wasn't there just now to welcome you. Right now, I'm afraid, you get a choice of one or the other of us. A bit like those plays when the same actor's playing two parts. You can't get both me and Emily in the same room at the same time. Rather childish, isn't it?'

'This is obviously a bad time for me to have come. I'll go away, straight after lunch. I'll stay with my Auntie Katie in Finchley.'

'What are you talking about? You're not listening. I just told you. I want you to do me a favour.'

'I thought that was your way of saying . . .'

'No, you idiot, *I*'m the one who has to clear out. I've got to go to a meeting in Frankfurt, I'm flying out this afternoon. I'll be back in two days, Thursday at the latest. Meanwhile, you stay here. You bring things round, make everything okay again. Then I come back, say a cheerful hello, kiss my darling wife like the last two months haven't happened, and we pick up again.'

At this point the waitress came to take our order, and after she'd gone Charlie seemed reluctant to take up the subject again. Instead, he fired questions at me about my life in Spain, and each time I told him anything, good or bad, he'd do this sour little smile and shake his head, like I was confirming his worst fears. At one point I was trying to tell him how much I'd improved as a cook – how I'd prepared the Christmas buffet for over forty students and teachers virtually single-handed – but he just cut me off in mid-sentence.

'Listen to me,' he said. 'Your situation's hopeless. You've got to hand in your notice. But first, you have to get your new job lined up. This Portuguese depressive, use him as a go-between. Secure the Madrid post, then ditch the apartment. Okay, here's what you do. One.'

He held up his hand and began counting off each instruction as he made it. Our food arrived when he still had a couple of fingers to go, but he ignored it and carried on till he'd finished. Then as we began to eat, he said:

'I can tell you won't do any of this.'

'No, no, everything you say is very sound.'

'You'll go back and carry on just the same. Then we'll be here again in a year's time and you'll be moaning about exactly the same things.'

'I wasn't moaning . . .'

'You know, Ray, there's only so much other people can suggest to you. After a certain point, you've got to take charge of your life.'

'Okay, I will, I promise. But you were saying earlier, something about a favour.'

'Ah yes.' He chewed his food thoughtfully. 'To be honest, this was my real motive in inviting you over. Of course, it's great to see you and all of that. But for me, the main thing, I wanted you to do something for me. After all you're my oldest friend, a life-long friend . . .'

Suddenly he began eating again, and I realized with astonishment he was sobbing quietly. I reached across the table and prodded his shoulder, but he just kept shovelling pasta into his mouth without looking up. When this had gone on for a minute or so, I reached over and gave him another little prod, but this had no more effect than my first one. Then the waitress appeared with a cheerful smile to check on our food. We both said everything was excellent and as she went off, Charlie seemed to become more himself again.

'Okay, Ray, listen. What I'm asking you to do is dead simple. All I want is for you to hang about with Emily for the next few days, be a pleasant guest. That's all. Just until I get back.'

'That's all? You're just asking me to look after her while you're gone?'

'That's it. Or rather, let her look after you. You're the guest. I've lined up some things for you to do. Theatre tickets and so on. I'll be back Thursday at the latest. Your mission's just to get her in a good mood and keep her that way. So when I come in and say, "Hello darling," and hug her, she'll just reply, "Oh hello, darling, welcome home, how was everything," and hug me back. Then we can carry on as before. Before all this horrible stuff began. That's your mission. Quite simple really.'

'I'm happy to do anything I can,' I said. 'But look, Charlie, are you sure she's in the mood to entertain visitors? You're obviously going through some sort of crisis. She must be as upset as you are. Quite honestly, I don't understand why you asked me here right now.'

'What do you mean, you don't understand? I've asked you because you're my oldest friend. Yes, all right, I've got a lot of friends. But when it comes down to it, when I thought hard about it, I realized you're the only one who'd do.'

I have to admit I was rather moved by this. All the same, I could see there was something not quite right here, something he wasn't telling me.

'I can understand you inviting me to stay if you were both going to be here,' I said. 'I can see how that would work. You're not talking to each other, you invite a guest as a diversion, you both put on your best behaviour, things start to thaw. But it's not going to work in this case, because you're not going to be here.'

'Just do it for me, Ray. I think it might work. Emily's always cheered up by you.'

'Cheered up by me? You know, Charlie, I want to help. But it's possible you've got this a bit wrong. Because I get the impression, quite frankly,

Emily isn't cheered up by me at all, even at the best of times. The last few visits here, she was . . . well, distinctly impatient with me.'

'Look, Ray, just trust me. I know what I'm doing.'

Emily was at the flat when we returned. I have to admit, I was taken aback at how much she'd aged. It wasn't just that she'd got significantly heavier since my last visit: her face, once so effortlessly graceful, was now distinctly bulldoggy, with a displeased set to the mouth. She was sitting on the living-room sofa reading the *Financial Times*, and got up rather glumly as I came in.

'Nice to see you, Raymond,' she said, kissing me quickly on the cheek, then sitting down again. The whole way she did this made me want to blurt out a profuse apology for intruding at such a bad time. But before I could say anything, she thumped the space beside her on the sofa, saying: 'Now, Raymond, sit down here and answer my questions. I want to know all about what you've been up to.'

I sat down and she began to interrogate me, much as Charlie had done in the restaurant. Charlie, meanwhile, was packing for his journey, drifting in and out of the room in search of various items. I noticed they didn't look at each other, but neither did they seem so uncomfortable being in the same room, despite what he'd claimed. And although they never spoke directly to each other, Charlie kept joining in the conversation in an odd, once-removed manner. For instance, when I was explaining to Emily why it was so difficult to find a flat-mate to share my rent burden, Charlie shouted from the kitchen:

'The place he's in, it's just not geared up for two people! It's for one person, and one person with a bit more money than he'll ever have!'

Emily made no response to this, but must have absorbed the information, because she then went on: 'Raymond, you should never have chosen an apartment like that.'

This sort of thing continued for at least the next twenty minutes, Charlie making his contributions from the stairs or as he passed through to the kitchen, usually by shouting out some statement that referred to me in the third person. At one point, Emily suddenly said:

'Oh, honestly Raymond. You let yourself be exploited left, right and centre by that ghastly language school, you let your landlord rip you off silly, and what do you do? Get in tow with some airhead girl with a drink problem and not even a job to support it. It's like you're deliberately trying to annoy anyone who still gives a shit about you!'

'He can't expect many of that tribe to survive!' Charlie boomed from the hall. I could hear he had his suitcase out there now. 'It's all very well behaving like an adolescent ten years after you've ceased to be one. But to carry on like this when you're nearly fifty!'

'I'm only forty-seven . . .'

'What do you mean, you're *only* forty-seven?' Emily's voice was unnecessarily loud given I was sitting right next to her. '*Only* forty-seven. This "only", this is what's destroying your life, Raymond. Only, only, only. Only doing my best. Only forty-seven. Soon you'll be only *sixty*-seven and only going round in bloody circles trying to find a bloody roof to keep over your head!'

'He needs to get his bloody arse together!' Charlie yelled down the staircase. 'Fucking well pull his socks up till they're touching his fucking balls!'

'Raymond, don't you ever stop and ask yourself who you are?' Emily asked. 'When you think of all your potential, aren't you ashamed? Look at how you lead your life! It's . . . it's simply infuriating! One gets so exasperated!'

Charlie appeared in the doorway in his raincoat, and for a moment they were shouting different things at me simultaneously. Then Charlie broke off, announced he was leaving – as though in disgust at me – and vanished.

His departure brought Emily's diatribe to a halt, and I took the opportunity to get to my feet, saying: 'Excuse me, I'll just go and give Charlie a hand with his luggage.'

'Why do I need help with my luggage?' Charlie said from the hall. 'I've only got the one bag.'

But he let me follow him down into the street and left me with the suitcase while he went to the edge of the kerb to hail a cab. There didn't seem to be any to hand, and he leaned out worriedly, an arm half-raised.

I went up to him and said: 'Charlie, I don't think it's going to work.'

'What's not going to work?'

'Emily absolutely hates me. That's her after seeing me for a few minutes. What's she going to be like after three days? Why on earth do you think you'll come back to harmony and light?'

Even as I was saying this, something was dawning on me and I fell silent. Noticing the change, Charlie turned and looked at me carefully.

'I think', I said, eventually, 'I have an idea why it had to be me and no one else.'

'Ah ha. Can it be Ray sees the light?'

'Yes, maybe I do.'

'But what does it matter? It remains the same, exactly the same, what I'm asking you to do.' Now there were tears in his eyes again. 'Do you remember, Ray, the way Emily always used to say she believed in me? She said it for years and years. I believe in you, Charlie, you can go all the way, you're really talented. Right up until three, four years ago, she was still saying it. Do you know how trying that got? I was doing all right. I *am* doing all right. Perfectly okay. But she thought I was destined for . . . God knows, president of the fucking world, God knows! I'm just an ordinary bloke who's doing all right. But she doesn't see that. That's at the heart of it, at the heart of everything that's gone wrong.'

He began to walk slowly along the pavement, very preoccupied. I hurried back to get his suitcase and began pulling it along on its rollers. The street was still fairly crowded, so it was a struggle to keep up with him without crashing the bag into other pedestrians. But Charlie kept walking at a steady pace, oblivious to my difficulties.

'She thinks I've let myself down,' he was saying. 'But I haven't. I'm doing perfectly okay. Endless horizons are all very well when you're young. But get to our age, you've got to . . . you've got to get some perspective. That's what kept going round in my head whenever she got unbearable about it. Perspective, she needs perspective. And I kept saying to myself, look, I'm doing okay. Look at loads of other people, people we know. Look at Ray. Look what a pig's arse he's making of *his* life. She needs perspective.'

'So you decided to invite me for a visit. To be Mr Perspective.'

At last, Charlie stopped and met my eye. 'Don't get me wrong, Ray. I'm not saying you're an awful failure or anything. I realize you're not a drug addict or a murderer. But beside me, let's face it, you don't look the highest of achievers. That's why I'm asking you, asking you to do this for me. Things are on their last legs with us, I'm desperate, I need you to help. And what am I asking, for God's sake? Just that you be your usual sweet self. Nothing more, nothing less. Just do it for me, Raymond. For me and Emily. It's not over between us yet, I know it isn't. Just be yourself for a few days until I get back. That's not so much to ask, is it?'

I took a deep breath and said: 'Okay, okay, if you think it'll help. But isn't Emily going to see through all this sooner or later?'

'Why should she? She knows I've got an important meeting in Frankfurt. To her the whole thing's straightforward. She's just looking after a guest, that's all. She likes to do that and she likes you. Look, a taxi.' He waved frantically and as the driver came towards us, he grasped my arm. 'Thanks, Ray. You'll swing it for us, I know you will.'

I returned to find Emily's manner had undergone a complete transformation. She welcomed me into the apartment the way she might a very aged and frail relative. There were encouraging smiles, gentle touches on the arm. When I agreed to some tea, she led me into the kitchen, sat me down at the table, then for a few seconds stood there regarding me with a concerned expression. Eventually she said, softly:

'I'm so sorry I went on at you like that earlier, Raymond. I've got no right to talk to you like that.' Then turning away to make the tea, she went on: 'It's years now since we were at university together. I always forget that. I'd never dream of talking to any other friend that way. But when it's you, well, I suppose I look at you and it's like we're back there, the way we all were then, and I just forget. You really mustn't take it to heart.'

'No, no. I haven't taken it to heart at all.' I was still thinking about the conversation I'd just had with Charlie, and probably seemed distant. I think Emily misinterpreted this, because her voice became even more gentle.

'I'm so sorry I upset you.' She was carefully laying out rows of biscuits on a plate in front of me. 'The thing is, Raymond, back in those days, we could say virtually anything to you, you'd just laugh and we'd laugh, and everything would be a big joke. It's so silly of me, thinking you could still be like that.'

'Well, actually, I *am* more or less still like that. I didn't think anything of it.'

'I didn't realize', she went on, apparently not hearing me, 'how different you are now. How close to the edge you must be.'

'Look, really Emily, I'm not so bad . . .'

'I suppose the passing years have just left you high and dry. You've like a man on the precipice. One more tiny push and you'll crack.'

'Fall, you mean.'

She'd been fiddling with the kettle, but now turned round to stare at me again. 'No, Raymond, don't talk like that. Not even in fun. I don't ever want to hear you talking like that.'

'No, you misunderstand. You said I'd crack, but if I'm on a precipice, then I'd fall, not crack.'

'Oh, you poor thing.' She still didn't seem to take in what I was saying. 'You're only a husk of the Raymond from those days.'

I decided it might be best not to respond this time, and for a few moments we waited quietly for the kettle to boil. She prepared a cup for me, though not for herself, and placed it in front of me.

'I'm so sorry, Ray, but I've got to get back to the office now. There are two meetings I absolutely can't miss. If only I'd known how you'd be, I wouldn't have deserted you. I'd have made other arrangements. But I haven't, I'm expected back. Poor Raymond. What will you do here, all by yourself?'

'I'll be terrific. Really. In fact, I was thinking. Why don't I get our dinner ready while you're gone? You probably won't believe this, but I've become a pretty good cook these days. In fact, we had this buffet just before Christmas . . .'

'That's terribly sweet of you, wanting to help. But I think it's best you rest just now. After all, an unfamiliar kitchen can be the source of so much stress. Why don't you just make yourself completely at home, have a herbal bath, listen to some music. I'll take care of dinner when I come in.'

'But you don't want to worry about food after a long day at the office.'

'No, Ray, you're just to relax.' She produced a business card and placed it on the table. 'This has got my direct line on it, my mobile too. I've *got* to go now, but you can call me any time you want. Now remember, don't take on anything stressful while I'm gone.'

*

For some time now I've been finding it hard to relax properly in my own apartment. If I'm alone at home, I get increasingly restless, bothered by the idea that I'm missing some crucial encounter out there somewhere. But if I'm left by myself in someone else's place, I often find a nice sense of peace engulfing me. I love sinking into an unfamiliar sofa with whatever book happens to be lying nearby. And that's exactly what I did this time, after Emily had left. Or at least, I managed to read a couple of chapters of *Mansfield Park* before dozing off for twenty minutes or so.

When I woke up, the afternoon sun was coming into the flat. Getting off the sofa, I began a little nose-around. Perhaps the cleaners had indeed been in during our lunch, or may be Emily had done the tidying herself; in any case, the large living room was looking pretty immaculate. Tidiness aside, it had been stylishly done up, with modern designer furniture and arty objects – though someone being unkind might have said it was all too obviously for effect. I took a browse through the books, then glanced through the CD collection. It was almost entirely rock or classical, but finally, after some searching, I found tucked away in the shadows a small section devoted to Fred Astaire, Chet Baker, Sarah Vaughan. It puzzled me that Emily hadn't replaced more of her treasured vinyl collection with their CD reincarnations, but I didn't dwell on this, and wandered off into the kitchen.

I was opening up a few cupboards in search of biscuits or a chocolate bar when I noticed what seemed to be a small notebook on the kitchen table. It had purple cushioned covers, which made it stand out amidst the sleek minimalist surfaces of the kitchen. Emily, in a big hurry just before she'd left, had been emptying and re-filling her bag on the table while I'd been drinking my tea. Obviously she'd left the notebook behind by mistake. But then in almost the next instant another idea came to me: that this purple book was some kind of intimate diary, and Emily had left it there on purpose, fully intending for me to have a peek; that for whatever reason, she'd felt unable to confide more openly, so had resorted to this way of sharing her inner turmoil.

I stood there for a while, staring at the notebook. Then I reached forward, inserted my forefinger into the pages at the mid-way point and gingerly levered it up. The sight of Emily's closely packed handwriting inside made me pull my finger out, and I moved away from the table, telling myself I had no business nosing in there, never mind what Emily had intended in an irrational moment.

I went back into the living room, settled into the sofa and read a few more pages of *Mansfield Park*. But now I found I couldn't concentrate. My mind kept going back to the purple notebook. What if it hadn't been an impulsive action at all? What if she'd planned this for days? What if she'd composed something carefully for me to read?

After another ten minutes, I went back into the kitchen and stared some more at the purple notebook. Then I sat down, where I'd sat before to drink my tea, slid the notebook towards me, and opened it.

One thing that became quickly apparent was that if Emily confided her innermost thoughts to a diary, then that book was elsewhere. What I had before me was at best a glorified appointments diary; under each day she'd scrawled various memos to herself, some with a distinct aspirational dimension. One entry in bold felt-tip went: 'If still not phoned Mathilda, WHY THE HELL NOT??? DO IT!!!'

Another one ran: 'Finish Philip Bloody Roth. Give back to Marion!'

Then, as I kept turning the pages, I came across: 'Raymond coming Monday. Groan, groan.'

I turned a couple more pages to find: 'Ray tomorrow. How to survive?'

Finally, written that very morning, amidst reminders for various chores: 'Buy wine for arrival of Prince of Whiners.'

Prince of Whiners? It took me some time to accept this really could be referring to me. I tried out all sorts of possibilities – a client? a plumber? – but in the end, given the date and the context, I had to accept there was no other serious candidate. Then suddenly the sheer unfairness of her giving me such a title hit me with unexpected force, and before I knew it, I'd screwed up the offending page in my hand.

It wasn't a particularly fierce action: I didn't even tear the page. I'd simply closed my fist on it in a single motion, and the next second I was in control again, but of course, by then, it was too late. I opened my hand to discover not only the page in question but also the two beneath it had fallen victim to my wrath. I tried to flatten the pages back to their original form, but they simply curled back up again, as though their deepest wish was to be transformed into a ball of rubbish.

All the same, for quite some time, I carried on performing a kind of panicked ironing motion on the damaged pages. I was just about coming to accept that my efforts were pointless – that nothing I now did could successfully conceal what I'd done – when I became aware of a phone ringing somewhere in the apartment.

I decided to ignore it, and went on trying to think through the implications of what had just happened. But then the answering machine came on and I could hear Charlie's voice leaving a message. Perhaps I sensed a lifeline, perhaps I just wanted someone to confide in, but I found myself rushing into the living room and grabbing the phone off the glass coffee table.

'Oh, you *are* there.' Charlie sounded slightly cross I'd interrupted his message.

'Charlie, listen. I've just done something rather stupid.'

'I'm at the airport,' he said. 'The flight's been delayed. I want to call the car service that's picking me up in Frankfurt, but I didn't bring their number. So I need you to read it over to me.'

He began to issue instructions about where I'd find the phone book, but I interrupted him, saying:

'Look, I've just done something stupid. I don't know what to do.'

There was quiet for a few seconds. Then he said: 'Maybe you're thinking, Ray. Maybe you're thinking there's someone else. That I'm going off now to see her. It occurred to me that might be what you were thinking. After all, it would fit with everything you've observed. The way Emily was when I left, all of that. But you're wrong.'

'Yes, I take your point. But look, there's something I have to talk to you about . . .'

'Just accept it, Ray. You're wrong. There's no other woman. I'm going now to Frankfurt to attend a meeting about changing our agency in Poland. That's where I'm going right now.'

'Right, I've got you.'

'There's never been another woman in any of this. I wouldn't look at anyone else, at least not in any serious way. That's the truth. It's the bloody truth and there's nothing else to it!'

He'd started to shout, though possibly this was because of all the noise around him in the departure lounge. Now he went quiet, and I listened hard to work out if he was crying again, but all I heard were airport noises. Suddenly he said:

'I know what you're thinking. You're thinking, all right, there's no other woman. But is there another *man*? Go on, admit it, that's what you're thinking, isn't it? Go on, say it!'

'Actually, no. It's never occurred to me you might be gay. Even that time after finals when you got really drunk and pretended to . . .'

'Shut up, you fool! I meant another man, as in Lover of Emily! Lover of Emily, does this figure bloody exist? That's what I'm getting at. And the answer, in my judgement, is no, no, no. After all these years, I can read her pretty well. But the trouble is, precisely because I know her so well, I can tell something else, too. I can tell she's started to think about it. That's right, Ray, she's looking at other guys. Guys like David bloody Corey!'

'Who's that?'

'David bloody Corey is a smarmy git of a barrister who's doing well for himself. I know exactly how well, because she tells me how well, in excruciating detail.'

'You think . . . they're seeing each other?'

'No, I just told you! There's nothing, not yet! Anyway, David bloody Corey wouldn't give her the time of day. He's married to a glamourpuss who works for Condé Nast.'

'Then you're okay . . .'

'I'm not okay, because there's also Michael Addison. And Roger Van Den Berg who's a rising star at Merrill Lynch who gets to go to the World Economic Forum every year . . .'

'Look, Charlie, please listen. I've got this problem here. Small by most standards, I admit. But a problem all the same. Please just listen.'

At last I got to tell him what had happened. I recounted everything as honestly as I could, though maybe I went easy on the bit about my thinking Emily had left a confidential message for me.

'I know it was really stupid,' I said, as I came to the end. 'But she'd left it sitting there, right there on the kitchen table.'

'Yes.' Charlie was now sounding much calmer. 'Yes. You've rather let yourself in for it there.'

Then he laughed. Encouraged by this, I laughed, too.

'I suppose I'm over-reacting,' I said. 'After all, it's not like her personal diary or anything. It's just a memo book . . .' I trailed off because Charlie had continued to laugh, and there was something a touch hysterical in his laughter. Then he stopped and said flatly:

'If she finds out, she'll want to saw your balls off.'

There was a short pause while I listened to airport noises. Then he went on:

'About six years ago, I opened that book myself, or that year's equivalent. Just casually, when I was sitting in the kitchen, and she was doing some cooking. You know, just flicked it open absent-mindedly while I was saying something. She noticed immediately and told me she wasn't happy about it. In fact, that's when she told me she would saw my balls off. She was wielding this rolling pin at the time, so I pointed out she couldn't very well do what she was threatening with a rolling pin. That's when she said the rolling pin was for afterwards. For what she'd do to them once she'd cut them off.'

A flight announcement went off in the background.

'So what do you suggest I do?' I asked.

'What *can* you do? Just keep smoothing the pages down. Maybe she won't notice.'

'I've been trying that and it just doesn't work. There's no way she won't notice . . .'

'Look, Ray, I've got a lot on my mind. What I'm trying to tell you is that all these men Emily dreams about, they're not really potential lovers. They're just figures she thinks are wonderful because she believes they've accomplished so much. She doesn't see their warts. Their sheer . . . *brutality*. They're all out of her league anyway. The point is, and this is what's so pathetically sad and ironic about all this, the point is, at the bottom of it all, she loves *me*. She still loves me. I can tell, I can tell.'

'So, Charlie, you don't have any advice.'

'No! I don't have any fucking advice!' He was shouting full blast again. 'You figure it out! You get on your plane and I'll get on mine. And we'll see which one crashes!'

With that, Charlie was gone. I slumped down into the sofa and took a deep breath. I told myself I had to keep things in proportion, but all the while I could feel in my stomach a vaguely nauseous sensation of panic. Various ideas ran through my mind. One solution was simply to flee the apartment, and have no contact with Charlie and Emily for several years, after which I'd send them a cautious, carefully worded letter. Even in my current state, I dismissed this plan as being a touch too desperate. A better plan was that I steadily work through the bottles in their drinks cabinet, so that when Emily arrived home, she'd find me pathetically drunk. Then I could claim to have looked through her diary and attacked the pages in an alcoholic delirium. In fact, in my drunken unreasonableness, I could even adopt the role of the injured party, shouting and pointing, telling her how bitterly hurt I'd been to read those words about me, written by someone whose love and friendship I'd always counted on, the thought of which had helped sustain me through my lousiest moments in strange and lonely countries. But while this plan had points to recommend it from a practical aspect, I could sense something there – something near the bottom of it, something I didn't care to examine too closely – that I knew would make it an impossibility for me.

After a time, the phone began to ring and Charlie's voice came onto the machine again. When I picked it up he sounded considerably calmer than before.

'I'm at the gate now,' he said. 'I'm sorry if I was a little flustered earlier on. Airports always make me that way. Can't ever settle until I'm sitting right by the gate. Ray, listen, there's just one thing that occurred to me. Concerning our strategy.'

'Our strategy?'

'Yes, our overall strategy. Of course, you've realized, this isn't the time for little tweakings of the truth to show yourself in a better light. Absolutely not the time for the small self-aggrandizing white lie. No, no. You're remembering, aren't you, why you were given this job in the first place. Ray, I'm depending on you to present yourself to Emily just as you are. So long as you do that, our strategy stays on course.'

'Well, look, I'm hardly on course here to come over like Emily's greatest hero . . .'

'Yes, you appreciate the situation and I'm grateful. But something's just occurred to me. There's just one thing, one little thing in your repertoire that won't quite do here. You see, Ray, she's got this idea that you have good musical taste.'

'Ah . . .'

'Just about the only time she ever uses *you* to belittle me is in this area of musical taste. It's the one respect in which you aren't absolutely perfect for your current assignment. So Ray, you've got to promise not to talk about this topic.'

'Oh, for God's sake . . .'

'Just do it for me, Ray. It's not much to ask. Just don't start going on about that . . . that croony nostalgia music she likes. And if *she* brings it up, then you just play it dumb. That's all I'm asking. Otherwise, you just be your natural self. Ray, I can count on you about this, can't I?'

'Well, I suppose so. This is all pretty theoretical anyway. I don't see us chatting about anything this evening.'

'Good! So that's settled. Now, let's move to your little problem. You'll be glad to hear I've been giving it some thought. And I've come up with a solution. Are you listening?'

'Yes, I'm listening.'

'There's this couple who keep coming round. Angela and Solly. They're okay, but if they weren't neighbours we wouldn't have much to do with them. Anyway they often come round. You know, dropping in without warning, expecting a cup of tea. Now here's the point. They turn up at various times in the day when they've been taking Hendrix out.'

'Hendrix?'

'Hendrix is a smelly, uncontrollable, possibly homicidal Labrador. For Angela and Solly, of course, the foul creature's the child they never had. Or the one they haven't had yet, they're probably still young enough for real children. But no, they prefer darling, darling Hendrix. And when they call round, darling Hendrix routinely goes about demolishing the place as determinedly as any disaffected burglar. Down goes the standard lamp. Oh dear, never mind, darling, did you have a fright? You get the picture. Now listen. About a year ago, we had this coffee-table book, cost a fortune, full of arty pictures of young gay men posing in North African casbahs. Emily liked to keep it open at this particular page, she thought it went with the sofa. She'd go mad if you turned over the page. Anyway, about a year ago, Hendrix came in and chewed it all up. That's right, sank his teeth into all that glossy photography, went on to chew up about twenty pages in all before Mummy could persuade him to desist. You see why I'm telling you this, don't you?'

'Yes. That is, I see a hint of an escape route, but . . .'

'All right, I'll spell it out. This is what you tell Emily. The door went, you answered it, this couple are there with Hendrix tugging at the leash. They tell you they're Angela and Solly, good friends needing their cup of tea. You let them in, Hendrix runs wild, chews up the diary. It's utterly plausible. What's the matter? Why aren't you thanking me? Won't quite do for you, sir?'

'I'm very grateful, Charlie. I'm just thinking it through, that's all. Look, for one thing, what if these people really turn up? After Emily's home, I mean.'

'That's possible, I suppose. All I can say is you'd be very, very unlucky if such a thing happened. When I said they came round a lot, I meant maybe once a month at most. So stop picking holes and be grateful.'

'But Charlie, isn't it a little far-fetched that this dog would chew just the diary, and exactly those pages?'

I heard him sigh. 'I assumed you didn't need the rest of it spelt out. Naturally, you have to do the place over a bit. Knock over the standard lamp, spill sugar over the kitchen floor. You have to make it like Hendrix did this whirlwind job on the place. Look, they're calling the flight. I've got to go. I'll check in with you once I'm in Germany.'

While listening to Charlie, a feeling had come over me similar to the one I get when someone starts on about a dream they had, or the circumstances that led to the little bump on their car door. His plan was all very well – ingenious, even – but I couldn't see how it had to do with anything I was really likely to say or do when Emily got home, and I'd found myself getting more and more impatient. But once Charlie had gone, I found his call had had a kind of hypnotic effect on me. Even as my head was dismissing his idea as idiotic, my arms and legs were setting out to put his 'solution' into action.

I began by putting the standard lamp down on its side. I was careful not to bump anything with it, and I removed the shade first, putting it back on at a cocked angle only once the whole thing was arranged on the floor. Then I took down a vase from a bookshelf and laid it down on the rug, spreading around it the dried grasses that had been inside. Next I selected a good spot near the coffee table to 'knock over' the wastepaper basket. I went about my work in a strange, disembodied mode.

I didn't believe any of it would achieve anything, but I was finding the whole procedure rather soothing. Then I remembered all this vandalism was supposed to relate to the diary, and went through into the kitchen.

After a little think, I took a bowl of sugar from a cupboard, placed it on the table not far from the purple notebook, and slowly tilted it until the sugar slid out. I had a bit of a job preventing the bowl rolling off the edge of the table, but in the end got it to stay put. By this time, the gnawing panic I'd been feeling had evaporated. I wasn't tranquil, exactly, but it now seemed silly to have got myself in the state I had.

I went back to the living room, lay down on the sofa and picked up the Jane Austen book. After a few lines, I felt a huge tiredness coming over me and before I knew it, I was slipping into sleep once more.

I was woken up by the phone. When Emily's voice came on the machine, I sat up and answered it.

'Oh goody, Raymond, you *are* there. How are you, darling? How are you feeling now? Have you managed to relax?'

I assured her I had, that in fact I'd been sleeping.

'Oh what a pity! You probably haven't been sleeping properly for weeks, and now just when you finally get a moment's escape, I go and disturb you! I'm so sorry! And I'm sorry too, Ray, I'm going to have to disappoint you. There's an absolute crisis on here and I won't be able to get home quite as quickly as I'd hoped. In fact, I'm going to be another hour at least. You'll be able to hold out, won't you?'

I reiterated how relaxed and happy I was feeling.

'Yes, you do sound really stable now. I'm so sorry, Raymond, but I've got to go and sort this out. Help yourself to anything and everything. Goodbye, darling.'

I put down the phone and stretched my arms. The light was starting to fade now, so I went about the apartment switching on lights. Then I contemplated my 'wrecked' living room, and the more I looked at it, the more it seemed overwhelmingly contrived. The sense of panic began to grow once more in my stomach.

The phone went again, and this time it was Charlie. He was, he told me, beside the luggage carousel at Frankfurt airport.

'They're taking bloody ages. We haven't had a single bag come down yet. How are you making out over there? Madam not home yet?'

'No, not yet. Look, Charlie, that plan of yours. It's not going to work.'

'What do you mean, it's not going to work? Don't tell me you've been twiddling your thumbs all this time mulling it over.'

'I've done as you suggested. I've messed the place up, but it doesn't look convincing. It just doesn't look like a dog's been here. It just looks like an art exhibition.'

He was silent for a moment, perhaps concentrating on the carousel. Then he said: 'I can understand your problem. It's someone else's property. You're bound to be inhibited. So listen, I'm going to name a few items I'd dearly love to see damaged. Are you listening, Ray? I *want* the following things ruined. That stupid china ox thing. It's by the CD player. That's a present from David bloody Corey after his trip to Lagos. You can smash that up for a start. In fact, I don't care what you destroy. Destroy everything!'

'Charlie, I think you need to calm down.'

'Okay, okay. But that apartment's full of junk. Just like our marriage right now. Full of tired junk. That spongy red sofa, you know the one I mean, Ray?'

'Yes. Actually I fell asleep on it just now.'

'That should have been in a skip ages ago. Why don't you rip open the covering and throw the stuffing around.'

'Charlie, you have to get a grip. In fact, it occurs to me you're not trying to help me at all. You're just using me as a tool to express your rage and frustration . . .'

'Oh shut up with that bollocks! Of course I'm trying to help you. And of course my plan's a good one. I guarantee it'll work. Emily hates that dog, she hates Angela and Solly, so she'll seize any opportunity to hate them even more. Listen.' His voice suddenly dropped to a near-whisper. 'I'll give you the big tip. The secret ingredient that'll ensure she's convinced. I should have thought of this before. How much time do you have left?'

'Another hour or so . . .'

'Good. Listen carefully. Smell. That's right. You make that place smell of dog. From the moment she walks in, she'll register it, even if it's only subliminally. Then she steps into the room, notices darling David's china ox smashed up on the floor, the stuffing from that foul red sofa all over . . .'

'Now look, I didn't say I'd . . .'

'Just listen! She sees all the wreckage, and immediately, consciously or unconsciously, she'll make the connection with the dog smell. The whole scene with Hendrix will flash vividly through her head, even before you've said a word to her. That's the beauty of it!'

'You're havering, Charlie. Okay, so how do I make your home pong of dog?'

'I know exactly how you create a dog smell.' His voice was still an excited whisper. 'I know exactly how you do it, because me and Tony Barton used to do it in the Lower Sixth. He had a recipe, but I refined it.'

'But why?'

'Why? Because it stank more like cabbage than dog, that's why.'

'No, I meant why would you . . . Look, never mind. You might as well tell me, so long as it doesn't involve going out and buying a chemistry set.'

'Good. You're coming round to it. Get a pen, Ray. Write this down. Ah, here it comes at last.' He must have put the phone in his pocket, because for the next few moments I listened to womb noises. Then he came back and said:

'I have to go now. So write this down. Are you ready? The middle-sized saucepan. It's probably on the stove already. Put about a pint of water in it. Add two beef stock cubes, one dessertspoon of cumin, one tablespoon of paprika, two tablespoons of vinegar, a generous lot of bay leaves. Got that? Now you put in there a leather shoe or boot, upside down, so the sole's not actually immersed in the liquid. That's so you don't get any hint of burning rubber. Then you turn on the gas, bring the concoction to the boil, let it sit there simmering. Pretty soon, you'll notice the smell. It's not an awful smell. Tony Barton's original recipe involved garden slugs, but this one's much more subtle. Just like a smelly dog. I know, you're going to ask me where to find the ingredients. All the herbs and stuff are in the kitchen cupboards. If you go to the understairs cupboard, you'll find a discarded pair of boots in there. Not the wellingtons. I mean the battered-up pair, they're more like built-up shoes. I used to wear them all the time on the common. They've had it and they're waiting for the heave. Take one of those. What's the matter? Look, Ray, you just do this, okay?

Save yourself. Because I'm telling you, an angry Emily is no joke. I've got to go now. Oh, and remember. No showing off your wonderful musical knowledge.'

Perhaps it was simply the effect of receiving a clear set of instructions, however dubious: when I put the phone down, a detached, business-like mood had come over me. I could see clearly just what I needed to do. I went into the kitchen and switched on the lights. Sure enough, the 'middle-sized' saucepan was sitting on the cooker, awaiting its next task. I filled it to halfway with water, and put it back on the hob. Even as I was doing this, I realized there was something else I had to establish before proceeding any further: namely, the precise amount of time I had to complete my work. I went into the living room, picked up the phone, and called Emily's work number.

I got her assistant, who told me Emily was in a meeting. I insisted, in a tone that balanced geniality with resolution, that she bring Emily out of her meeting, 'if indeed she is in one at all'. The next moment, Emily was on the line.

'What is it, Raymond? What's happened?'

'Nothing's happened. I'm just calling to find out how you are.'

'Ray, you sound odd. What is it?'

'What do you mean, I sound odd? I just called to establish when to expect you back. I know you regard me as a layabout, but I still appreciate a timetable of sorts.'

'Raymond, there's no need to get cross like that. Now let me see. It's going to be another hour . . . Maybe an hour and a half. I'm awfully sorry, but there's a real crisis on here . . .'

'One hour to ninety minutes. That's fine. That's all I need to know. Okay, I'll see you soon. You can get back to your business now.'

She might have been about to say something else, but I hung up and strode back into the kitchen, determined not to let my decisive mood evaporate. In fact, I was beginning to feel distinctly exhilarated, and I couldn't understand at all how I'd allowed myself to get into such a state of despondency earlier on. I went through the cupboards and lined up, in a neat row beside the hob, all the herbs and spices I needed. Then I measured them out into the water, gave a quick stir, and went off to find the boot.

The understairs cupboard was hiding a whole heap of sorry-looking footwear. After a few moments of rummaging, I discovered what was certainly one of the boots Charlie had prescribed – a particularly exhausted specimen with ancient mud encrusted along the rim of its heel. Holding it with fingertips, I took it back to the kitchen and placed it carefully in the water with the sole facing up to the ceiling. Then I lit a medium flame under the pan, sat down at the table and waited for the water to heat. When the phone rang again, I felt reluctant to abandon the saucepan, but then I heard Charlie on the machine going on and on. So I eventually turned the flame down low and went to answer him.

'What were you saying?' I asked. 'It sounded particularly self-pitying, but I was busy so I missed it.'

'I'm at the hotel. It's only a three-star. Can you believe the cheek! A big company like them! And it's a poxy little room too!'

'But you're only there for a couple of nights . . .'

'Listen, Ray, there's something I wasn't entirely honest about earlier. It's not fair on you. After all, you're doing me a favour, you're doing your best for me, trying to heal things with Emily, and here I am, being less than frank with you.'

'If you're talking about the recipe for the dog smell, it's too late. I've got it all going. I suppose I might be able to add an extra herb or something . . .'

'If I wasn't straight with you before, that's because I wasn't being straight with myself. But now I've come away, I've been able to think more clearly. Ray, I told you there wasn't anyone else, but that's not strictly true. There's this girl. Yes, she *is* a girl, early thirties at most. She's very concerned about education in the developing world, and fairer global trade. It wasn't really a sexual attraction thing, that was just a kind of by-product. It was her untarnished idealism. It reminded me of how we all were once. You remember that, Ray?'

'I'm sorry, Charlie, but I don't remember you ever being especially idealistic. In fact, you were always utterly selfish and hedonistic . . .'

'Okay, maybe we were all decadent slobs back then, the lot of us. But there's always been this other person, somewhere inside of me, wanting to come out. That's what drew me to her . . .'

'Charlie, when was this? When did this happen?'

'When did what happen?'

'This affair.'

'There was no affair! I didn't have sex with her, nothing. I didn't even have lunch with her. I just . . . I just made sure I kept seeing her.'

'What do you mean, kept seeing her?' I'd drifted back into the kitchen by this time and was gazing at my concoction.

'Well, I kept seeing her,' he said. 'I kept making appointments to see her.'

'You mean, she's a call girl.'

'No, no, I told you, we've never had sex. No, she's a dentist. I kept going back, kept making things up about a pain here, discomfort of the gums there. You know, I spun it out. And of course, in the end, Emily guessed.' For a second, Charlie seemed to be choking back a sob. Then the dam burst. 'She found out . . . she found out . . . because I was flossing so much!' He was now half-shrieking. 'She said, you *never, ever* floss your teeth that much!'

'But that doesn't make sense. If you look after your teeth more, you've less reason to go back to her . . .'

'Who cares if it makes sense? I just wanted to please her!'

'Look, Charlie, you didn't go out with her, you didn't have sex with her, what's the issue?'

'The issue is, I so wanted someone like that, someone who'd bring out this other me, the one that's been trapped inside . . .'

'Charlie, listen to me. Since the last time you called, I've pulled myself together considerably. And quite frankly, I think you should pull yourself together too. We can discuss all of this when you get back. But Emily will be here in an hour or so, and I've got to have everything ready. I'm on top of things here now, Charlie. I suppose you can tell that from my voice.'

'Fucking fantastic! You're on top of things. Great! Some fucking friend . . .'

'Charlie, I think you're upset because you don't like your hotel. But you should pull yourself together. Get things in perspective. And take heart. I'm on top of things here. I'll sort out the dog business, then I'll play my part up to the hilt for you. Emily, I'll say. Emily, just look at me, just look how pathetic I am. The truth is, most people are just as pathetic. But Charlie, he's different. Charlie is in a different league.'

'You can't say that. That sounds completely unnatural.'

'Of course I won't put it literally like that, idiot. Look, just leave it to me. I've got the whole situation under control. So calm down. Now I've got to go.'

I put the phone down and examined the pot. The liquid had now come to the boil and there was a lot of steam about, but as yet no real smell of any sort. I adjusted the flame until everything was bubbling nicely. It was around this point I was overcome by a craving for some fresh air, and since I hadn't yet investigated their roof terrace, I opened the kitchen door and stepped out.

It was surprisingly balmy for an English evening in early June. Only a little bite in the breeze told me I wasn't back in Spain. The sky wasn't fully dark yet, but was already filling with stars. Beyond the wall that marked the end of the terrace, I could see for miles around the windows and back yards of the neighbouring properties. A lot of the windows were lit, and the ones in the distance, if you narrowed your eyes, looked almost like an extension of the stars. This roof terrace wasn't large, but there was definitely something romantic about it. You could imagine a couple, in the midst of busy city lives, coming out here on a warm evening and strolling around the potted shrubs, in each other's arms, swapping stories about their day.

I could have stayed out there a lot longer, but I was afraid of losing my momentum. I went back into the kitchen, and walking past the bubbling pot, paused at the threshold of the living room to survey my earlier work. The big mistake, it struck me, lay in my complete failure to consider the task from the perspective of a creature like Hendrix. The key, I now realized, was to immerse myself within Hendrix's spirit and vision.

Once I'd started on this tack, I saw not only the inadequacy of my previous efforts, but how hopeless most of Charlie's suggestions had been. Why would an over-lively dog extract a little ox ornament from the midst of hi-fi equipment and smash it? And the idea of cutting open the sofa and throwing around the stuffing was idiotic. Hendrix would need razor teeth to achieve an effect like that. The capsized sugar bowl in the kitchen was fine, but the living room, I realized, would have to be re-conceptualized from scratch.

I went into the room in a crouched posture, so as to see it from something like Hendrix's eyeline. Immediately, the glossy magazines piled up on the coffee table revealed themselves as an obvious target, and so I pushed them off the surface along a trajectory consistent with a shove from a rampant muzzle. The way the magazines landed on the floor looked satisfyingly authentic. Encouraged, I knelt down, opened one of the magazines and scrunched up a page in a manner, I hoped, would find an echo when eventually Emily came across the diary. But this time the result was disappointing: too obviously the work of a human hand rather than canine teeth. I'd fallen into my earlier error again: I'd not merged sufficiently with Hendrix.

So I got down on all fours, and lowering my head towards the same magazine, sank my teeth into the pages. The taste was perfumy, and not at all unpleasant. I opened a second fallen magazine near its centre and began to repeat the procedure. The ideal technique, I began to gather, was not unlike the one needed in those fairground games where you try to bite apples bobbing in water without using your hands. What worked best was a light, chewing motion, the jaws moving flexibly all the time: this would cause the pages to ruffle up and crease nicely. Too focused a bite, on the other hand, simply 'stapled' pages together to no great effect.

I think it was because I'd become so absorbed in these finer points that I didn't become aware sooner of Emily standing out in the hall, watching me from just beyond the doorway. Once I did realize she was there, my first feeling wasn't one of panic or embarrassment, but of hurt that she should be standing there like that without having announced her arrival in some way. In fact, when I remembered how I'd gone to the trouble of calling her office only several minutes earlier precisely to pre-empt the sort of situation now engulfing me, I felt the victim of a deliberate deception. Perhaps that was why my first visible response was simply to give a weary sigh without making any attempt to abandon my all-fours posture. My sigh brought Emily into the room, and she laid a hand very gently on my back. I'm not sure if she actually knelt down, but her face seemed close to mine as she said:

'Raymond, I'm back. So let's just sit down, shall we?'

She was easing me up onto my feet, and I had to resist the urge to shake her off.

'You know, it's odd,' I said. 'No more than a few minutes ago, you were about to go into a meeting.'

'I was, yes. But after your phone call, I realized the priority was to come back.'

'What do you mean, priority? Emily, please, you don't have to keep holding my arm like that, I'm not about to topple over. What do you mean, a priority to come back?'

'Your phone call. I recognized it for what it was. A cry for help.'

'It was nothing of the sort. I was just trying to . . .' I trailed off, because I noticed Emily was looking around the room with an expression of wonder.

'Oh, Raymond,' she muttered, almost to herself.

'I suppose I was being a little clumsy earlier on. I would have tidied up, except you came back early.'

I reached down to the fallen standard lamp, but Emily restrained me.

'It doesn't matter, Ray. It really doesn't matter at all. We can sort it all out together later. You just sit down now and relax.'

'Look, Emily, I realize it's your own home and all that. But why did you creep in so quietly?'

'I didn't creep in, darling. I called when I came in, but you didn't seem to be here. So I just popped into the loo and when I came out, well, there you were after all. But why go over it? None of it matters. I'm here now, and we can have a relaxing evening together. Please do sit down, Raymond. I'll make some tea.'

She was already going towards the kitchen as she said this. I was fiddling with the shade of the standard lamp and so it took me a moment to remember what was in there – by which time it was too late. I listened for her reaction, but there was only silence. Eventually I put down the lampshade and made my way to the kitchen doorway.

The saucepan was still bubbling away nicely, the steam rising around the upheld sole of the boot. The smell, which I'd barely registered until this point, was much more obvious in the kitchen itself. It was pungent, sure enough, and vaguely curryish. More than anything else, it conjured up those times you yank your foot out of a boot after a long sweaty hike.

Emily was standing a few paces back from the cooker, craning her neck to get as good a view of the pot as possible from a safe distance. She seemed absorbed by the sight of it, and when I gave a small laugh to announce my presence, she didn't shift her gaze, let alone turn around.

I squeezed past her and sat down at the kitchen table. Eventually, she turned to me with a kindly smile. 'It was a terribly sweet thought, Raymond.'

Then, as though against her will, her gaze was pulled back to the cooker.

I could see in front of me the tipped-up sugar bowl – and the diary – and a huge feeling of weariness came over me. Everything felt suddenly overwhelming, and I decided the only way forward was to stop all the games and come clean. Taking a deep breath, I said:

'Look, Emily. Things might look a little odd here. But it was all because of this diary of yours. This one here.' I opened it to the damaged page and showed her. 'It was really very wrong of me, and I'm truly sorry. But I happened to open it, and then, well, I happened to scrunch up the page. Like this . . .' I mimicked a less venomous version of my earlier action, then looked at her.

To my astonishment, she gave the diary no more than a cursory glance before turning back to the pot, saying: 'Oh, that's just a jotter. Nothing private. Don't you worry about it, Ray.' Then she moved a step closer to the saucepan to study it all the better.

'What do you mean? What do you mean, don't worry about it? How can you say that?'

'What's the matter, Raymond? It's just something to jot down stuff I might forget.'

'But Charlie told me you'd go ballistic!' My sense of outrage was now being added to by the fact that Emily had obviously forgotten what she'd been writing about me.

'Really? Charlie told you I'd be angry?'

'Yes! In fact, he said you'd once told him you'd saw his balls off if he ever peeked inside this little book!'

I wasn't sure if Emily's puzzled look was due to what I was saying, or still left over from gazing at the saucepan. She sat down next to me and thought for a moment.

'No,' she said, eventually. 'That was about something else. I remember it clearly now. About this time last year, Charlie got despondent about something and asked what I'd do if he committed suicide. He was just testing me, he's far too chicken to try anything like that. But he asked, so I told him if he did anything like that I'd saw his balls off. That's the only time I've said that to him. I mean, it's not like a refrain on my part.'

'I don't get this. If he committed suicide, you'd do that to him? Afterwards?'

'It was just a figure of speech, Raymond. I was just trying to express how much I'd dislike him topping himself. I was making him feel valued.'

'You're missing my point. If you do it afterwards, it's not really a disincentive, is it? Or maybe you're right, it would be . . .'

'Raymond, let's forget it. Let's forget all of this. There's a lamb casserole from yesterday, there's over half of it left. It was pretty good last night, and it'll be even better tonight. And we can open a nice bottle of Bordeaux. It was awfully sweet of you to start preparing something for us. But the casserole's probably the thing for tonight, don't you think?'

All attempts to explain now seemed beyond me. 'Okay, okay. Lamb casserole. Terrific. Yes, yes.'

'So . . . we can put *this* away for now?'

'Yes, yes. Please do. Please put it away.'

I got up and went into the living room – which of course was still a mess, but I no longer had the energy to start tidying. Instead, I lay down on the sofa and stared at the ceiling. At one point, I was aware of Emily coming into the room, and I thought she'd gone through to the hall, but then I realized she was crouched in the far corner, fiddling with the hi-fi. The next thing, the room filled with lush strings, bluesy horns, and Sarah Vaughan singing 'Lover Man'.

A sense of relief and comfort washed over me. Nodding to the slow beat, I closed my eyes, remembering how all those years ago, in her college room, she and I had argued for over an hour about whether Billie Holiday always sang this song better than Sarah Vaughan.

Emily touched my shoulder and handed me a glass of red wine. She had a frilly apron on over her business suit, and was holding a glass for herself. She sat down at the far end of the sofa, next to my feet, and took a sip. Then she turned down the volume a little with her remote.

'It's been an awful day,' she said. 'I don't mean just work, which is a total mess. I mean Charlie going, everything. Don't imagine it doesn't hurt me, to have him go off abroad like that when we haven't made up.

Then to cap it all, you finally go and tip over the edge.' She gave a long sigh.

'No, really, Emily, it's not as bad as that. For a start, Charlie thinks the world of you. And as for me, I'm fine. I'm really fine.'

'Bollocks.'

'No, really. I feel fine . . .'

'I meant about Charlie thinking the world of me.'

'Oh, I see. Well, if you think that's bollocks, you couldn't be more wrong. In fact, I know Charlie loves you more than ever.'

'How can you know that, Raymond?'

'I know because . . . well, for a start he more or less told me so, when we were having lunch. And even if he didn't spell it out, I can tell. Look, Emily, I know things are a bit tough right now. But you've got to hang onto the most important thing. Which is that he still loves you very much.'

She did another sigh. 'You know, I haven't listened to this record for ages. It's because of Charlie. If I put this sort of music on, he immediately starts groaning.'

We didn't speak for a few moments, but just listened to Sarah Vaughan. Then as an instrumental break started, Emily said: 'I suppose, Raymond, you prefer her other version of this. The one she did with just piano and bass.'

I didn't reply, but just propped myself up a little more so as to sip my wine better.

'I bet you do,' she said. 'You prefer that other version. Don't you, Raymond?'

'Well,' I said, 'I really don't know. To tell you the truth, I don't remember the other version.'

I could feel Emily shift at the end of the sofa. 'You're kidding, Raymond.'

'It's funny, but I don't listen to this kind of stuff much these days. In fact, I've forgotten almost everything about it. I'm not even sure what song this is right now.' I did a little laugh, which perhaps didn't come out very well.

'What are you talking about?' She sounded suddenly cross. 'That's ridiculous. Short of having had a lobotomy, there's no way you could have forgotten.'

'Well. A lot of years have gone by. Things change.'

'What are you talking about?' There was now a hint of panic in her voice. 'Things can't change that much.'

I was pretty desperate to get off the subject. So I said: 'Pity things are such a mess at your work.'

Emily completely ignored this. 'So what are you saying? You're saying you don't like *this*? You want me to turn it off, is that it?'

'No, no, Emily, please, it's lovely. It . . . it brings back memories. Please, let's just get back to being quiet and relaxed, the way we were a minute ago.'

She did another sigh, and when she next spoke her voice was gentle again.

'I'm sorry, darling. I'd forgotten. That's the last thing you need, me yelling at you. I'm so sorry.'

'No, no, it's okay.' I heaved myself up to a sitting position. 'You know, Emily, Charlie's a decent guy. A very decent guy. And he loves you. You won't do better, you know.'

Emily shrugged and drank some more wine. 'You're probably right. And we're hardly young any more. We're as bad as one another. We should count ourselves lucky. But we never seem to be contented. I don't know why. Because when I stop and think about it, I realize I don't really want anyone else.'

For the next minute or so, she kept sipping her wine and listening to the music. Then she said: 'You know, Raymond, when you're at a party, at a dance. And it's maybe a slow dance, and you're with the person you really want to be with, and the rest of the room's supposed to vanish. But somehow it doesn't. It just doesn't. You know there's no one half as nice as the guy in your arms. And yet . . . well, there are all these people everywhere else in the room. They don't leave you alone. They keep shouting and waving and doing daft things just to attract your attention. "Oi! How can you be satisfied with that?! You can do much better! Look over here!" It's like they're shouting things like that all the time. And so it gets hopeless, you can't just dance quietly with your guy. Do you know what I mean, Raymond?'

I thought about it for a while, then said: 'Well, I'm not as lucky as you and Charlie. I don't have anyone special like you do. But yes, in some ways, I know just what you mean. It's hard to know where to settle. What to settle to.'

'Bloody right. I wish they'd just lay off, all these gatecrashers. I wish they'd just lay off and let us get on with it.'

'You know, Emily, I wasn't kidding just now. Charlie thinks the world of you. He's so upset things haven't been going well between you.'

Her back was more or less turned to me, and she didn't say anything for a long time. Then Sarah Vaughan began her beautiful, perhaps excessively slow version of 'April in Paris', and Emily started up like Sarah had called her name. Then she turned to me and shook her head.

'I can't get over it, Ray. I can't get over how you don't listen to this kind of music any more. We used to play all these records back then. On that little record player Mum bought me before I came to university. How could you just forget?'

I got to my feet and walked over to the french doors, still holding my glass. When I looked out to the terrace, I realized my eyes had filled with tears. I opened the door and stepped outside so I could wipe them without Emily noticing, but then she was following right behind me, so maybe she noticed, I don't know.

The evening was pleasantly warm, and Sarah Vaughan and her band came drifting out onto the terrace. The stars were brighter than before, and the lights of the neighbourhood were still twinkling like an extension of the night sky.

'I love this song,' Emily said. 'I suppose you've forgotten this one too. But even if you've forgotten it, you can dance to it, can't you?'

'Yes. I suppose I can.'

'We could be like Fred Astaire and Ginger Rogers.'

'Yes, we could.'

We placed our wine glasses on the stone table and began to dance. We didn't dance especially well – we kept bumping our knees – but I held Emily close to me, and my senses filled with the texture of her clothes, her hair, her skin. Holding her like this, it occurred to me again how much weight she'd put on.

'You're right, Raymond,' she said, quietly in my ear. 'Charlie's all right. We should sort ourselves out.'

'Yes. You should.'

'You're a good friend, Raymond. What would we do without you?'

'If I'm a good friend, I'm glad. Because I'm not much good at anything else. In fact, I'm pretty useless, really.'

I felt a sharp tug on my shoulder.

'Don't say that,' she whispered. 'Don't talk like that.' Then a moment later, she said again: 'You're such a good friend, Raymond.'

This was Sarah Vaughan's 1954 version of 'April in Paris', with Clifford Brown on trumpet. So I knew it was a long track, at least eight minutes. I felt pleased about that, because I knew after the song ended, we wouldn't dance any more, but go in and eat the casserole. And for all I knew, Emily would re-consider what I'd done to her diary, and decide this time it wasn't such a trivial offence. What did I know? But for another few minutes at least, we were safe, and we kept dancing under the starlit sky.

JACKIE KAY

Physics and Chemistry

Before Physics and Chemistry's life altered completely and forever one morning in June, Chemistry added a couple of drops of vinegar to the small pan, then slid Physics's egg in, slowly. Poaching was a talent. Physics hadn't bothered trying to poach an egg for about ten years. Even on school mornings Physics and Chemistry made sure they had a good breakfast. These days the division of domestic tasks in the house was quite simple: Chemistry poached eggs, roasted chicken, made the salad dressing, sent the cards, dusted, chose the new curtains, or the shade of emulsion; Physics made the bed, put the bin out, changed the light bulbs, serviced the car, wrapped the presents, did the ironing, wired the plugs. Chemistry washed, Physics dried. Neither believed in dishwashers – though, at home, in private, they marvelled at those in their staff room who claimed the dishwasher had saved their marriage.

Physics and Chemistry smiled small scientific smiles in the staff room when the subject of marriage came up. One of the more insensitive teachers, Mrs Fife (home economics, big apron) once famously said to Chemistry:

'You are not the kind of spinster I feel embarrassed talking about marriage to. I mean, I would have thought you could have easily got married, if you'd wanted to.'

In the staff room that day, quite some time ago now, there was a gigantic embarrassed silence. It seeped round the staff room making everybody blush. The odd thing was that everyone, the history teacher, the English teacher, the maths teacher, the PE teacher, felt a peculiar mixture of glee and shame, just like they might have for a member of their own family, for Mrs Fife's faux pas. She herself was blissfully unaware. Almost charmingly so.

73

'Oh dear, have I put my foot in it?' she finally said when the big wallop of silence was too much even for her not to notice. It was down to Chemistry to summon all of her generosity and say, 'I think I prefer the term single woman, it sounds more modern.' Physics fumed by the kettle, stirring her coffee.

When Mrs Fife made her gaffes, when pupils referred to Physics and Chemistry as *the Science Spinsters*, Physics always, always pretended not to hear. Physics was tall with long bones in her face, a long nose, large hands, and thick short hair, greying now. She had more hair than she would wish around her top lip. Recently, she noticed, it was even more of a presence than ever, perhaps it was her age. Still, there was nothing she could do about it; she was not going to subject herself to electrolysis, she'd heard that was painful and Physics hated pain. A coward, pain-wise, Chemistry said so. Physics had never been in hospital or had anything much wrong with her, but the slightest ache would have her moaning for days. Physics overheard one pupil say to another, 'Look at that moustache. She looks like a man.' And again she had stared straight ahead. Every day, in her own silent way, Physics kept something to herself.

At home in their Wimpey house, in Gleneagles Gardens, off the main Kirkintilloch Road, not too far from Bishopbriggs High School, where they both taught, Physics pulled the strings to shut the curtains, and put her slippers on. Physics and Chemistry had identical moccasin slippers, which they replaced every Christmas. At home, slippers on, fire lit – a fake gas fire that attempted to look like a real one, but never really fooled anybody – the *Scotsman* in hand, Physics felt herself physically relaxing. Most of the long school day, she stayed unlit and dangerous as one of Chemistry's experiments, the potential to blow up, to turn suddenly pink, to sparkle and spit, never far from her surface. At home, Physics would tell Chemistry some of the things she had pretended not to hear that day and Chemistry would tell Physics things back; sympathy and hilarity bubbled between them; and Chemistry's eyes lit up like a blue flame.

Some nights they sat at dinner – Physics in her chair by the kitchen door and Chemistry in the one opposite, and the weight of all the things they'd listened to in silence moved around them like molecules. The dinner in the middle of the table, the organic vegetables cooked in lemon grass and coconut oil, sat between them, a bright, colourful wok of strange ingredients as far as Physics was concerned. If Physics had her way, she would have a roast lamb, two veg and mashed potatoes and a nice wee jug of gravy. She ate all these unfamiliar, oddly upsetting, foods out of love. Her very palate had transformed since Chemistry's culinary habits had turned foreign a few years back. Chemistry always wanted to do things differently. Physics had to be forced to change. In the kitchen, the flushed pleasure on Chemistry's cheeks, the brightness of her voice and eyes, when she held out a spoon and said try this and pronounced some strange words like *gadoh gadoh* or *sayur lemak* or *sambal tauco*, made Physics want to drop to her knees with love and disappointment.

Physics was not an enthusiastic woman herself, but she admired the quality in others, marvelled at the way Chemistry could stretch her arms out and shout *Yippee*, or do a little skip or clap her hands loudly together and shriek *Yes!* when Evonne Goolagong won Wimbledon. Physics's mother had never smiled much; she thought that people who grinned widely were ignorant or idiotic; Physics's father had wanted a boy. She had never been hugged in her life until she met Chemistry. Even now she was uncomfortable if Chemistry touched her anywhere but in bed.

They sat at dinner, Chemistry boldly eating her Malaysian food with clever chopsticks; Physics clinging to a fork. A bottle of chilled Alsace in a bucket on the table. This wine bucket was another Christmas present from Chemistry to Physics, so that they could have, at home, a semblance of a restaurant. Why go out? Why ever go out? Most nights, Chemistry cooked. At weekends, they had special meals with wine. Physics always opened and poured the wine. During the week, they had quick meals with water or a cup of tea. After dinner, they did their marking. After marking, they'd watch the news. After the news, they might watch one of their favourite programmes, *Frost* or *Morse*, *The Street*, or *Panorama*. Usually Chemistry would fall asleep on the chair and Physics would smoke a cigarette outside the back door. Chemistry was an ex-smoker, the worst kind. Physics usually waited till Chemistry nodded off, sneaked out of the back door and smoked one or two Benson and Hedges. She enjoyed figuring out the constellations on such smoking nights on her own back door-step, puffing upwards towards the brilliant plough. After, she'd lock the door carefully, double-check by shaking the door and then shoogle Chemistry gently awake. Up the stairs they'd go to brush their teeth and go to bed. Physics brushed her teeth for a longer time than Chemistry to try to get rid of the smell of smoke.

Sometimes they had two teachers from Lenzie High School round – Rosemary and Nancy, PE and music, who also, like them, lived together and bought each other comfortable slippers for Christmas. Neither Rosemary and Nancy nor Physics and Chemistry, ever, ever, mentioned the nature of their relationship to each other. Every Boxing Day for the past eight years Rosemary and Nancy came round for dinner. They brought their slippers with them and the four of them sat drinking sweet white sparkling wine with identical moccasins on their feet, enjoying each other's company. Physics, when she had guests round, was always rather proud of Chemistry's adventurous cooking. 'Oh she gets all the proper ingredients, lemon grass, fresh chillies, coriander, glass noodles.'

Rosemary looked flushed and horrified. 'Is that what that taste is – cor-i-an-der?' Rosemary said, exchanging an oh-for-a-turkey-sandwich look with Nancy. 'Which taste?' Chemistry asked, beetroot with pleasure and effort and heat from the cooker.

'That sharpish taste,' said Rosemary, barely hiding her distaste.

'Oh, that'll be lemon grass, definitely,' Chemistry said with authority.

Physics beamed with pride and poured Rosemary and Nancy a little more festive wine. Rosemary covered Nancy's glass with her hand. 'Not for her, she's driving.'

But mostly it was the pair of them alone at the dining table. Sometimes they'd play music after their dinner. Shirley Bassey was a great favourite. One night at the beginning of their relationship, Chemistry had become a little tipsy and had sung along to *Goldfinger*, flourishing her arms in the air and tossing her hair like Shirley Bassey. Then she swung her hips and Physics watched open-mouthed as Chemistry's ample breasts bounced from side to side. It had shocked Physics to the core and excited her. One year Chemistry got them both tickets to go and see Shirley Bassey as a birthday present for Physics. When they came home that night, Chemistry, bubbling, sang *Hey Big Spender* dancing up and down their living room whilst Physics smoked a rare cigarette indoors. Chemistry leaned right over her when she sang *spend a little time with me* and she sounded, to Physics's ears, exactly like Shirley Bassey. What a woman, what a voice, Physics thought to herself, now as devoted to Bassey as Chemistry was. Physics blew a perfect smoke ring.

That night in bed, Chemistry slid her golden fingers through the fly of Physics's pyjamas and touched her gently at first, then firmer, faster; until she felt Physics's whole body stiffen and tremble. Then she lay her hand on Physics's flat stomach and waited until Physics lifted her nightdress with alarming speed, and pushed into her quickly, Physics's long fingers going up and up, deeper and deeper; Chemistry holding on to Physics for dear life. It was so much, first Shirley Bassey, then this, so much she felt she could explode. Outside, the sparkling, experimental stars lit up the suburban sky.

They never discussed these nights. Not a word. Not a single word was spoken or ever had been spoken about such nights. Physics had never ever said the dreaded word out loud for fear of it. The word itself spread terror within her. Chemistry was like her flesh and blood, heart of her heart, a part of her. Chemistry was Physics. Everything was relative. What they did in the dark at night in their own small house in Gleneagles Gardens was immaterial. In the morning Physics could almost feel it disappear like a ghost. But Chemistry knew better. The transformation could be seen on Physics's face, a face that was usually pale and pinched became brighter, more effusive somehow. Her eyes became even more familiar, sparkly. The morning after the night before, Chemistry could not but notice that Physics drove their Mini Metro to school in quite a cavalier fashion, spinning and abruptly whirling the car to a stop in the school car park.

Physics and Chemistry's life altered completely and forever one morning in June when Physics walked into the staff room as usual during the morning break and all the teachers stopped talking. Mr Ferguson coughed awkwardly and Mrs Cameron said loudly, 'The Head wants to see you. I'm afraid a parent has been up.'

'Which parent?' Physics asked.

'Sandra Toner.'

Sandra Toner was Physics's favourite and most talented pupil, a girl she encouraged, gave extra homework to, and had promised to spend thirty minutes extra every Tuesday with her.

'What's the problem?'

Mr Ferguson coughed and said, 'We've no idea.'

Physics looked out of the window in the headmaster's, Mr Smart's, office. There was a blur of pupils beyond the glass at break time, one uniform part of another, as if they shared cells. There was the sound of them, high, hysterical, bouncing off the windowpane and back into the playground like a rubber ball. Chemistry was on playground duty; Physics thought she saw her, small and round, in the distance. Mr Smart's face in front of her had changed. There was no doubt about it. It was like witnessing a strange conversion. A man reducing himself. His nose became sharper before Physics's very eyes. He kept moving his tie from side to side as if his collar was much too tight and was about to strangle him any second. His neck lengthening and rising above the collar, appearing for a moment like a snake, high and long, to get some relief, to taste the air. Why don't men like him wear the correct collar size? Physics thought to herself as he informed her he was giving her notice.

'You must understand,' he was saying. 'You must understand it from our point of view as a school. Even if the rumours are unfounded, you understand it is a delicate business, working with young people . . .' Physics, who rarely said more than a sentence to anybody except Chemistry and her students, kept quite, quite quiet. What was it about?

According to Mr Smart, the school gossiped about the pair of them, saying that they had a lesbian relationship, shared a house, a car, a bed. The whole school. It was time for them to go. He could no longer take the risk. Sandra Toner's father had come to him and said he did not want a lesbian teaching his daughter, especially out of school hours. Physics suddenly came to life. Mr Smart, said, didn't he, the *pair* of them. 'Do you mean to say that you have also sacked Chemistry?' she asked, appalled. 'Who?' Mr Smart asked, puzzled. 'Miss Gibson, you know, Iris. Have you sacked Iris?'

'That's . . . that's what I've been saying,' said Mr Smart, stuttering a bit now. 'Maybe you're too upset to take it all in. I can understand. You've both been exemplary teachers, but I've got the parents to think of.' But Physics wasn't listening any longer. She lunged forward; a voice came out of her as she grabbed hold of his collar and shook him; and shook him again. He was wearing a blue-and-white striped tie. She got hold of the tie and pulled it even tighter. 'You hypocritical bastard! How dare you sack Chemistry,' she shouted at him. 'She is a wonderful teacher. How dare you!' Mr Smart had his arm in the air and was trying to get out of her stranglehold. My God but she was strong for a woman. Suddenly, Physics let go. She gave him one final push and walked out of the head-master's office, past the school secretary's office, aware that she was being watched, with her head held high, taking long, long strides down the corridor.

Physics and Chemistry's life was never the same since the day they were sacked. Physics now kissed Chemistry in the kitchen over a sizzling wok. Physics stopped wearing skirts altogether. She put all of her checked and pleated and tartan skirts in a big black binbag and drove them to the Cancer Research shop in Springburn. Their new life became experimental, unpredictable. Once they pulled the strings of their curtains closed and lay down on their living room carpet and made love. Sometimes they had been seen at Bishopbriggs Cross, arm in arm at the traffic lights. They opened up a wool shop in Milngavie and called it *Close Knit* – the name made Rosemary and Nancy laugh when they came for their Christmas drink as if they were in on some big secret. It was a strange relief really. Being out of the classroom, the staff room, and the school, selling brightly coloured wool; Shetland wool, Botany wool, mohair, merino, angora, cashmere, cotton, nylon, rayon, wild silk, silk cotton, and patterns, and bobbles and buttons. Plain did the accounts, the opening and closing, the labelling. Purl did the selling, the smiling, the recommending, the order-ing. From the very first time, twenty-five years ago, when they had first met, they had this thing between them, this spark. It could always change colour.

GRAHAM SWIFT

Remember This

They were married now and had been told they should make their wills, as if that was the next step in life, so one day they went together to see a solicitor, Mr Reeves. He was not as they'd expected. He was soft-spoken, silver-haired and kindly. He smiled at them as if he'd never before met such a sweet newly married young couple, so plainly in love yet so sensibly doing the right thing. He was more like a vicar than a solicitor, and later Nick and Lisa shared the thought that they'd wished Mr Reeves had actually married them. Going to see him was in fact not unlike getting married. It had the same mixture of solemnity and giggly disbelief – are we really doing this? – the same feeling of being a child in adult's clothing.

They'd thought it might be a rather grim process. You can't make a will without thinking about death, even when you're twenty-four and twenty-five. They'd thought Mr Reeves might be hard going. But he was so nice. He gently steered them through the delicate business of making provision for their dying together, or with the briefest of gaps in between. 'In a car accident say,' he said, with an apologetic smile. That was like contemplating death indeed, that was like saying they might die tomorrow.

But they got through it. And, all in all, the fact of having drafted your last will and testament and having left all your worldly possessions – pending children – to your spouse was every bit as significant and as enduring a commitment as a wedding. Perhaps even more so.

And then there was something . . . Something.

Though it was a twelve-noon appointment and wouldn't take long, they'd both taken the day off and, without discussing it but simultaneously, dressed quite smartly, as if for a job interview. Nick wore a suit and tie.

Lisa wore a short black jacket, a dark red blouse and a black skirt which, though formal, was also eye-catchingly clingy. They both knew that if they'd turned up at Mr Reeves' office in jeans and T-shirts it wouldn't have particularly mattered – he was only a high street solicitor. On the other hand this was hardly an everyday event, for them at least. They both felt that certain occasions required an element of ceremony, even of celebration. Though could you celebrate making a will?

In any case, if just for themselves, they'd dressed up a bit, and perhaps Mr Reeves had simply been taken by the way they'd done this. Thus he'd smiled at them as if, so it seemed to them, he was going to consecrate their marriage all over again.

It was a bright and balmy May morning, so they walked across the common. There was no point in driving (and when Mr Reeves said that thing about a car accident they were glad they hadn't). There was no one else to think about, really, except themselves and their as yet unmet solicitor. As they walked they linked arms or held hands, or Nick's hand would wander to pat Lisa's bottom in her slim black skirt. The big trees on the common were in their first vivid green and full of singing birds.

They were newly married, but it had seemed to make no essential difference. It was a 'formality', as today was a formality. Formality was a lovely word, since it implied the existence of informality and even in some strange way gave its blessing to it. Nick let his palm travel and wondered if his glad freedom to let it do so was in any way altered, even enhanced, now that Lisa was his wife and not just Lisa.

Married or not, they were still at the stage of not being able to keep their hands off each other, even in public places. As they walked across the common to see Mr Reeves, Nick found himself considering that this might only be a stage – a stage that would fade or even cease one day. They'd grow older and just get used to each other. They wouldn't just grow older, they'd age, they'd *die*. It was why they were doing what they were doing today. And it was the deal with marriage.

It seemed necessary to go down this terminal path of thought even as they walked in the sunshine. Nonetheless, he let his palm travel.

And in Mr Reeves' office, though it was reassuring that Mr Reeves was so nice, one thing that helped Nick, while they were told about the various circumstances in which they might die, was thinking about Lisa's arse and hearing the tiny slithery noises her skirt made whenever she shifted in her seat.

It was a beautiful morning, but he'd heard a mixed forecast and he'd brought an umbrella. Having your will done seemed, generally, like remembering to bring an umbrella.

When they came out – it took less than half an hour – the clouds had thickened, though the bright patches of sky seemed all the brighter. 'Well, that's that,' Nick said to Lisa, as if the whole thing deserved only a relieved shrug, though they both felt an oddly exhilarating sense of accomplishment. Lisa said, 'Wasn't he *sweet*,' and Nick agreed immediately, and they both felt also, released back into the spring air, a great sense of animal vitality.

There was a bloom upon them and perhaps Mr Reeves couldn't be immune to it.

They retraced their steps, or rather took a longer route via the White Lion on the edge of the common. It seemed appropriate, however illogical, after what they'd done, to have a drink. Yes, to celebrate. Lunch, a bottle of wine, why not? In fact, since they both knew that, above all, they were hungry and thirsty for each other, they settled for nothing more detaining than two prawn sandwiches and two glasses of Sauvignon. The sky, at the window, meanwhile turned distinctly threatening.

By the time they'd crossed back over the common the rain had begun, but Nick had the umbrella, under which it was necessary to huddle close together. As he put it up he had the fleeting thought that its stretched black folds were not unlike women's tight black skirts. He'd never before had this thought about umbrellas, only the usual thoughts – that they were like bats' wings or that they were vaguely funereal – and this was like other thoughts and words that came into his head on this day, almost as if newly invented. It was a bit like the word kindly suddenly presenting itself as the exact word to describe Mr Reeves.

As they turned the corner of their street it began to pelt down and they broke into a run. Inside, in the hallway, they stood and panted a little. It was dark and clammy and with the rain beating outside a little like being inside a drum. They climbed the stairs to their flat, Lisa going first. Nick had an erection and the words 'stair rods' came into his mind.

It was barely two o'clock and the lower of the two flats was empty. Nick thought – though very quickly, since his thoughts were really elsewhere – of how incredibly lucky they were to be who they were and to have a flat of their own to go to on a rainy afternoon. It was supposed to be a 'starter home' and they owed it largely to Lisa's dad. It was supposed to be a first stage. He thought of stages again, if less bleakly this time. Everything in life could be viewed as a stage, leading to other stages and to having things you didn't yet have. But right now he felt they had everything, the best life could bring. What more could you want? And they'd even made their wills.

He'd hardly dropped the sopping umbrella into the kitchen sink than they were both, by inevitable progression, in the bedroom, and he'd hardly removed his jacket and pulled across the curtains than Lisa had unbuttoned her red blouse. She'd let him unzip her skirt, she knew how he liked to.

It rained all afternoon and kept raining, if not so hard, through the evening. They both slept a bit, then got up, picked up the clothes they'd hastily shed, and thought about going for a pizza. But it was still wet and they didn't want to break the strange spell of the day or fail to repeat, later, the manner of their return in the early afternoon. It seemed, too, that they might destroy the mood if they went out dressed in anything less special than what they'd worn earlier. But just for a pizza?

So – going to the other extreme – they took a shared bath, put on bathrobes, and settled for Welsh rarebit. They opened the only bottle of wine they had, a Rioja that someone had once brought them. They found a red twisty candle left over from Christmas. They put on a favourite CD. Outside, the rain persisted and darkness, though it was May, came early. The candle flame and their white-robed bodies loomed in the kitchen window.

Why this day had become so special, a day of celebration, of formality mixed with its flagrant opposite, neither of them could have said exactly. It happened. Having eaten and having drunk only half the bottle, it seemed natural to drift back to bed, less hurriedly this time, to make love again more lingeringly.

Then they lay awake a long time holding each other, talking and listening to the rain in the gutters and to the occasional slosh of a car outside. They talked about Mr Reeves. They wondered what it was precisely that had made him so sweet. They wondered if he was happily married and had a family, a grown-up family. Surely he would have all those things. They wondered how he'd met Mrs Reeves – they decided her name was Sylvia – and what she was like. They wondered if he'd been perhaps a little jealous of their own youth or just, in his gracious way, gladdened by it.

They wondered if he found wills merely routine or if he could be occasionally stopped short by the very idea of two absurdly young people making decisions about death. He must have made his own will. Surely – a good one. They wondered if a good aim in life might simply be to become like Mr Reeves, gentle, courteous and benign. Of course, that could only really apply to Nick, not to Lisa.

Then Lisa fell asleep and Nick lay awake still holding her and thinking. He thought: What is Mr Reeves doing now? Is he in bed with Mrs Reeves – with Sylvia? He wondered if when Mr Reeves had talked to them in his office he'd had any idea of how the two of them, his clients (and that was a strange word and a strange thing to be), would spend the rest of the day. He hoped Mr Reeves had had an inkling.

He wondered if he really might become like Mr Reeves when he was older. If he too would have (still plentiful and handsome) silver hair.

Then he forgot Mr Reeves altogether and the overwhelming thought came to him: Remember this, remember this. Remember this always. Whatever comes, remember this.

He was so smitten by the need to honour and consummate this thought that even as he held Lisa in his arms his chest felt full and he couldn't prevent his eyes suddenly welling. When Lisa slept she sometimes unknowingly nuzzled him, like some small creature pressing against its mother. She did this now, as if she might have quickly licked the skin at the base of his neck.

He was wide awake. Remember this. He couldn't sleep and he didn't want to sleep. The grotesque thought came to him that he'd just made his last will and testament, so he could die now, it was all right to die. This might be his deathbed and this, with Lisa in his arms, might be called dying happy – surely it could be called dying happy – the very thing that no will or testament, no matter how prudent its provisions, could guarantee.

But no, of course not! He clasped Lisa, almost wanting to wake her, afraid of his thought.

Of course not! He was alive and happy, intensely alive and happy. Then he had the thought that though he'd drafted his last testament it was not in any real sense a testament, it was not even *his* testament. It was only a testament about the minor matter of his possessions and what should become of them when he was no more. But it was not the real testament of his life, its stuff, its story. It was not a testament at all to how he was feeling *now*.

How strange that people solemnly drew up and signed these crucial documents that were really about their non-existence, and didn't draw up anything – there wasn't even a word for such a thing – that testified to their existence.

Then he realized that in all his time of knowing her he'd never written a love letter to this woman, Lisa, who was sleeping in his arms. Though he loved her completely, more than words could say – which was perhaps the simple reason why he'd never written such a thing. Love letters were classically composed to woo and to win, they were a means of getting what you didn't have. What didn't he have? Perhaps they were just silly wordy exercises anyway. He hardly wrote letters at all, let alone love letters, he hardly *wrote* anything. He wouldn't be any good at it.

And yet. And yet the need to write his wife a love letter assailed him. Not just a random letter that might, in theory, be one among many, but *the* letter, the letter that would declare to her once and for all how much he loved her and why. So it would be there always for her, as enduring as a will. The testament of his love, and thus of his life. The testament of how his heart had been full one rainy night in May when he was twenty-five. He would not need to write any other.

So overpowering was this thought that eventually he disengaged his arms gently from Lisa and got out of bed. He put on his bathrobe and went into the kitchen. There was the lingering smell of toasted cheese and there was the unfinished bottle of wine. They possessed no good-quality notepaper, unless Lisa had a private stash, but there was a box of A4 by the computer in the spare room and he went in and took a couple of sheets and found a blue roller-ball pen. He'd never had a fountain pen or used real ink, but he felt quite sure that this thing had to be handwritten, it would not be the thing it should be otherwise. He'd noticed that Mr Reeves had a very handsome fountain pen. Black and gold. No doubt a gift from Sylvia.

He returned to the kitchen, poured a little wine and very quickly wrote, so it seemed like a direct release of the thickness in his chest:

My darling Lisa,
  One day you walked into my life and I never thought something so wonderful could ever happen to me. You are the love of my life . . .

The words came so quickly and readily that, not being a writer of any kind, he was surprised by his sudden ability. They were so right and complete and he didn't want to alter any of them. Though they were just the beginning.

But no more words came. Or it seemed that there were a number of directions he might take, in each of which certain words might follow, but he didn't know which one to choose, and didn't want, by choosing, to exclude the others. He wanted to go in all directions, he wanted a totality. He wanted to set down every single thing he loved about his wife, every moment he'd loved sharing with her – which was almost *every* moment – including of course every moment of this day that had passed: the walk across the common, the rain, her red blouse, her black skirt, the small slithery sounds she made sitting in a solicitor's office, which of course were the sounds any woman might make shifting position in a tight skirt, but the important thing was that *she* was making them. She was making them even as she made her will, or rather as they made *their* wills, which were really only wills to each other.

But he realized that if he went into such detail the letter would need many pages. Perhaps it would be better simply to say, 'I love everything about you. I love all of you. I love every moment spent with you.' But these phrases, on the other hand, though true, seemed bland. They might be said of anyone by anyone.

Then again, if he embarked on the route of detail, the letter could hardly all be written now. It would need to be a thing of stages – stages! – reflecting their continuing life together and incorporating all the new things he found to commemorate. That would mean that it would be all right if he wrote no more now, he could pick it up later. And he'd written the most important thing, the beginning. But then if he picked it up later, it might become an immense labour – if truly a labour of love – a labour of years. There'd be the question: When would he stop, when would he bring it to its conclusion and deliver it?

A love letter was useless unless it was delivered.

He'd hardly begun and already he saw these snags and complications, these reasons why this passionate undertaking might fail. And he couldn't even think of the next thing to say. Then the words that he'd said to himself silently in his head, even as he held Lisa in his arms, rushed to him, as the very words he should write to her now and the best way of continuing:

I never thought something so wonderful could happen to me. You are the love of my life. Remember this always. Whatever comes, remember this . . .

Adding those words, in this way, made his chest tighten again and his eyes go prickly. And he wondered if that in itself was enough. It was entirely true to his feelings and to this moment. He should just put the date on it and sign it in some way and give it to Lisa the next morning. Yes, that was all he needed to do.

But though emotion was almost choking him, it suddenly seemed out of place – so big, if brief, a statement looking back at him from a kitchen table, with the smell of toasted cheese all around him. Suppose the mood tomorrow morning was quite different, suppose he faltered. Then again, that 'whatever comes' seemed ominous, it seemed like tempting fate, it seemed when you followed it through even to be about catastrophe and death. It shouldn't be there at all perhaps. And yet it seemed the essence of the thing. 'Whatever comes, remember this.' That was the essence.

Then he reflected that the essence of love letters was that they were about separation. It was why they were needed in the first place. They were about yearning and longing and distance. But he wasn't separated from Lisa – unless being the other side of a wall counted as separation. He could be with her whenever he liked, as close to her as possible, he'd made love to her twice today. Though as he'd written those additional words, 'whatever comes', he'd had the strange sensation of being a long way away from her, like a man in exile or on the eve of battle. It was what had brought the tears to his eyes.

In any case there it was. It was written. And what was he supposed to do with it? Just keep it? Keep it, but slip it in with the copy of his will – the 'executed' copy – so that after his death Lisa would read it? Read what he'd written on the night after they'd made their wills. Is that what he intended?

And how did he know he would die *first*? He'd simply had that thought so it would enable Lisa to read the letter. But how did he know she wouldn't die first? And he didn't want to think about either of them dying, he didn't want to think of dying at all. And even supposing Lisa read these words – these very words on this bit of paper! – after his death, wouldn't they in one undeniable and inescapable sense be too late? Though wouldn't that moment, after his death, be in another sense precisely the right moment?

Love letters are written out of separation.

He didn't know what to do. He'd written a love letter and it had only brought on this paralysis. But he couldn't cancel what he'd written. He folded the sheet of A4 and, returning to the spare room, found an envelope, on which he wrote Lisa's name, simply her name: Lisa. Without sealing the envelope, he put the letter in a safe and fairly secret place. There were no really secret places in the flat and he would have been glad to declare that he and Lisa had no secrets. Had the opportunity arisen, he might have done so to Mr Reeves. But now – it was almost like some misdeed – there was this secret.

But he couldn't cancel it. Some things you can't cancel, they stare back at you. There was nothing experimental or feeble or lacking about those words. His heart had spilled over in them.

He went back to bed. He fitted himself against Lisa's body. She'd turned now onto her other side, away from his side of the bed, but she was fast asleep. He kissed the nape of her neck. He wanted to cradle her and protect her. Thoughts came to him that he might add to the letter, if he added to it. But the letter was surely already complete.

His penis stiffened, contentedly and undemandingly, against his wife.

She knew nothing about it, or about his midnight session with pen and paper. He thought again about Mr Reeves and about last wills and testaments. Pen. Penis. It was funny to think about the word penis and the word testament in the same breath, as it were. Words were strange things. He thought about the word testicle.

The rain was still gurgling outside and whether it stopped before he fell asleep or he fell asleep first he didn't remember.

The truth is he did nothing with the letter the next morning. He might have propped it conspicuously, after sealing the envelope, on the kitchen table, but he didn't want to disturb the tender atmosphere that still lingered from yesterday, even though that same tenderness gave him his licence. Wouldn't the letter only endorse it? He felt a little cowardly, though why? For what he'd put in writing?

He looked adoringly, perhaps even rather pleadingly, at Lisa, as if she might have helped him in his dilemma. She looked slightly puzzled, but she also looked happy. She was hardly going to say, 'Go on, give me the letter.'

His line of thought to himself was still that the letter wasn't finished. Yes, he'd add to it later. It would be premature, at this point, to hand it over. Though he also knew there was no better point. And the moment was passing.

It was a Saturday morning. Outside, the rain had stopped, but a misty breath hung in the air, and over them hung still the curiously palpable, anointing fact that they were people who'd made their wills.

The truth is he could neither keep nor deliver, nor destroy, nor even resume the letter. It was simply there. Though he did keep it, by default. His hesitation over delivering it, a thing at first of just minutes and hours, became a prolonged, perennial reality, a thing of years, like his excuse that he'd continue it.

And one day, one bad day, he did, nearly, destroy it. It was a long time later, but the letter was still there, still as it was on that wet night in May, still in the envelope with the single word 'Lisa' on it, but now like a piece of history.

And his will, now, would certainly need altering. But not yet. Not yet.

He thought of destroying the letter. It had suddenly and almost accusingly come into his mind – that letter! But the thought of destroying a love letter seemed almost as melodramatic and sentimental as writing one.

How did you destroy a love letter? The only way was to burn it. The smell of Welsh rarebit reinvaded his nostrils. You found some ceremonial-looking dish and set light to the letter and watched it burn. Though the *real* way to burn a love letter was to fling it into a blazing fire and for good measure thrust a poker through it. And to do this you should really be sitting at a hearthside, rain at the window, in a long finely quilted silk dressing gown . . .

Then his chest filled and his eyes melted just as they'd done when he first penned the letter.

The truth is they separated. Then they needed lawyers, in duplicate, to decide on the settlement and on how the two children would be provided for. And, in due course, to draw up new wills. He didn't destroy the letter, and he didn't send it on finally to its intended recipient, as some last-ditch attempt to resolve matters and bring back the past, or even as some desperate act of guilt-inducement, of warped revenge. This would have betrayed its original impulse, and how hopeless anyway either gesture would have been. She might have thought it was all a fabrication, that he hadn't really written the letter on the 10th of May all those years ago – if so, why the hell hadn't he delivered it? – that he'd concocted it only yesterday. It was another, rather glaring, example of his general instability.

He didn't destroy it, he kept it. But not in the way he'd waveringly and wonderingly kept it for so many years. He kept it now only for himself. Who else was going to look at it?

Occasionally, he took it out and read it. He knew the words, of course, by heart, but it was important now and then, even on every 10th of May, to see them sitting on the paper. And when he looked at them it was like looking at his own face in the mirror, but not at a face that would obligingly and comfortingly replicate whatever he might do – wrinkle his nose, bare his teeth. It was a face that had found the separate power to smirk back at him when he wasn't smirking himself, and to have an expression in its eyes, which his own eyes could never have mustered, that said, 'You fool, you poor sad fool.'

JANE GARDAM

Dangers

Jake was six and lived in America in the city of Boston where he had never seen a cow. Or a sheep. Or a waddling goose. Or a dazzle-coloured pheasant in the garden. (He had no garden.) Or a rabbit. Or a mole with tiny hands. Or hens scratching about and laying eggs and talking to each other in rusty voices.

Jake's granny lived in England down a country lane. Pheasants came marching through her garden. Rabbits hopped about in it. Cows loitered down past her gate four times a day, to and fro, to the milking shed. Sheep leaned against her fence, broke it down and ate her apple trees. The cows ate her blackcurrants and raspberries, stretching out their necks over the stone walls. When this happened Jake's granny went tearing out of her cottage flailing towels in the air. When Jake came on a visit, he thought it was very funny.

On Granny's birthday everyone went for a picnic by the river. The river was toffee-coloured with swirls of creamy bubbles rushing noisily in circles. Jake could not believe that he could just walk in up to his knees and play, and watch the fishes the size of needles examining his toes. When he wiggled his toes all the fishes turned together in the same direction and darted off in fright. Soon Jake began to make a great deal of noise in the river with a pretend gun.

Then Granny fell in the river.

Or, at any rate, she fell down the river bank, down on to the fat white pebbles. She fell sideways and downwards from a light canvas chair that had been placed not so much on the river bank as on what looked like a river bank but was really a web of tree roots covered in grass. Under the tree roots the river had scooped out a hole and round the sides of the hole was a honeycomb of rabbit holes. Granny had actually been sitting on air.

Bang, bang, bang went Jake's imaginary gun from the middle of the river. Sometimes he pointed the gun at Granny for fun. He pointed it at Granny and she fell slowly sideways down upon the stones.

'Dead?' called Jake in a nonchalant way.

Granny had hurt her finger and had to go to the doctor. Jake became quiet and that night cried when he went to bed.

He thought that he had tried to kill Granny.

'Of *course* not,' she said. 'It was an *imaginary* gun. Mind, you should never point a gun at anyone, ever, not even an imaginary gun.'

'I never will,' said Jake.

The next night it was pheasant for supper and he didn't like it. He had a tummy ache. Granny searched about in an old cupboard and found some arrowroot to tempt his appetite, which had been lost. He spat out the arrowroot and said that the pheasant was better than that. His mother and father said, 'You are being rude to Granny. Apologize.' And Jake did. But that night he had dreams and said it was the poison.

'What poison?'

'The poison in the pheasant when they killed it.'

'Of *course* there was no poison. It was shot.'

'With a gun?'

'Yes.'

'Was it a real gun or an imaginary gun?'

'A real gun.'

'I will never *use* a real gun.'

'I agree with you,' said Granny.

The next day Granny and Jake went for a walk together along the lane. Jake couldn't believe a lane could be so empty of people and cars. 'I expect they're watching out for us,' he said from Granny's white wicket gate. 'I'd better take my rod.'

'Who's watching out for us?' asked Granny, nursing her finger, which had turned purple.

'The gunmen,' said Jake.

'Oh, come on,' said Granny. 'We're not pheasants.'

'I'll still take my rod.'

'Do you mean a fishing rod?'

'No, I'll catch fish with my pretend rod. This is just a rod,' and he went back into the cottage and rattled about in the umbrella stand where there were some mysterious things.

A shepherd's crook with bits of fluff in it.

Three tall walking sticks.

And a folded kite. A queer long branch with a 'v' at the end. You were supposed to hold tight to the 'v', one bit in each hand, and then the other end would twitch when you held it over invisible water, like a metal detector that doesn't twitch but screams. Jake knew you should try to have the water-finding stick with you whenever you are in a desert but as it was nearly always raining at Granny's – soaking, sparkling, lovely rain – the stick was seldom used. It was called a dowse.

'That's a dowse,' said Granny, 'not a rod.'

'No. This is what I have to take,' said Jake, burrowing about among thin sticks with little flags on them that other children had once run off with during a bike race. 'Here!' And he brought out a metal rod a metre long with orange plastic rings and a spike on one end. It was heavy.

'I don't like the look of that,' said Granny. 'I think we could do without it on this walk. It might go in someone's eye. Oh, all right then, but keep it pointing down.' They set off.

Soon the cows came thoughtfully along the lane. Jake jumped for the stone wall and flourished the rod. The cows stumbled a bit and swung away but on the whole decided that he was just being foolish.

'I'm protecting us,' he said and held the rod high, like a harpoon.

'I hate that thing,' said Granny. 'Wherever did we get it? Give it to me to carry.'

'I want to protect us.'

They came upon a heap of brown and green moss that somebody had dumped under a red rowan tree. Jake prodded the heap with the rod. 'It's a dead cow,' he said. 'We don't have horrible things like that in America.'

'It is a heap of beautiful moss,' said Granny. 'Now give me the rod and we'll pick blackberries. See how perfect they are, black, red, pink, green, white.'

'They're full of seeds,' said Jake.

'Of course they are, but we only pick the ripe ones. We cook them with sugar and they're lovely with cream.'

'What is cream? We don't have cream in America, only ice cream.'

'You'll see. It's delicious. It comes from cows.'

'From cows? I think it wouldn't agree with me. You'd give me more horrible arrowroot.'

'Here,' said the exhausted Granny, 'my finger hurts. *You* can pick the blackberries. I wish you'd throw away that iron rod.'

'OK,' said Jake and suddenly did so. He flung the rod sideways so fast that it vanished like a needle-fish. It vanished through the stones of the field wall. It was gone in a second.

'Goodness!' said Granny. 'That was a quick decision. Had you had enough of it?'

'Oh, I'll get it back some time, I expect.'

They all ate blackberries and cream for dinner and Jake, after a few sips of the juice on the edge of the spoon, said they were very good and finished them up. 'I'll carry the bowl next time we go picking,' he said. 'I shan't mind not having the iron rod.'

'What iron rod?' asked Grandpa, walking in.

'Something he found in the stick stand,' said Jake's mother. 'I'm afraid it seems to have disappeared through a hole in a wall.'

'That would be the arrow we found,' said Grandpa, 'last year, lying in the stream at the foot of the ghyll near the waterfall. We couldn't think how it got there. It was a real archery arrow. A very dangerous thing.'

'Had it real feathers on it when you found it?' asked Jake. 'Like cowboys and Indians?'

'That is history,' said Grandpa. 'We've not had that sort of arrow in England for a long time.'

'Yes. There are none in Boston,' said Jake. 'It's quite dull there really, compared to here.'

Before he went home to America, Jake and Granny had another walk down the lane. The blackberries were over but the rowan trees still blazed red. Jake put an eye to various chinks along the stone wall but neither he nor Granny could remember exactly where they had been standing.

'I think it went right through the wall and swish, *pang*! Deep into the grass on the other side. Like in films. But I hope it didn't hit a sheep or a cow or a hen.'

'I think we'd have heard,' said Granny, holding her hand out to him and saying as she jumped him into the lane again, 'Not too tight now because of my finger.'

'I'm sorry about your finger.'

'It wasn't your fault.'

'Do you think my arrow will grow?' he asked, 'over the wall in the field? Will it grow an arrow root?'

'I expect something will grow,' she said, 'maybe a story. When you get home.'

STORY

ALI SMITH

The Universal Story

There was a man dwelt by a churchyard.

Well, no, okay, it wasn't always a man; in this particular case it was a woman. There was a woman dwelt by a churchyard.

Though, to be honest, nobody really uses that word nowadays. Everybody says cemetery. And nobody says dwelt any more. In other words:

There was once a woman who lived by a cemetery. Every morning when she woke up she looked out of her back window and saw –

Actually, no. There was once a woman who lived by – no, in – a second-hand bookshop. She lived in the flat on the first floor and ran the shop which took up the whole of downstairs. There she sat, day after day, among the skulls and the bones of second-hand books, the stacks and shelves of them spanning the lengths and breadths of the long and narrow rooms, the piles of them swaying up, precarious like rootless towers, towards the cracked plaster of the ceiling. Though their bent or riffled or still chaste spines had been bleached by years of anonymous long-gone light, each of them had been new once, bought in a bookshop full of the shine of other new books. Now each was here, with too many possible reasons to guess at when it came to the question of how it had ended up sunk in the bookdust which specked the air in which the woman, on this winter's day, sat by herself, sensing all round her the weight of it, the covers shut on so many millions of pages that might never be opened to light again.

The shop was down a side street off the centre of a small rural village which few tourists visited in the summer and in which business had slowed considerably since 1982, the year the Queen Mother, looking frail and holding her hat on her head with one hand because of the wind, had cut the ribbon on the bypass which made getting to the city much quicker and stopping in the village quite difficult. Then the bank had closed and eventually the post office. There was a grocer's but most people drove to the supermarket six miles away. The supermarket also stocked books, though hardly any.

Occasionally someone would come into the second-hand bookshop looking for something he or she had heard about on the radio or read about in the papers. Usually the woman in the shop would have to apologize for not having it. For instance, it was February now. Nobody had been into the shop for four days. Occasionally a bookish teenage girl or boy, getting off the half-past four school bus which went between the village and the town, used to push, shy, at the door of the shop and look up with the kind of delight you can see even from behind in the shoulders and back and the angle of head of a person looking up at the endless promise of books. But this hadn't happened for a while.

The woman sat in the empty shop. It was late afternoon. It would be dark soon. She watched a fly in the window. It was early in the year for flies. It flew in veering triangles then settled on The Great Gatsby by F. Scott Fitzgerald to bask in what late winter sun there was.

Or – no. Wait:

There was once a fly resting briefly on an old paperback book in a second-hand bookshop window. It had paused there in a moment of warmth before launching back into the air, which it would do any second now. It wasn't any special or unusual kind of fly or a fly with an interesting species name – for instance, a robber fly or an assassin fly, a bee fly or a thick-headed fly, a dance fly, a dagger fly, a snipe fly or a down-looker fly. It wasn't even a stout or a cleg or a midge. It was a common house fly, a *musca domesticus linnaeus*, of the diptera family, which means it had two wings. It stood on the cover of the book and breathed air through its spiracles.

It had been laid as an egg less than a millimetre long in a wad of manure in a farmyard a mile and a half away and had become a legless maggot feeding off the manure it had been laid in. Then, because winter was coming, it had wriggled by sheer muscle contraction nearly a hundred and twenty feet. It had lain dormant for almost four months in the grit round the base of a wall under several feet of stacked hay in the barn. In a spell of mild weather over the last weekend it had broken the top off the pupa and pulled itself out, a fly now, six millimetres long. Under an eave of the barn it had spread and dried its wings and waited for its body to harden in the unexpectedly springlike air coming up from the Balearics. It had entered the rest of the world through a fly-sized crack in the roof of the barn that morning then zigzagged for over a mile looking for light, warmth and food. When the woman who owned the shop had opened her kitchen window to let the condensation out as she cooked her lunch, it had flown in. Now it was excreting and regurgitating, which is what flies do when they rest on the surfaces of things.

To be exact, it wasn't an it, it was a female fly, with a longer body and red slitted eyes set wider apart than if she had been a male fly. Her wings were each a thin, perfect, delicately veined membrane. She had a grey body and six legs, each with five supple joints, and she was furred all over her legs and her body with minuscule bristles. Her face was striped velvet-silver. Her long mouth had a sponging end for sucking up liquid and for liquefying solids like sugar or flour or pollen.

She was sponging with her proboscis the picture of the actors Robert Redford and Mia Farrow on the cover of the Penguin 1974 edition of The Great Gatsby. But there was little there really of interest, as you might imagine, to a house fly which needs urgently to feed and to breed, which is capable of carrying over one million bacteria and transmitting every-thing from common diarrhoea to dysentery, salmonella, typhoid fever, cholera, poliomyelitis, anthrax, leprosy and tuberculosis; and which senses that at any moment a predator will catch her in its web or crush her to death with a fly-swat or, if she survives these, that it will still any moment now simply be cold enough to snuff out herself and all ten of the gener-ations she is capable of setting in motion this year, all nine hundred of the eggs she will be capable of laying given the chance, the average twenty days of life of an average common house fly.

No. Hang on. Because:

There was once a 1974 Penguin edition of F. Scott Fitzgerald's classic American novel The Great Gatsby in the window of a quiet second-hand bookshop in a village that very few people visited any more. It had a hun-dred and eighty-eight numbered pages and was the twentieth Penguin edition of this particular novel – it had been reprinted three times in 1974 alone; this popularity was partly due to the film of the novel which came out that year, directed by Jack Clayton. Its cover, once bright yellow, had already lost most of its colour before it arrived at the shop. Since the book had been in the window it had whitened even more. In the film-still on it, ornate in a twenties-style frame, Robert Redford and Mia Farrow, the stars of the film, were also quite faded, though Redford was still dapper in his golf cap and Farrow, in a very becoming floppy hat, suited the sepia effect that the movement of sun and light on the glass had brought to her quite by chance.

The novel had first been bought for 30p (6/-) in 1974 in a Devon book-shop by Rosemary Child who was twenty-two and who had felt the urge to read the book before she saw the film. She married her fiancé Roger two years later. They mixed their books and gave their doubles to a Corn-wall hospital. This one had been picked off the hospital library trolley in Ward 14 one long hot July afternoon in 1977 by Sharon Patten, a fourteen-year-old girl with a broken hip who was stuck in bed in traction and bored because Wimbledon was over. Her father had seemed pleased at visiting hour when he saw it on her locker and though she'd given up reading it halfway through she kept it there by the water jug for her whole stay and smuggled it home with her when she was discharged. Three years later, when she didn't care any more what her father thought of what she did, she gave it to her schoolfriend David Connor who was going to university to do English, telling him it was the most boring book in the world. David read it. It was perfect. It was just like life is. Everything is beautiful, everything is hopeless. He walked to school quoting bits of it to himself under his breath. By the time he went up north to university in Edinburgh two years later, now a mature eighteen-year-old, he admired it, as he said several times in the seminar, though he found it a little adolescent and believed the underrated Tender Is the Night to be Fitzgerald's real masterpiece. The tutor, who every year had to mark around a hundred and fifty abysmal first-year essays on The Great Gatsby, nodded sagely and gave him a high pass in his exam. In 1985, having landed a starred first and a job in personnel management, David sold all his old literature course books to a girl called Mairead for thirty pounds. Mairead didn't like English – it had no proper answers – and decided to do economics instead. She sold them all again, making a lot more money than David had. The

Great Gatsby went for £2.00, six times its original price, to a first-year student called Gillian Edgbaston. She managed never to read it and left it on the shelves of the rented house she'd been living in when she moved out in 1990. Brian Jackson, who owned the rented house, packed it in a box which sat behind the freezer in his garage for five years. In 1995 his mother, Rita, came to visit and while he was tidying out his garage she found it in the open box, just lying there on the gravel in his driveway. The Great Gatsby! she said. She hadn't read it for years. He remembers her reading it that summer, it was two summers before she died, and her feet were up on the sofa and her head was deep in the book. She had a whole roomful of books at home. When she died in 1997 he boxed them all up and gave them to a registered charity. The registered charity checked through them for what was valuable and sold the rest on in auctioned boxes of thirty miscellaneous paperbacks, a fiver per box, to second-hand shops all over the country.

The woman in the quiet second-hand bookshop had opened the box she bought at auction and had raised her eyebrows, tired. Another Great Gatsby.

The Great Gatsby. F. Scott Fitzgerald. Now a Major Picture. The book was in the window. Its pages and their edges were dingy yellow because of the kind of paper used in old Penguin Modern Classics; by nature these books won't last. A fly was resting on the book now in the weak sun in the window.

But the fly suddenly swerved away into the air because a man had put his hand in among the books in the window display in the second-hand bookshop and was picking the book up.

Now:

There was once a man who reached his hand in and picked a second-hand copy of F. Scott Fitzgerald's The Great Gatsby out of the window of a quiet second-hand bookshop in a small village. He turned the book over as he went to the counter.

How much is this one, please? he asked the grey-looking woman.

She took it from him and checked the inside cover.

That one's £1, she said.

It says thirty pence here on it, he said, pointing to the back.

That's the 1974 price, the woman said.

The man looked at her. He smiled a beautiful smile. The woman's face lit up.

But, well, since it's very faded, she said, you can have it for fifty.

Done, he said.

Would you like a bag for it? she asked.

No, it's okay, he said. Have you any more?

Any more Fitzgerald? the woman said. Yes, under F. I'll just – .

No, the man said. I mean, any more copies of The Great Gatsby.

You want another copy of The Great Gatsby? the woman said.

I want all your copies of it, the man said, smiling.

The woman went to the shelves and found him four more copies of The Great Gatsby. Then she went through to the storeroom at the back of the shop and checked for more.

Never mind, the man said. Five'll do. Two pounds for the lot, what do you say?

His car was an old Mini Metro. The back seat of it was under a sea of different editions of The Great Gatsby. He cleared some stray copies from beneath the driver's seat so they wouldn't slide under his feet or the pedals while he was driving and threw the books he'd just bought over his shoulder on to the heap without even looking. He started the engine. The next second-hand bookshop was six miles away, in the city. His sister had called him from her bath two Fridays ago. James, I'm in the bath, she'd said. I need F. Scott Fitzgerald's The Great Gatsby.

F what's the what? he'd said.

She told him again. I need as many as possible, she said.

Okay, he'd said.

He worked for her because she paid well; she had a grant.

Have you ever read it? she asked.

No, he'd said. Do I have to?

So we beat on, she'd said. Boats against the current. Borne back ceaselessly into the past. Get it?

What about petrol money, if I'm supposed to drive all over the place looking for books? he'd said.

You've got five hundred quid to buy five hundred books. You get them for less, you can keep the change. And I'll pay you two hundred on top for your trouble. Boats against the current. It's perfect, isn't it?

And petrol money? he'd said.

I'll pay it, she'd sighed.

Because:

There was once a woman in the bath who had just phoned her brother and asked him to find her as many copies of The Great Gatsby as possible. She shook the drips off the phone, dropped it over the side on to the bathroom carpet and put her arm back into the water quick because it was cold.

She was collecting the books because she made full-sized boats out of things boats aren't usually made out of. Three years ago she had made a three-foot long boat out of daffodils which she and her brother had stolen at night from people's front gardens all over town. She had launched it, climbing into it, in the local canal. Water had come up round her feet almost immediately, then up round her knees, her thighs, till she was midriff-deep in icy water and daffodils floating all round her, unravelled.

But a small crowd had gathered to watch it sink and the story had attracted a lot of local and even some national media attention. Sponsored by Interflora, which paid enough for her to come off unemployment benefit, she made another boat, five feet long and out of mixed flowers, everything from lilies to snowdrops. It also sank, but this time was filmed for an arts project, with her in it, sinking. This had won her a huge arts commission to make more unexpected boats. Over the last two years she had made ten-and twelve-footers out of sweets, leaves, clocks and photographs and had launched each one with great ceremony at a different UK port. None of them had lasted more than eighty feet out to sea.

The Great Gatsby, she thought in the bath. It was a book she remembered from her adolescence and as she'd been lying in the water fretting about what to do next so her grant wouldn't be taken away from her it had suddenly come into her head.

It was perfect, she thought, nodding to herself. So we beat on. The last line of the book. She ducked her shoulders under the water to keep them warm.

And so, since we've come to the end already:

The seven-foot boat made of copies of The Great Gatsby stuck together with waterproof sealant was launched in the spring in the port of Felixstowe.

The artist's brother collected over three hundred copies of The Great Gatsby and drove between Wales and Scotland doing so. It is still quite hard to buy a copy of The Great Gatsby second-hand in some of the places he visited. It cost him a hundred and eighty three pounds fifty exactly. He kept the change. He was also a man apt to wash his hands before he ate, so was unharmed by any residue left by the fly earlier in the story on the cover of the copy he bought in the quiet second-hand bookshop.

This particular copy of The Great Gatsby, with the names of some of the people who had owned it inked under each other in their different handwritings on its inside first page – Rosemary Child, Sharon Patten, David Connor, Rita Jackson – was glued into the prow of the boat, which stayed afloat for three hundred yards before it finally took in water and sank.

The fly which had paused on the book that day spent that evening resting on the light fitting and hovering more than five feet above ground level. This is what flies tend to do in the evenings. This fly was no exception.

The woman who ran the second-hand bookshop had been delighted to sell all her copies of The Great Gatsby at once, and to such a smiling young man. She replaced the one which had been in the window with a copy of Dante's The Divine Comedy and as she was doing so she fanned open the pages of the book. Dust flew off. She blew more dust off the top of the pages then wiped it off her counter. She looked at the book dust smudged on her hand. It was time to dust all the books, shake them all open. It would take her well into the spring. Fiction, then non-fiction, then all the sub-categories. Her heart was light. That evening she began, at the letter A.

The woman who lived by a cemetery, remember, back at the very beginning? She looked out of her window and she saw – ah, but that's another story.

And lastly, what about the first, the man we began with, the man dwelt by a churchyard?

He lived a long and happy and sad and very eventful life, for years and years and years, before he died.

NEIL GAIMAN

Troll Bridge

They pulled up most of the railway tracks in the early sixties, when I was three or four. They slashed the train services to ribbons. This meant that there was nowhere to go but London, and the little town where I lived became the end of the line.

My earliest reliable memory: eighteen months old, my mother away in hospital having my sister, and my grandmother walking with me down to a bridge, and lifting me up to watch the train below, panting and steaming like a black iron dragon.

Over the next few years they lost the last of the steam trains, and with them went the network of railways that joined village to village, town to town.

I didn't know that the trains were going. By the time I was seven they were a thing of the past.

We lived in an old house on the outskirts of the town. The fields opposite were empty and fallow. I used to climb the fence and lie in the shade of a small bulrush patch, and read; or if I were feeling more adventurous I'd explore the grounds of the empty manor beyond the fields. It had a weed-clogged ornamental pond, with a low wooden bridge over it. I never saw any groundsmen or caretakers in my forays through the gardens and woods, and I never attempted to enter the manor. That would have been courting disaster, and, besides, it was a matter of faith for me that all empty old houses were haunted.

It is not that I was credulous, simply that I believed in all things dark and dangerous. It was part of my young creed that the night was full of ghosts and witches, hungry and flapping and dressed completely in black.

The converse held reassuringly true: daylight was safe. Daylight was always safe.

A ritual: on the last day of the summer school term, walking home from school, I would remove my shoes and socks and, carrying them in my hands, walk down the stony flinty lane on pink and tender feet. During the summer holiday I would put shoes on only under duress. I would revel in my freedom from footwear until school term began once more in September.

When I was seven I discovered the path through the wood. It was summer, hot and bright, and I wandered a long way from home that day.

I was exploring. I went past the manor, its windows boarded up and blind, across the grounds, and through some unfamiliar woods. I scrambled down a steep bank, and I found myself on a shady path that was new to me and overgrown with trees; the light that penetrated the leaves was stained green and gold, and I thought I was in fairyland.

A little stream trickled down the side of the path, teeming with tiny, transparent shrimps. I picked them up and watched them jerk and spin on my fingertips. Then I put them back.

I wandered down the path. It was perfectly straight, and overgrown with short grass. From time to time I would find these really terrific rocks: bubbly, melted things, brown and purple and black. If you held them up to the light you could see every colour of the rainbow. I was convinced that they had to be extremely valuable, and stuffed my pockets with them.

I walked and walked down the quiet golden-green corridor, and saw nobody.

I wasn't hungry or thirsty. I just wondered where the path was going. It travelled in a straight line, and was perfectly flat. The path never changed, but the countryside around it did. At first I was walking along the bottom of a ravine, grassy banks climbing steeply on each side of me. Later, the path was above everything, and as I walked I could look down at the treetops below me, and the roofs of the occasional distant houses. My path was always flat and straight, and I walked along it through valleys and plateaus, valleys and plateaus. And eventually, in one of the valleys, I came to the bridge.

It was built of clean red brick, a huge curving arch over the path. At the side of the bridge were stone steps cut into the embankment, and, at the top of the steps, a little wooden gate.

I was surprised to see any token of the existence of humanity on my

path, which I was by now convinced was a natural formation, like a vol-
cano. And, with a sense more of curiosity than anything else (I had, after
all, walked hundreds of miles, or so I was convinced, and might be *anywhere*), I climbed the stone steps, and went through the gate.

I was nowhere.

The top of the bridge was paved with mud. On each side of it was a
meadow. The meadow on my side was a wheatfield; the other field was
just grass. There were the caked imprints of huge tractor wheels in the
dried mud. I walked across the bridge to be sure: no trip-trap, my bare
feet were soundless.

Nothing for miles; just fields and wheat and trees.

I picked a stalk of wheat, and pulled out the sweet grains, peeling them
between my fingers, chewing them meditatively.

I realized then that I was getting hungry, and went back down the
stairs to the abandoned railway track. It was time to go home. I was not
lost; all I needed to do was follow my path home once more.

There was a troll waiting for me, under the bridge.

'I'm a troll,' he said. Then he paused, and added, more or less as an
afterthought, 'Fol rol de ol rol.'

He was huge: his head brushed the top of the brick arch. He was
more or less translucent: I could see the bricks and trees behind him,
dimmed but not lost. He was all my nightmares given flesh. He had huge
strong teeth, and rending claws, and strong, hairy hands. His hair
was long, like one of my sister's little plastic gonks, and his eyes bulged.
He was naked, and his penis hung from the bush of gonk hair between
his legs.

'I heard you, Jack,' he whispered, in a voice like the wind. 'I heard you
trip-trapping over my bridge. And now I'm going to eat your life.'

I was only seven, but it was daylight, and I do not remember being
scared. It is good for children to find themselves facing the elements of a
fairy tale – they are well-equipped to deal with these.

'Don't eat me,' I said to the troll. I was wearing a stripy brown T-shirt
and brown corduroy trousers. My hair also was brown, and I was missing
a front tooth. I was learning to whistle between my teeth, but wasn't there
yet.

'I'm going to eat your life, Jack,' said the troll.

I stared the troll in the face. 'My big sister is going to be coming down the path soon,' I lied, 'and she's far tastier than me. Eat her instead.'

The troll sniffed the air, and smiled. 'You're all alone,' he said. 'There's nothing else on the path. Nothing at all.' Then he leaned down, and ran his fingers over me: it felt like butterflies were brushing my face – like the touch of a blind person. Then he snuffled his fingers, and shook his huge head. 'You don't have a big sister. You've only a younger sister, and she's at her friend's today.'

'Can you tell all that from smell?' I asked, amazed.

'Trolls can smell the rainbows, trolls can smell the stars,' it whispered, sadly. 'Trolls can smell the dreams you dreamed before you were ever born. Come close to me and I'll eat your life.'

'I've got precious stones in my pocket,' I told the troll. 'Take them, not me. Look.' I showed him the lava jewel rocks I had found earlier.

'Clinker,' said the troll. 'The discarded refuse of steam trains. Of no value to me.'

He opened his mouth wide. Sharp teeth. Breath that smelled of leaf mould and the underneaths of things. 'Eat. Now.'

He became more and more solid to me, more and more real; and the world outside became flatter, began to fade.

'Wait.' I dug my feet into the damp earth beneath the bridge, wiggled my toes, held on tightly to the real world. I stared into his big eyes. 'You don't want to eat my life. Not yet. I – I'm only seven. I haven't *lived* at all yet. There are books I haven't read yet. I've never been on an airplane. I can't whistle yet – not really. Why don't you let me go? When I'm older and bigger and more of a meal I'll come back to you.'

The troll stared at me with eyes like headlamps.

Then it nodded.

'When you come back, then,' it said. And it smiled.

I turned around and walked back down the silent straight path where the railway lines had once been.

After a while I began to run.

I pounded down the track in the green light, puffing and blowing, until I felt a stabbing ache beneath my rib cage, the pain of stitch; and, clutching my side, I stumbled home.

*

The fields started to go, as I grew older. One by one, row by row, houses sprang up with roads named after wildflowers and respectable authors. Our home – an aging, tattered Victorian house – was sold, and torn down; new houses covered the garden.

They built houses everywhere.

I once got lost in the new housing estate that covered two meadows I had once known every inch of. I didn't mind too much that the fields were going, though. The old manor house was bought by a multinational, and the grounds became more houses.

It was eight years before I returned to the old railway line, and when I did, I was not alone.

I was fifteen; I'd changed schools twice in that time. Her name was Louise, and she was my first love.

I loved her grey eyes, and her fine light brown hair, and her gawky way of walking (like a fawn just learning to walk which sounds really dumb, for which I apologize): I saw her chewing gum, when I was thirteen, and I fell for her like a suicide from a bridge.

The main trouble with being in love with Louise was that we were best friends, and we were both going out with other people.

I'd never told her I loved her, or even that I fancied her. We were buddies.

I'd been at her house that evening: we sat in her room and played *Rattus Norvegicus*, the first Stranglers LP. It was the beginning of punk, and everything seemed so exciting: the possibilities, in music as in everything else, were endless. Eventually it was time for me to go home, and she decided to accompany me. We held hands, innocently, just pals, and we strolled the ten-minute walk to my house.

The moon was bright, and the world was visible and colourless, and the night was warm.

We got to my house. Saw the lights inside, and stood in the driveway, and talked about the band I was starting. We didn't go in.

Then it was decided that I'd walk *her* home. So we walked back to her house.

She told me about the battles she was having with her younger sister, who was stealing her makeup and perfume. Louise suspected that her sister was having sex with boys. Louise was a virgin. We both were.

We stood in the road outside her house, under the sodium-yellow streetlight, and we stared at each other's black lips and pale yellow faces.

We grinned at each other.

Then we just walked, picking quiet roads and empty paths. In one of the new housing estates, a path led us into the woodland, and we followed it.

The path was straight and dark, but the lights of distant houses shone like stars on the ground, and the moon gave us enough light to see. Once we were scared, when something snuffled and snorted in front of us. We pressed close, saw it was a badger, laughed and hugged and kept on walking.

We talked quiet nonsense about what we dreamed and wanted and thought.

And all the time I wanted to kiss her and feel her breasts, and hold her, and be held by her.

Finally I saw my chance. There was an old brick bridge over the path, and we stopped beneath it. I pressed up against her. Her mouth opened against mine.

Then she went cold and stiff, and stopped moving.

'Hello,' said the troll.

I let go of Louise. It was dark beneath the bridge, but the shape of the troll filled the darkness.

'I froze her,' said the troll, 'so we can talk. Now: I'm going to eat your life.'

My heart pounded, and I could feel myself trembling.

'No.'

'You said you'd come back to me. And you have. Did you learn to whistle?'

'Yes.'

'That's good. I never could whistle.' It sniffed, and nodded. 'I am pleased. You have grown in life and experience. More to eat. More for me.'

I grabbed Louise, a taut zombie, and pushed her forward. 'Don't take me. I don't want to die. Take *her*. I bet she's much tastier than me. And she's two months older than I am. Why don't you take her?'

The troll was silent.

It sniffed Louise from toe to head, snuffling at her feet and crotch and breasts and hair.

Then it looked at me.

'She's an innocent,' it said. 'You're not. I don't want her. I want you.'

I walked to the opening of the bridge and stared up at the stars in the night.

'But there's so much I've never done,' I said, partly to myself. 'I mean, I've never. Well, I've never had sex. And I've never been to America. I haven't . . .' I paused. 'I haven't *done* anything. Not yet.'

The troll said nothing.

'I could come back to you. When I'm older.'

The troll said nothing.

'I *will* come back. Honest I will.'

'Come back to me?' said Louise. 'Why? Where are you going?'

I turned around. The troll had gone, and the girl I had thought I loved was standing in the shadows beneath the bridge.

'We're going home,' I told her. 'Come on.'

We walked back, and never said anything.

She went out with the drummer in the punk band I started, and, much later, married someone else. We met once, on a train, after she was married, and she asked me if I remembered that night.

I said I did.

'I really liked you, that night, Jack,' she told me. 'I thought you were going to kiss me. I thought you were going to ask me out. I would have said yes. If you had.'

'But I didn't.'

'No,' she said. 'You didn't.' Her hair was cut very short. It didn't suit her.

I never saw her again. The trim woman with the taut smile was not the girl I had loved, and talking to her made me feel uncomfortable.

I moved to London, and then, some years later, I moved back again, but the town I returned to was not the town I remembered: there were no fields, no farms, no little flint lanes; and I moved away as soon as I could, to a tiny village ten miles down the road.

I moved with my family – I was married by now, with a toddler – into an old house that had once, many years before, been a railway station.

The tracks had been dug up, and the old couple who lived opposite us used the ground where the tracks had been to grow vegetables.

I was getting older. One day I found a grey hair; on another, I heard a recording of myself talking, and I realized I sounded just like my father.

I was working in London, doing A&R for one of the major record companies. I was commuting into London by train most days, coming back some evenings.

I had to keep a small flat in London; it's hard to commute when the bands you're checking out don't even stagger onto the stage until midnight. It also meant that it was fairly easy to get laid, if I wanted to, which I did.

I thought that Eleanora – that was my wife's name; I should have mentioned that before, I suppose – didn't know about the other women; but I got back from a two-week jaunt to New York one winter's day, and when I arrived at the house it was empty and cold.

She had left a letter, not a note. Fifteen pages, neatly typed, and every word of it was true. Including the PS, which read: *You really don't love me. And you never did.*

I put on a heavy coat, and I left the house and just walked, stunned and slightly numb.

There was no snow on the ground, but there was a hard frost, and the leaves crunched under my feet as I walked. The trees were skeletal black against the harsh grey winter sky.

I walked down the side of the road. Cars passed me, travelling to and from London. Once I tripped on a branch, half hidden in a heap of brown leaves, ripping my trousers, cutting my leg.

I reached the next village. There was a river at right angles to the road, and a path I'd never seen before beside it, and I walked down the path, and stared at the partly frozen river. It gurgled and plashed and sang.

The path led off through fields; it was straight and grassy.

I found a rock, half buried, on one side of the path. I picked it up, brushed off the mud. It was a melted lump of purplish stuff, with a strange rainbow sheen to it. I put it into the pocket of my coat and held it in my hand as I walked, its presence warm and reassuring.

The river meandered away across the fields, and I walked on in silence.

I had walked for an hour before I saw houses – new and small and square – on the embankment above me.

And then I saw the bridge, and I knew where I was: I was on the old railway path, and I'd been coming down it from the other direction.

There were graffiti painted on the side of the bridge: BARRY LOVES SUSAN and the omnipresent NF of the National Front.

I stood beneath the bridge in the red brick arch, stood among the ice-cream wrappers, and the crisp packets, and watched my breath steam in the cold afternoon air.

The blood had dried into my trousers.

Cars passed over the bridge above me; I could hear a radio playing loudly in one of them.

'Hello?' I said quietly, feeling embarrassed, feeling foolish. 'Hello?'

There was no answer. The wind rustled the crisp packets and the leaves.

'I came back. I said I would. And I did. Hello?'

Silence.

I began to cry then, stupidly, silently, sobbing under the bridge.

A hand touched my face, and I looked up.

'I didn't think you'd come back,' said the troll.

He was my height now, but otherwise unchanged. His long gonk hair was unkempt and had leaves in it, and his eyes were wide and lonely.

I shrugged, then wiped my face with the sleeve of my coat. 'I came back.'

Three kids passed above us on the bridge, shouting and running.

'I'm a troll,' whispered the troll in a small, scared voice. 'Fol rol de ol rol.'

He was trembling.

I held out my hand and took his huge clawed paw in mine. I smiled at him. 'It's okay,' I told him. 'Honestly. It's okay.'

The troll nodded.

He pushed me to the ground, onto the leaves and the wrappers, and lowered himself on top of me. Then he raised his head, and opened his mouth, and ate my life with his strong sharp teeth.

When he was finished, the troll stood up and brushed himself down. He put his hand into the pocket of his coat and pulled out a bubbly, burnt lump of clinker rock.

He held it out to me.

'This is yours,' said the troll.

I looked at him: wearing my life comfortably, easily, as if he'd been wearing it for years. I took the clinker from his hand, and sniffed it. I could smell the train from which it had fallen, so long ago. I gripped it tightly in my hairy hand.

'Thank you,' I said.

'Good luck,' said the troll.

'Yeah. Well. You too.'

The troll grinned with my face.

It turned its back on me and began to walk back the way I had come, towards the village, back to the empty house I had left that morning; and it whistled as it walked.

I've been here ever since. Hiding. Waiting. Part of the bridge.

I watch from the shadows as the people pass: walking their dogs, or talking, or doing the things that people do. Sometimes people pause beneath my bridge, to stand, or piss, or make love. And I watch them, but say nothing; and they never see me.

Fol rol de ol rol.

I'm just going to stay here, in the darkness under the arch. I can hear you all out there, trip-trapping, trip-trapping over my bridge.

Oh yes, I can hear you.

But I'm not coming out.

MARTIN AMIS

The Unknown Known

Even as we enter the age of cosmic and perhaps eternal war, it remains remarkable: the nuanced symbiosis between East and West. Here at Strategic Planning, or 'the "Prism" ', there are three sectors, and these three sectors used to be called, not very imaginatively, Sector Three, Sector Two, and Sector One. Sector Three dealt with daily logistics, Sector Two with long-term missions, and Sector One with conceptual breakthroughs. But now, following certain remarks by the American Secretary of Defence, the three sectors have been renamed as follows: Known Knowns, Known Unknowns, and Unknown Unknowns – a clear improvement. There is of course (this goes without saying) no sector called Unknown Knowns. That would be preposterous and, moreover, a complete waste of time. Only a madman would give the idea any serious thought. There are no such things as Unknown Knowns – though I have to say that I can imagine such a category, such a framework, when I contemplate my physical extinction (which, I admit, I am increasingly inclined to do). I work in Sector One: Unknown Unknowns.

Our camp lies on the Northern Border. Picking up on certain remarks in the Western press, other groups in the region – affiliates, rivals, enemies – have seen fit to call 'the "Prism" ' a 'jungle gym' operation, a mere 'rope ladder' or 'monkey puzzle' bivouac which the Americans, should they ever find out about it, wouldn't take the trouble to destroy. According to them, we're not worth so much as a cruise missile – or even, if you please, a Hellfire warhead from a Predator drone. They call us 'daydreamers'; they call us 'sleepwalkers'. Well, all that is about to change. Soon the whole world will whisper it – in the East with tears of pride, in the West with bitterness and horror: *the "Prism"* . . .' I refer of course to my own initiative, my 'baby' if you will. Its codename is UU: CRs/G,C.

To the right of the drill-yard, the first longhouse: Known Knowns. This is where we all started out. When you think about human society in a certain way – i.e., with the sole objective of hurting it – the entire planet resembles a pulsing bullseye. The continents themselves hang there like great soft underbellies, almost pleading to be strafed and scorched and slashed. True, our activities here in Known Knowns are hands-on and bread-and-butter: shells, landmines, grenades, petrol bombs. But one's induction will include action in the field: oh yes. And it goes on being dangerous work, what with the frequent gas leaks and accidental fires and the almost daily explosions.

Later, when, with some pomp, you cross the yard and enter the second longhouse, Known Unknowns, you begin to understand that civilization isn't *entirely* defenceless. It is no walk in the park, trolling around North Korea in search of the fabled twenty-five kilograms of uranium; it is no picnic, going from factory to factory in Uzbekistan in search of weapons-grade anthrax or aerosolized asphyxiants. True, doing that is better than actually being in Known Unknowns. In *Bio*, for example, the conditions are far from sanitary. In one stall a comrade tests a sarin compound on a donkey; in the next stall along, another channels a 'mosaic' toxin of small-pox and VX into a garden sprinkler. The regular and lethal epidemics are not always easy to contain. Accordingly the breath of a Sector Two comrade always has a tell-tale tang, that of potent cough-drops, moving about as he does among vats of acids and tubs full of raw pesticides.

Unknown Unknowns is not to be found in a third longhouse. In fact, there isn't a third longhouse. No. For Unknown Unknowns you go behind the wash-huts and over the sheepdip and then you see it, a deceptively modest wooden cabin, called, sinisterly, 'Hut A'. An outsider, putting his head round the door, might find the atmosphere somewhat casual and unfastidious – even somewhat torpid and scurf-blown. But these are the necessary motes and postures of intense concentration. The thinking, here, is pointed-end, cutting-edge. Synergy, maximalization – these are the kind of concepts that are tossed from cushion to floor mat in Unknown Unknowns. Now a comrade argues for the dynamiting of the San Andreas Fault; now another envisages the large-scale introduction of rabies (admixed with smallpox, angel dust, and steroids) to the fauna of Central Park. A pensive silence follows. Sometimes these silences can last for days on end. We sit there and think. All you can hear is the occasional swatting palm-slap, or the crackle of a beetle being ground underfoot.

Every evening, after prayers, I flex my impeccable English, reading aloud our write-ups in *The New York Times* and elsewhere on a faulty and outmoded computer borrowed from *Cyber* in Known Unknowns.

Paradigm-shift is what we're in the business of. But paradigm-shift represents a window, and windows will close. The much-ballyhooed operation of September 2001, to take the obvious example, is now unrepeatable. Indeed, the tactic was obsolete by ten o'clock the same morning. Its efficacy lasted for exactly seventy-one minutes: from 8.46, when American 11 hit the North Tower, until 9.57, and the rebellion on United 93. The passengers on the fourth plane grasped the new reality, and acted. They didn't linger for long in the vanished praxis of the 1970s (and how antique and diffident that now seems!): the four-day siege on the tropical tarmac, the shortages of food and water, the festering toilets, the airing of 'conditions' and 'demands', the phased release of the children and the women – then the surrender, or the clambering commandos. No. They rose up. And United 93 came down on its back at 580 miles per hour, twenty minutes from the Capitol.

For different reasons, UU: CRs/G,C, launched but not yet completed, is also unrepeatable. From the outset it relied on something we may never have again: the full resources of a nation state. That's gone, thanks to the biblical, the mountain-flattening rage of the Americans. Indeed, given the heavy price we have had to pay for it, many of us, here in Unknown Unknowns, regard September as almost criminally lax. We would have deployed scores of planes nationwide, and our targeting would have been much more adventurous. Not just the landmarks: we would have sent a message about all the other things we hate – nightclubs, music halls, women's institutes, sports arenas. Think of it. A 767, in the evening glitter, descending like an incensed seraph on Yankee Stadium . . .

UU: CRs/G,C was launched in July 2001. If everything had gone according to schedule there would have been a second 'September surprise' for the Americans. Now, four years later, my actors are at last on US soil and poised to strike: my CRs are at last homing in on G,C. The difficulties along the way have been unexpectedly numerous. I don't know – twice a day I have attacks of fluttering uncertainty; I mistake the dawn for a sunset, the sunset for a dawn, and a part of my mind involuntarily anticipates failure, if not fiasco. Thereafter it is hardly the work of a moment to refresh my belief that God will smile on UU: CRs/G,C.

On top of all this I am not getting on very well with my wives.

Last night I had a visitor: a colleague from Unknown Unknowns. Now might be a good time to explain about our aliases. We in 'Hut A' have, over the years, become theorists and visionaries, but we all started out in Known Knowns, seeing action in various theatres (Chechnya, Thailand, Kashmir), and our aliases are reminders of the way we made our bones on the front line. Again the 'nuanced symbiosis': for these names are taken from our coverage in the Anglophone media, and then lightly transliterated. I cannot exaggerate the ineffable reverence, the tender solemnity, with which we murmur our *noms de guerre*. My visitor, my colleague – *his* name is of the very best: bold, virile, and self-explanatory. Unlike mine. I didn't say anything when they gave it to me, but I have grown increasingly unhappy with it. My name's 'Ayed', and it derives from Improvised Explosive Device. But Ayed's *already* a name. The little Tajik who limps into the village once a month, to grind the knives, *his* name's Ayed . . .

'I had a message today, "Ayed",' said my guest, 'from the One Eyed One.'

The tea I was drinking abruptly changed direction and came sneezing out of my nose. 'Continue, "Truqbom",' I said when I was able. As was now my habit, I'd been hoping that the One Eyed One was dead.

'He asks after UU: CRs/G,C. He asks: "When will the great day come? When will it be, this day?"'

'. . . *July 29!*' I always imagined that, when I said those words for the first time, they would echo with geo-historical resonance (this, after all, this was a date that would for ever burn in the soul of the West); but it came out as something of a whinny. It was now July 25, and my CRs were still in a pit near a swamp in East Texas.

'July 29 of this year?'

'Definitely. I virtually guarantee it.'

'He understands, "Ayed" – *we* understand – that there have been setbacks.'

I laughed with unexpected shrillness, and found myself saying, 'It is so, is it not, comrade, that you've never been introduced to my wives?'

And before he could answer I summoned them from the kitchen with a mighty clap of my hands. In they filed. I had spent my lunch hour, that day, sadly gazing into the small pond, or large puddle, under the plane trees behind the wash-huts. And it now seemed to me that my wives resembled four gigantic tadpoles. What would they eventually mutate into?

'Oh, we're very advanced here you know,' I cried. 'Oh yes. My wives quite often "meet". Have some purified water, comrade, cooled in my refrigerator.'

He left at once, naturally, stalking off on that noisy tin leg of his. This afforded me some temporary relief, and then of course I gave the wives the rough edge of my tongue.

All night I sat there on the lumpy hassock with my face in my hands. What extraordinary behaviour: my wives most certainly do *not* 'meet'! And now I have offended the notoriously sensitive and traditionalist 'Truqbom', with his ugly muscles – my patron and my peer.

It was he, you see, who sponsored my initial audience with the One Eyed One (aka the One with One Eye, the Mullah, the Emir, the Commander of the Faithful) that June: the June that preceded September. There has been much speculation in the press about this – about whether the Mullah actually approved the attack on America. The truth is that he voiced his doubts and, at first, withheld his blessing. And his doubts were not the obvious ones – that he would a) forfeit his country, and b) spend the rest of his life in hiding.

No. What worried *him* were considerations best described as 'ideological' (I quote from *The 9/11 Commission Report*, which, with rather exaggerated nonchalance, we are all passing around). The One Eyed One wanted the autumn initiative 'to attack Jews' (ibid.). Already aware of this settled emphasis of the Mullah's, I mildly exaggerated the anti-Semitic component (at that point non-existent) of UU: CRs/G,C when I came to make my presentation. The prospect of September 11, by the way, did not deter the Mullah from going ahead with, or getting started on, his autumn campaign against the Northern Alliance, solemnly inaugurated on September 10.

Having made the six-day journey to our second city, I joined the queue in the back yard of the One Eyed One's modest villa. Many of my fellow supplicants were representatives of organizations similar to but much grander than 'the "Prism"', and I heard the usual sly remarks about swings and hammocks and treetop dens. My clothes were creased from successive nights on packed buses, and I would have dearly liked a minute alone with a cloth and a faucet. Overall, my confidence was far from high. I had, as it were, auditioned CRs/G,C (it did not yet bear the 'UU' imprimatur) before the thinkers of 'Hut A', and it was greeted without the slightest sign of enthusiasm, to put it mildly; it was greeted, in fact, with chilled dismay and then outright mockery. I also had an unpleasant suspicion that 'Truqbom' had intervened on my behalf in a facetious spirit, to bring upon me not only much trouble and expense but also humiliation and perhaps even punishment. Despite all this, I cherished the hope that the One Eyed One would somehow grasp the wayward, the vaulting genius of CRs/G,C.

Once I got inside it was possible to watch the petitioners as they took their leave of the fabled chamber. You could see them backing away, and then turning towards the open front doors. Some came out looking almost farcically gratified; some (I counted nine) seemed utterly crushed – and two of *them* were promptly marched off by the guards. The overwhelming majority, admittedly, were neither happy nor sad: they were merely caricatures of bafflement. But by this time I had a near-irresistible desire to bolt: I could feel my body trying to do it, trying to burst away from itself and be gone. My turn came and I stumbled in.

The warrior poet lay half-submerged by the heaped cushions, an imposing figure in his dishdash and his flip-flops. I found it difficult to return his one-eyed gaze, and during my presentation I looked elsewhere, at the rugs, the tea tray, the large tin box brimming with US dollars. When I eventually fell silent and straightened my neck, Mullah Omar said slowly,

'Answer me this. What should we do with the buggerers? Some scholars say they should be thrown from a high roof. Others maintain that these sinners should be buried in a hole and a wall should be toppled on them. Which?'

I said with hesitation, 'The hole and the wall sounds more unnatural, and thus more pious, my Leader.'

And I saw that he was smiling at me. A strange smile, combining serenity and severity. Perhaps this is the way God smiles.

I returned to the north-east in a two-door Datsun pickup. Brashly I sounded the horn, and watched the unloading of my recent purchases (the water purifier, the battery-operated refrigerator), suitably impressing my wives.

UU: CRs/G,C? It's simple. We're going to scour all the prisons and madhouses for every compulsive rapist in the country, and then unleash them on Greeley, Colorado.

Ah, my wives. As I keep saying to all my temporary wives, 'My wives don't understand me.'

And they don't. For instance, I am of that breed of men which holds that a husband should have sex with his wives every night. Or, to put it slightly more realistically, every twenty-four hours – without fail, except for the usual calendric exemptions. My wives have of course never denied me, but they sometimes show a certain resistance (more by demeanour than by word or deed) to my forthright amatory style. It is fairly clear by now, I think, that what they object to is my invariable use of the 'RodeoMaMa'.

The 'RodeoMaMa' is a Western frippery I picked up, by mail order, during my sojourn in the United States and didn't have the heart to leave behind. It consists of a 'weight belt' and the prow of a leather saddle. You attach it to your wives' waists, so that the saddle hovers over the lower back. If the 'RodeoMaMa' has a fault, it is its unwieldiness, or its bulk. My wives always know when I am off to see one of my temporary wives, because I take my 'RodeoMaMa' with me in its ragged old sack.

I was fourteen when my father, a gifted poppy-grower, took me to America. One day I was a contented young student, never happier than when about my tasks of recitation and memorization; the next, I was hurled into the hellhouse of Greeley, Colorado. I arrived in midwinter, which muffled the shock – in several applications of that verb. A mother blimplike in her padded parka, an infant daughter, as rigid as a capital aitch, in hers; and the snow, seen at first from above, like a flood made of milk, then on the ground like a sugar coating that also imparted silence. The shock was muffled, but it came. Scarcely crediting my senses, I began to notice that there were women motorists, women police officers, women *soldiers*; I felt all this as a multiple, a compound ignominy. Yet nothing prepared me for the spring and the summer.

A thousand times a day I would whisper it ('But her *father* . . . her *brothers* . . .'), every time I saw a luminously bronzed *poitrine*, the outline of underwear on a tightly packaged rump, a thin skirt rendered transparent by a low sun, a pair of nipples starkly staring through a pullover, a white bra strap contending with a murky armpit, a stocking top arresting the architecture of an upper thigh, or the very crux of a woman sliced in two by a wedge of denim or dungaree. They strolled in swirly print dresses across the Walkway, indifferent to the fact that anyone standing below, in the thicket of nettles and poison ivy, could see the full scissoring of their legs and their shamelessly brief underpants. And when, in all weathers, I took a late walk along the back gardens, the casual use of a buttress or a drainpipe would soon confront me with the sight of a woman quite openly undressing for bed.

Worst was Drake Square in early July: the students, in the week before summer recess. A slum of bubblegum, sweet drinks, cigarettes, and naked flesh; the girls on towels and blankets, with limbs and midriffs raw to the sun, waiting to be *checked out* (such is the brutal patois) by any man with eyes to see. Sitting on a bench, trying to apply myself to a book, I would despairingly conclude that in the universal war between the flesh and the spirit, the spirit was tasting ruin, its armies crushed and broken-winged. And yet the birds sang, and the grey squirrels bobbed across the green. On the way to Drake Square from the bus stop I would pass, each morning, an inanimate reminder of what a woman ought to look like, cherished, sequestered, exalted: I mean the curve-cornered matt-black postbox (check *that* out) in front of Thurgood Assurance on City Boulevard, which I would often glance at as I sprinted by.

It was at this time, too, that I received a cruel blow to my self-esteem. Back home, every little boy, at the age of five or six, experiences that lovely warm glow of pride when he realizes that his sisters are, in one important respect, just like his mother: *they* can't read or write either. Well, that pride was painfully retracted in Greeley, Colorado; and there were other familial developments that caused enormous suffering for me and for my brothers – and for my poor father. What can you do when your daughters start consorting with *kaffirs*, with *koofs*? You can't live with them, and you can't kill them (not in America); so the women stayed, and the men came home.

I wonder. Will there one day be a book called *The 7/29 Commission Report*, running to 567 pages, including 118 pages of notes? I still believe there will. And what a tortuous tale it will tell.

The One Eyed One, the One with One Eye, referred me to another one with one eye, his Justice Minister, who referred me to his Justice Minister (another one with one eye). The initial scouring of all the country's prisons and madhouses yielded 423 CRs. It was a hazardous journey they faced (there would be attrition), so I authorized a second sweep with a different kind of inmate in mind: compulsive paedophiles. This realized an additional 62. The 485 compulsives were corralled in a barracks near the capital and prepared for departure with heroin and straitjackets. As a further refinement, those who didn't have it already were infected with syphilis D.

When I went to America, I went there by plane. But I hardly needed telling that the unscheduled arrival of a jumbo jet crammed with scrofulous sociopaths would have raised some eyebrows at US Immigration. The first leg of the compulsives' journey, then, was a 900-mile drive in the trunks of old taxis. When we performed a 'test run', using a dozen assorted criminals and lunatics, the fatality rate turned out to be one hundred per cent, so we were careful, next time, to poke a few more holes in the back panelling, and we reluctantly reduced each load from four to two. This meant that the drivers had to come back for a second batch while the first took its ease in holding kennels at the port. Although I was inflexibly resolved to lead UU: CRs/G,C myself, a sudden indisposition forced me to stand down; so all authority in the field devolved upon the ferocious figure of Colonel Gul, commander of the First Mechanized Battalion. On August 3, 2001, chained to the hold of a disused container ship, my compulsives boldly set sail for Somalia.

*

NOTE: At which point (for reasons I will later mention) I abandoned this skeletal typescript of 'The Unknown Known'. The much fuller manuscript version followed the compulsives on their sanguinary journey to Greeley, Colorado (Greeley, after all, is the cradle of Islamism: it was there that Sayyid Qutb's Milestones, *known as the Islamists'* Mein Kampf, *was decisively shaped). The disused container ship is hijacked by Filipino pirates; the surviving compulsives spend two years in a punishment block in Mogadishu; they are then death-marched across Ethiopia into Sudan, where they encounter a host of some 30,000* janjaweed, *who kill all the compulsives under thirty 'as a warning'; the remainder (now consisting entirely of paedophiles, plus the implacable Colonel Gul) continue west by bus and on foot; they are severely mauled by a child militia in Congo, armed with* pangas . . . *And so on. Finally, one CR makes it to Greeley, Colorado, where, half-dead with syphilis D, he is found weeping in a cinema car park. Meanwhile, Ayed's marriages decline to the point where he retools his RodeoMaMa in the outhouse called Known Knowns, and resolves on a paradigm shift, an Unknown Unknown, which is sure to succeed: a suicide operation in his own home. The unknown known of the title is of course God.*

I abandoned the story for many reasons, all of them strictly extraneous. As I have said, Islamism is a total *system, and like all such it is eerily amenable to satire. But in the end I felt that the piece was premature, and therefore a hostage to fortune; certain future events might make it impossible to defend. If I live to be very old, I may one day pull it out of my desk – at the other end of the Long War.*

CHINA MIÉVILLE

Entry Taken from a Medical Encyclopaedia

NAME: *Buscard's Murrain*, or *Wormword*.

COUNTRY OF ORIGIN: Slovenia (probably).

FIRST KNOWN CASE: Primoz Jansa, a reader for a blind priest in the town of Bled in what is now northern Slovenia. In 1771 at the age of thirty-six Jansa left Bled for London. The first record of his presence there (and the first description of Buscard's Murrain) is in a letter from Ignatius Sancho to Margaret Cocksedge dated 4th February 1774.*

SYMPTOMS: The disease incubates for up to three years, during which time the infected patient suffers violent headaches. After this, full-blown Buscard's Murrain is manifested in slowly failing mental faculties and severe mood swings between three conditions: near full lucidity; a feverish seeking out of the largest audience possible; and a state of loud, hysterical glossolalia. Samuel Buscard infamously denoted these states *torpid*, *prefatory* and *grandiloquent* respectively, thereby appearing to take the side of the disease.

After between three and twelve years, the patient enters the terminal

---

* 'I doubt not that you have heard of Mister *Jansa* – a fellow of lamentable aspect – who is daily seen around the squares of his adopted city where his intense bearing entices crowds of the curious; when surrounded the fellow excoriates 'em in obscure tongues such as would shame the most *pious* and ecstatic of quakers. Those gathered mock the afflicted with mummery. But horrors! A number of those who have mimicked poor Jansa have fallen to his brain-fever, and are now partners in his *unorthodox ministry*.' (Kate Vinegar [ed.], *The London Letters of Ignatius Sancho* [Providence 1954], p. 337.)

phase of the disease. The so-far gradual mental collapse speeds up mark-edly, leaving him or her in a permanent vegetative state within months.

Those present during the nonsensical 'grandiloquence' of a murrain sufferer report that one particular word – the wormword – is repeated often, followed by a pause as the sufferer waits for a response. If any of those listening repeats the word, the sufferer's satisfaction is obvious.

Later, it is from among these mimics that the next batch of the infected will be found.

HISTORY: At the insistence of the respected Dr William Haygarth, all murrain sufferers were released into the care of Dr Samuel Buscard in 1775.* During postmortem investigations on the brains of infected victims Buscard discovered what he thought were parasitic worms, which he named after himself. When a committee of aetiologists examined his evidence, they found that the vermiform specimens were made of cerebral matter itself. Buscard was denounced amid claims that he had made the 'worms' himself by perforating the brains with a cheese-screw. The com-mittee renamed the disease 'gibbering fever', and half-heartedly claimed it to be the result of 'bad air'.

Samuel Buscard was ordered to surrender Jansa to the committee, but he produced papers showing that his patient had succumbed and been buried. The disgraced doctor then disappeared from public view and died in 1777.

His research was continued by his son Jacob, also a doctor. In 1782 Jacob Buscard astounded the medical establishment with the publication of his famous pamphlet proving that the brain-tissue 'worms' were capable of independent motion in the head, and that the cerebrums of sufferers were riddled with convoluted tunnels. 'The first Dr Buscard was thus correct,'

---

* There is no record of Haygarth fraternizing with or even mentioning Dr Buscard before or after this time, and the reasons behind his 1775 recommendation are opaque. In his diaries, Haygarth's assistant William Fin noted 'a disparity between Dr H's *words* and his *tone* when he claimed Dr Buscard as his *very good friend*' (quoted in Marcus Gadd's *A Buscardology Primer* [London 1972], p. iii). De Selby, in his unpublished 'Notes on Buscard', claims that Buscard was blackmailing Haygarth. What incriminating material he might have held on his more esteemed colleague remains unknown.

he wrote. 'Not *bad air* but a voracious parasite – a *murrain* – afflicts the gibberers.'

There is a word, which when spoken inveigles its way into the mind of the speaker and manifests itself in his flesh. It forces its bearer to speak itself again and again, in the company of others, that they might be tempted to echo it. With each utterance another wormword is born, until the brain is tunnelled quite through: and when those listening repeat what they have heard, in curiosity or mockery, if their utterance is just so, a wormword is hatched in their heads. Not quite the parasite envisaged by my wronged father, but a parasite nonetheless.*

Jacob Buscard's pamphlet dates his revelation to 1780, during one of his numerous interrogations of Jansa in his 'torpid' state. Jansa told Buscard that his illness had started one day while he was reading to his master in Bled. Between the pages of the book he had found a slip of paper on which was written two words. Jansa read the first word aloud, and thus started the earliest known outbreak of wormword. His ensuing headache caused him to drop the paper, which was subsequently lost. 'With the translation of those few letters into sound,' Jacob Buscard wrote, 'the wretched Jansa became midwife and host to the wormword.'†

The younger Buscard's breakthrough won him a tremendous reputation, marred by his admissions that he and his father had forged Jansa's death certificate and kept him alive and imprisoned as an experimental subject for the past seven years. Jansa was found in the Buscard basement in the advanced stages of his disease and taken to a madhouse, where he died two months later. Jacob Buscard escaped prosecution for kidnapping, torture, and accessory to forgery by fleeing to Munich, where he disappeared.‡

London suffered periodic outbreaks of Buscard's Murrain until the

---

* *A Posthumous Vindication of Dr Samuel Buscard: Proof That 'Gibbering Fever' Is Indeed Buscard's Murrain.* (London 1782), p. 17.

† Ibid., p. 25.

‡ His last known letter (to his son Matthew) is dated January 1783, and contains a hint as to his plans. Jacob complains 'I have not even the money to finish this. Carriage to Bled is a scandalous expense!' (Quoted in Ali Khamrein's *Medical Letters* [New York 1966], p. 232.)

passage of the Gibbering Act of 1810 legalized the incarceration of the infected in soundproof sanatoria.* The era of mass infection was over, and only occasional isolated cases have been recorded since.

It took the late twentieth century and the work of Jacob Buscard's great-great-great-great-great granddaughter Dr Mariella Buscard conclusively to dispel the superstitious notions about 'evil words' that have clouded even scholarly discussions of the disease. In her seminal 1995 *Lancet* article 'It's the Synapses, Stupid!', the latest Dr Buscard proves the murrain to be simply an unpleasant (though admittedly unusual) biochemical reaction.

She points out that with every action of the human body, including speech, a unique configuration of thousands of minute chemical reactions occurs in the brain. Dr Buscard shows that when the wormword is spoken with a precise inflection, the concomitant synaptic firing has the unfortunate property of reconfiguring nerve-fibres into discrete self-organizing clusters. The tiny chemical reactions, in other words, turn nerves into parasites. Boring through the brain and using their own newly independent bodies to reroute neural messages, these marauding lengths of brain matter periodically take control of their host. They particularly affect his or her speech, in an attempt to fulfil their instincts to reproduce.

Following the format established in Jacob Buscard's pamphlet, the wormword is traditionally rendered *yGudluh*. This is recorded with some trepidation: the main vector for the transmission of Buscard's Murrain over the last two centuries has been the literature about it.†

CURES: Randolph Johnson's claims about bergamot oil in *Confessions of a Disease Junkie* are spurious: there is no known cure for Buscard's

* These notorious 'Buscard Shacks' loom large in popular culture of the time. See for example the ballad 'Rather the Poorhouse than a Buscard Shack' (reproduced in Cecily Fetchpaw's *Hanoverian Street Songs: Populism and Resistance* [Pennsylvania 1988], p. 677).
† Contrary to the impression given by the media after the 1986 Statten-Dogger incident, *deliberate* exposure to the risks of wormword is neither common nor new. Ully Statten was (no doubt unwittingly) continuing a tradition established in the late eighteenth century. In what could be considered a late Georgian extreme sport, London's young rakes and coffeehouse dandies would take turns reading the word aloud, each risking correct pronunciation and thereby infection.

Murrain.* There is, however, persistent speculation that the second word on Jansa's lost paper, if spoken, might engender some cure in the brain: perhaps a predatory 'hunter' synapse to devour the wormwords. Several 'Jansa's papers' have appeared over the decades, all forgeries.† Despite numerous careful searches, Jansa's paper remains lost.‡

* This will come as no surprise to those familiar with Johnson's work. The man is a liar, a fraud, and a bad writer (whose brother is Britain's third-largest importer of bergamot oil).
† There is a comprehensive list in Gadd, op. cit., p. 74.
‡ 'Years of Violent Ransacking Leave Slovenia's Historic Churches in Ruins', *Financial Times*, 3/7/85.

PETER HOBBS

Winter Luxury Pie

Row One – Baby Blue Hubbard to Hong Kong Long Dong

For the best part of two hundred years the women in my family have run farms. We're a late, great, matriarchal agricultural dynasty. Grandma was the last of the doyennes, what with my father not really cutting it in the gender stakes, and myself not having much of a realm to preside over. But the fun stops here, I'm the last – not because I'll never have children, simply because after this there will be nothing more to bequeath.

I was raised principally as a farmer, but allowed out on odd days to go to school. My parents, traditional and untraditional in equal measure, made it clear that a woman's place was running the family business, for which I didn't need too many brains. Just enough, perhaps. And so I was spared the indignities of home-schooling inflicted with great and sedulous care on my two brothers. Da and Ma both had a fixation with education, which ran against a somewhat inauspicious legacy. Family tradition, after all, has it that F-A-R-M spells 'work'. Jer, the youngest of us, could speak Greek and Latin by the age of five, and solve quadratic equations in about the time it took him to blink. He'd answer in Urdu, and not particularly to show off, simply because that was what he usually counted in. He still has a phenomenal memory, particularly for statistics. He's like a walking *Harper's Index* when he gets going. Aged eight he came third in the National Spelling Bee, devastating my Da who assumed he'd walk it – and he in fact might have, his failure at the final hurdle being primarily the fault of the announcer, who struggled with *aphaeresis*, unintentionally pronouncing the word as though it were in the plural – Jer misunderstood, and rushed in with an entirely correct spelling of *aphaereses*. He was inconsolable when it was called wrong. Being the only person present who realized the reason for his mistake, he protested in vain.

He's never really recovered from those years, even though he left home and didn't return to the farm until my parents had gone. He hardly ever washes, and has worn the same clothes – the entire set, I mean, socks, pants, underwear, shirt – every day for perhaps a decade. His hair long ago got to the state where it was washing itself. He's quite charming, though given to pressure of speech, and he panics a little in company. He collects tomato seeds. He isn't good at conversation, though he can talk for hours about his tomatoes, or battles fought between peoples long since dead. He has this sad and unfortunate tendency to fall in love with girls who have large vocabularies – pretty or ugly, old or young, continent or no. They run a mile, of course. The last of these was Emily, a girl from the *nice* farm down the road, and achingly beautiful – tall where I'm short, willowy where I'm kinda gnarled. She has a laugh which tames wild horses – mine tends to startle tame ones. Whoever she marries, it's hard to imagine her children being anything other than demi-gods. She actually liked Jer, I should say – it wasn't entirely unrequited. Farm girls after all are used to that kind of smell, maybe even get to like it. Where she got her (admittedly impressive) vocabulary from is anyone's guess. But it all ended over the winter. Jer phoned up – and he *hates* using the phone – to tell me about it.

'I really like you, Jer,' she said, 'but dontcha think all this physical stuff is, like, kinda banausic?' He's still not over her. It would have been kinder to have rejected him in monosyllables, really. Of course what he really needs is a girl who won't understand a word he's on about when he goes on one of his rants, who will just smile and go run a bath for him, a girl who's sweet and kind but not too bright, a girl who doesn't use the word *heterophyllous* in casual conversation.

Row Two – Untreated Autumn Queen to Gourdgeous Tricolor

And here the two of us are, back on Grandma's farm. Out through Esperanza ('We're beyond hope,' Jer says), east four miles along the highway. Third right after the gas station – a track more than a road. Past the sign advertising Taxidermy & Deer Processing. Next farm, the green gate, you've got it. This particular farm has been in the family about 120 years, before which we were over in the Appalachians. I guess my ancestors fancied a change of scenery.

My great-grandfather who bought the place committed suicide by drowning himself in a puddle. He just lay down and put his face in the muddy water. There were rumors he'd caught syphilis from a dancing girl up in Taylorville. He never really cut it as a farmer, the lure of the city dragging him ceaselessly away. Alcohol, gambling and dancing girls, the usual vices. Great-grandma never let on exactly what it was, so we're very much down to speculation. She just got on with running the farm – she got that at least from her husband's money – and expanded it into a significant empire. They already had two daughters: Hattie, who lived and worked there for forty years before marrying an India-rubber salesman from Cincinnati and moving to California (I heard once that there's a whole lost branch of the family still out there so I guess that, contrary to what they say, rubber don't bounce back); and Grandma, who never married. She told me once that she'd been in love, and after that never wanted anyone else. When I asked her how it felt to be celibate so long she laughed. 'Well there were *men*, honey, of course. Your father didn't come from nowhere. But they were distractions. After a month or so I'd get thinking back to Harry. I met some wonderful people, some wonderful men. I just didn't fall in love, and wasn't prepared to settle for anything less. I mean, your father did, obviously, but he's not like us, is he?'

My Da then was another who had his heart broken when young, another who drifted away from the farm. He went off to Chicago, educated himself between working jobs in a tax office by day and a bar by night, and turned himself around. Then having been broken down and torn apart and his heart turned to cynicism and his life to the common bleakness of existence, he met my mother, and without falling in love understood perfectly well that here was a woman who would do, who he could be happy with. Ma was easily enough pleased with him. She came from a poor background, but was possessed of a great urge for self-improvement and was thus entirely complicit in the thorough education of her male offspring. Da saw too she came from hard-working stock and would make (or at least produce) a good farmer. And unlike his paternal ancestry, he came back to the farm, at least until failing health took him away again.

My mother was philoprogenitive, in both senses of the word. Heterophyllous too, bearing the three of us as though we were different species. Like strikes of lightning hitting the same place we emerged with an unlikely forty-minute gap between first and last, Harry, myself and Jer.

The three of us, some facts: Hair colors: black, mousy and blonde (when he gets round to washing it). Eye colors: Brown, green-in-certain-lights and blue. Heights: 6 feet 3 inches, 5 feet 2-ish inches, 5 feet 6 inches. IQs: 110-ish, mind your own business, 160-ish. Handedness: ambi-, right, left. Careers: lawyer, farmer, none. You get the idea. No palingenesis. You could put the three of us together for photos and it would look like a gathering of the races. However, the family has always stuck together and defended its own.

Row Three – Rupp's Green – Striped Cushaw

In fact the only one we never liked was our cousin on my mother's side, Freddy. There was something in his (black) eyes, something about the loss of his (ginger) hair that we never trusted. By the age of twenty he had just clumps or tufts of rusted fur across his head, a distressing crop he concealed beneath a backwards baseball cap which he wore with accompanying white-trash accent. For Freddy a trailer was just the *height* of sophistication, a great bold step up from the ditch.

He never really made an effort to be liked. Family gatherings when we were young he'd make presents to me of dead birds, telling me they were asleep, and would wake up if I treated them right. I can still feel the slimy guilt of failing them today. He tripped Harry when he walked past, then would offer a bare-faced apology, without much effort at coming over sincere. Harry was so honest he thought it was all an accident, and at the wake when he'd been a bit pressed for something to say, all he could come out with was: 'He was always a bit clumsy, our Freddy.' I mean, *Jesus*. I hated him most though because he put maggots into Jer's cot when Jer was still just a tiny child. So don't get me wrong – we like *everybody*. It's just Freddy. Even his parents, Aunt Jean and Uncle Pete, didn't like him enough to go to his funeral. He wasn't actually their son, of course, had been adopted as a baby when it was clear Aunt Jean's problem with her tubes wasn't going to get fixed. Our side of the family we were always suspicious that Freddy had been put into adoption because his Da had been a serial killer or somesuch and had gone away for a very long time. Not that he was ever told about his uncertain parentage – they were tempted, mind, to use it as a constant disclaimer against anything he did. (That whispered confession: '*Of course he's not really ours . . .*') Personally I think Freddy knew, deep inside, despite not being overly bright. I don't think it helped. Slow, dawning realization is a killer. It's *always* better to be told. Finding out by yourself is a horrible thing, and even the small lies get found out, in the end. He died at twenty-three from sudden heart failure over in Ariola Square Mall, gasping something about how terribly lonely it was in the dark. The irony of it was that there were probably more people concerned for his welfare at that particular moment, he having collapsed in front of a crowd of surprised shoppers, than ever before in his truncated life.

Uncle Pete almost died of relief, in fact, suffering a stroke the day after the funeral. He lasted another three years, but in poor health. In later years Aunt Jean got so lonely and weirded out that she sat at home by herself waiting for the phone to ring. She got rid of her TV, moved the armchair out into the hallway where the phone table was, and settled down every day to wait for calls. Sometimes she knitted (my inheritance from her – which to be fair was more than I expected – was measured in scarves), occasionally she read one of the free household shopping magazines that came through her door. Of course she didn't tell anyone that she was waiting for calls, and our whole side of the family has a thing about phones, so *we* never called her. I didn't find out about this until her own funeral, when my mother tearfully explained what had been going on. And my mother didn't find out until a couple weeks before that. So who called my aunt? Well, as far as I understand, aside from pestilent telesales reps (to whom she gave short shrift), she waited for people to call the wrong number. Based on an entirely unrepresentative survey of my own phone, I can't imagine this occurring more than once a month. And when they called, she didn't try too hard to draw them into conversation, it was just, 'Oh, there's no one here of that name, perhaps you have the wrong number? Well, this is 476- . . . No, no trouble at all. Goodbye, now.' For Aunt Jean I guess it was enough, the contact.

Ma told me all this not so as to spread gossip, and not to make my heart blur with sympathy. Merely to say, 'There but for the grace of God and your Da go I.' Married siblings are always grateful, and always a little embarrassed, when it comes to get-togethers with unmarried siblings. Harry, happily married for ten years, always stands in front of his wife, Sue, when they call at the door, so as to avoid drawing attention to her or appearing smug. It's astonishing to see. My parents too are apologetic whenever they talk about Harry. 'Of course,' they say, 'he was so *lucky* to find her.' This is to make me feel better, because all girls need to be married.

Row Four – *Show King Bag 1, Show King Bag 2, Genital Improved Hubbard*

When I was young, and after learning one day in school about erosion, I became pretty certain that the end of the world was nigh. Some say the world will end in fire, some say in ice. I developed this terrible fear that it would just wear away. This was precisely not the kind of fear to mention to my dad – he shouted for Jer and then got us to calculate (without the aid of a calculator – which with Jer around is not so much of a handicap), about how long it *would* take for the world to erode, given a posited rate. *Taking account of the different types of rock that make up the earth.* Taking into account too countervailing processes, such as the diagenesis of sediment. Coming up with a number with a name bigger than I remember somehow didn't allay my fears, but I did learn to keep them to myself next time.

Thanks to working with Jer, and helping him learn the long lists of words which are required cramming for spelling-bee entrants, I was doing pretty well at school. Three concurrent educations – on the farm, in school, and vicariously through Jer, while not exactly giving me clear direction in life, have provided me an essential sciolism.

For a while there it looked like I might escape the farm. The acreage then was shrinking anyway, and everything that remained still being run by Grandma with some help from Ma, and I was able to get to college, a year after Harry, where I majored in French.

My love life has been sparse. Remitting, perhaps, is a better word. The action has always fallen a little short of the required standard, and I never really thought my standards were unreasonable. Let me name and shame, for example, Thom the football player. After pursuing me a couple of weeks he came back to my room one night, a bit nervous and overcompensating with fraudulent assurance. After a while he took off his shirt and did a few push-ups, then asked me if I wanted to sleep with him. Let me elaborate on that one – in fact what he actually did was flex his muscles and say: 'You won't get a chance to sleep with a body like this very often.' I felt terribly, terribly sorry for him. It was painfully clear that no one would ever compete with the love he so clearly got from his mirror. Or take Mike, who one night in bed went through a whole bright pleiad of names before he landed on mine, then later, after a minute's recuperation from a sudden interfemoral intervention by my knee, claimed to have been joking. Neither is my worst experience, not by a clear country mile.

For me there was a boy once. A boy who changed everything while he was around. Everything in my life gained meaning or lost it according to whether I shared it with him. He left. I still imagine myself pointing things out to him as I walk the fields. The cobalt bluebirds beneath the willows. Flame-breasted cardinals on the fence post. One or two rare helobious species visiting from the lowlands, and myriad chromatic butterflies crowding like a ticker-tape parade. It all just seems like wasted beauty, without him. I can't say his name. All I'll say is there's not one of us without shit in our soul, somewhere.

And then lately there's Bob. Persistence is his middle name. Hope, unfortunately, is in fact his last. He wore me down, in a sweet kinda way. It happened one night, as the movie has it. My last year in college. Thereafter he seemed to assume I was the girl for him. Sometimes he acts like we're already married. I think he's puzzled when I run away, find space for myself, but I think too he tells himself that it's just one of my quirks, just me and not him, and puts up with it. I didn't tell him I was coming back to the farm, and he doesn't know where it is, but it's only a matter of time. With Bob everything is just a matter of time. It all wears away, however long it takes.

Row Five – Stokes' Tricolor to Kitchenette

Home-schooling hell aside, the three of us had as golden a childhood as might be believed. From which I don't retain too much. The lingering, slightly fibrous taste of tomatoes straight from the vine. A happiness which rises only when I'm surrounded by farmland or countryside. Great memories of pre-Christmas pig-slaughtering ceremonies. The ability to operate a tractor. Well-developed upper-body strength from every menial task you care to name – and subsequently a right hook a fair degree more dangerous than you'd expect from looking. In fact I only got good things out of it, my upbringing, while it seems to have finished off my parents. On an organic patch at least the farm-life is a pretty healthy one (no organo-phosphates), once the stresses of actually making a living are removed, but it cut a swathe through their generation.

Da has recently received a new heart. Following the recrudescence of what was always a suspiciously idiopathic illness. The doctors doubted, but could see something wasn't right, so relented, and gave him one. I always wondered if transplants were the one final way to mend a broken heart. Unless the donor's heart were broken too. Either way, I'm pretty clear that there's more to the heart than just a pump.

Da, I think, was never really built for this life, nor any other, perhaps, but circumstances have allowed him to survive more comfortably than he otherwise might have done.

Ma joined him in hospital after her back gave out. For eighteen months she lay flat, the duration of two pregnancies. 'You're *not* getting fat,' was all she really wanted to hear from me when I visited. Post-hospital, she and Da moved to the city for access to reliable health care and firmer mattresses.

Grandma then was ninety-five, the oldest human being I ever saw, and complaining of decrepitude, manifested in her recently acquired inability to climb trees. Grandma had been climbing trees all her life, until a year or two back. It was simply what she did, the way other people worked out at the car plant or one of the gas stations up by the highway. In the end her hips gave out. It seemed entirely possible that she'd levitate up into the branches anyway through sheer force of will, hips or no, and God knows she tried, standing by the trunks of her favorite pieces of living timber, and gazing upwards at a lost world. She battled it for months, then finally admitted defeat. She was never the same after that, and died two months ago, her body in the end decaying enough to catch her unawares, asleep. Not the kind of woman who'd be careless enough to go out awake, Da said.

That meant that we were finally able to put in motion selling the farm, the house, and getting out of the agricultural vice. Debts have been mounting. The last of the animals were shipped out last year and sold for prices lower than we'd brought them in at, never mind the work and feed. Even the guinea fowl are gone. I have a feeling Jer ate the last couple, though he must have had some help in killing them. He has whole strata of earth beneath his fingernails, but won't get his hands dirty by precipitating the premature end of livestock. Pig-killing season he'd stay indoors and cry. Anyways. Just this year's crop to be rid of, then we can all go home.

I feel it's important, however, we get this last bit right. Financially, partly, but also to go out on a high. History deserves it. Which is the reason I'm here doing it all and not Harry, or even Jer. Jer was the first choice, and is probably the only one of us sufficiently versed in agronomy, but he hasn't really got the required concentration. Once he'd run out of projects to keep him interested (renumbering the rows in Urdu, re-writing all the names as anagrams – projects it didn't take me *too* long to straighten out again), he let it all go to seed. Harry's in Alaska with a family to look after. Ma and Da are up in town nursing their respective ailments (and very much on the mend, now they're settled in their urban idyll). So they called me back to take over. There's a moral there. Try as you might you can't separate a woman from the soil of her destiny.

Row Six – Sweet Dumpling and Small Wonder

I don't mind being here. It's good to be home. It's good to work with living stuff, stuff that's grown from seed and needs nurturing. Good for the soul. And for the first few weeks no one had the number here, because we only really use it for outgoing emergency calls, so they couldn't phone. Bob tracked it down eventually, of course.

'Uh, where *are* you?'

'I'm on the farm.'

'On a what?'

'A farm. We own a farm, remember?'

'Oh. I thought you were joking about that.'

He said he'd come over, but I think he's getting worried whether he made the right choice with me after all. He doesn't think it's natural, going off to live on a farm for a few months. Not that I'm lonely – Jer's still around, cutting an increasingly aristulate figure. He sleeps a lot during the day, and sometimes when I wake in the night I come down to find him researching recondite strains of tomato. He's a terrible insomniac, or rather a very good one. I think lately his emotional troubles have begun having a detrimental effect on his health. He's a sensitive lad, and we brought in a TV – the first TV this farm has ever seen – especially so he could watch it daytimes when he's awake to feel numb and quell the rising nausea.

Evenings we rendezvous in the kitchen, and he cooks dinner. He's a great cook, though refuses to countenance any recipe which involves the butchery of innocent tomatoes. That aside, his chief responsibility around the place is to keep the fire burning there – it's an enormous fireplace, recessed like a small room, the natural claw of the hearth holding a row of smoldering logs we take turns to bring in. A great blackened streak up the back bricks. It's not cold – just coming into autumn now – but we've nothing else to cook on. He counts his seeds sitting in the window seat, his index finger on his left hand separating them with an untypical dexterity. Jer's left-handedness was his one act of apostasy against a rigorous learning regime. When he was young he used to write with the sheet of paper perpendicular to him, his left arm curling round it. Ma and Da couldn't shake the habit, and eventually conceded the point. I thought his being left-handed was cool. I still have an over-riding impression that *gauche* means *cool*, even though I know it doesn't.

From that window though you can see the patch. A six- by four-hundred-yard low-level jungle. I walk up the rows three or four times a day, keeping an eye out for slugs or snails. We're organic here so there's no pesticides, and the alternative preventative treatments are never certain. The patch is like critter central. There are bean bugs, which disintegrate disgustingly to the touch, setiferous spiders – variously-armed with poison spikes or wicked fangs – and evil, invisible, egg-laying monsters known as chiggers. Some enormous praying mantises too, eight inches or so – the kind town-folk see and start raving about first contact and alien encounters. And we get cockroaches. I mean real cockroaches, somewhere near the size of turtles.

Then there are the usual (and preternaturally destructive) snails and slugs. Weird things, when you think about it. A slug pretty much *is* its own foot. Put that in your mouth.

I talk to the crop. Grandma was a firm believer in that. 'Words change everything,' she said. 'So talk nicely when you're on the patch.' Harry once got the hiding of his life when he got his foot stuck beneath a particularly robust root, tripped, fell and swore.

Harry though, I should probably say, was the one anomaly of our impeccably agricultural ancestry, an aberration. A man never meant for the farm. A man born to cliché. Captain of his high school football team, dating (and later marrying) the prom queen, a football scholarship to college, law school. He was resistant to an unusual degree to home-schooling, but evinced a compensating aptitude at sports. Da thus kicked him out of his development program (transferring his remaining hopes in the brain department to Jer), sent him to school, and with the collusion of the head coach there fast-streamed him into the sporting life. He's currently working in Anchorage in a building with no windows on three sides. Sends me postcards of blue glaciers. They already have two kids, twins aged eight and a half, and once a few years ago a fortune teller told Sue that one would go on to get a doctorate in physics, and the other end up in and out of jail for the rest of his life. Both, I would say, are well on their way.

Row Seven – Big Autumn

Lately I have come to wonder if I am becoming like Grandma, who though she was happy and faced up to her losses in life, never really found a way of leaving them behind and moving on. Maybe, I think, I should climb trees. See what it was she found there. I'm not sure though there's anything that could make all that much difference. Leaves? Snails? I can't help but think I'd just get more dirt on my hands, and no less shit in my soul.

And I've come to wonder too if I'm wasting my time dwelling on my family, and these stories. There's a thousand things I haven't told you: that Harry once admitted to me that what he really wanted to do professionally was ice-dance, that he and Sue have been taking lessons four nights a week; that when Da was born he was a twin, and his baby sister died of TB; that Ma once had an affair with a rutabaga farmer from the Two Valleys. That I had my first sexual experience when I was twelve, in the hay barn one sunny summer afternoon, when I went all the way with my best friend, a girl called Carol. These stories don't seem to fit in anywhere else. But telling them keeps me from getting bored, when I have nothing to do for the next few weeks months except walk the rows and wait for the approach of Halloween, when I can finally sell all these damn pumpkins.

MEN

THOMAS MORRIS

All the Boys

The best man won't tell them it's Dublin until they get to Bristol Airport. He'll tell them to bring euros and don't bother packing shorts. The five travelling from Caerphilly will drink on the minibus. And Big Mike, the best man, will spend the first twenty minutes reading and rereading the A4 itinerary he typed up on MS Word. The plastic polypocket will be wedged thick with flight tickets and hostel reservations. It will be crumpled and creased from the constant hand-scrunching and metronome swatting against his suitcase – the only check-in bag on the entire trip. He'll spend the journey to the airport telling Gareth, and anyone who listens, that Rob had better never marry again, that he couldn't handle the stress of organizing another one of these.

'You should see my desk in work,' Big Mike will say. 'It's covered in notes for this fuckin stag. It's been like a full-time job.'

Gareth will nod and Gareth will sympathize. He'll just be glad to get out of Caerphilly for the weekend; he's been waiting months for this, has imagined how it all might go. He'll take a swig of his can, and look to Rob's father. Rob's father will be fifty-four in two weeks and will think there's something significant about the fact, about being twice the age of his son. He had two kids and a house by the time he was twenty-seven, and he'll think about that as he listens to Larry telling the story about the woman he picked up at the Kings. She'd taken Larry back to her place, and in the middle of the night he'd heard sex noises coming from the room next to hers. Larry said to the woman, 'Your housemate's a bit wild', and the woman replied, 'I don't have a housemate, love. That's my daughter.'

Hucknall and Peacock, travelling from London, will arrive at Bristol before the others. They'll sit in the bar getting drunk and studying departures screens. Hucknall will have spent the whole morning moaning about the fact they're flying from Bristol, and why couldn't Big Mike have just told them where they're going?

'Bet you it's Dublin,' Hucknall will say, leaning back in his chair, his knees spread wide, his hands smoothing his tan chinos. 'Bet Big Mike's too scared to book somewhere foreign.'

'Don't make a difference to me,' Peacock will say. 'I'll clear up wherever we go.'

When the Caerphilly boys join the now-London ones at the airport bar, Big Mike will confirm that it's Dublin they're headed to. And he'll loudly declare the weekend's drinking rule: pints must always be held in the left hand. If you find yourself holding two drinks, your own drink must be in your left hand. Failure to adhere will result in a forfeit, as decided by Lead Ruler Larry. The boys will all say that's easy, and start suggesting additional rules, but Big Mike will be defiant: the left-hand rule is king.

'You sure no one here's a secret leftie, though?' Hucknall will ask.

'I've done my research,' Big Mike will say. 'Rob's dad is left-footed, but he's definitely right-handed. I made him write his name out earlier.'

When Peacock – with perfect stubble and coiffed hair – goes to the airport bar, everyone will laugh at his shoes that seem to be made of straw.

'Couldn't believe it when I met him at Paddington,' Hucknall will say. 'Doesn't he look benter than a horseshoe?'

'I've seen straighter semicircles,' Rob will say.

Gareth will shout to Peacock: 'Mate, why don't you do yourself a favour and just come out?'

Peacock will stand there, between table and bar, and kiss his own biceps. He'll accept the jibes, and say none of the boys has any idea about style. He'll take the piss out of Caerphilly's clothes shops, and say David Beckham wore a pair of shoes just like these to the *Iron Man 3* premiere. And that will be it: Peacock will be called Iron Man Three for the rest of the trip.

When they board the plane, Larry will tell the air stewardess that Peacock's ticket isn't valid, that his name is Iron Man Three.

When they get to the hostel in Temple Bar – and Hucknall has finally stopped going on about the ten-minute wait for Big Mike's suitcase, he'll ask if Iron Man Three has a reservation.

And in Fitzsimons on the first night, to every girl that Peacock talks to, one of the boys will come up and say, 'Don't bother, Iron Man's gay.'

Peacock will laugh. 'They're just jealous,' he'll tell the girl from Minneapolis or Wexford or Rome. 'They wouldn't know fashion if it woke them up in the morning and gave them a little kiss.'

Gareth, meanwhile, will be at the bar ordering shots. He'll have his arm around Rob and he'll tell him that he loves him, that he's really happy he's happy. He'll make Rob do shots with him – sambuca, whiskey and vodka – and Rob will say he can't handle any more after the apple sours.

'Who's for shots?' Gareth will say, looking around '*Shotiau?*'

He'll order shots for whoever's beside him at the bar. He'll buy randomers shots. And he'll persuade the English barman to have a shot with him. He's not meant to, but he'll do one just to shut Gareth up.

At a table, Rob's father will have his arm around his son.

'I love Rachel, you know,' Rob will say, his eyes ablaze. 'I really love her.'

'Just pace yourself,' his father will say quietly. 'The boys are getting wrecked. They won't even notice if you don't drink the stuff they're giving you.'

He'll offer to drink his son's drinks; he'll get wasted so that his son may be saved.

Big Mike will be careering around the pub making sure everyone's alright. He'll always have a pint in his left hand. And he'll be going from boy to boy, just to make sure everyone's okay. This first night he'll be torn between keeping steady and getting absolutely bollocksed. He'll decide on ordering half-pints but asking the barman to pour them into pint glasses.

'Dun want anyone thinking I'm gay,' he'll say, and he'll order another pint for Rob, and place it down at his table without saying a word.

And Larry? He'll be getting attacked by an English girl for calling her sugar-tits. When her friends pull her off, he'll retouch his hair and say, 'Fair play, my dear, that was lovely. Can we do that back at yours?'

The night will become an ungodly mess. All the boys will be pouncing on each other for holding pints in their right hand, and drinking shots as forfeits, and drinking faster as the night slips by. They'll make moves on girls on hen-do's from Brighton and Bangor and Mayo. By eleven, Hucknall will be puking in the corner of the dance floor, and Rob's father, after a quiet word in Big Mike's ear, will take Rob back to the hostel. Peacock will go missing, talking to some girl somewhere, his deep V-neck shirt showing off his tonely chest and glimmering sunbed tan. And Rob, the groom (lest we forget), will be flat-out on the hostel bed, fully clothed, but shoeless, his father having taken them off while his drunken twenty-seven-year-old son lay half-comatose. He'll send a text to the boy's mother: *'all gd here, back at the hostel. Rob's safe and asleep.'*

Outside McDonald's, Larry'll coax the boys to take turns hugging the Polish dwarf in a leprechaun costume.

Larry will say: 'Cracking job this would be for you, Mikey-boy.'

Big Mike will laugh and grab at his own hair. He'll slur, 'I'm small. I know I'm small. But at least I'm *not* fucking ginger.'

Gareth will ask the Polish dwarf if Big Mike can try on his hat, but the man will decline.

'No hat, no job,' he'll say.

So they'll take turns to photograph each other hugging the Polish dwarf in a leprechaun costume. They'll ask a passer-by to take photos of them hugging the Polish dwarf in a leprechaun costume. And when the Polish man points at the little pot-of-gold money box and asks for two euro, Larry will say – actually, Larry won't say anything the leprechaun will understand. Larry will be speaking Welsh. When abroad, all the boys slag everyone in Welsh.

At Zaytoon, Gareth, Big Mike and Larry will queue for food while Hucknall sits on the pavement outside, his head arched between his legs, his vomit softly coating the kerb and cobblestones like one of Dali's melted clocks. A blonde girl will ask the boys if they're from Wales. She'll say she loves the accent, and Larry will say he likes hers too – where's she from? But when she answers, she'll be looking at Gareth, not Larry. She'll say she likes his quiff.

'Cheers,' Gareth will say. 'I grew it myself.'

She'll be asking about the tattoo of a fish on Gareth's arm when Larry will tell her that Gareth has a girlfriend called Carly, that they're buying together a house in Ystrad Mynach. The girl will lose interest, not immediately – she won't be that obvious – but she'll allow herself to be pulled back into the gravitational force of her friends who lean against the restaurant window.

'Cheers,' Gareth will say to Larry. 'You're such a twat.'

'Any time,' Larry will say. 'have you seen *Iron Man Three*?'

Big Mike will have his hands on the glass counter, his head resting like a small bundle in his arms. Gareth will be looking at Big Mike's tiny little frame, his tiny little shoes against the base of the counter, and Gareth will think he should text Carly back.

'I ain't seen Peacock all night,' he'll say. 'Probably shagging some bloke somewhere.'

Larry will smile. 'Aye,' he'll say. 'Wouldn't surprise me.'

all the boys

Saturday, the hostel room smelling like sweated alcohol and men, heavy tongues will wake stuck to the roofs of dry mouths. Set up a microphone, and this is what you'll hear: waking-up farts and morning groans; zips and unzips on mini-suitcases and sports bags; the library-*shhhhhhh* of Lynx sprays; and the sounds of the bathroom door opening and slamming, its lock rotating clockwise in the handle. Pop your nose through the door, and this is what you'll smell: dehydrated shit mingling with the minty hostel shower gel in the hot, steamy air. And back in the room, more sounds now: the beginning of last night's stories, the where-did-you-go-tos, the how-the-hell-did-I-get-backs and Larry inviting the boys to guess if the skin he's pulling over his boxers belongs to his cock or balls.

Big Mike will be first to breakfast, the others dripping behind. All the boys will be scrolling through iPhones for photos from last night, with Rob's father doing the same on his digital camera. There'll be sympathetic bleats for headaches and wrenched stomachs, with paracetamol handed around like condiments. Big Mike will be urging the boys to get a move on or they'll never make it to Croke Park. Hucknall will ask why the hell are they going there anyway? And Big Mike, tapping the inventory in its polypocket, will say: 'Culture, mate. Culture.' Fried breakfasts and questions: how's an Irish breakfast different to an English? When you buying the house then, Gareth? And seriously, Peacock, where the hell did you end up last night?

Peacock's story will be confusing and confused. He got in a taxi with a girl, and she was well up for it – he was fingering her in the backseat. ('Backseat?' Larry'll say. 'Up the arse, like?' and Peacock will go, 'No, the backseat of the taxi, you dickwad.') Anyway, when they got to her place she realized she didn't have her keys ('Sure this wasn't a bloke?' Rob will say.) So Peacock and the girl walked for like an hour to somewhere – Cadbra or some random place – and when they arrived she told him he couldn't come in because it was her nan's house. She just went in and closed the door on him. When he finally found a taxi, he didn't have enough cash so the driver dropped him off at some random ATM in a 24-hour shop, but Peacock got talking to some random guy about London for ages ('Oh yeah, bet you did,' Gareth'll say) and when he came out, the taxi had gone, so he – ('He's holding his glass in his right hand!' Rob's father will say. 'It's orange juice,' Peacock will say. 'It don't matter,' Larry will say. 'Down it!') – so he found the tram stop and –

'Gay Boy Robert Downey Junior,' Hucknall will say. 'I'm bored now. Worst Man, when we going to Croke Park?'

Big Mike will be glaring. He'll say: 'As soon as you've finished your fucking breakfast.'

All the boys will be surprised and impressed by Croke Park's size, by the vastness of the changing rooms, the way the training centre gleams. When the guide takes them out onto the edge of the pitch, he'll point to the stand at the far end, and tell them about the Bloody Sunday Massacre in 1920, how the British army opened fire on the crowd during a Gaelic football match. Fourteen were killed, he'll say. Two players were shot. There'll be a silence. Rob's father will be nodding – he'll have read about all this in the guide book he bought at the Centra in Temple Bar. Three of the boys will be wearing Man Utd shirts. And the guide will go on, explaining how Gaelic football and hurling – he'll just call it GAA, and it'll take a few minutes for the boys to fully get what he's talking about – are not sports, but expressions of resistance. But they're also more than that, they're not just reactive things. It's in the blood, he'll say. And Gareth will be sort of startled. Something the guide says, something of its tone, will resonate. Though resonate isn't quite how Gareth would put it; he won't even know what he's thinking. He'll just be looking out to the far stand, trying to picture how it all happened.

'They were boys,' the guide will say. 'The ones who fought for independence, they were younger than all you.'

The sky will be white, and there'll be silence and rapture. When the guide leaves them at the museum, Hucknall will say to the boys, 'Fucking hell, I thought he'd never shut up.'

And Larry will put on an Irish accent and go: '*GAA is in the blood.*'

And Hucknall will laugh and go: '*And they killed all our boys* . . . Yeah, nice one, Worst Man. Most depressing stag-do in the world. You got any other crap trips in that suitcase of yours?'

Big Mike will be quiet, he won't know what to say.

'I enjoyed it,' Rob will say, and his father will thank Big Mike for bringing them.

Gareth will send a text to Carly. '*Miss you too*', it'll say.

Peacock will be using his iPhone to check his hair.

They'll get a taxi back into town, then they'll walk around and look at things. Larry'll be in hysterics when he sees the place called Abrakebabra, insisting that one of the boys take his photo next to the sign. They'll walk in a group, taking up half the width of Westmoreland Street, wondering what the hell goes on in the massive white building with the huge columns that look as if they belong in Rome.

'It's a bank,' Rob's father will say, and Big Mike will go, 'No wonder things are so fucking expensive.'

When they pass Trinity College, Rob's father will say there's meant to be a nice library in there, he read about it in his guide book. And Gareth will point ahead at Hucknall and Larry as they eye up a group of Spanish-looking tourists, and he'll say: 'I've got a feeling the boys aren't really in the mood for a good read.'

Before they know it, they'll be in Temple Bar again. In Gogarty's they'll order bouquets of Guinness, and Hucknall will insist that they should have gone to the Guinness Factory instead of Croke Park.

Big Mike will say: 'If you know so much, why dun you be fucking best man?' And the boys will do a handbags-*oooooh*, and laugh until their already-aching kidneys hurt. A greying man on a guitar will sing 'Whiskey in the Jar' and 'The Wild Rover' ('The Clover song!' Peacock will say), and when the boys request 'Delilah', he'll oblige, and all the boys will sing-shout along, all the while pushing more pints in front of Rob. Rob will be singing loudest now. He'll have decided that tonight's the night he's going to properly go for it. Leaving Croke Park, he'll have felt something stirring, and he'll have told his father he was ready to have one more final night of going nuts.

Gareth will sing along too, but he'll be thinking of his small bedroom at home, of the journey back to Wales tomorrow night.

'By the way,' Big Mike will tell the group when talk turns to eating, 'before we go for food, we've gotta go back to the hostel.'

'How come, Worst Man?' Hucknall will say.

'Costumes for tonight, butt. And if you call me Worst Man one more time I'm gonna knock you out, you ginger prick.'

'Sorry, Worst Man.'

The boys will be awkward-quiet, and Rob's father will ask where they're gonna get the costumes from. And Big Mike will smile now. He'll say, 'Why the hell do you think I checked in a suitcase?'

'A fucking potato?' Hucknall will say. 'Are you fucking serious?'

They'll all be back at their room, and Big Mike will have his suitcase open on the bed, the bag bulging with bumpy, creamy-brown potato costumes.

'Aye,' Big Mike will say. 'Got a problem with that as well, have you?'

Peacock will take a costume from the suitcase and place it over himself in the mirror. 'These gonna make us look fat, you reckon?'

'No way am I wearing a potato costume,' Hucknall will say. 'We're in Ireland, for fuck's sake.'

'Exactly,' Big Mike'll go. 'They love potatoes. *Dirty-tree potatoes.*'

And the boys will shake their heads, will say all sorts.

'Are they all the same size?' Larry'll go.

'All the same,' Big Mike will say, 'except for Rob's. He's wearing something else. Oh, and you all owe me fifteen quid.'

Rob will beam, his teeth visible, a smile in his voice. 'What the fuck you got me?'

A plunging arm into the suitcase depths and Big Mike will pull out something black in cellophane.

Wordless, he'll hand the package to Rob.

Rob will tear at the cellophane. There'll be some kind of dress: green-and-orange and hideous. It'll take a moment for Rob to click: he's been given a woman's Irish dance costume. There'll be white socks to go with it too.

'*Rrrrriverdance!*' Big Mike will scream, doing an odd, high-kneed jig on the hostel floor.

And all the boys will laugh, and Hucknall will say fair play, that's a good un. And once they see that Rob looks the biggest tit, they won't mind dressing up like potatoes. At least we'll all be warm, Rob's father will say.

They'll drink the cans left over from last night, and Gareth will find himself at the point of drunkenness where he wants to fight. He'll offer arm wrestles to everyone. Using Big Mike's suitcase for a table – and at Gareth's insistence – they'll take turns to lie on the floor and arm-wrestle each other. And when he's not competing, Gareth will come up behind Larry, give him a bear hug and lift him off the ground. He'll do the same to Hucknall and Peacock and Rob. They'll be laughing at first, but by the end they'll be properly pushing him off.

In Temple Bar, with the boys dressed like potatoes, and Rob dressed like a female Irish dancer (but wearing his own brown Wrangler boots), they'll argue over where to go for dinner. Foreign girls with dark hair and dinner menus will approach, trying to coax them into their restaurants. Passers-by will cheer and laugh, and tourists – German, American, Chinese – will ask for photos with all the boys. And they'll begin to get into it, begin to feel like Dublin's central attraction.

'We should start charging,' Larry'll say, as Rob poses for a photo with a girl from Cincinnati. 'Two quid per photo, whadyou reckon?'

At some point in the night someone will say that the euro feels like Monopoly money, and everyone will agree.

After forty minutes of wandering and arguing, they'll land on Dame Street, at an empty Chinese restaurant.

'Never a good sign when it's empty,' Rob's father will say, but they'll have been walking around for too long, and will be too hungry to go elsewhere.

Before they've even ordered, Hucknall will suggest they split the bill. Hucknall is an accountant, Hucknall can afford to say such things. And for reasons beyond them, to save hassle perhaps, everyone will agree. They'll order pints immediately, but the food will take deliberation. They'll all ask each other what they're going to order, as if each boy's afraid of getting the wrong dish, of getting the whole eating-out thing wrong. They'll wind up the waitress who takes their orders, ask her if she'll be joining them for starters, and then they'll make her stand at the table for photos with them all.

The potato costumes will be chunky and clunky, so the chairs will have to be set some distance from the tables, and Gareth will find that to eat he has to lean forward, his back arched like a capital C. His arms will be free, though – he'll have that at least.

'When you buying this place with your missus, then?' Larry will ask.

'We'll see,' Gareth will say, taking a swig of his pint. 'No rush, is there?'

'I heard she wants somewhere by the summer,' Big Mike'll say.

'Carly talks too fucking much,' Gareth will say, and the table will laugh, giddy. Gareth'll say: 'What? It's true. She shouldn't talk about stuff like this with other people. I dun know what's wrong with her.'

Peacock will be smiling like a bag of chips, brimming over, as if he can't believe they're allowed to slag off their partners publicly. He'll think he could handle having a girlfriend if he could just slag her off all the time.

Gareth will finish off his pint and call to the waitress for another. Rob, his arms beginning to itch in the dance dress, will be watching Gareth's left leg. Under the white tablecloth, it'll be shaking.

The boys will chant football songs as they eat. They'll recall stories from school, from holidays, and from other stag trips. And all the boys will laugh as Larry pretends to cry and goes *'I'm soooooo hungry!'* – in imitation of the time Hucknall passed out in Malaga and woke to find his wallet had been stolen. When the boys found him, he'd been walking the streets for three hours and he was a quivering, starving mess. At some point, some food will be thrown at someone. A man and a woman will sit down at a table across from the boys, then promptly leave. Of all the boys, Rob's father will be the only one to notice. But the restaurant manager won't mind the noise because the boys are buying so many drinks and extra portions of egg-fried rice and chips.

'Alright then,' Rob will shout across the table, raising his glass. And it'll take Big Mike and Hucknall to quiet everyone down. 'I should have done this earlier,' Rob will shout, 'but I just wanna say thanks for all this. I know you're all wankers, but I've known you all so long –'

'So he's gonna dump Rachel and marry us!' Gareth will yell, and the boys will cheer.

'Dump the girl,' will come the shout from Larry, and Gareth will shout it too, and they'll both chant the words, banging the table. Hucknall will tell them to shut up, and Big Mike will be annoyed because that's his job, really, not Hucknall's.

Rob's father will smile and tell his son to go on with the speech.

'If I could,' Rob will say, 'I'd marry you all.'

'A toast to us!' Gareth will shout. And though his glass will be empty, he'll raise it anyway. And Rob won't realize he never said what he wanted to say.

In Gogarty's, Gareth will be doing his bear-hug-picking-up-mates routine again, but the place will be packed and he'll be banging into everyone. It won't help matters that they're all dressed like potatoes. Big Mike will take Gareth aside and tell him to calm the fuck down.

Upstairs, in the smoking area, Larry and Rob – neither smoke – will be reminiscing.

'Getting older's mad, innit?' Rob will say, taking a swig of his pint. He'll almost have forgotten he's dressed like a woman, and he'll be repeatedly confused by all the looks he's getting.

'Yeah,' Larry will say. 'I can't believe we're twenty-seven. Innit sad thinking about all the things we'll never do? I was thinking about it the other day. Like, at this age, I will never be the victim of paedophilia.'

Rob will laugh and bury his head in his hands. Between his fingers, he'll see the cream foam collecting on the inside of his glass. He'll take a swig and look at Larry. 'Incredible,' he'll say.

'It's not real, though,' Larry will say. 'I reckon we're in *The Matrix*. We're gonna wake up and we're gonna be five years old and it's gonna be the end of our first day at school again and –'

'Yeah,' Rob will say.

'But back to the issue,' Larry will say. 'Any pre-match doubts?'

'What, about Rachel?'

'Yeah. Any niggles?'

'Nah, all good, mate. All good.'

'I dunno how you do it,' Larry will say – and he'll mean it now, he'll be sincere. 'My record is three weeks and four days.'

Downstairs, Rob's father will be standing on a table with a Welsh flag around his head, singing 'Don't Look Back in Anger'.

'I'm telling you,' Gareth will shout at Hucknall at the bar, 'I'm not buying a house.'

'You been with Carly five years now, though, mate.'

'I know, but I'm not buying a house.'

'Look, you bender,' Hucknall will say, 'you can't live at home all your life. I'm spending shitloads on rent in London. I know that. But at least I'm not living with my fucking parents.'

'I know,' Gareth will say, and when Hucknall turns to fetch his pint from the bar, Gareth will put his arms around Hucknall's potato waist, pick him up, and launch him into a group of French guys in the corner. Pints will be knocked over, and Hucknall will be winded. He'll get up, confused, and make apologies to the jostling French men. He'll push his way through, smile at Gareth, and gesture for him to come back. And when Gareth takes a step forward, Hucknall will smack him square in the nose. Gareth will feel the cartilage snap, the muscle tear from the bone, and he'll be buckled over when he sees Hucknall lining up another.

He'll bound for the doors then. He'll leg it out, down the lane, down Merchant's Arch. He'll dodge and weave through the traffic, and lunge up to the bridge. He'll put his hand to his nose and there'll be blood wetting his fingers. He'll keep running until he's on the other side, on Lower Liffey Street. He'll take a seat at the bench.

He'll be sat there, watching the boardwalk, seething and lost, when a girl who's smoking outside the Grand Social will come sit beside him.

'Have a chip on your shoulder, do you?'

'What?' he'll say.

'You're a potato,' she'll say. 'Chips. Potatoes.' She'll look at him, see the nose. 'God, you're bleeding.'

'I know,' he'll say.

The taxis will be piling up beside the Liffey, glowing. Gareth will be staring at them, at the thin whistle of white lights, at the dark night, at the starless sky, at all the people on the boardwalk, and he'll think that only yesterday morning he was leaving his mother's house to get on the minibus. He'll feel small now, as if he's shrinking even, as if he's been dragged down from that vast sky and put here in Dublin, with his past and everything he knows about himself left behind. It's as if they've just brought the shell of his body over to Ireland, as if the rest of him might still be on the plane. He'll realize he hasn't looked up at the girl in some time.

'You alright?' she'll say.

He'll pause for a moment, unsure if he'll actually say it. This isn't how he imagined it. This isn't how he thought it all might go. But he'll look down at his bobbly potato body and think *fuck it.*

'I'm gay,' he'll say, and he'll feel there's no returning now.

'Good for you,' the girl will say. 'I was just asking if you're alright.'

He'll shift over on the bench, put a hand on her shoulder. 'No, you don't get it. My friends don't know I am. No one knows.'

'Oh God,' she'll say, watching the blood dribble from his nose, past his lips. 'I bet you're having a long night.'

'Yeah,' he'll say, getting up. 'I've got to go tell the boys.'

He'll leave the girl then, he'll rise, and he'll cross the bridge, and he'll wait at the beeping traffic lights before crossing the road. He'll wipe the blood with the sleeve of his potato costume – red streaks on the creamy-brown. He'll walk through the arch and over the cobbles to Gogarty's. The bouncers won't let him back in because he'll be too drunk, so he'll sit outside on the pavement and ring the boys. He'll call and he'll text, and Larry will come out and Gareth will go to say it, will go to tell him everything. He'll look at Larry, his fringe gelled upwards, and Gareth will open his mouth, he'll go to say how it's been like this since he was fifteen – but Larry will speak first.

'You alright?' he'll say. 'All the boys are off to find a strip club now – are you comin or what?'

There'll be a pause, a moment of nothing.

'Aye,' Gareth will finally say, 'I could probably do with seeing some tits.'

all the boys

They'll wake late on the Sunday. They'll be rushing to check out of the hostel. They won't all have breakfast together because the London boys will have an earlier flight. All the boys will hug and high-five, and the Caerphilly boys will say bye to Hucknall and Peacock as the two leave in search of a taxi.

Big Mike still won't be talking to Gareth and there'll be a tough silence in the group until Rob tells them to sort it out cos it's getting depressing. Gareth will apologize for 'ruining Gogarty's', and say he was wrecked, he doesn't remember any of last night now. He'll buy Big Mike a make-up pint and Big Mike will accept.

'Don't get me wrong,' Big Mike will say, 'Hucknall's a prick, but you don't go chucking your mates around a pub.'

Big Mike will say there's still time for them to see a little bit more of the city, but the boys won't be up for it. They've got their bags to carry, and Man Utd are on at 12.30, and can't they just watch the match at Fitzsimons? They're sure the place has Sky.

So they'll watch the United game at Fitzsimons, and they'll nurse slow pints, and they'll keep looking at their phones, sending texts to their girlfriends and wives. They'll decide to leave earlier than they need to because they're just killing time now, aren't they? There's no point waiting around here, they're better off getting to the airport than staying around here. At least they know they won't miss the flight then.

So they'll get the taxi, and they'll wait at departures, and they'll board their flight, and they'll sit there as the plane carries them over the water, over from Dublin to Bristol, and they'll wait at Bristol Airport for their minibus to pick them up, and they'll get on the minibus, and they'll tell stories about the weekend to each other, and they'll try and clear up some details that are hazy, like how much did it actually cost to get into the strip club? Did anyone else see Rob Senior on the table in Gogarty's? And Gareth, where did you get to last night, mate? What happened to you?

And when they cross the Severn Bridge, and see the *Welcome to Wales* sign, all the boys will cheer.

DAVID ROSE

A Nice Bucket

Right, couple of spades each, trowels, barrow's in the van already, now, buckets. Grab us two buckets. Best you can find. Best'll be gone by now. Just the best you can find. I was reading, on telly like, these cooks, top cooks, their pans, pans they use for pancakes, omelettes like, they never clean them. Reckon they cook better for not cleaning. Now it's different with buckets. You need a good clean bucket so's the amalgam don't stick, eases out sweet as dough. Tar's okay, any old tin'll do, but this new stuff . . . Yeah, and a rake, find us a rake.

The best he can find in the pile in the depot. He puts one bucket inside the other, carefully, drops his sandwiches into the inner, picks up a rake, walks slowly to the van. Sharkey's in the driver's seat by now. He shows him the buckets.

– Right, sling them in. Hang about, don't leave your sarnies in there, be squashed to buggery. Bung them under the seat. All set, then? Ron and Mickser'll meet us there. They're in the lorry with the asphalt. Wearing their pith helmets. Asphalt jungle, get it? Sydney Poitier. Never seen it? Wind down the window, get some carbon monoxide into your lungs.

The sun is out, it's almost warm on his arm. From a tree behind a wall a bird calls, a ringing, repeated call. A woodpecker? It couldn't be. (It's a great tit. This is urbia.) He watches sunlight bouncing off the bumpers ahead, shimmered by exhaust. He thinks of the walls absorbing the warmth. Old, some of them, Victorian, more than a century of cold and warmth, heat and frost. Solid, established.

A girl waits to cross the road. Short jacket, pleated skirt. Her fringe parts and lifts in the breeze of the traffic. Her mouth describes a smile that seems part of her, defining, an openness, warmth maybe. But maybe not. It may be the sun, she is screwing up her eyes.

– Look at the legs on that. Should've offered her a lift, kidder. I'd've stopped.

He feels the tremble of the engine as they wait for the lights.

Off the main road and into a sidestreet, long, curving, residential, quiet. He sees the lorry already there, Ron and Mickser smoking in the cab, the asphalt smoking in the back.

They unload the van – wheelbarrow, rake, spades, stand them up along the wall. Sharkey joins Ron and Mickser in a cigarette. He guards the tools as instructed, standing against the wall, hands in his pockets, leaning back, the bricks hard to his shoulders, reassuring.

Then they start work and he can relax. The squares have already been cut in the road. Mickser lifts down the metal frame from the lorry, a square smaller than the square in the road. He puts the frame in the square, centres it with the rake, puts four boards along the inner sides.

Now they can unload the asphalt into the barrow, wheel it across, shovel it into the frame, level it off. He stands ready with the rake, reaching over as it mounds up, pulling it even, turns the rake prongs-up and smooths it off. Sharkey and Mickser lift down the whacker plate, trundle it over.

– Get the water, kidder.

He climbs up into the lorry, swinging himself up by the tail-board, fills the watering can from the barrel behind the cab, jumps down.

As the whacker plate moves across the asphalt, he follows with the watering can, the spray a nice even curve, keeping pace.

The four of them, a side each, lift the frame, then kick out the boards from the asphalt mound.

– Bumps in the bloody road. Bloody bumps in the bloody road. Wait till I tell the ma. She thinks I'm laying motorway. 'You're putting *in* bumps, you say? And what will they be for?' 'To stop the traffic.' 'I thought that was what roads was for.' 'That's the English.'

– You going over this year?

– I might if I've a mind.

– We'll be on something fuckn else by then. There's word of a hospital car park.

– Would've been handy last week, like, when Gerry lost those two toes. Took us an hour in the van.

– Serve him fuckn right. *Desert* boots. Fuckn ponce.

After a cigarette, they load up the van and lorry and move down to the next square. Like a wagon train breaking camp, he thinks.

They do another square, then another, and it's time for lunch.

Sharkey boils a kettle on the burner used to melt the tar. They all pool their sandwiches so they have some variety. His chicken are all taken, he's left with an egg-and-salt, and one which appears to be empty, but he keeps his coconut cake back for himself, for after his mug of tea.

– Leave mine for the time. I'm slipping to the high street.

– Mitching off, Mickser?

– I've to get some skin lotion.

– Moisturizer, like?

They sit on the pavement, smoking, drinking the tea, the sun on their faces. There's a squabble of sparrows in the hedge opposite, the whine of the first mower of spring. A car passes slowly in the far lane.

– Tell you what, these fuckn humps are a waste of fuckn time down here. Traffic calming. Wants something to boister them up.

– No, look, here's another one, like. Hey look, a bloody nodding dog. That'll be bloody antique, that. Haven't seen a nodding dog for years. My brother-in-law had one in his Escort, only instead of nodding it lifted its leg. Got it in Wallasey. So he *said*. Bloody hell, look at that.

She had come, presumably, from one of the houses across the road, appearing suddenly, walking quickly, skirt swinging. Something in her movement reminds him of Susan. He thinks of the warm hardness of her lips, the pressure of a breast, as she walks away, smiling. Sharkey whistles.

– Should've seen the one I saw last night at the snooker club. Put me right off my stroke. Keep suggesting to the manager they have mixed topless tournaments. Bump up the membership. *And* save ironing the tables.

– You'd be alright for that.

– What you mean? I'm not fat. Just got thick bones. Hey, here's Mickser.

– About fuckn time.

– Get your moisturizer, then?

– I did.

– Rubbed it well in, like?

– It's easily absorbed.

– Well let's get some more fuckn humps done, shall we? They're giving *me* the fuckn hump, I can tell you.

They pick up their shirts, spades, stow the kettle and teapot on the lorry, stuff the used tea-bags in the hedge, move on to the next RAMP sign, some distance away, beyond a crossroads.

They do three more squares, about to begin the fourth after a tea break. Sharkey jumps up.

– Sodding hell, it's the old man.

– Alright, are we, lads? Getting stuck in, I see. I thought you'd be in Jesmond Road by now. Looking for you there.

– We've had problems, like. Hold-ups. I think you've had a bad batch of asphalt there. Inferior grade, like.

– That right? Sticks to the spade, does it?

– That's it.

– You'd find it helps to move the spade. In, up, tip. Got the idea? Now, when you've reached the end, leave Jesmond Road, go back and finish off this morning's, alright? How are you doing, lad?

He's been standing, rake poised, the other arm behind his back. He moves forward slightly.

– Fine, sir, thanks.

– Just do your fair share, no more. All right?

– Right, sir.

They set to with a scraping of spades until they're sure the old man's gone.

– The crafty old bollockser, creeping up on us like he did.

– Jesmond fuckn Road already? What's he think we're on, the Burma fuckn Railway?

– Like Alec Guinness, like.

– Someone mention Guinness?

– Wrong liquid, Mickser.

– He's got enough of a fuckn head on him.

They finish the mound of the last square, cone it off, and drive back to the first square of the morning.

They heap asphalt around and over the central mound, hardened by now, compress and smooth it with the whacker plate to form a gentle hill. Then they mix up the amalgam on a board on the lorry, shovel it into the buckets.

Ron and Mickser prepare the next batch of amalgam while he and Sharkey apply the first batch to the hump with trowels.

– Buggering hell, these buckets are bloody knackered. They're flaking off into the amalgam. See what I mean, like? It'll give us a sod of a surface. May as well use it straight off the board. Hey, Ron, lift the board down, will you, over here?

– Fuck off, it's far too heavy. You're not icing a fuckn cake, you know. It's just a hump in the road, to be driven over, right?

– But if the old man sees that, he'll go spare about quality penalties.

– Take it on your spades, then.

– They're worse than the buckets.

– Then *you* lift the fuckn board down.

– We'll just spread this the best we can.

They trowel on the rest of the amalgam, the crushed mica glinting in the oblique sunlight.

– Gerry would've lifted the board down, no problem.

– He's a strong lad, I'll give you that. Despite his fuckn desert boots.

– And probably talked the old man into buying some new buckets.

– Hey, remember Gerry and the Pacemakers? Fe-rry. Cross the Mersey. They're still going. Probably all *got* pacemakers now. They were good, though. They were great times, them. I was still at school, like. On and off. Out every night, not a care in the world.

– And what cares have you now, exactly?

– It's just not the same now. As you get older, it changes, like.

– What about the rest of this amalgam?

– Sod it. Dump it. It'll be hard by now, anyway. We'll do some fresh in the morning.

They load up the van and lorry, light up a last cigarette.

He and Sharkey get into the van. Sharkey calls across to Ron.

– Don't forget to stop off and dump the amalgam before the old man sees it.

It feels good to be going home after a day's work. He leans his head back, allowing the vibration to throb down his spine.

The light is hazy with the dust of the day. He thinks about his sand-wiches, the nodding dog, the girl they watched, the roll of her buttocks as she walked away. He sits up.

– Can you drop me off, along here?

– Anywhere you like, kidder. Got a date?

– Just some shopping.

The morning is sunny, with a spring chill but promise of warmth. He enters the depot, his bucket rattling, sparkling. Ron and Mickser are sit-ting on piled scaffold boards with some of the others, smoking. He walks across and sits with them.

Mickser tosses his cigarette end into the bucket, then kicks at it.

– That's a grand-looking bucket.

– It's bloody brand new. Where'd you fuckn find that?

– I bought it.

– What you mean, bought it? You mean, paid fuckn money for it?

– You *bought* it? Where from?

– Homebase.

– You seen this? He's gone and bought a fuckn bucket. Will you take it home and polish it every night?

– Why not a spade too?

– We'll have a whipround, buy him a silver-plated crowbar.

– With his initials engraved.

– Don't let the old man see it. It'll give him ideas. He'll have us all forking out for our own fuckn tools.

They get up, disperse to their different gangs.

– Ignore them, kidder. It's a nice bucket, is that. Just keep hold of it.

– I thought we could share it.

– Yeah. Great.

It's warm enough now for them to take off their shirts. He trowels out the amalgam as Sharkey spreads and smooths. The sunlight sparkles off the amalgam, shivers off the bucket. The handle flashes as he picks it up.

They stop for a cigarette, sitting in the gutter. The road is deserted, silent in the mid-morning sun. In either direction, rows of front doors, identical but for their colours, glossy, repelling the light. They curve away into the distance, holding themselves in, secretive, like a picture by an Italian painter (he means de Chirico). Yet each door holds a life, each house could tell a story – many stories, each room, each floor, stories stacked up in storeys. He laughs – quietly – at the joke.

And in the front door opposite, in the black gloss, he sees their reflections, his, Ron's, Mickser's, Sharkey's. They are there too on the brass letterbox and the spherical knocker, distorted, looming and shrinking as they move.

And he finds himself wondering what difference the loss of two toes would make. Not to his balance but just in general. To life, like.

DAVID SZALAY

Chapter 2 (from *All That Man Is*)

The office, showroom and warehouse occupy adjoining units of an industrial estate in the suburbs of Lille, within earshot of the E42 motorway. It is here that Bérnard has been spending his days this spring, working for his uncle Clovis, who sells windows. The office is as dull a space as it is possible to imagine – laminate floor, air-freshener smell, lightly soiled furniture.

Five fifteen on Wednesday afternoon.

From the large windows, listless spring light, and the sounds of the industrial estate. Bérnard is waiting for his uncle to lock up. He is already wearing his jacket, and sits there staring at the objects on the desk – next to a depressed-looking plant, the figurine of the little fairy maiden, winged and sitting under a drooping flower head with a melancholy smile on her heart-shaped face.

Clovis arrives and makes sure that all the drawers are locked.

'Cheer up,' he says unhelpfully.

Bérnard follows him down the spare, Clorox-smelling stairs.

Outside they take their places in the BMW, parked as always in the space nearest the door.

There is no way that Clovis would have taken Bérnard on if he wasn't his sister's son. Clovis thinks his nephew is a bit thick. Slow, like his father, the train driver. Easily pleased. Able to stare for hours at something like rain running down a window. It is typical of him, Clovis thinks, that he should have *dropped out* of university. Clovis's own attitude to university is ambivalent. He suspects that it is mostly just a way for well-to-do kids to avoid working for a few more years. Still, they must learn *something* there. Some of them, after all, end up as surgeons, as lawyers. So to spend two whole years at university and then *drop out*, as Bérnard did, with nothing to show for it, seems like the worst of all worlds. A pathetic waste of time.

They leave the estate and feed onto the E42.

The kid smokes pot. That's not even a secret any more. He smokes it in his room at home – he still lives with his parents, in their narrow brick house in a quiet working-class residential district. He shows no sign of wanting to leave. His meals are made for him, his washing is done. And how old is he now? Twenty-one? Twenty-two? Unmanly, is the word.

He once tried to have a talk with him, Clovis did, for his sister's sake. (The boy's father was obviously not going to do it.) He sat him down in a bar with a beer and said, in so many words, 'You've got to grow up.'

And the boy just stared at him out of his vague blueish eyes, his blond hair falling into them, and said, in so many words, 'What d'you mean?'

And, in so many words, Clovis said, 'You're a loser, mate.'

And the boy – if that was the word, his chin was thick with orange stubble – drank his beer and seemed to have nothing more to say for himself.

So Clovis left it at that.

And then Mathilde said to him, when he was trying to tell her, post their drink together, what he thought of her son, 'Well, if you want to help so much, Clovis, why don't you give him a job?'

So he had to make a place for him – first in the warehouse, and then, where there was less scope for him to do any damage (they sent the wrong windows to a site once, which Bérnard had loaded onto the truck), in the office. Though he is totally forbidden to answer the phone. And not allowed anywhere near anything to do with money. Which means there isn't much, in the office, for him to do. He tidies up. And for that, for a bit of ineffectual tidying, he is paid two hundred and fifty euros a week.

Clovis sighs, audibly, as they wait at a traffic light on their way into town. His fingers tap the steering wheel.

They stop at a petrol station to fill up, the Shell station which Clovis favours on Avenue de Dunkerque.

Bérnard, in the passenger seat, is staring out of the window.

Clovis pays for the petrol, V-Power Nitro+, and some summer

windscreen-wiper fluid, which he sees they have on sale, and takes his seat in the BMW again.

He is just strapping himself in when his nephew says, speaking for the first time since they left the office, 'Is it okay if I go on holiday?'

The presumptuous directness of the question, the total lack of supplicatory preamble, are shocking.

'Holiday?' Clovis says, almost sarcastically.

'Yes.'

'You've only just started.'

To that, Bérnard says nothing, and Clovis has to focus, for a few moments, on leaving the petrol station. Then he says, again, 'You've only just started.'

'I get holidays though, don't I?' Bérnard says.

Clovis laughs.

'I worry about your attitude,' he says.

Bérnard meets that statement with silence.

Holding the steering wheel, Clovis absorbs waves of outrage.

The silly thing is, he would be more than happy to have his nephew out of the way for a week or two. Or – who knows? – for ever.

'You planning to go somewhere?' he asks.

'Cyprus,' Bérnard says.

'Ah, Cyprus. And how long,' Clovis asks, 'do you plan to spend in Cyprus?'

'A week.'

'I see.'

They travel about a kilometre. Then Clovis says, 'I'll think about it, okay?'

Bérnard says nothing.

Clovis half-turns to him and says again, 'Okay?'

Bérnard, for the first time, seems slightly embarrassed. 'Well. I've already paid for it. That's the thing. The holiday.'

A further, stronger wave of outrage, and Clovis says, 'Well, that was a bit silly.'

'So I need to go,' Bérnard explains.

'When is it, this holiday?' Clovis asks, no longer trying to hide his irritation – if anything, playing it up, enjoying it.

'It's next week.'

'Next week?' Said with a theatrical expression of surprise.

'Yeah.'

'Well, you need to give at least a month's notice.'

'Do I? You didn't tell me that.'

'It's in your contract.'

'Well . . . I didn't know.'

'You should read documents,' Clovis says, 'before you sign them.'

'I didn't think you'd try to take advantage of me . . .'

'Is *that* what I'm doing?'

'Look,' Bérnard says, 'I've already paid for it.'

Clovis says nothing.

'You're not really going to try and stop me?'

'I worry about your attitude, Bérnard.'

They have arrived in Bérnard's parents' street, the featureless street of narrow brick houses.

The BMW stops in front of one of them and first Bérnard, and then, more slowly, Clovis, emerges from it.

Unusually, Clovis comes into the house.

Bérnard's parents are both there. His father, in a vest, is drinking a beer. He has, within the last half-hour, returned from work. He is short, blond, with a moustache – Asterix, basically. He is sitting at the table in the front room, the room into which the front door directly opens, with a single window onto the street, in the light of which he is studying *La Voix du Nord*. Bérnard's mother, further back in the same space, where the kitchen is, is doing the washing-up.

On Bérnard's entrance, neither of them looks up from what they are doing.

'*Salut*,' he says.

They both murmur something. His father has a swig from the brown bottle in his hand.

'André,' Clovis says to him.

At that, André looks up from the paper. Mathilde, too, looks across from the neon puddle of the kitchen. She smiles to see her brother.

André does not smile.

If happiness is having one euro more than your brother-in-law, then Clovis is happy a million times over.

And André – André is fucked.

Clovis steps forward into the room.

'To what do we owe the honour?' André says.

Mathilde asks her brother if he'd like something.

'No, thank you,' Clovis says.

Having left the harsh light of the kitchen, she kisses him on the face.

'I find myself in a difficult position,' Clovis says.

His sister indicates that he should sit. Again, he declines.

'I wanted to help,' he says. 'I tried to help. But Bérnard has made it clear that he does not want the sort of help that I am able to offer him.'

At the sound of his name, Bérnard, who has been peering into the fridge, looks at his uncle.

'I'm afraid so,' Clovis says sadly.

'What do you mean?' André asks.

Clovis looks at him and says, 'I'm sacking your son.'

He half-turns his head in the direction of the kitchen and says, 'Yes, that's right, Bérnard – you can go where you like now.'

Bérnard, still illuminated by the open fridge, just stares at his uncle.

Mathilde is already pleading with him.

He is shaking his head. 'No, no,' he is saying. 'No, I've made up my mind.'

'I knew this would happen,' André murmurs furiously.

'What?' Clovis asks him. 'What did you know?'

Through a friend at the Chambre de Commerce et d'Industrie, he had, a few years ago, found André a job as a Eurostar driver; the interview would have been a formality. André, saying something about the long hours, had turned the opportunity down, and still spends his days trundling back and forth between Lille and Dunkerque, Lille and Amiens. The stopping service. Local routes. Not even the Paris gig.

'What did you know?' Clovis asks him, looming over the table where André is sitting with his paper.

André says, clinging to his beer, 'You didn't really want to help, did you?'

'Oh, I did,' Clovis tells him. 'I did indeed. Your son is lazy.' He throws his voice towards the kitchen. 'Yes, Bérnard. I'm sorry to say it, but you are. You have no ambition. No desire to improve yourself, to move up in the world . . .'

'Please, Clovis, please,' Mathilde is still saying.

He silences her with a lightly placed hand – her shoulder. 'I'm sorry. I am sorry,' he says. 'Despite what your husband says, I did want to help. And I tried. I did what I could. And I will pay him,' he says, drawing himself up like a monarch in his suede jacket, 'a month's wages in lieu of notice.'

'Clovis . . .'

'There is only so much I can do,' he tells her. 'What can I do? What do you want me to do?'

'Give him one more chance.'

'If I thought it would help *him*, I would.'

André mutters something.

'What?'

'Bollocks,' André says more distinctly.

'No. No, André, it is not *bollocks*,' Clovis says, speaking quietly, in a voice trembling with anger. 'How have I benefited in any way from taking Bérnard on? Tell me how I have benefited.'

There is a tense silence.

Then Clovis, in a sad voice, says, 'I'm sorry, Bérnard.'

Bérnard, now eating a yoghurt, just nods. He is not as upset as either of his parents seem to be.

He is not actually upset at all. The main facts, as he sees them, are: 1) he does not have to go to work tomorrow, or ever again, and 2) he is getting a thousand euros for nothing.

His mother's near-tearfulness, his father's smouldering fury, are just familiar parts of the family scenery.

He is aware that there exists between his father and his uncle some terrible issue, some fundamental unfriendliness – it is not something, however, that he understands. It has always been there. It is just part of life.

Like the way his parents argue.

They are arguing now.

From his room on the top floor of the house he hears them, far below.

When they argue it is either about money – which is always tight – or about Bérnard.

They worry about him, that he understands. They are arguing now out of their worry, shouting at each other.

He does not worry about himself. *Their* worry, however, sets off a sort of unwelcome humming in his psyche; like the high-pitched pulse of an alarm somewhere far off down the street, leaking anxiety into the night. Their voices now, travelling up through two floors, are like that. They are arguing about him, about what he is going 'to do with his life'.

To him, the question seems entirely abstract.

He is playing a first-person shooter, listlessly massacring thousands of monstrous enemies.

After an hour or so he tires of it, and decides to visit Baudouin.

Baudouin is also playing a first-person shooter, albeit on a much larger and more expensive display – a vast display, flanked by muscular speakers. His father, also Baudouin, is a dentist, and the younger Baudouin is himself studying dentistry at the university. He is the only university friend with whom Bérnard is still in touch.

In keeping with his impeccably provisioned life, Baudouin always has a substantial stash of super-skunk – imported from Holland, and oozing crystals of THC – and Bérnard skins up while his friend finishes the level.

He says, 'I've been sacked.'

Baudouin, the future dentist, takes out half a dozen zombies. 'I thought you worked for your uncle,' he says.

'Yeah. He sacked me.'

'What a twat.'

'He is a twat.'

Baudouin stretches out a white hand for the spliff.

Bérnard obliges him. 'I don't give a shit,' he says, as if worried that his friend might think he did.

Baudouin, blasting, grunts.

'I get a month's pay. Severance or whatever.' Bérnard says that with some pride.

Baudouin, however, seems unimpressed: 'Yeah?'

'And now I can come to Cyprus for sure.'

Passing him the spliff again, and without looking at him, Baudouin says, 'Oh, I need to talk to you about that.'

'What?'

'I can't go.'

'What d'you mean?'

'I didn't pass Biochemistry Two,' Baudouin says. 'I need to take it again.'

'When's the exam?' Bérnard asks.

'In two weeks.'

'So why can't you go?'

'My dad won't let me.'

'Fuck that.'

Baudouin laughs, as if in agreement. Then he says, 'No, he says it's important I don't fail again.'

Bérnard, sitting somewhat behind him on one of the tatami mats that litter the floor, has a pull on the spliff. He feels deeply let down. 'You seriously not coming then?' he asks, unable to help sounding hurt.

What makes it worse, the whole thing was Baudouin's idea.

It had been he who found, somewhere online, the shockingly inexpensive package that included flights from Charleroi airport and seven nights at the Hotel Poseidon in Protaras. It had been he who persuaded Bérnard – admittedly, he needed little persuading – that Protaras was a hedonistic paradise, that the weather in Cyprus would be well hot enough in mid-May, and that it was an excellent time for a holiday. He had stoked up Bérnard's enthusiasm for the idea until it was the only thing on which he fixed his mind as he tried to survive the interminable afternoons on the greyish-brown industrial estate.

And now he says, still mostly focused on the screen in front of him, 'No. Seriously. I can't.'

His hand, stretched out, is waiting for the spliff.

Bérnard passes it to him, silently.

'What am I supposed to do?' he asks after a while.

'Go!' Baudouin says, over the manic whamming of the speakers. 'Obviously, go. Why wouldn't you? I would.'

'On my own?'

'Why wouldn't you?'

'Only saddoes,' Bérnard says, 'go on holiday on their own.'

'Don't be stupid . . .'

'It's true.'

'It's not.'

Bérnard has the spliff again, what's left of it, an acrid stub. 'It so is.' He says, 'I'll feel like a fucking loser.'

'Don't be stupid,' Baudouin says, finishing the level finally and saving his position. He turns to Bérnard. 'Think Steve McQueen,' he says. Baudouin is a fan of the late American actor. He has a large poster of him – squinting magisterially astride a vintage motorbike – on the wall of the room in which they sit. 'Think Belmondo.'

'Whatever.'

'Do you think I'm pleased I can't go?' Baudouin asks. A Windows Desktop, weirdly vast and static, now fills the towering screen.

'Whatever,' Bérnard says again.

While he moodily sets to work on the next spliff, massaging the tobacco from one of his friend's Marlboro Lights, Baudouin starts an MP4 of *Iron Man 3* – a film which has yet to arrive in the Lille cinemas.

'You seen this?' he asks, after drinking at length from a bottle of Evian.

'What is it?'

'*Iron Man Three.*'

'No.'

'It's got Gwyneth Paltrow in it,' Baudouin says.

'Yeah, I know.'

They watch it in English, which they both speak well enough for the dialogue to present no major problems.

Whenever Gwyneth Paltrow is on screen Baudouin stops talking and starts devotedly ogling. He has, as they say, a 'thing' about her. It is not a 'thing' his friend understands, particularly – not the full hormonal, worshipping intensity of it.

'She's alright,' Bérnard says.

'You, my friend, are working class.'

'She's got no tits,' Bérnard says.

'That you should say that,' Baudouin tells him, 'does sort of prove my point.'

Then he says, in a scholarly tone, 'In *Shakespeare in Love* you see her tits. They're not as small as you might think.'

Willing to be proven wrong, Bérnard makes a mental note to torrent the film when he gets home.

Which he does, and discovers that his friend has a point – there is indeed something there, something appreciable. And, hunched over himself, a hand-picked frame on the screen, he does appreciate it.

2

At four o'clock on Monday morning, on the bus to Charleroi airport he feels sad, loserish, very lonely. Dawn arrives on the empty motorway. The sun, smacking him in the face. Shadows everywhere. He stares through smarting eyes, at the landscape as it passes – its flatness, its shimmer. There is an exhilarating whisper of freedom, then, that lasts until he sees a plane hanging low in the sky, and again finds himself facing the affront to his ego of having to holiday alone.

3

From Larnaca airport – newer and shinier than Charleroi – a minibus operated by the holiday firm takes him, and about twelve other people, to Protaras. A dusty, unpleasant landscape. No sign of the sea. He is, on that air-conditioned bus, with little blue curtains that can be closed against the midday sun, the only person travelling on his own.

The drop-offs start.

He is the last to be dropped off.

Most of the others are set down at newish white hotels next to the sea, which did eventually appear, hotels that look like the top halves of cruise ships.

Then, when he is alone on the bus, it leaves the shore and starts inland, taking him first through some semi-pedestrianized streets full of lurid impermanent-looking pubs and then, the townscape thinning out, past a sizeable Lidl and into an arid half-made hinterland, without much happening, where the Hotel Poseidon is.

The Hotel Poseidon.

Three storeys of white-painted concrete, studded with identical small balconies. Broken concrete steps leading up to a brown glass door.

It is now the heat of the day – the streets around the hotel are empty and shadowless as the sun drops straight down on them. In the lobby the air is hot and humid. At first he thinks there is no one there. Then he sees the two women lurking in the warm semi-darkness behind the desk.

He explains, in English, who he is.

They listen, unimpressed.

Having taken his passport, one of them then leads him up some dim stairs to the floor above, and into a narrow space with a single window at one end and two low single beds placed end to end against one wall.

A sinister door is pointed to. 'The bathroom,' she says.

And then he is alone again.

He is able to hear, indistinctly, voices, from several directions. From somewhere above him, footsteps. From somewhere else, a well-defined sneeze.

He stands at the window: there are some trees, some scrubby derelict land, some walls.

Far away, a horizontal blue line hints at the presence of the sea.

He is standing there feeling sorry for himself when there is a knock on the door.

It is a short man in an ill-fitting suit. Unlike the two women in the lobby, he is smiling. 'Hello, sir,' he says, still smiling.

'Hello,' Bérnard says.

'I hope you are enjoying your stay,' the man says. 'I just wanted to have a word with you please about the shower.'

'Yes?'

'Please don't use the shower.'

After a short pause, Bérnard says, 'Okay.' And then, feeling obscurely that he should ask, 'Why not?'

The man is still smiling. 'It leaks, you see,' he says. 'It leaks into the lobby. So please don't use it. I hope you understand.'

Bérnard nods and says, 'Sure. Okay.'

'Thank you, sir,' the man says.

When he has left, Bérnard has a look at the bathroom. It is a window-less shaft with a toilet, a sink, a metal nozzle in the wall over the toilet and what seems to be an associated tap – which is presumably the unusable shower – a flaky drain in the middle of the floor, and a sign in Greek, and also in Russian, Bérnard thinks, of which the only thing he can understand are the numerous exclamation marks. He switches off the light.

Sitting on one of the single beds, he starts to feel that it is probably unacceptable for him not to have access to a shower, and decides to speak to someone about it.

There is no one in the lobby, though, so after waiting for ten minutes, he leaves the hotel and starts to walk in what he thinks is the direction of the sea.

In addition to the shower, there is something else he feels might be unsatisfactory: he was sure the hotel was supposed to have a pool. Bau-douin had talked about afternoons spent 'vegging next to the pool', had even sent him a link to a picture of it – the picture had shown what appeared to be some sort of aqua park, with a number of different pools and water slides, populated by smiling people. The whole thing had seemed, from the picture, to be more or less next to the sea.

And that was another thing.

The hotel was advertised as five minutes' walk from the sea, yet he has been trudging for at least double that through the desolate heat and is only just passing the Lidl.

In fact, to walk to the sea takes half an hour.

Once there he hangs about for a while – stands at the landward margin of a brown beach, thick with sun umbrellas down to the listless flop of the surf.

He has a pint in a pub hung with Union Jacks and England flags, and advertising English football matches, and then walks slowly back to his hotel. The Lidl is easy to find: there are signs for it throughout the town. And from the Lidl he is able, with only one or two wrong turnings, to find the Hotel Poseidon.

In the hot lobby he walks up to the desk, where there is now someone on duty, intending to talk about the shower situation and the lack of a swimming pool on the premises.

It is the smiling man, who says, 'Good afternoon, sir. There is a message for you.'

'For me?'

'For you, sir.' The smiling man – middle-aged, with a lean, tanned face – pushes a slip of paper across the desk.

It is a handwritten note:

Dropped by – you weren't in. I'll be in Waves from 5 if you wanna meet up and talk things through. Leif

Bérnard looks up at the smiling man's kind, avuncular face.

'Are you sure this is for me?' he asks.

Still smiling kindly, the man nods.

Looking at the note again, Bérnard asks him if he knows where Waves is.

It is near the sea, the man tells him, and explains how to get there. 'It's a popular place with *young* people,' he says.

Bérnard thanks him. It is already five, and he is about to set off again when he remembers the shower, and turns back. He does not know exactly how to put it, how to express his dissatisfaction. He says, uncertainly, 'Listen, um. The shower . . .'

Immediately, as soon as the word *shower* has been spoken, the smiling man says, 'The problem will be sorted out tomorrow.' For the first time, he is not smiling. He looks very serious. His eyes are full of apology. 'I'm very sorry, sir.'

'Okay,' Bérnard says. 'Thank you.'

'I'm sorry, sir,' the man says again, this time with a small deferential smile.

'There is one other thing,' Bérnard says, emboldened.

'Yes, sir?'

'There is a swimming pool?'

The man's expression turns sad, almost mournful. 'At the moment, no, sir, there is not,' he says. He starts to explain the situation – something about a legal dispute with the apartments next door – until Bérnard interrupts him, protesting mildly that the hotel had been sold to him as having a pool, so it seems wrong that there isn't one.

The smiling man says, 'We have an arrangement with the Hotel Vangelis, sir.'

There is a moment of silence in the oppressive damp heat of the lobby.

'An arrangement?'

'Yes, sir.'

'What sort of arrangement?'

The arrangement turns out to be that for ten euros a day inmates of the Poseidon can use the pool facilities of the Hotel Vangelis, which are extensive – the aqua park pictured on the Poseidon's website, and also in the leaflet which the smiling man is now pressing into Bérnard's hand.

The smiling man has a moustache, Bérnard notices at that point. 'Okay,' he says. 'Thank you. What time is supper?'

'Seven o'clock, sir.'

'And where?'

'In the dining room.' The smiling man points to a glass door on the other side of the lobby. Dirty yellow curtains hang on either side of the door. Next to the door there is an empty lectern. The room on the other side of the door is dark.

'You wanna party, yeah?' Leif asks, smiling lazily, as Bérnard, with a perspiring Keo, the local industrial lager, takes a seat opposite him.

Bérnard nods. 'Of course,' he says, fairly seriously.

A tall, tanned Icelander, only a few years older than Bérnard, Leif turned out to be the company rep.

Now he is telling Bérnard about the night life of Protaras. He is talking about some nightclub – Jesters – and the details of a happy-hour offer there. 'And then three cocktails for the price of two from seven till eight,' he says. 'Take advantage of it. Like I told the others, it's one of the best offers in the resort.'

'Okay,' Bérnard says.

Leif is drinking a huge smoothie. He keeps talking about 'the others', and Bérnard wonders whether he missed some prearranged meeting that no one told him about.

Who were these 'others'?

'Kebabs,' Leif says, as if it were a section heading. 'The best place is Porkies, okay? It's just over there.' He takes his large splayed hand from the back of his shaved head and points up the street. Bérnard looks and sees an orange sign: *Porkies.*

'Okay,' he says.

They are sitting on the terrace of Waves, he and Leif. Inside, music thumps. Although it is only just six, there are already plenty of drunk people about. A drinking game is in progress somewhere, with lots of excitable shouting.

'It's open twenty-four hours,' Leif says, still talking about Porkies.

'Okay.'

'And be careful – the hot sauce *is* hot.'

He says this so seriously that Bérnard thinks he must be joking and laughs.

Just as seriously, though, Leif says, 'It is a really fucking hot sauce.' He tips the last of his smoothie into his mouth. There is a sort of very faint disdain in the way he speaks to Bérnard. His attention always seems vaguely elsewhere; he keeps slowly turning his head to look up and down the street, which is just starting to acquire its evening hum, though the sun is still shining, long-shadowedly.

'So that's about it,' he says. He has the air of a man who gets laid effort-lessly and often. Indeed, there is something post-coital about his exaggeratedly laid-back manner. Bérnard is intimidated by him. He nods and has a sip of his beer.

'You here with some mates?' Leif asks him.

'No, uh . . .'

'On your own?'

Bérnard tries to explain. 'I was supposed to be with a friend . . .' He stops. Leif, obviously, is not interested.

'Okay,' Leif says, looking in the direction of Porkies as if he is expect-ing someone.

Then he turns to Bérnard again and says, 'I'll leave you to it. You have any questions just let me know, yeah.'

He is already standing up.

Bérnard says, 'Okay. Thanks.'

'See you round,' Leif says.

He doesn't seem to hear Bérnard saying, 'Yeah, see you.'

As he walks away the golden hair on his arms and legs glows in the low sun.

Bérnard finishes his drink quickly. Then he leaves Waves – where the music is now at full nightclub volume – and starts to walk, again, towards the Hotel Poseidon.

He feels slightly worse, slightly more isolated, after the meeting with Leif. He had somehow assumed, when he first sat down, that Leif would show him an evening of hedonism, or at least provide *some* sort of entrée into the native depravity of the place. That he did not, that he just left him on the terrace of Waves to finish his drink alone, leaves Bérnard feeling that he has failed a test – perhaps a fundamental one.

This feeling widening slowly into something like depression, he walks into the dead hinterland where the Hotel Poseidon is.

It is just after seven when he arrives at the hotel. The lobby is sultry and unlit. The dining room, on the other hand, is lit like a hospital A&E department. It doesn't seem to have any windows, the dining room. The walls are hung with dirty drapes. He sits down at a table. He seems to be the last to arrive – most of the other tables are occupied, people lowering their faces towards the grey soup, spooning it into their mouths. It is eerily quiet. Someone is speaking in Russian. Other than that the only sound, from all around, is the tinking of spoon on plate. And a strange humming, quite loud, that lasts for twenty or thirty seconds, then stops, then starts again. A waiter puts a plate of soup in front of him. Bérnard picks up his spoon, and notices the encrustations on its cloudy metal surface, the hard deposits of earlier meals. With a napkin – which itself shows evidence of previous use – he tries to scrub them off. The voice is still speaking in Russian, monotonously. Having cleaned his spoon, he turns his attention to the soup. It is a strange grey colour. And it is cold. He looks around, as if expecting someone to explain. No one explains. What he does notice, however, is the microwave on the other side of the room – the source of the strange intermittent humming – and the queue of people waiting to use it, each with a plate of soup. He picks up his own soup and joins them.

He is preceded in the queue by a woman in her mid-forties, probably, who is quite short and very fat. She has blonde hair, and an orange face – red under her eyes and along the top of her nose. He noticed her sitting at a table near him when he sat down – she is the sort of fat person it is hard to miss. What makes her harder to miss is that she is with another woman, younger than her and even fatter. This younger woman – her daughter perhaps – is actually fascinatingly huge. Bérnard tried not to stare.

After they have been standing in the microwave queue for a few minutes, listening to the whirr of the machine and taking a step forward every time it stops, the older woman says to him, in English, 'It's a disgrace, really, isn't it?'

'Mm,' Bérnard agrees, surprised at being spoken to.

The woman is sweating freely – the dining room is very warm. 'Every night the same,' she says.

'Really?'

'Really,' she says, and then it is her turn and she shoves her plate into the microwave.

4

Iveta. Ah, Iveta.

He first sees her the next morning, in Porkies.

He has had almost no sleep, is tipsy with fatigue. It was a *nuit blanche*, nearly. He wasn't out late, it wasn't that – he had a few lonely drinks on the lurid stretch, tried unsuccessfully to talk to some people, was humiliatingly stung in a hostess bar, and then, feeling quite depressed, made his way back to the Poseidon. At that point he was just looking forward to getting some sleep. And that's when the problems started. Though the hotel seemed totally isolated, there was at least one place in the immediate vicinity which thudded with dance music till the grey of dawn. Within the hotel itself, doors slammed all night, and voices shouted and sang, and people fucked noisily on all sides.

Finally, just as natural light started to filter through the ineffectual curtains, everything went quiet.

Bérnard, sitting up, looked at his watch. It was nearly five, and he had not slept at all.

And then, from the vacant lot next door, where people would illegally park, they started towing the cars.

He must have fallen asleep somehow while they were still doing that, while the alarms were still being triggered, one after another – when he next sat up and looked at his watch it was ten past ten.

Which meant he had missed the hotel breakfast.

So he went out into the morning, which was already hot, to find something to eat, and ended up in Porkies.

Porkies, even at ten thirty a.m., is doing a steady trade. Many of the people there, queuing for their kebabs, are obviously on the final stop of a night out. Hoarsely, they talk to each other or, still damp from the foam disco, stare in the fresh sunlight near the front of the shop, where a machine is loudly extracting the juice from orange halves.

With his heavy kebab Bérnard finds a seat at the end of the counter, the last of the stools that are there.

Next to him, facing the brown-tinted mirror tiles and still in their party kit with plenty of flesh on show, is a line of young women, laughing noisily as they eat their kebabs, and speaking a language he is unable to place.

He gets talking to the one sitting next to him when he asks her to pass him the squeezable thing of sauce and then, taking it from her, says, 'It was a nice night?'

'Where are you from?' he asks her next – the inevitable Protaras question.

She is Latvian, she says, she and her friends. Bérnard isn't sure where Latvia is. One of those obscure Eastern European places, he supposes.

He informs her that he is French.

She is on the small side, with a slightly too-prominent forehead, and spongy blonde hair – a cheap chemical blonde, displaced by something mousier near the roots. Still, he likes her. He likes her little arms and shoulders, her childish hands holding the kebab. The tired points of glitter on her nose.

He introduces himself. 'Bérnard,' he says.

Iveta, she tells him her name is.

'I like that name,' he says. He smiles, and she smiles too, and he notes her nice straight white teeth.

'You have very nice teeth,' he says.

And then learns that her father is a dentist.

He says, mildly bragging, 'I know a guy, his father is a dentist.'

She seems interested. 'Yes?'

There is something effortless about this, as they sit there eating their kebabs. Effortlessly, almost inadvertently, he has detached her from the others. She has turned away from them, towards him.

'You like Cyprus?' he asks.

Eating, she nods.

This is her second time in Protaras, he discovers. 'Maybe you can show me around,' he suggests easily. 'I don't know it. It's my first time here.'

And she just says, with a simplicity which makes him feel sure he is onto something here, 'Okay.'

'Where are you staying?' he asks.

She mentions some youth hostel, and he feels proud of the fact that he is staying in a proper hotel – proud enough to say, as if it were a totally natural question, 'What are you doing today?'

Her friends are starting to leave.

'Sleeping!'

She says that with a laugh that unsettles him, makes him feel that maybe their whole interaction has been, for her, a sort of joke, something with no significance, something that will lead nowhere. And he wants her now. He wants her. She is wearing denim hot pants, he sees for the first time, and sandals with a slight heel.

'What about later?' he says, trying not to sound desperate. The sense of effortlessness has evaporated. It evaporated the moment she seemed happy to leave without any prospect of seeing him again.

Now, however, she lingers.

Her friends are leaving, and yet she is still there, lingering.

'You want to meet later?' she says, with some seriousness.

'I want to see you again.'

She looks at him for a few moments. 'We'll be in Jesters tonight,' she says. 'You know Jesters?'

'I heard of it,' Bérnard says. 'I never been there.'

'Okay,' she says, still with this serious look on her face. And she tells him, in unnecessary detail, and making sure he understands, how to find it.

'Okay,' he says, smiling easily again. 'I'll see you there. Okay?'

She nods, and hurries to join her friends, who are waiting near the door.

He watches them leave and then, squirting more sauce onto it, un-
hurriedly finishes his kebab.

His mood, of course, is totally transformed. He fucking loves this place
now, Protaras. Walking down the street in the sun, everything looks different, everything pleases his eye. He wonders whether he's in love, and
then stops at the pharmacy next to McDonald's for a ten-pack of Durex.

'Hello, my friend,' he says to the smiling man, who is on duty in the
humid lobby of the Hotel Poseidon.

'Good morning, sir. You slept well, sir?'

'Very well,' Bérnard says, without thinking. 'Yesterday you said something, about another hotel, the swimming pool . . . ?'

'The Hotel Vangelis, yes, sir.'

'Where is that?'

Bérnard, eventually finding the Hotel Vangelis, says he is staying at the
Hotel Poseidon, pays ten euros, gets stamped on the hand with a smudged
logo, and then follows a pointed finger down a passage smelling of pool
chemicals to a locker room, and the sudden noise and dazzle of the aqua
park.

In knee-length trunks, he swims. His skin is milky from the Lille
winter. He does a few sedate laps of the serious swimmers' pool, then
queues with kids for a spin on the water slide. Next he tries the wave-
machine pool, lifting and sinking in the water, in the chlorine sparkle,
one wet head among many, all the time thinking of Iveta.

And still thinking of her afterwards, drying on a sunlounger. His eyes
are shut. His hair looks orangish when it is wet. There is a tuft of it in
the middle of his flat, white chest. His arms and legs are long and smooth.
The trunks hang wetly on his loins and thighs, sticking to them
heavily.

Slowly, the sun swings round.

One of the pools features a bar – a circular, straw-roofed structure in
the shallow end, the seats of the stools that surround it set just above the
surface of the water. Where it touches the side of the pool, there is a gate
that allows the barman to enter the dry interior, where the drinks are kept
in a stainless-steel fridge.

Some time in the afternoon, Bérnard is wallowing in this shallow pool, thinking of Iveta, when, on a whim, he paddles over and takes a seat on one of the stools. His legs, still in the water, look white as marble. He orders a Keo. He is impatient for evening, for Iveta. The day has started to be tiresome.

He is sitting there, under the thatch, holding his plastic pot of lager and looking mostly at his blue-veined feet, when a voice quite near him says, 'Hello again.'

A woman's voice.

He looks up.

It is the woman from the Hotel Poseidon, the fat one he spoke to in the microwave queue last night. She and her even fatter daughter are wading towards him through the shallow turquoise water of the pool – and weirdly, though they are in the pool, they are both wearing dresses, simple ones that hang from stringy shoulder straps, sticking wetly to their immense midriffs, and floating soggily on the waterline.

'Hello again,' the mother says, reaching the stool next to Bérnard's, her face and shoulders and her colossal cleavage sunburnt, her great barrel of a body filling the thin wet dress.

'Hello,' Bérnard says.

The daughter, moving slowly in the water, has arrived at the next stool along. She, it seems, is more careful in the sun than her mother – her skin everywhere has a lardy pallor. Only her face has a very slight tan.

'Hello,' Bérnard says to her, politely.

He wonders – with a mixture of amusement and pity – whether she will be able to sit on the stool. Surely not.

Somehow, though, she manages it.

Her mother is already in place. She says, 'Not bad, this, is it?'

Bérnard is still looking at the daughter. 'Yeah, it's good,' he says.

'Better than we expected, I have to say.'

'It's good,' Bérnard says again.

When the two of them have their sweating plastic tankards of Magners, the older woman says, 'So what do you think of the Hotel Poseidon then?' The tone in which she asks the question suggests that she doesn't think much of it herself.

'It's okay,' Bérnard answers.

'You think so?'

'Yeah. Okay,' he admits, 'maybe there are some problems . . .'

The woman laughs. 'You can say that again.'

'Yeah, okay,' Bérnard says. 'Like my shower, you can say.'

'Your shower? What about your shower?'

Bérnard explains the situation with his shower – which the smiling man this morning again warned him against using. It would, he promised Bérnard, be sorted out by tomorrow.

The older woman turns to her daughter. 'Well, that's just typical,' she says, 'isn't it? Isn't it?' she says again, and the younger woman, who is drinking her Magners through a straw, nods.

'We've had no end of things like that,' the mother says to Bérnard. 'Like what happened with the towels.'

'The towels?'

'One morning the towels go missing,' she tells him. 'While we're downstairs. They just disappear. Don't they?' she asks her daughter, who nods again.

'And then,' the mother says, 'when we ask for some more, they tell us we must have stolen them. They say we've got to pay forty euros for new ones, or we won't get our passports back.'

Bérnard murmurs sympathetically.

He has a swig of his drink. He is still fascinated by the daughter's body – by the pillow-sized folds of fat on her sitting midriff, the way her elbows show only as dimples in the distended shapes of her arms. How small her head seems . . .

Her mother is talking about something else now, about some Bulgarians in the next room. 'Keep us up half the night, shouting and God knows what,' she says. 'The walls are like paper. We can hear everything – and I do mean everything. We call them the *vulgar Bulgars*, don't we?' she says to her daughter. 'You know what we saw them doing? We saw them stealing food from the dining room.'

Bérnard laughs.

'Why they would want to steal that food I don't know. It's awful. Well, you experienced it last night. You ask if they've any fish – I mean we are next to the sea, aren't we – they bring you a tin of tuna. It's unbelievable. And the flies, especially at lunchtime. I've never seen anything like it. It's not fit for human consumption. We were both down with the squits for a few days last week,' she says, and Bérnard, unwilling to dwell on that idea, lets his thoughts drift again to Iveta – her thin tanned thighs, her pretty feet in the jewelly sandals – while the fat Englishwoman keeps talking.

They are English, these two, he has worked that out now.

'One day we thought, enough's enough, we're going to eat somewhere else,' the older woman says. 'So we asked our rep about good places to eat and he suggested this place, the Aphrodite . . . Do you know it?'

Bérnard shakes his head.

'Well, we went there on Saturday,' she says, 'and after spending over fifty euros on drinks and dinner, I went to the toilet and was told I had to pay a euro to use it. Well, I wasn't happy and I told the woman I was a customer. And she said that doesn't matter, you still have to pay. And I said well, I'm not paying, and when I tried to go into the toilet anyway, she pushed me away. She physically pushed me away. Wouldn't let me use it. So I asked to speak to the manager, and after about fifteen minutes this man appears – Nick, he says his name is – and when I explain to him what happened, he just laughs, laughs in my face. And when that happened . . . Well, I got so angry. He just laughed in my face. Can you imagine. The Aphrodite,' she says. 'Stay away from it.'

'I will,' Bérnard tells her.

'We love Cyprus,' she says, moving on her stool. 'Every year we come here. Don't we? I'm Sandra, by the way. And this is Charmian.'

'Bérnard,' says Bérnard.

They stay there drinking for two hours, until the hotel's shadow starts to move over them. They get quite drunk. And then Bérnard, whose thoughts have never been far from Iveta and what will happen that evening, notices the time and says he has to leave.

The two women have just ordered another pair of Magners – their fourth or fifth – and Sandra says, 'We'll see you at supper then.'

Bérnard is wading away. 'Okay,' he says.

Showering in the locker room a few minutes later, he has already forgotten about them.

*

When he wakes up it is dark. He is in his room in the Hotel Poseidon. The narrow room is very hot and music thuds from the place nearby.

It was about six when he got back from the Hotel Vangelis, and having a slight headache, he thought he would lie down for a while before supper. He must have fallen into a deep sleep. Sitting up suddenly, he looks at his watch, fearful that it might be too late to find Iveta at Jesters. It is only ten, though, and he lies down again. He is sweating in the close heat of the room. Last night he tried the air conditioning, and it didn't work.

He washes, as best he can, at the sink.

The light in the bathroom is so dim he can barely see his face in the mirror.

Then he tidies up a bit. It is his assumption that Iveta will be in this room later, and he does not want it littered with his dirty stuff.

He spends quite a lot of time deciding what to wear, finally opting for the dressier look of the plain white shirt, and leaving the horizontally striped polo for another night. He leaves the top three buttons of the shirt undone, so that it is open down to the tuft of hair on his sternum, and digs in his suitcase for the tiny sample of Ermenegildo Zegna Uomo that was once stuck to a magazine in his uncle's office. He squirts about half of it on himself, and then, after inquisitively sniffing his wrists, squirts the other half on as well.

Satisfied, he turns his attention to his hair, combing back the habitual mop to the line of his skull – thereby disclosing, unusually, his low forehead – and holding the combed hair in place with a generous scoop of scented gel.

In the buzzing light of the bathroom he inspects himself.

He buttons the third button of his shirt.

Then he unbuttons it again.

Then he buttons it again.

His forehead, paler than the rest of his face, looks weird, he thinks.

Working with the comb he tries to hide it, but that just makes it look even weirder.

Finally, impatient with himself, he tries to put the hair back the way it was before.

There is still something weird about it, and he worries as he hurries down the stairs to the lobby and, in a travelling zone of Uomo, out into the warm night.

It is nearly eleven now, and he has not eaten anything. It's not that he is hungry – far from it – it's just that he feels he ought to 'line' his stomach.

He stops at Porkies and eats part of a kebab, forcing a few mouthfuls down. He is almost shaking with excitement, with anticipation. He tries to still his nerves with a vodka-Red Bull, and with the memories of how easily they talked in the morning, of how eagerly she had told him how to find Jesters – she practically drew him a map. The memories help.

He abandons the kebab and starts for Jesters, through the heaving streets.

He finds it easily, following a pack of shirtless singing youths to its shed-like facade, outlined in hellish neon tubes. The looming neon cap-and-bells, the drunken queue.

Five euros, he hands over.

Inside, he looks for her.

Moving through strobe light, through a wall of throbbing sound, he looks for her.

The place is solid flesh. Limbs flickering in darkness. He could search all night, he thinks, and not find her.

Holding his expensive Beck's, he scans the place with increasing desperation. For the first time it occurs to him that she might not actually be there.

He has a nervous pull of the lager and pushes his way through a hedge of partying anonymity.

Some girls, on heat, are flaunting on a platform.

At their feet, a pool of staring lads in sweat-wet T-shirts. He watches for a moment, up-skirting with the other males, and then, with a shock of adrenalin, he sees someone, a face he sort of knows – one of her friends from this morning, he thinks it is, moving away from him.

He follows her. His eyes stuck to the skin of her exposed back, its dull shine of perspiration, he tears a path through interlacing limbs.

And she leads him to Iveta. She leads him to Iveta. He sees her in a pop of light as the music winds up. She does not see him. Her eyes are shut. She is in a man's hands, mouths melting together.

And then the hit crashes into its chorus.

5

The Hotel Vangelis, the next afternoon. Waist deep in water he is at the in-pool bar, drinking Cypriot lager and absorbing sunburn. He still smells of Ermenegildo Zegna Uomo. He had welcomed the arrival, about an hour before, of Sandra and Charmian. They are stationed next to him now, huge on their submerged stools, and Sandra is talking. She is telling him how the man she always refers to as 'Charmian's father' died horrifically after falling into a vat of molten zinc – he worked in an industrial installation of some sort – and how heartbroken she was after that. Tasting his Keo, Bernard appreciates the parity she seems to accord that event and his finding a girl he had only just met snogging someone else in a nightclub.

Already quite drunk, and exhausted by a night spent wandering the litter-strewn streets of Protaras, he had told them about that. He found he wanted to talk about it. And when he had finished his story, Sandra sighed and said she knew how he felt, and told him the story of her husband's death.

It was awful enough to be on the news – she is telling him how upsetting it was to see strangers talking about it on the local TV news.

'And the worst thing,' she says, 'is they think he was *alive* for up to twenty seconds after he fell in.'

'When did it happen?' Bérnard asks her morosely.

'Nine years ago,' Sandra says, sighing again. 'And I miss him every single day.'

Bérnard finishes his Keo and hands the empty plastic pot to the barman.

'What do you do, Bernard?' Sandra asks him, pronouncing his name the English way.

He tells her he was working for his uncle, until he was sacked.

'Why'd he sack you then?' she asks.

'He sounds like a tosser,' she says, when he has told her what happened.

'I don't know,' he says. 'What is it, a tosser?'

'A tosser?' Sandra laughs, and looks at Charmian. 'How would you explain?'

'Sort of like an idiot?' Charmian suggests.

'But what's it mean literally?'

'Literally?'

'Yes.'

'Well, it's like wanker, isn't it?'

Sandra laughs again. 'How do we explain that to Bernard?'

'I don't know.'

Sandra says, turning to Bérnard, 'Literally, it means someone who plays with himself.'

'Okay.'

'You know what I mean?' Sandra is smirking.

Charmian seems embarrassed – her face has turned all pink, and she is urgently sucking up cider and looking the other way.

'I think so,' Bérnard says, smiling slightly embarrassedly himself.

'But really it just means an idiot, someone we don't like.'

'Then he is a tosser, my uncle.'

'He sounds like it.' She turns to Charmian again. 'Imagine sacking your own nephew, just because he wants to go on holiday!'

Charmian nods. She looks quickly at Bérnard.

Warming to the subject, Bérnard starts to tell them more about his uncle – how he lives in Belgium to pay less tax, how he . . .

'Where you from then, Bernard?' Sandra asks him.

'Lille.'

'Where's that then?'

'It's sort of near Belgium, isn't it?' Charmian ventures shyly.

Bérnard nods.

'How'd you know that then?' Sandra asks her, impressed.

Charmian says, 'The Eurostar goes through there sometimes, doesn't it?' The question is addressed, somewhat awkwardly, to Bérnard.

Who just says, 'Yeah,' and turns his head towards the sparkle of the pool.

'We're from Northampton,' Sandra tells him. 'It's famous for shoes.'

They swim together, later. The ladies, still in their billowing dresses, letting the water lift them, and Bérnard moving more vigorously, doing little displays of front crawl, and then lolling on his back in the water, letting the sun dazzle his chlorine-stung eyes. Sandra encourages him to do a handstand in the shallow end. Not totally sober, he obliges her. He surfaces to ask how it was, and she shouts at him to keep his legs straight next time, while Charmian, still bobbing about nearby, staying where she can find the cool blue tiles with her toes, looks on. He does another handstand, unsteady in his long wet trunks. The ladies applaud. Triumphant, he dives again, into watery silence, blue world, losing all vertical aplomb as his big hands strive for the tiles. His legs thrash to drive him down. His lungs keep lifting his splayed hands from the tiles. His face feels full of blood. Streams of bubbles pass over him, upwards from his nostrils. And then he is in air again, squatting shoulder deep in the tepid water, the water sharp and bright with chemicals streaming from orange slicks of hair that hang over his eyes. He feels queasy for a moment. All those Keo lagers . . . He fears, just for a moment, that he is going to throw up.

Then he notices a lifeguard looming over them, his shadow on the water. He is talking to Sandra. He has just finished saying something, and he moves away, and takes his seat again, up a sloping ladder, like a tennis umpire.

'We've been told off,' Sandra says, hanging languidly in the water, only her sunburnt head, with its mannish jawline and feathery blonde pudding-bowl, above the surface.

Bérnard isn't sure what's going on. He still feels light-headed, vaguely unwell. 'What?'

'We've been told off,' Sandra says again.

Bérnard, from his crouch in the water, which feels chilly now that he has stopped moving, just stares at her. His body is bony. Individual vertebrae show on his white back. Sandra is still saying something to him. Her voice sounds muffled. '. . . told to stop being so immature . . .' he hears it say.

She has started to swim away from him – her head moving away on a very slow, lazy breaststroke.

The surface of the pool, which had been all discomposed by his antics, is smoothing itself out again, is slapping the sides with diminishing vigour.

*

After the horseplay they lie on the side, on sunloungers. Sandra just about fits onto one. Charmian, however, needs to push two together. Bérnard helps her. Then, without saying anything, he takes his place on his own lounger and shuts his eyes. It is late afternoon. The sun has a dull heat. In their dripping dresses, Sandra and Charmian are smoking cigarettes and talking about food. Bérnard isn't really listening.

Then Sandra's voice says, 'Bernard,' and he opens his eyes.

They are both looking at him.

Charmian, however, quickly looks away.

'We're going out for a meal tonight,' Sandra says. 'Want to come?'

*

They meet in the lobby of the hotel. Bérnard is talking to the smiling man – who is telling him that his shower will definitely be fixed tomorrow – when the ladies appear. There is an awkwardness. Unlike the previous night, Bérnard has made absolutely no effort at all with his preparations. The ladies, on the other hand, have to some extent dressed up. He sees that immediately. They have make-up on – quite a lot of make-up – and though Sandra is wearing a dress similar to the one she swims in, hanging from flimsy shoulder straps, its green-and-white floral pattern straining to hold the enormities of her figure, Charmian, extraordinarily, is in a pair of jeans and a blouse with delicate lacy details.

'All set then?' Sandra says, as Bérnard turns to them.

The smiling man watches tactfully as they leave.

They proceed in silence, initially, through the plain half-made streets near the hotel. The evening is no more than pleasantly warm – the nights are still mild sometimes, this early in the season. Even so, and in spite of the fact that they are walking downhill, Charmian, in particular, is soon shedding sheets of watery sweat.

'It's not far,' Sandra says, panting.

'What . . . what sort of place is it?' Bérnard asks.

'Typical Greek,' Sandra tells him.

It turns out to be a long single-storey construction on an arid stretch of road, painted deep red, and covered with signage.

In the huge air-conditioned interior they are shown to a table. Music is playing, the latest international hits, and on screens attached to the walls men are playing golf in America. It is still too early for the place to be very full. The waitress brings big laminated menus, which they study in silence. There are pictures of each item – unappealingly documentary images like police evidence photos.

Things loosen up once the wine starts to take effect – a large jug of it that Sandra orders, which tastes faintly of pine trees.

'I love this stuff,' she says.

A stainless-steel plate of stuffed vine leaves also appears, leaking olive oil, and dishes of taramasalata and hummus, and a plate of warm pitta bread.

Bérnard pours himself some more of the weird wine, and then tops the others up as well. He is telling them about his experience in the hostess bar, his first night there, when he was intimidated into emptying his wallet on overpriced drinks for a pair of haughty, painted ladies. Sandra had told him how the taxi driver had tried to overcharge them on the way home from the Hotel Vangelis that afternoon, and he is offering his own tale of unscrupulous piracy. Mopping up the last of the tarama with the last piece of pitta, Sandra says, 'You don't need to take that, Bernard.'

'It's okay,' Bérnard says mellowly. 'Shit happens.' He drinks some more wine.

'You *shouldn't* take it,' she says. 'A hundred euros?'

'Yes.'

'I tell you what we're going to do,' she says, looking around for the waiter. 'When we've finished here, we're going to go over there and get your money back.'

Bérnard laughs quietly.

'I'm not joking,' Sandra says. 'We're going to go over there and get your money back. You can't let them get away with that, Bernard.'

Bérnard sighs. 'They won't give it back,' he says.

'Yes,' Sandra says, 'they will. When we tell them we're going to the police they'll give it back. Remember what happened to us that time in Turkey?' she asks Charmian, who nods. Charmian has hardly said a word all evening, has only eaten half-heartedly four or five stuffed vine leaves. She seems out of sorts. Turning to Bérnard again, Sandra starts on the Turkish story. 'This man tried to rip us off changing money in the street. Well, he shouldn't have picked on us, should he . . .'

Then the main course arrives.

There is enough food, Bérnard thinks, for eight or ten people.

Platters of grilled lamb, chicken, fish. A huge dish of rice. Portions of fries for everyone and a heap of Greek salad which would on its own have fed a whole family. Also another jug of the wine, even though the first one is still half-full.

With some help from Bérnard the ladies obliterate the spread in under half an hour.

Sandra pours out the last of the wine.

Bérnard is drunk. Quite how drunk, he didn't understand until he went to the toilet – his shiny face in the mirror stared back at him with eerie impassivity, then suddenly put out its tongue.

The others, however, seem unaffected, except that Sandra looks even redder than usual.

The place has filled up a bit and a band has started playing.

Sandra and the waiter have some sort of dispute over the bill – the manager is summoned – and when that is finally sorted out, she pays and they leave.

Bérnard had tried to offer some money, and on the pavement outside, he tries again. He says, with his wallet once more in his hand, 'So . . . ?'

'I think I'm just going to use the lav,' Sandra says, apparently not having heard him, and leaves him there with Charmian.

He pockets his wallet.

Charmian isn't looking at him. She is facing the other way, as if she does not want to be associated with him. He wonders whether he has offended her somehow.

He stands there, drunk, looking at her, the slabs of her arms protruding from the frilly sleeves of her blouse, the grotesque inflations of her jeans.

When Sandra rejoins them, he is still just standing there, and Charmian is still staring off down the street.

In the end, he is unable to find the hostess bar. They spend about half an hour looking for it, on the fringes of Protaras's nightlife, in the streets where the neon stops. They drop into a snack bar for pizza slices, sit eating them in a plastic booth. Then a place with live music – some zithering 'traditional' band and older couples swaying under a turning glitter ball.

Bérnard, badly drunk now, gives Sandra a spin on the dance floor, treading on her feet, feeling the immense swell of her side hot and damp under his hand. He offers to do the same for Charmian but she just shakes her head.

'Oh, go on!' Sandra says to her, sweating dangerously, her vast red cleavage shining as if with varnish.

Charmian shakes her head again.

'You are sure?' Bérnard asks, out of breath.

When Charmian just ignores him, Sandra says, 'Don't be so rude!'

She gives Bérnard an apologetic, exasperated look.

Then they sit down to finish the red wine.

Their final stop of the evening is Porkies, for a kebab. Bérnard does not have one. He just watches the others eat. In his state of extreme drunkenness, Charmian has taken on a strange, fascinating quality. Sitting opposite her, he watches her eating the kebab with what seem to be modest flickers of desire. They surprise him. Her face, admittedly, is nice enough and there is nothing wrong with the pale blue of her long-lashed eyes . . .

He looks away, wondering what to make of this. What, if anything, to *do* about it.

He is still wondering in the taxi that takes them back to the Hotel Poseidon. He is sitting in the front, next to the driver. The surprising question presses itself on him: Should he make some sort of move?

Awkward, with her mother there.

The taxi stops at the crumbling concrete steps of the Poseidon.

With difficulty, with Bérnard helping, heaving heavy flesh, the ladies extract themselves from its low seats.

And then they are in the lobby.

And he almost says to Charmian something about whether she wants to see his room.

And then it is too late.

Sandra has kissed him goodnight.

He is alone in his room, which starts to turn if he shuts his eyes.

He tries a wank, but he is too drunk.

In the morning he lies there on the single bed, imprisoned in his hangover, trying to piece together the fragments of the evening and feeling that he nearly did something very, very silly.

He opens his eyes.

The heat of the sun throbs from the closed curtains and the sounds of the street intrude into the painful stillness of the dim, narrow room. He lies there for most of the morning, instantly feeling sick if he moves at all.

At some point he falls asleep again, and when he wakes up he feels okay.

He is able to move.

To sit.

To stand.

To peel back the edge of the curtain and squint at the white, fiery day – the glare of the vacant lot next door.

The sky's merciless scream of blue.

It is eleven fifty, nearly time for lunch, and he is hungry now.

He feels strange, as if in a dream, as he descends the cool stairs.

Descending the cool stairs, he really feels as if he is still in bed, and dreaming this.

The dining room.

Murmur of voices – Russian, Bulgarian.

The buffet of congealed brown food.

The microwave queue.

And there they are, Sandra and Charmian, at their usual table, which is where he sits now too.

As he approaches – feeling weightless, as if he is floating over the filthy carpet – Sandra says, 'We didn't see you at breakfast, Bernard.'

She seems more or less unaffected by the night's drinking – her ruddiness only slightly attenuated, her voice only marginally hoarser than normal.

Charmian, sitting next to her, looks quite pale.

'No, I, er . . .' Bérnard mumbles, taking a seat. 'I was sleeping.'

'Last night too much for you, was it?'

Bérnard laughs weakly. Then there is a short pause. The thought of eating has lost most of its appeal. 'It was good,' he says finally.

'It was, wasn't it,' Sandra says.

She has already eaten – the emptied plate is on the table in front of her. Charmian too is just finishing up.

Bérnard opens his can of Fanta and pours most of it into a greasy glass.

'You not having anything?' Sandra asks him, moving her faint blonde eyebrows in the direction of the buffet.

'Later, maybe,' Bérnard says. He is starting to think that this was a mistake, making an appearance here. He feels less normal than he thought he did. The taste of the Fanta – a tiny sip, the first thing to have passed his lips today – makes him feel slightly more grounded.

Charmian stands abruptly.

He finds it hard to believe, now, that he considered making some sort of move on her last night.

He is pretty sure he didn't actually say anything, or do anything. Still, even just having had the idea embarrasses him.

She is off to the buffet for seconds. He watches, briefly, her cumbersome waddle as she passes among the tables. Others are watching her too, he sees.

Somewhere near him, Sandra's voice says, 'I don't know if you've noticed, but Charmian really likes you.'

Bérnard feels, again, that he is still in bed upstairs and just dreaming this.

'I don't know if you've noticed,' Sandra says, when he turns to her, with a look of pale incomprehension on his face.

'Have you?' she asks.

He shakes his head.

Sandra looks away and a few seconds pass. Some Russians laugh at something.

Then Sandra says, 'Do you like sex, Bernard?'

Bérnard tries to steady himself with another sip of Fanta. 'Sex?' he says.

'Yes.'

'Of course . . .'

Sandra chuckles. 'Spoken like a true Frenchman.'

He is not sure what she means by this, or even if he heard her properly. 'I'm sorry . . . ?' he asks.

'Why don't you ask Charmian up to your room after lunch?' Sandra says. 'I think she'd like that.'

Puzzled, Bérnard says, 'To my room?'

'Yes. I think she'd like that.'

He does not have time to ask any more questions – Charmian is there again, has taken her place at the table without a word, without looking at Bérnard, and is tucking into her next plate of microwaved lunch.

They are in the lobby afterwards when he says to her, 'You would like to see my room?'

The words, flat and matter-of-fact, just seem to escape him. He had not planned to say them, or to say anything.

She looks at her mother.

Sandra says, 'I'm going to have a little lie-down.'

She starts up the stairs on her own.

After a few moments, without saying anything else, they follow her.

They follow her as far as the first floor. She is taking a breather where the stairs turn and just nods at them as they leave her there in the stairwell window's soiled light and enter, with Bérnard one pace ahead, the shadows of the passageway.

They stop, in semi-darkness, at Bérnard's door. He operates the key, and lets Charmian precede him into the room.

He is aware, following her into it, that the narrow room smells quite strongly. The curtains are drawn and his dirty clothes are all over the floor.

'I am sorry about the mess,' he says, shutting the door.

'Our room's just the same,' she tells him.

'Yes?'

They stand there, in the soupy air. He has that feeling, again, that he's dreaming this. She is huge. Her hugeness makes the whole situation seem more dreamlike.

'What do you want to do then?' she asks, still taking the place in – looking at the open suitcase still half-full of stuff on the neatly made bed, the one he doesn't sleep in, nearer the door.

He shrugs, as if he hasn't any idea what he wants to do, as if he hasn't even thought about it.

'Do you want to have a shower?' she asks without obvious enthusiasm, looking at him now.

'The shower doesn't work.'

'Oh, yeah – you said.'

'Yes.'

They stand there for a while longer, and then she says, 'Do you want to see my tits?'

After hesitating for a second, he says, 'Okay.'

In the dim light she takes her top off – a frilly-edged shirt like the one she was wearing last night – and extricates herself from the colossal bra. The tits hang down. Doughy, blue-veined, they sit on the shelf of the next tier of her, each one equivalent, more or less, to Bérnard's head. The nipples are pale pink, very pale, and the size of saucers – they occupy meaningful territory.

It is a strange moment – him just standing there, looking, while she waits.

He notices, eventually, that he has an erection.

She notices too, and with slow movements, she kneels in front of him and slides down the zip of his jeans.

Her mouth is soft and warm.

'You have done this before,' he says after a while, sincerely impressed.

She just shrugs. She wipes her mouth and moves back a bit. With a fair amount of shoving and tugging she gets herself out of her jeans.

Her legs do not quite have the overwhelmingly vertical quality of a normal leg – they have a definite and assertive horizontal dimension too. And not much in the way of knees. When she drags down her lace-edged pants, he sees, for a moment, somewhere among all the whitish flesh, a soft tuft of hair the colour of peanut butter.

She takes his hand and pulls him towards the bed where he sleeps, its sweaty mess of sheets.

While she stands there waiting, he sits on the edge of the bed and pulls his own jeans over his feet, his horizontally striped polo shirt over his head.

They are both naked now, and his hard-on is almost embarrassingly fervent. It almost hurts. She tries to lie back on the bed and open her legs. She needs to open her legs as wide as they will go or the flesh, pouring in from every direction, will obstruct him. The single bed, however, in its position flush to the wall, is simply too narrow for her to do that. She hardly fits onto it with her legs held parallel. After a few moments of frustration, Bérnard says, 'I know. We put the mattress on the floor, okay?'

They stand up and start to move the mattress onto the floor.

Bérnard's aching erection knocks against his stomach as he struggles with his end of the mattress.

They put it down on the brown tiles.

For a moment she stands there, in the veiled light, naked, looking like a huge melted candle, all drips and slumps of round-shaped waxy flesh. Pendulous surrenders. Those pale pink nipples the size of his face. There is just so much of her, it seems to him, standing at his end, stunned by how much he wants her now, so much of her, a quantity of woman nearly equal, if that were possible, to his need to possess it, physically, in every way imaginable. Though in fact at this moment that need seems infinite. His member nodding, his lungs pulling at the air, it seems that there is nothing else to him, that that is all he is.

She takes her place on the mattress.

And then it starts.

*

It lasts all afternoon, and into the evening. The light softens in the folds of the curtains. Finally they sleep for a while, and when he opens his eyes, she is dressing herself. Though she is wearing her shirt, she seems to be naked from the waist down.

'What time is it?' he asks.

'Seven,' she says. 'You coming to supper?'

She pulls one of the curtains open and admits a wedge of light in which she immediately finds her enormous knickers. Sitting heavily on the second bed, she manoeuvres them on.

'I don't think so,' Bérnard says. He is lying naked on the mattress on the floor, supine. Worn out by orgasms – at least five of them, he isn't sure exactly how many – he feels sleepy and immobile. The idea of dressing, of dragging himself down to the dining room, seems impossible.

'Fair enough,' Charmian says, working her jeans on now.

'I'll see you later then?' she says, when she is dressed, and standing at the door.

'Yes, see you,' Bérnard says.

When she has left, he lies there still, the air warm on his skin, his eyes fixed on the soiled paintwork of the ceiling as darkness slowly hides it.

Sounds arrive at the window

a moped's noisy whirr

a snatch of music

very distant shouts

7

At lunch the next day he is shy and embarrassed. The women are normal, the same as always. Charmian, focusing on the food, hardly says anything, hardly looks at him. Sandra talks. She says, 'You weren't at the pool this morning, Bernard.'

He says he went to the beach.

'Was that nice?' Sandra asks.

He says it was.

'We don't really like the sea, do we?'

Charmian says, trying to force some last strings of meat from a scrawny, bleeding chicken leg, 'It's okay.'

'I'm scared of sharks,' Sandra says.

'That is not a problem here, I think,' Bérnard tells her.

Sandra is adamant – 'Oh, there are sharks here. And anyway I always end up with my knickers full of sand. Sand everywhere. You know what I mean? Still finding it when we get home. Still finding it *weeks* later.'

'Okay,' Bérnard says.

'They sorted out your shower yet?' she asks him.

'No.'

'*No?* It's just disgraceful. You need to be more assertive, Bernard.'

'Yes,' he agrees, 'I think so . . .'

'You've been here nearly a week now and they still haven't sorted it out. It's just not acceptable.'

'No.'

Bérnard looks shyly at Charmian again. She seems to be avoiding his eye.

'We're going horse-riding this afternoon.' Sandra announces, improbably.

'Horse-riding?'

'Yes. Our rep sorted it out for us.'

'There is horse-riding?' Bérnard asks.

'Apparently.'

After lunch, while they wait in the lobby, Bérnard says to Charmian, 'I will see you later? You will come to my room?'

Despite the exhaustiveness of yesterday's session he finds, slightly to his own surprise, that he wants more.

She is eating a pack of toffee popcorn, the sort of thing she always has on her, in her handbag. She looks at him for a moment as if she doesn't know what he's talking about. Then she says, 'Yeah, okay.'

'Okay,' Bérnard says, feeling pleased with himself. 'I will see you later.'

He looks quickly at Sandra – it was awkward, somehow, to speak out with her there. She doesn't seem to have heard, though. She is just fanning herself with a brochure, and looking towards the brown glass door.

The afternoon passes slowly. Bérnard sprawls on the pummelled, stained mattress on the floor of his room. He looks out the window. Nothing interests him. The only thing he is able to think about is what will happen later, when Charmian shows up.

Finally, at about five there is a knock on the door.

He opens it, wearing only his pants.

It is not Charmian.

It is her mother – feathery blonde pudding-bowl, red face, even redder cleavage.

'Hello, Bernard,' she says.

He swings the door mostly shut, leaving only his shocked face visible to her. He doesn't know what to say. He doesn't even manage hello.

'Can I come in then?' Sandra asks.

'I need . . . I need to get dressed.'

'Don't bother about that,' Sandra says authoritatively. 'Come on – let me in.'

He opens the door and stands aside and Sandra advances, with obvious interest, into the narrow stale-smelling room.

The thin sundress drapes her distended physique.

Her face is papery, parched, especially around the eyes.

'Our room's just like this,' she says.

Bérnard is standing there in his pants.

'You look worried, Bernard,' she says. She looks at the mattress in its odd position on the floor. 'You've got nothing to worry about.' Her eyes stay on the mattress for a few seconds, as if inspecting it, and then she says, 'I've heard good things about you, Bernard.'

He looks puzzled.

'Oh, yes, very good things.'

'What things?' he asks worriedly.

She laughs at the expression on his face. 'Well, what d'you think? You know why I'm here, don't you?' she says, looking him in the eye.

It takes him a few seconds.

Then he understands.

'That's more like it,' she says, immediately noticing. She smiles, showing her small yellow teeth. 'She said you were insatiable, and you are as well,' She puts her hand on his smooth chest and says, 'Charmian'll be back tomorrow, don't worry. She's a bit sore today. Didn't think she was up to it. So I asked her if it was alright if I had a go. I've never had a Frenchman before,' she says, almost tremulously. 'I want you to show me what all the fuss is about – alright?' She is looking up at him, her hand on his face now. 'Will you do that for me, Bernard?' Her sea-green eyes are full of imploration. 'Will you?'

*

She leaves after dark – she was more eager, more humble, than the younger woman – and he sleeps until eight in the morning, without waking once.

When he does wake, still lying on the mattress on the floor, the room is full of sunlight.

He walks to Porkies and has an egg roll, a Greek coffee.

And then, already in his trunks, and equipped with one of the Poseidon's small, scratchy towels, he makes his way to the sea.

As he had the previous day, he woke with a desire to swim in the sea.

It is still too early for the beach to be full. The Russians are there, of course, with their pungent cigarettes, their Thermoses of peat-coloured tea.

He walks down to the low surf – it is quite far from the road, the tide is out – and takes off his shirt and shoes. He puts his wallet in one of the shoes, and puts his shirt on top of them, weighing it down with an empty bottle he finds. The sand feels cold between his toes. The wind is quite strong and also feels cold when it blows. The waves, flopping onto the shore, are greenish. He lets the foaming surf wash the powdery sand from his white feet.

He wades out into the waves until they wet his long trunks, lifting his arms as the cloudy water rises around him, and lowering them as it sinks away. His skin puckers in the water, the windy air. An oncoming wave pours over him. For a moment, pouring over him, it obliterates everything in noise and push of water.

He feels its strength, feels it move away, and then he is in the smoother water on the far side of the falling waves. He is lying on the shining surface, the sea holding him, sun on his face and whispering salt water filling his ears. With his eyes shut, it seems to him that he can hear every grain of sand moving on the sea floor.

The tumbling surf feels warm now. It slides up the shore, stretching as far as its energy will take it, laying a lace of popping foam on the smoothed, shining sand.

Further up the sand is hot.

Tingling, he lies on it, lungs filling and emptying.

Arm over eyes, mouth open. Heart working.

Mind empty.

He is aware of nothing except the heat of the sun. The heat of the sun. Life.

IRVINE WELSH

Catholic Guilt (You Know You Love It)

It was a steaming, muggy day. The heat baked you slowly. My eyes were fuckin streaming from the pollutants in the air, carried around on the pollen. Nippy tears for souvenirs. Fuckin London. I used to like the sun and the heat. Now it was taking everything, sucking out my vital juices. Just as well something was. The lassies in this weather, the wey they dress. Fuckin torture, man, pure fuckin torture.

I'd been helping my mate Andy Barrow knock two rooms into one at his place over in Hackney and my throat was dry from graft and plaster dust. I'd come over a bit faint, probably because I'd hammered it a bit on the piss the last couple of nights. I decided to call it an early day. By the time I'd got back to Tufnell Park and up to my second-floor flat I felt better and in the mood to go out again. Nobody was home though; Selina and Yvette, they were both out. No note, and in this case no note is really a note which says: GIRLS' NIGHT OUT. FUCK OFF.

But Charlie had left me a message on the machine. He was as high as a kite. – Joe, she's had it. A girl. I'm down at the Lamb and Flag. Be there till about six. Come down if you get this in time. And get a fucking mobile, you tight Jock cunt.

Mobile my hole. I fuckin hate mobile phones. And the cunts that use them. The ugly intrusiveness of the strange voice: everywhere pushing their business in your face. The last time I was in Covent Garden on a brutal comedown all those fuckin tossers were standing in the street talking to themselves. The yuppies are now emulating the jakeys; drinking outside in the street and blethering shite to themselves, or, rather, into those small, nearly invisible microphones connected to their mobiles.

But I didnae need too much persuasion tae head down there, no with this fuckin thirst on me. I nip out sharpish, breathless in the heat after a few yards, feeling the grime and fumes of the city insinuating itself intae me. By the time I get down to the tube station I'm sweating like the cheese on yesterday's pizza. Thankfully it's cooler doon here, at least it is until you get on that fuckin train. There's a couple of queers sitting opposite me; the camp, lisping type, their voices burrowing into my skull. I clock two sets of those dead, inhuman, Boy Scout eyes; a lot of poofters seem to have them. Bet ye these cunts have got mobile phones.

Makes me think back to a couple of months ago when Charlie and I were over at the Brewers in Clapham, in that fairy pub by the park. We went in, only because we were in the area and it was open late. It was a mistake. The poncing and flouncing around, the shrill, shrieking queer voices disgusted me. I felt a sickness build in my gut and slowly force its way into my throat, constricting it, making it hard for me to breathe normally. I grimaced at Charlie and we finished our drinks and left.

We walked over the Common in silent shame and embarrassment, the weakness of our curiosity and laziness oppressing us. Then I saw one of *them* coming towards us. I clocked a twist of that diseased mouth, fuck knows what that's had in it, and it was pouting at *me*. Those sick, semi-apologetic queer eyes seemed to look right into my soul and interfered with my essence.

That cunt, looking at me.

At me!

I just fuckin well lashed out. The pressure of my body behind the shot told me it was a good one. My knuckle ripped against queer teeth as the fag staggered back, holding his mouth. As I inspected the damage on my hand, relieved that the skin hadn't drawn blood and merged with plague-ridden essence of pansy, Charlie flew in, no questions asked, smacking the cunt a beauty on the side of his face and knocking him over. The poof fell heavily onto the concrete path.

Charlie's a good mate, you can always rely on that cunt tae provide backup, no that I needed it here, but I suppose that what ah'm sayin is that he likes to get involved. Takes an interest. Ye appreciate that in a cunt. We stuck the boot into the decked pansy. Groaning, gurgling noises escaped from his burst faggot mouth. I wanted to obliterate the twisted puppet features of the fairy, and all I could do was boot and boot at his face until Charlie pulled me away.

Charlie's eyes were wide and wired, and his mouth was turned down.

– Enough, Joe, where's yer fucking head at? he reprimanded me.

I glanced down at the battered, moaning beast on the deck. He was well done. So aye, fair enough, I'd lost it awright, but I didnae like poofs. I told Charlie that, as we headed off across the park, swiftly into the dusky night, leaving that thing lying whining back there.

– Nah, I don't see it that way, he telt us, buzzing with adrenalin. – If every other geezer was a queer, it'd be an ideal world for me. No competition: I'd ave me pick orf all the skirt, wouldn't I?

Glancing furtively aroond, I felt we'd got away undetected. Darkness was falling and the Common seemed still deserted. My heartbeat was settling down. – Look at the fairy on the groond back thaire, I thumbed behind me as the night air cooled and soothed me. – Your bird's expecting a kid. Ye want some pervert like that teaching your kid in the classroom? Ye want that faggot brainwashing him that what *he* does is fucking normal?

– Come on, mate, you belted the geezer so I was in with ya, but I'm a live-and-let-live-type of cunt myself.

What Charlie didnae understand was the politics ay the situation; how those cunts were taking over everything. – Naw, but listen tae this, I tried to explain tae him. – Up in Scotland they want tae get rid of that Section 28 law, the only thing that stops fuckin queers like that interfering with kids.

– That's a load of old bollocks, Charlie said, shaking his head. – They didn't have no Section fucking nothing when I was at school, nor me old man, nor his old man. We didn't need it. Nobody can teach you who you want to fucking well shag. It's there or it ain't.

– What d'ye mean? I asked him.

– Well, you know you don't want to shag blokes, not unless you're a bit like that in the first place, he said, looking at me for a second or two, then grinning.

– What's that meant tae mean?

– Well, you Jocks might be different cause you wear fucking skirts, he laughed. He saw ah wisnae joking so he punched me lightly on the shoulder. – C'mon, Joe, I'm only pulling your leg, you uptight, narky cunt, he said. – We was out of order but we got a fucking result. Let's move on.

I mind that I wisnae that chuffed about this. There's certain things that ye dinnae joke about, even if ye are mates. I decided it was nothing though, and that I was just being a bit paranoid in case somebody might have seen us stomp the queer. Charlie was a great mate, a good old boy; we wound each other up a bit for a laugh, but that was as far as it went. Charlie was a fuckin sound cunt. So we did move on; to a late nightspot that he knew, and we thought no more about it.

It all comes back to me during this tube ride though. Just looking over at the nauseating pansies across fae me. Ughhh. My guts flip over as one of them gives me what seems to be a sly smile. I look away and try to control my breathing. My fingers dig into the upholstery of the seat. The two fairies get off at Covent Garden, which is ma fuckin stop. I let them go ahead and into the lift, which will take us up to street level. It's mobbed, and just being in such close vicinity of those arse bandits would make my skin crawl, so I elect to hold on for the next lift. As it is, I'm feeling sick enough when I get out and head for the Lamb and Flag.

I move up to the bar and Charlie's talking into his mobile phone. Twat. Seems to be with this lassie, who looks a bit familiar. He hasn't seen me come in. – A little girl. Four twenty this morning. Five pounds eleven. Both fine. Lily . . . He clocks me and breaks into a broad grin. I squeeze his shoulder and he nods over at the bird, who I instantly take to be his sister. – This is Lucy.

Lucy smiles at me, cocking her head to the side, presenting her cheek for a greeting kiss, which I'm happy to deliver. My first impression is that she's fuckin fit. Her hair is long and dark brown, and she has a pair of shades pushed up on top of her head. She wears blue jeans and a light blue top. My second impression (which should be contradictory) is that she looks like Charlie.

I knew Charlie had a twin sister, but I'd never met her before. Now she was standing with us at the bar and it was disconcerting. The thing was that she really *did* look like him. I could never, ever imagine a woman looking like Charlie. But she looked like him. A much slimmer, female, infinitely prettier version, but otherwise just like Charlie.

She smiles at me and gives me a sizing-up look. I suck in my beer gut. – You're the famous Joe, I take it? Her voice is high, a wee bit nasal, but a softer version of Charlie's south London twang. Charlie's south London accent is *so* south London that when I first met him I thought that he just had to be a posh cunt, trying it on.

– Aye. So you're Lucy then, I state in obvious approval, looking over towards Charlie, who's still blabbering into the mobby, then back to his sister. – Is everything okay?

– Yeah, a little girl. Four twenty this morning. Five pounds eleven.

– Is Melissa okay?

– Yeah, she had to work pretty hard, but at least Charlie was there. He went away during the contractions and –

Charlie's off the wobbly and we're hugging and he's gesturing for drinks as he takes up the tale. He looks happy, exhausted and a bit bewildered. – I was there, Joe! I just went out for a coffee, then I came back up and I heard them say, 'The head's coming,' so I thought I'd better get in there sharpish. Next thing I knew it was in me arms!

Lucy looks at him disapprovingly; her thick, black eyebrows are just like his. – *It* is a *she*. Lily, remember?

– Yeah, we're calling her Lily – Charlie's mobile rings again. He raises his eyebrows and shrugs. – Hi, Dave . . . Yeah, a little girl . . . Four twenty this morning . . . Five pounds eleven . . . Lily . . . Probably the Roses . . . I'll call yer in an hour . . . Cheers.

Just as he went to draw breath, the phone rang again.

– It's funny how we've never met, Lucy says, – because Charlie's always talking about you.

I think about this. – Yeah, he'd asked me to be best man at the wedding but my old man was pretty ill at the time and ah had tae go back up the road. Ah think it was better though, one of ehs mates fae the manor daein it, somebody that knew the family n that.

The old man pulled through okay. No that he was keen to see me in any case. He never forgave me for no going to our Angela's communion. Couldnae tell him but, couldnae tell him it was because of that priest cunt. No now. Too much water under the bridge. But that cunt'll get his one day.

– I dunno, might have been nice to have seen you in a kilt, she giggles. Laughter makes her face dance. I realize that she's little drunk and emotional but she's actively flirting with me. Her resemblance to Charlie makes this unnerving, but strangely exciting. The thing is, I mind that cunt casting aspersions, just after we'd battered that poof on the Common. I'm now wondering how he'd feel if his sister and me got it on.

As Lucy and I chat to each other, I can sense Charlie picking up the vibe. He's still talking on the phone, but it's charged with urgency now; he's trying to end the conversations asap so he can work out what's going with us. I'll show that cunt. Casting aspersions. English bastard.

– Nigel . . . you heard. Good news travels fast. Four twenty this morning . . . A little girl . . . Five eleven . . . Both doing well . . . Lily . . . The Roses . . . Probably nine but I'll phone you in an hour. Bye, Nige.

I catch the barman's attention and signal for three Beck's and three Smirnoff mules. Charlie raises a brow. – Steady on, Joe, it's going to be a long night. We're going down the Roses tonight, to wet the baby's head.

– Sound by me.

Lucy pulls on my arm and says, – Me n Joe's started already.

I'm thinking that Charlie's done a good PR job on me cause I've as good as pulled his sister without saying a fuckin word. By the look on the poor cunt's face he thinks so as well; thinks he's done *too* good a job.

– Yeah, well, I got to get back, he whines, get some things sorted out for Mel and the baby coming home tomorrow. I'll see you two later on down the Roses. Try not to get too sozzled.

– Awright, Dad, I say in a deadpan manner, and Lucy laughs, maybe a bit too loudly. Charlie smiles and says, – Tell ya wot, Joe, I could tell she was Millwall. She came out kicking!

I think about this for a second. – Call her Milly instead of Lily.

Charlie pushes down his bottom lip, raises his brow and rubs his jaw as if he's actively considering this. Lucy pushes him in his chest. – Don't you dare! Then she turns to me and says, – You're as bad as he is, you are, encouraging him! She's quite loud for a quiet pub and a few people turn round, but nobody's bothered, they know we're just enjoying a harmless high. I'm right into her now. I fancy her. I like the way she moved that one extra wee step forward into my space. I like the way she leans into you when she talks, the way her eyes dart about, how her hands move when she gets excited. Okay, it is an emotional time, but she's a banger, game as fuck, you can tell. I'm liking her more and more, and seeing less and less of Charlie in her as the drink takes effect. I like that mole on her chin; it's no a mole, it's a fuckin beauty spot, and her long, luxuriant, dark brown hair. Aye, she'll dae awright.

– See ya, Charlie goes. He gives me a bear hug, then breaks it and kisses and hugs Lucy. As he departs, the mobile goes off. – Mark! Hello! . . . A little girl . . . Four twenty . . . Sorry, Mark, you're breaking up a bit, mate, wait till I get outside . . .

Lucy and I leisurely finish our drinks before deciding to move on. We're off around the West End and go down Old Compton Street and, as usual, the place is teeming with arse bandits. Everywhere you look. I'm disgusted, but I say nowt to her. It's almost obligatory for a bird in London to have a fag mate these days. A loyal accessory for when the real man in her life fucks off. Cheaper than a dog and you don't have to feed it or take it for walks. Mind you, you don't have to listen to an Alsatian lisping and bleating doon the phone that its Border collie partner sucked off a strange Rottweiler in the local park.

Dirty fuckin . . .

I get up off the stool and have to sit down again for a bit cause I feel faint. My heartbeat's racing and there's a pain in my chest. I'll have to take things easier; drinking heavily in this heat always fucks me.

– You okay, Joe? Lucy asks.

– Never better, I smile, composing myself. But I'm thinking about how I had to sit down for a bit earlier today, over at Andy's. I picked up the sledgehammer and was itching to let fly at his wall. Then I felt this kind of spasm in my chest and I honestly thought I was going to pass out. I sat down for a bit and I was fine. Just been caning it a bit lately. That's what being single again does for you.

I get up and I'm a bit edgy in the next pub, but I concentrate on Lucy, blacking out all the queer goings-on around us. We have another couple of beers, then decide to go for a pizza at Pizza Express to soak up some of the booze. – It's weird that we haven't met before, you being one of Charlie's closest mates – Lucy considers.

– And you being his twin, I interject. – Tell ye what though, you're a lot better looking than him.

– So are you, she says, with a cool, evaluating stare. We look at each other across the table for a couple of seconds. Lucy's quite a skinny lassie, but she's got a bust on her. That never fails to impress, that one: substantial tits on a skinny bird. Never ceases to cause me to take a deep breath of admiration. She takes her shades from her head and sweeps her hair back out of her eyes in that Sloaney gesture which, for all its camp, let's face it, never fails to get the hormones racing. No that she's a posh bird or nowt like that, she's just a salt-of-the-earth type, like her brother.

Charlie's sister.

– I think that's what's called an awkward silence, I smile.

– I don't want to go to Lewisham, Lucy says to me with a toothy grin, as she stoops forward in the chair. She's sitting on her hands, to stop them flying about, I think. She's quite expressive that way – they were fairly swooping around in that last pub.

But aye, fuck south London the now. – Nah, I'm no that bothered either. I'm enjoying it with just the pair of us, to be honest.

Then she says to me, – You don't say very much but when you do it's really sweet.

I think of the smashed poof in the park and clench my teeth in a smile. Sweet talk. – You're sweet, I tell her.

Sweet talk.

– Where do you stay? she quizzes, raising her eyebrows.

– Tufnell Park, I tell her. I should say more, but there isnae any point. She's doing fine for the both of us, and I sense that I can only talk myself out of a shag right now, and I'm no about tae dae that. Not with the way my sex life's been lately.

It's a bummer sharing a gaff with two fit birds and no going oot wi anybody. Everybody says, lucky bastard, but it's sheer torture. But I find that the more you say that you're not shagging either of them, the less inclined people are to believe you. I feel like that *Man About the House* cunt.

Aye, ah could dae wi a ride.

So could she, by the sound ay things. – Let's get a cab, Lucy urges.

In the taxi I kiss her on the lips. In my celibate paranoia I'm expecting them to be cold and tight, like I've misread the signs, but they're open, warm and lush, and before I know it we're eating each other's faces. The snatches of conversation when we come up for air reveal that we're both in the process of getting over other people. We urgently rap out those monologues, both knowing that if we weren't so close to Charlie we wouldn't have bothered, but in the circumstances it seems only manners to be up to speed with each other's recent history. But whether we're really over our exes or not, it's nae bother: rebound rides are better than okay if celibacy is the only alternative.

I remember with satisfaction and relief that I recently visited the launderette and washed a new duvet, which I've got on my bed. So when we get back to mines I'm delighted that Selina and Yvette are both still out and I don't have to go through tiresome introductions. We shoot straight through to the bedroom and I'm fucking one of my best mates' twin sister. I'm on top of her and she's chewing her bottom lip, like . . . like Charlie when we were in Ibiza last year. We'd pulled these two lassies from York and we were riding them back in the room, and I looked over and saw Charlie biting his lower lip in concentration. Her eyes, her brows, so like his.

It's putting me off, I can feel myself going a bit soft.

I pull out and gasp, – From behind now.

She turns over, but she doesn't get up on her knees, just lies flat and smiles wickedly. I wonder for a second whether or not she wants it up her arse. I'm not into that. She looks good though, and I am rock hard again, the troubling Charlie associations all gone from my nut. All I can see is that long hair, slender body and peach of an arse, spread out before me. I struggle to push into her fanny, trying to keep some of my weight on my arms as I thrust into her.

It's going in though, and soon we're fucking away again for all we're worth. Lucy gives the odd appreciative groan, without making a big fuss. I like that. I'm looking at a spot on the headboard to avoid getting too turned on and blowing early, it's been a while and I . . .

I'm feeling . . .

WHOOSH . . .

PHOAH . . .

OH . . .

OOOOHHH . . .

No . . .

I think I've blown it there for a bit, the room seems to darken and spin, but I come to my senses and we're still at it.

The strange thing is that I'm suddenly aware that her dimensions seem to have changed. Her body is like it's rounder and fuller. And she's quiet now, it's as if she's passed out.

And . . . there's somebody in the bed next to us!

It's Melissa! Charlie's wife, and she's asleep. I look at Lucy, but it *isn't* Lucy. It's Charlie: I am . . . I am . . . I am fucking Charlie up his arse . . .

I AM FUCK –

A spasm of horror shoots through me, the rigidness going from my erection to my body. My cock instantly goes limp, as God's my witness, and I pull out, sweating and trembling.

I realize, to my further shock, that I'm not at home any more. I am in Charlie's flat.

WHAT THE FUCK IS THIS . . . ?

I slide out of the bed. I look around. Charlie and Melissa seem to be in a deep sleep. There's no sign of Lucy. I can't find my clothes, all my gear has gone. Where the fuck is this? How the fuck did I get here?

I grab a smelly old Millwall top with *South London Press* on it and a pair of jogging trousers that lie in a heap on a laundry basket. Charlie likes to run, he's a fitness fanatic. I look at him back there, still dozing, out for the count.

I pull on the clothes and go through to the front room. This is Charlie and Melissa's place alright. I can't think straight, but I know I have to get out of there fast. I promptly leave the flat and I run like fuck through the streets of Bermondsey until I get to London Bridge. I head to the tube station but I realize that I have no money. So I trot over London Bridge towards the city.

My head is buzzing with the obvious questions. What the fuck has happened? How did I get to south London? To Charlie's bed? To Char – it's obvious that my drink was spiked in some way, but who the fuck set me up? I can't remember!

I CANNAE FUCKIN REMEMBER!

I'M NO AN ARSE BANDIT!

That fuckin Lucy. She's a weirdo. But no her brother, surely no. Me and Charlie . . . I can't believe it.

I can't . . .

But the strangest thing is that just when I ought to be fuckin suicidal,

I am, in spite of myself, settling into this weird calmness. I feel tranquil, but strangely ethereal; somehow disassociated from the rest of the city. Although I'm still at a loss to work out what has happened, it all seems secondary, because I am cocooned in this floaty bubble of bliss. I must be daydreaming, as I cross the road at the Bishopsgate, because I don't see a cyclist come careering into me . . .

FUCKIN . . .

WHOOSH . . .

Then there's a flash and a ringing in my ears and miraculously I am standing at Camden Lock. There is absolutely no sense of any impact having taken place with the boy on the bike. Something is up here, but I'm not bothered. That is the thing. I feel fine, I don't care. I head up Kentish Town Road, towards Tufnell Park.

The door of my flat is locked and I have no keys. The girls might be in. I go to rap at the door, and bang – a whoosh of air in my ears and I am standing inside the living room. Yvette is ironing, while watching the television. Selina is sitting on the couch, skinning up a joint.

– I could handle some of that, I say. – You're no gaunny believe the night I've had . . .

They ignore me. I speak again. No reaction. I walk in front of them. No recognition.

They can't see or hear me!

I go to touch Selina, to see if I can elicit some response, but then I pull my hand away. It might break the spell. There is something exciting, something empowering, about this invisibility.

But there is something wrong with the pair of them. They seem in as much shock as I am. It must have been some night they've had as well. Aye, girls: we pay for our fun.

– I still can't believe it, Yvette says. – A bad heart. Nobody knew he had a bad heart. How can something like that not be picked up?

– Nobody knew he had *any* heart, Selina snorts. Then she shrugs, as if in guilt. – That's not fair . . . but . . .

Yvette looks sharply at her. – You fucking cold cow, she hisses in anger.

– Sorry, I . . . Selina starts, before slapping her forehead in confusion.

– Oh fuck, I'm going to take a shower, she suddenly decides and leaves the room.

I opt to follow her into the bathroom, to watch her take her clothes off. Yes. I'm going to enjoy this invisibility lark. Just as she starts to undress . . .

WHOOSH . . .

I'm not in the bathroom any more. I am pumping away . . . yes . . . ye-es . . . I'm fucking somebody . . . they're starting to come into focus . . .

It must be Lucy, it was all some fuckin daft hallucination, some acid flashback or the like, it was all . . .

But no . . .

NO!

I am on top of my mate Ian Calder, shagging him up his arse. He is unconscious, and I am giving him one. I can see we are on the couch in his house back in Leith. I am back up in Scotland, shagging one of my oldest pals up his fuckin hole, like I'm some kind of queer rapist!

OH NO, MY GOD . . . NO IN FUCKIN SCOTLAND . . .

I feel as if I'm going to throw up all over him. I withdraw, as Ian starts to make those delirious sounds, like he's having a bad dream. There is blood on my cock. I pull up the bottoms on my tracksuit and run out the house into the street.

I am in Edinburgh, but nobody can see me. I am going mad as I run screaming, up Leith Walk, down Princes Street, trying to avoid people. But as I pick up speed on the corner of Castle Street I collide with this old woman and a Zimmer frame . . .

Then . . .

WHOOSH . . .

I am in a prison cell, but I am fuckin well shagging this guy up his arse. He lies unconscious on the bed underneath me.

OH FOR FUCK SAKE . . .

It's my old buddy Murdo. He's inside for dealing coke.

YUK . . .

I pull out and jump down from the top bunk. I am sick, but in dry, racking coughs, holding myself against the cell wall. Nothing will come up. I look about as Murdo comes to, his face twisted in pain and confusion. He turns round, touches his arse, sees the shit and blood on his fingers and starts screaming. He jumps down, and I start to shout, crippled with fear: – I can explain, mate . . . it's no what it seems . . .

But Murdo ignores me and moves over to his sleeping cell mate in the lower bunk, launching into a savage attack on the poor cunt. His fist thrashes into the startled jailbird's face. – YOU, AH KEN YOU! YOU DID SOMETHING TAE ME! AH KEN YOU! YA DIRTY FUCKIN SICK BUFTIE BASTARD! YA FUCKIN BEAST!

– AAGGHH! IT'S HOOSEBREKIN AH'M IN FIR – the boy protests through his shock.

WHOOSHHH . . . The guy's screams fade as I am . . .

I am standing in a chapel of rest, at the back of the hall. The crematorium; Warriston, or Monktonhall, or the Eastern. I dinnae ken, but they are all there; my ma n dad, my brother Alan and my wee sister Angela. In front of the coffin. And I know, straight away, just who is inside that coffin.

I am at my ain fuckin funeral.

I'm screaming at them: what is this, what's happening to me?

But again, nobody can hear me. No, that's no quite right. There's one fucker who seems to be able to; this fat old boy with white hair, who's wearing a dark blue suit. He gives me the thumbs up. The old cunt seems to have a glow about him, with shards of incandescent light emanating from him.

I move across to him, completely invisible to the rest of the congregation, just as he seems to be. – You . . . you can hear me. You ken the Hampden Roar here. What the fuck is this?

The old guy just smiles and points at the coffin at the front of the mourners. – Nearly late for yir ain fuckin funeral thaire, mate, he laughs.

– But how? What happened tae me?

– Aye, ye died when you were on the job with your mate's sister. Congenital heart problem you didn't even know about.

Fuck me. I wis mair ill than I thought. – But . . . who are you?

– Well, the old boy grins, – I'm what you'd call an angel. I'm here to assist you in your passage over to the other side. He coughs, raising his hand to his face, stifling a laugh. – Pardon the pun, he chuckles. – I've had all sorts of names in different cultures. It might help you tae think of me as one of the ones I'm least fond of: St Peter.

The confirmation ay my death induces in me a bizarre elation, and no small relief. – So I'm deid! Thank fuck for that! It means I never shagged my mates up the arse. Ye hud me worried for a bit there!

The old angel cunt shakes his heid slowly and grimly. – You're not over to the other side yet.

– What d'ye mean?

– You're a restless spirit, wandering the Earth.

– How come?

– Punishment. This is your penance.

I'm no having this. – Punishment? Me? What the fuck have ah done wrong? I ask the bastard.

The auld guy smiles like a double-glazing salesman who's about tae tell me there's nowt they can dae aboot their crappy installation. – Well, Joe, the truth is that you're not a bad guy, but you have been a bit misogynistic and homophobic. So your punishment is to make you walk the Earth as a homosexual ghost buggering your old mates and acquaintances.

– No way! No way am ah gaunny dae that! You cannae fuckin well make me . . . I say, lamely tailing off as I realize that the sick old bastard has been doing exactly that.

– Aye, this is your punishment for being a queer basher, the angel gadge smiles again. – I'm going to watch and laugh at you being crippled with guilt. Not only am I going to make you do it, Joe, I'm going to make you *keep* doing it until you enjoy it.

– No way. You must be fuckin joking. I'll never enjoy that. I point at myself. – Never! You cunt . . . I spring at the bastard, ready to throttle him, but in another swish of sound and flash of light he's gone.

I sit at a vacant seat at the back of the chapel, my head in my hands. I look around at the congregation. Lucy has come up for it, she's sitting quite close to me. That's nice of her. Must've been a fuckin shock for her. One minute you've a stiffer inside ye, the next it's just a stiff. Charlie's there too, he's with Ian and Murdo at the back of the hall.

They are all standing up.

Then I see him. That dirty old cunt of a priest.

Father Brannigan. Him, putting me to rest! That filthy, evil auld cunt!

I'm looking over at my parents, screaming silently at them for this appalling betrayal. I mind of me saying to them, I dinnae want tae be an altar boy any mair, Ma, and my mother being so disappointed. My old man never gave a fuck. Let the laddie dae what eh wants, he said. But when I didnae come tae our Angela's communion and I couldnae tell them why . . .

Aw fuck . . . that dirty old cunt touching me, and worse, making me do things to him . . .

I never would, never *could* say. Never. Never even thought about it. I always vowed he'd fuckin well get it one day. Now he's here, he's sending me off, his pious lies ringing throughout this chapel.

– Joseph Hutchinson was a kind, sensitive, young Christian man, taken untimely from us. But, through our grief and loss, we should not fail to remember that God has a plan, no matter how obscure this may seem to we mortals. Joseph, who once served at the altar of this very house of the Lord, would have understood this divine truth more than most of us . . .

I want to roar the truth at them all, to tell them what that dirty old cunt did tae me . . .

WHOOSHHHH . . .

Then I'm on auld Brannigan and he's screaming under my weight; his old skinny, smelly bones, crushed under my bulk. I'm giving it to the dirty old cunt; pummelling him right up his arse and he's screaming. I'm snarling in demented rage: – You cannae tell anybody, or God will punish you for being a sinner, and I'm fucking him and fucking him harder and harder. He's screeching beyond agony and bang! . . . his heart stops, I feel it stop as his last breath escapes him. Brannigan's body judders underneath me and his eyes roll towards heaven. I feel his essence rise up through his body and through mine, planting a thought into my psyche that says YOU CUNT as he floats away, a soundless cry coming from his spirit like a balloon farts out air as it flies into space.

I'm sobbing and crying to myself, saying over and over again in my self-disgust, – When will it be over? When will this nightmare end?

WHOOSH . . .

And then I'm with my best mate Andy Sweeney; we grew up together, did almost everything together. He was always more popular than me – better looking, brighter, good job – but he was my best mate. As I said, we did everything together – well, almost everything. But now I'm on top of him and I'm shagging the arse off him . . . and it's horrible.

– WHEN, I'm screaming, – WHEN WILL THIS FUCKIN NIGHTMARE END?

And he's in the room with us, the auld St Peter boy from the funeral. He's just sitting in the armchair watching us in a studied, detached manner. – When you start to enjoy it, when you cease to feel the guilt, that's when it'll end, he tells me coldly.

So there I am shagging my best mate up his arse. God, am I feeling disgusted and crippled with revulsion, loathing and guilt . . .

. . . feeling sick and ugly, in constant torture as I am compelled to pump away like a rancid fuck machine from hell, feeling like my soul is being ripped apart . . .

. . . going to a place beyond fear, humiliation and torture, and hating it, loathing it, detesting it so fuckin much . . . a pain so great and pervasive that I'll never, ever grow to feel anything other than this sheer horror . . .

. . . or so I keep telling that daft cunt of an angel.

WOMEN

LUCY CALDWELL

Poison

I saw him last night. He was with a girl half his age, more than half, a third of his age. It was in the bar of the Merchant Hotel, and they were together on the raspberry crushed-velvet banquette. Her arm was flung around his shoulder, and he had an arm around her, too, an easy hand on her waist. She was laughing, her face turned right up to his, enthralled, delighted. They kept clinking glasses: practically every time they took a sip of their cocktails they clinked glasses. I was alone, in a high seat at the bar, waiting for my friends – friends I hadn't seen in years but who, even years ago, were always late. I'd ordered a glass of white wine while I waited; I picked it up with shaking hands. It was him. There was no doubt about it. His face had got pouchy, and his hair, though still black – dyed, surely – was limp and thinning. When he stood up, he was shorter than I remembered.

But it was him.

I hadn't seen him in years. I scrambled to work out the numbers in my head. Sixteen – seventeen – almost eighteen. All those years later, and there he was, entwined with a girl a fraction of his age. He must be nearly sixty now.

I bent my head over the cocktail list as he walked towards me, letting my hair fall partly over my face, but I couldn't take my eyes off him. His eyes slid over the women he passed, thin, fake-tanned bare backs and sequinned dresses, stripper shoes. He didn't look once at me. I'd lived away too long, and I'd forgotten how dressed up people got for a Saturday night: I was in skinny jeans and a blazer, and not enough make-up. I watched him walk along the candy-striped carpet and out towards the toilets, and then I turned to look at his companion.

She had her head bowed over her phone, and she was jiggling one leg and rapidly texting. She suddenly looked very young indeed. I'd put her in her mid-twenties, but it was less than that. I felt a strange tightness in my chest. She put her phone away and uncrossed her legs, recrossed them, tugged at the hem of her little black dress. She picked up her empty glass and tilted her head right back and drained the dregs, coughed a little, set the glass back down and slung her hair over the other shoulder. She had too much make-up on: huge swipes of blusher, exaggerated cat-eyes. She glanced around the bar, then she took out her phone again, flicked and tapped at it. She wasn't used to being alone in a bar like this. It was an older crowd and she felt self-conscious, you could tell. The men in the chairs opposite her were in their forties at least, heavy-jowled, sweating in their suits, tipping back their whiskey sours. I watched the relief on her face when he appeared again, how she wriggled into him and kissed him on the cheek. As they studied the menu together, giggling, their heads bent confidentially together, I suddenly realized she wasn't his lover.

She was his daughter.

She was Melissa. Seventeen years. She'd be eighteen now. Perhaps they were out tonight celebrating her eighteenth birthday. With a surge of nausea I realized, then, that what I'd been feeling wasn't outrage that she was too young for him, or contempt, or disgust. It was simpler, and much more complicated, than that.

*

I don't remember whose idea it was to go to Mr Knox's house. One minute we were giggling over him, nudging elbows and sugar-breath and damp heads bent together, and the next minute someone was saying they knew where he lived, something about a neighbour and church and his wife, and suddenly, almost without the decision being made, it was decided we were going there.

Was it Tanya?

There were four of us: Donna, Tanya, Lisa and me. We were fourteen, and bored. It was a Baker day, which meant no school, and we had nothing else to do. It was April, and chilly, rain coming in gusty, intermittent bursts. The Easter holidays had only just ended, and none of us had any pocket money left. We'd met in Cairnburn Park just after nine, but at that time on a wet Monday morning it was deserted. We'd wandered down to the kiddie playground, but the swings were soaking, and, after a half-hearted couple of turns on the roundabout, we'd given up. The four of us had trailed down Sydenham Avenue and past our school – it was strange to see the lights on in the main building and the teachers' cars all lined up as usual.

Then, more out of habit than anything else, we crossed the road to the Mini-Market. We pooled our spare change to buy packets of strawberry bon-bons and Midget Gems, and Donna nicked a handful of fizzy cola bottles. We ate them as we trudged on down towards Ballyhackamore. The rain was getting heavier, and none of us had umbrellas, so we ended up in KFC, huddled over the melamine table, slurping a shared Pepsi.

We were the only ones in there. The sugar and the rain and the boredom made us restless, and snide. We'd started telling a story, in deliberately too-loud voices, about someone who'd ordered a plain chicken burger and complained when it came with mayo. There's no mayo in it, the person behind the counter had said. Oh yes there is. Oh no there isn't. And it turned out that the mayo was actually a burst sac of pus from a cyst growing on the chicken breast.

The girl behind the counter was giving us increasingly dirty looks, and we realized that if she chucked us out we really had nowhere to go, so we changed tack then and started slagging each other, boys we'd fancied, boys we'd seen or wanted to see.

And then the conversation, almost inevitably, turned to Mr Knox.

We all fancied Mr Knox. No one even bothered to deny it. The whole school fancied him. He was the French and Spanish teacher, and he was part French himself, or so the rumours went. He was part something, anyway: he had to be – he was so different from the other teachers. he had dark hair that he wore long and floppy over one eye and permanent morning-after stubble, and he smoked Camel cigarettes. Teachers couldn't smoke anywhere in the school grounds, not even in the staffroom, but he smoked anyway, in the staff toilets in the Art Block or in the caretakers' shed, girls said, and if you had him immediately after break or lunch you smelt it off him. He drove an Alfa Romeo, bright red, and where the other male teachers were rumpled in browns and greys, he wore coloured silk shirts and loafers. On Own Clothes Day at the end of term he'd worn tapered jeans and a polo neck and Chelsea boots and, even though it was winter, mirrored aviator sunglasses, like an off-duty film star. He had posters on his classroom walls of Emmanuelle Béart and a young Catherine Deneuve and Soledad Miranda, and he lent his sixth-formers videos of Pedro Almodóvar films.

But that wasn't all. A large part of his charge came from the fact that he'd had an affair with a former pupil, Davina Calvert. It had been eight years ago, and they were married now. He'd left his wife for her, and it was a real scandal. He'd almost lost his job over it, except in the end they couldn't dismiss him because he'd done nothing strictly, legally wrong.

It had happened before we joined the school, but we knew all the details: everyone did. It was almost a rite of passage to cluster as first- or second-years in a corner of the library poring over old school magazines in search of her, hunting down grainy black-and-white photographs of year groups, foreign exchange trips, prize days, tracking her as she grew up to become his lover.

Davina Calvert, Davina Knox. She was as near and as far from our lives as it was possible to get.

Davina, the story went, was her year's star pupil. She got the top mark in Spanish A Level in the whole of Northern Ireland and came third in French. Davina Calvert, Davina Knox. Nothing happened between them while she was still at school – or nothing anyone could pin on him, at least – but when she left she went on a gap year, teaching English in Granada, and he went out to visit her. We knew this for sure because Lisa's older sister had been two years below Davina Calvert and was in Mr Knox's Spanish A-Level class at the time. After Hallowe'en half-term, he turned up with a load of current Spanish magazines, *Hola!* and *Diez Minutos* and Spanish *Vogue*. They asked him if he'd been away, and where he'd been, and he answered them in a teasing torrent of Spanish that none of them could quite follow. But it went around the school like wildfire that he'd been in Granada, visiting Davina Calvert, and, sure enough, when she was back for Christmas, at least two people saw them in his Alfa Romeo, parked up a side street, kissing, and by the end of the school year he and his wife were separated, getting divorced.

The following year, he didn't even pretend to hide it from his classes: when they talked about what they'd done at the weekend, he'd grin and say, in French or Spanish, that he'd been visiting a special friend in Edinburgh. Everyone knew it was Davina.

We used to picture what it must have been like, when he first visited her in Granada. The winding streets and white medieval buildings. The blue and orange and purple sky. They would have walked together to Lorca's house and the Alhambra, and, afterwards, clinked glasses of sherry in some cobbled square with fountains and Gypsy musicians. Perhaps he would have reached under the table to stroke her thigh, slipping a hand under her skirt and tracing the curve of it up, and, when he withdrew it, she would have crossed and uncrossed her legs, squeezing and releasing her thighs, the tingling pressure unbearable.

I imagined it countless times, but I could never quite settle on what would have happened next. What would you do, in Granada, with Mr Knox? Would you lead him back to your little rented room, in the sweltering eaves of a home-stay or a shared apartment? No: you'd go with him instead to the hotel that he'd booked, a sumptuous four-poster bed in a grand and faded parador in the Albayzin – or more likely an anonymous room in the new district where the staff wouldn't ask questions, a room where the bed had white sheets with clinical corners, a room with a bathroom you could hear every noise from. The shame of it – the excitement.

And in the KFC on the Upper Newtownards Road, on that rainy Monday Baker day in April, we knew where Mr Knox and Davina lived. It was out towards the Ice Bowl, near the golf club, in Dundonald. It was a forty-, forty-five-minute walk. We had nothing else to do. We linked arms and set off.

It was an anticlimax when we got there. We'd walked down the Kings Road, passing such posh houses on the way; somehow, with the sports car and the sunglasses and the designer suits, we'd expected his house to be special too. But most of the houses on his street were just like ours: bungalows, or small red-brick semis, with hedges and lawns and rhododendron bushes. We walked up one side and down the other. There was nothing to tell us where he lived: no sign of him.

We were starting to bicker by then. The rain was coming down relent-less, and Tanya was getting worried that someone might see us and report us to the school. We slagged her – how would anyone know we were doing anything wrong, and how would they know which school we went to anyway, we weren't in uniform – but all of us were slightly on edge. It was only mid-morning, but what if he left school for some reason, or came home for an early lunch? All four of us were in his French class, and me and Lisa had him for Spanish too: he'd recognize us.

We should go: we knew we should go. The long walk back in the rain stretched ahead of us. We sat on a low wall to empty our pockets and purses and work out if we had enough to pay for a bus ticket each. When it turned out there was only enough for three, we started squabbling: Tanya had no money left, but she'd paid for the bon-bons, and almost half of the Pepsi, so it wasn't fair if she had to walk. Well, it wasn't fair for everyone to have to walk just because of her. Besides, she lived nearest: there was least distance for her to walk. But it wasn't fair! Back and forth it went, and it might have turned nasty – Donna had just threatened to slap Tanya if she didn't quit whingeing.

Then we saw Davina.

It was Lisa who recognized her, at the wheel of a metallic-blue Peugeot. The car swept past us and round the curve of the road, but Lisa swore it had been her at the wheel. We leapt up, galvanized, and looked at each other. 'Well, come on,' Donna said.

'Donna!' Tanya said.

'What, are you scared?' Donna said. Donna had thick glasses that made her eyes look small and mean, and she'd pushed her sister through a patio door in a fight. We were all a little scared of Donna.

'Come on,' Lisa said.

Tanya looked as if she was about to cry.

'We're just going to look,' I said. 'We're just going to walk past and look at the house. There's no law against that.' Then I added, 'For fuck's sake, Tanya.' I didn't mind Tanya, if it was just the two of us, but it didn't do to be too friendly with her in front of the others.

'Yeah, Tanya, for fuck's sake,' Lisa said.

Tanya sat back down on the wall. 'I'm not going anywhere,' she said. 'We'll be in such big trouble.'

'Fine,' Donna said. 'Fuck off home, what are you waiting for?' She turned and linked Lisa's arm, and they started walking down the street.

'Come on, Tan,' I said.

'I have a bad feeling,' she said. 'I just don't think we should.' But when I turned to go after the others, she pushed herself from the wall and followed.

We found the house where the Peugeot was parked, right at the bottom of the street. It was the left-hand side of a semi, and it had an unkempt hedge and a stunted palm tree in the middle of the little front lawn. You somehow didn't picture Mr Knox with a miniature palm tree in his garden. We clustered on the opposite side of the road, half hidden behind a white van, giggling at it. And then we realized that Davina was still in the car. 'What's she at?' Donna said. 'Stupid bitch.'

We stood and watched a while longer, but nothing happened. You could see the dark blur of her head and the back of her shoulders, just sitting there.

'Well, fuck this for a game of soldiers,' Donna said. 'I'm not standing here all day like a big fucking lemon.' She turned and walked a few steps down the road and waited for the rest of us to follow.

'Yeah,' Tanya said. 'I'm going too. I said I'd be home for lunch.'

Neither Lisa nor I moved.

'What do you think she's doing?' Lisa said.

'Listening to the radio?' I said. 'Mum does that, sometimes, if it's *The Archers*. She doesn't want to leave the car until it's over.'

'I suppose,' Lisa said, looking disappointed.

'Come on,' Tanya said. 'We've seen where he lives, now let's just go.'

Donna was standing with her hands on her hips, annoyed that we were ignoring her. 'Seriously,' she shouted. 'I'm away on.'

They were expecting me and Lisa to follow, but we didn't. As soon as they were out of earshot, Lisa said, 'God, Donna's doing my fucking head in today.' She glanced at me sideways as she said it.

'Hah,' I said, vaguely. It didn't do to be too committal: Lisa and Donna were thick as thieves these days. Lisa's mum and mine had gone to school together, and the two of us had been friends since we were babies. There were photographs of us in the bath together, covered in bubbles, bashing each other with bottles of Mr Matey. We'd been inseparable through primary school, and into secondary. Recently though Lisa had started hanging out more with Donna, smoking Silk Cuts nicked from Donna's mum and drinking White Lightning in the park at weekends. Both of them had gone pretty far with boys. Not full-on sex, but close, or so they both claimed. I'd kissed a boy once. It was better than Tanya – but still; it made me weird and awkward around Lisa when it was just the two of us. I'd always imagined we'd do everything together, like we always had done.

I could feel Lisa still looking at me. I scuffed the ground with the heel of one of my gutties.

'I mean, seriously doing my head in,' she said, and she pulled a face that was recognizably an impression of Donna, and I let myself start giggling. Lisa looked pleased. 'Here,' she said, and she slipped her arm through mine. 'What do you think Davina's like? I mean, d' you know what I mean?'

I knew exactly what she meant. 'Well, she's got to be gorgeous,' I said.

'You big lesbo,' Lisa said, digging me in the ribs.

I dug her back. 'No, being serious. She's got to be: he left his wife for her. She's got to be gorgeous.'

'What else?'

'Well, she doesn't care what people think. I mean, think of all the gossip. Think of what you'd say to your parents and that.'

'My dad would go nuts.'

'Yeah,' I said.

We were silent for a moment then, watching the blurred figure in the Peugeot.

'D' you think anything did happen while they were at school?' Lisa suddenly said. 'I mean, it must have, mustn't it? Otherwise why would you bother going all that way to visit her? I mean, like, lying to your wife and flying all the way to Granada.'

'I know. I don't know.'

I'd wondered about it before – we all had. But it was especially strange, standing right outside his house, his and Davina's. Did she linger at his desk after class? Did he stop and give her a lift somewhere? Did she hang around where he lived and bump into him, as if by chance, or pretend she was having problems with her Spanish grammar? Who started it? And how exactly did it start? And did either of them ever imagine it would end up here?

'She might have been our age,' Lisa said.

'I know.'

'Or only, like, two or three years older.'

'I know.'

We must have been standing there for ten minutes by now. A minute longer and we might have turned to go. But all of a sudden the door of the Peugeot swung open, and Davina got out. There she was: Davina Calvert, Davina Knox.

Except that the Davina in our heads had been glamorous, like the movie sirens on Mr Knox's classroom walls, but this Davina had messy hair in a ponytail and dark circles under her eyes, and she was wearing baggy jeans and a raincoat. And she was crying: her face was puffy, and she was crying, openly, tears just running down her face.

I felt Lisa take my hand and squeeze it. 'Oh my God,' she breathed.

We watched Davina walk around to the other side of the car and unstrap a toddler from the back seat. She lifted him to his feet and then hauled a baby car seat out.

We had forgotten – if we'd ever known – that Mr Knox had babies. He never mentioned them, or had photos on his desk like some of the other teachers. You somehow didn't think of Mr Knox with babies.

'Oh my God,' Lisa said again.

The toddler was wailing. We watched Davina wrestle him up the drive and into the porch, the car seat over the crook of her other arm. She had to put it down while she found her keys, and we watched as she scrabbled in her bag and then her coat pockets before locating them, unlocking the door and going inside. The door swung shut behind her.

We stood there for a moment longer. Then, 'Come on,' I found myself saying. 'Let's knock on her door.' I have no idea where the impulse came from, but as soon as I said it I knew I was going to do it.

Lisa turned to face me. 'Are you insane?'

'Come on,' I said.

'But what will we say?'

'We'll say we're lost, we'll say we're after a glass of water – I don't know. We'll think of something. Come on.'

Lisa stared at me. 'Oh my God, you're mad,' she said. But she giggled. And then we were crossing the road and walking up the driveway, and there we were, standing in Mr Knox's porch. 'You're not seriously going to do this?' Lisa said.

'Watch me,' I said, and I fisted my hand and knocked on the door.

I can still picture every moment of what happens next.

Davina opens the door (Davina Calvert, Davina Knox) with the baby in one arm and the toddler hanging off one of her legs. We blurt out – it comes to me, inspired – that we live just round the corner, and we're going door to door to see does anyone need a babysitter. All at once, we're like a team again, me and Leese. I start a sentence, she finishes it. She says something, I elaborate. We sound calm, and totally plausible. Davina says thank you, but the baby's too young to be left. Lisa says can we leave our details anyway, for maybe in a few months' time? Davina blinks and says okay, sure, and the two of us inch our way into her hallway while she gets a pen and notelet from the phone pad. Lisa calls me Judith, and I call her Carol. We write down Judith and Carol and give a made-up number. We are invincible. We are on fire. Davina says what school do we go to, and Lisa says, not missing a beat, Dundonald High. Why aren't you at school today, Davina asks, and I say it's a Baker day. I suddenly wonder if all schools have the same Baker days, and a dart of fear goes through me, but Davina just says, Oh, and doesn't ask anything more.

We sense she's going to usher us out now, and before she can do it, Lisa asks what the baby's called, and Davina says, Melissa. That's a pretty name, I say, and Davina says thank you. So we admire the baby, her screwed-up little face and flexing fingers, and I think of having Mr Knox's baby growing inside you, and a huge rush of heat goes through me. When Davina says, as we knew she was going to, Girls, as I'm sure you can see, I've really got my hands full here, and Lisa says, No, no, of course, we'll have to be going – and she's getting the giggles now, I can see them rising in her, the way the corners of her lips pucker and tweak – I say, Yes, of course, but do you mind if I use your toilet first? Davina blinks again, her red-raw eyes, as if she can sense a trap but doesn't know quite what it is, and then she says no problem, but the downstairs loo's blocked, wee Reuben has a habit of flushing things down it, and they haven't got round to calling out the plumber, I'll have to go upstairs. It's straight up the stairs and first on the left. I can feel Lisa staring at me, but I don't meet her eye, I just say, Thank you, and make my way upstairs.

The bathroom is full – just humming – with Mr Knox. There's his dressing gown hung on the back of the door, his electric razor on the side of the sink, his can of Lynx deodorant on the window sill. There's his toothbrush in a mug, and there's flecks of his stubble in the sink, and there's his dirty clothes in the laundry basket. I kneel and open it and recognize one of his shirts, a slippery pale-blue one with yellow diamond patterning. I reach over and flush the toilet so the noise will cover my movements, and then I open the mirrored cabinet above the sink and run my fingers over the bottles on what must be his shelf, the shaving cream, the brown plastic bottle of prescription drugs, a six-pack of Durex condoms, two of them missing.

The skin all over my body is tingling, tingling in places I didn't know could tingle, in between my fingers, the backs of my knees. I ease one of the condoms from the strip, tugging gently along the foil perforations, and stuff it into my jeans. Then I put the box back, exactly as it was, and close the mirrored cabinet.

I stare at myself in the mirror. My face looks flushed. I wonder, again, what age she was when he first noticed her. I realize that I don't know how long I've been in here. I run the tap, and look around me one last time. And then, without planning to, without knowing I'm going to until I've done it, I find my hand closing around one of the bottles of perfume on the window sill and rearranging the others so the gap doesn't show. You're not supposed to keep perfume on the window sill anyway – even I know that. I slide it into the inside pocket of my jacket and arrange my left arm over it so the bulge doesn't show, then I turn off the tap and go downstairs to where Lisa's shooting me desperate glances.

Outside, she can't believe what I've done. None of them can. We catch up with Donna and Tanya still waiting for us on the main road. Although it feels like a lifetime has passed, it's only been ten minutes or so since they left us.

'You'll never believe what she did,' Lisa says, and there's pride in her voice as she tells them how we knocked on the door and went inside, inside Mr Knox's house, and talked to Davina, and touched the baby, and how I used his bathroom. I take over the story then. The condom I keep quiet about – that's mine, just for me – but I show them the perfume. It's a dark glass bottle, three-quarters full, aubergine, almost black, with a round glass stopper. In delicate gold lettering, it says, 'POISON, Dior'.

'I can't believe you nicked her fucking perfume!' Donna says.

Tanya stares at me as if she's going to be sick.

Donna takes the bottle from me and uncaps the lid. She aims it at Lisa.

'Fuck off,' Lisa says. 'You're not spraying that shit on me.'

'Spray me then,' I say, and they all look at me. 'Go on,' I say, 'spray me.' I roll up the sleeve of my jumper to bare my wrist.

Donna aims the nozzle. A jet of perfume shoots out, dark and heady and forbidden-smelling.

'Eww,' says Tanya, 'that smells like fox. Why would anyone want to smell like that?'

I press my wrists together carefully and raise them to my neck, dab both sides. It's the strongest perfume I've ever smelt. The musty green scent makes me feel slightly nauseous. It doesn't smell like a perfume you'd imagine Davina Calvert choosing: he must have bought it for her; it must be him that likes it. I wonder if he sprays it on her before they go out, if she holds up her wrists and bares her throat for him.

'What are you going to do with it?' Lisa says.

'We could bring it into school,' I say, and all at once my heart is racing again. 'We could bring it into school and spray it in his lesson. We could see what he does.'

'You're a fucking psycho,' Donna says, and she laughs, but for the first time ever it's tinged with awe.

'You can't,' Tanya's saying, 'I'm not having anything to do with this,' but we're all ignoring her now.

'Me and Lisa have Spanish tomorrow,' I say, 'straight after lunch. We'll do it then. Right, Leese?'

'What do you think he'll do?' Lisa says, wide-eyed.

'Maybe,' I say, 'he'll keep us behind after class and shag our brains out on his desk.' I say it as if I'm joking, and she and Donna laugh, and I laugh too, but I think of the condom hidden in my pocket and the tingling feeling returns.

*

That night, I lie in bed and squeeze my eyes closed and play the scene of them meeting in Granada with more intensity than ever before, and when I get to the part where he undoes her halter-neck top and eases her skirt off and lies her down on the bed, my whole body starts shaking.

The next day in Spanish, we did it, just as we'd planned. Before class started, we huddled over my bag and sprayed the Poison, unknotting our ties to mist it in the hollow of our throats. We were feverish with excitement.

He didn't know how close to him we'd got.

I had his condom with me too. I'd slept with it under my pillow, and now it was zipped into the pocket of my school skirt. I could feel the foil edge rubbing against my thigh when I crossed my legs.

Mr Knox came in, sat on the edge of his desk and asked us what we'd been doing over the weekend.

My heart was thumping. I suddenly wished I'd prepared something clever to say, something that would get his attention, or make him smile, but I hadn't, and I found myself saying the first thing that came into my head, just to be the one that spoke.

'Voy de compras,' I said.

'I'm sure you go shopping all the time, but in this instance it was in the past tense.' He looked straight at me as he said it, his crinkled eyes, a teasing smile. He seemed surprised, or amused, to see me talking. I was never one of the confident ones who spoke up in class without prompting. 'Otra vez, Señorita.'

Señorita. I'd never been one of the girls he called *señorita* before. I imagined he'd called Davina *señorita*. His accent in Spanish was rolling and sexy. Hers would be too, of course. They'd probably had conversations of their own, over and above everyone else's heads.

'Fui de compras,' I said, locking eyes with him.

'Muy bien, fuiste de compras, y qué compraste?'

'What did I buy?' The cloying smell of the perfume was making me dizzy, and I couldn't seem to straighten my thoughts.

'Sí – qué compraste?'

'Compré – compré un nuevo perfume.'

'Muy bien.' He grinned at me. 'Fuiste de compras, y compraste un nuevo perfume. Muy bien.'

'Do you want to smell it, Mr Knox?' Lisa blurted.

'Lisa!' I hissed, delighted and appalled.

'Gracias, Lisa, pero no.'

'Are you sure? I think you'd like it.'

'Gracias, Lisa. Who's next?' He gazed around the room, waiting for someone else to put their hand up. I'd said it: I couldn't believe I'd said it. I felt the colour rising to my face. Lisa was stifling a fit of giggles beside me, but I ignored her and kept my eyes on Mr Knox. He hadn't flinched.

At the end of class, we hung about, taking our time to pack our bags and wondering if he'd keep us behind, but he didn't. We left the room and fell into each other's arms in fits of giggles, but we were exaggerating, both of us kidding ourselves that we weren't disappointed. Or at least I was. Maybe for Lisa it was just a big joke. I don't know what I'd expected, exactly, but I'd expected something – a moment of recognition, something.

My last lesson of the day was Maths, where I sat with Tanya – none of our other friends were taking Higher Maths. We walked out of school together. Tanya lived up by Stormont, and it was out of my way, but I sometimes walked home with her anyway. My mum had gone back to work since my dad moved out, and I didn't like going back to an empty house. And today there was the increased attraction of knowing that this was the way Mr Knox must drive home.

We walked down Wandsworth and crossed the busy junction, then up the Upper Newtownards Road. When we got to the traffic lights at Castlehill Road, by Stormont Presbyterian, I kept us hanging about. I made sure I was standing facing the traffic. I was waiting for the Alfa Romeo to pass us. I knew in my bones that it would, knew that it had to. When it did, I turned to watch it and didn't take my eyes from it until it was gone completely from sight. And by the time I turned back, something inside me had shifted.

I spent an hour that night learning extra French vocab and practising my Spanish tenses, determined to impress him the following day, to make him notice me. The next day, I walked home with Tanya again, and the day after that, and pretty soon I was walking home with her every day. It was a twenty-minute walk from school to hers, and most days by the time we reached the Upper Newtownards Road his car would be long gone. But I took to noticing which days he held his after-school language club for sixth-formers, or had staff meetings, and on those days I'd try to time our journey, persuading Tanya to come to the Mini-Market with me and killing time there choosing sweets and looking at the magazines, then lingering at the traffic lights by the church in the hope of seeing his car.

On the days that I did, even just a flash of it as it sped past through a green light, I'd feel I was flying all the way home.

Lisa and Donna were friends again, and Lisa still didn't invite me on their Cairnburn nights, but suddenly I didn't care. Three Saturday evenings in a row I let my mum think I was going to Lisa's, and I walked the whole way to Mr Knox and Davina's house, and I walked past two, three, four, five times and saw both cars in their driveway and the lights in their windows and once even caught a glimpse of him in an upstairs room.

It had to happen. I knew it had to happen.

The days you were most likely to see his car, I'd worked out, were Tuesdays and Wednesdays, and one Wednesday, as I kept Tanya hanging about at the end of her road, Mr Knox's Alfa Romeo finally pulled up at the lights.

He was right beside us. Metres away. It was real. It was happening. For a moment, I couldn't breathe. 'There he is,' I said, and Tanya followed my gaze and said, 'No, wise up, what are you doing?'

'Mr Knox!' I yelled, and I waved at the car. 'Mr Knox!'

His windows were wound halfway down – he was smoking – and he ducked to look out, then pressed a button to wind them down fully. 'Hello?' he said. 'What is it, is everything okay?'

'Mr Knox,' I said, 'We need a lift, will you give us a lift?'

'Stop it!' Tanya hissed at me.

'Please, Mr Knox!' I said. 'We're really late and it's important.'

The lights were still red, but any moment they'd go amber, and green.

'Please, Mr Knox,' I said. 'You have to, please, you have to.' I had taken to wearing a dab of Poison every day I had a French or Spanish lesson – even though Lisa told me I was a weirdo – and I could still smell the perfume, Davina's perfume, on me, and I wondered if he could too, creeping from me in a slow green spiral.

He took a drag of his cigarette and dropped it out of the window. 'Where are you going?'

Tanya hissed again and grabbed my arm, but I wrenched it free. The lights were amber, and, as they turned green, I was opening the passenger seat and getting in. There I was, in Mr Knox's Alfa Romeo. It was happening.

'Where do you need to go?' he said again, and I said, 'Anywhere.' He looked at me and raised an eyebrow and snorted with laughter, and I thought he might tell me to get out, but he didn't, he just revved the engine and then accelerated away, and in the wing mirror I caught a glimpse of Tanya's stricken face, open-mouthed, and I looked at Mr Knox beside me – Mr Knox, I was there, now, finally, in Mr Knox's car, me and Mr Knox – and I started laughing too.

Afterwards, I couldn't resist telling Tanya. I told her how he kissed me, gently at first, and his lips were soft. Then harder, with his tongue. I told her how he undid my tie and unbuttoned my shirt, and how his fingers were cool on my skin. I told her how he slipped his hand underneath my skirt and traced his fingertips up, then hooked his fingers under my panties and tugged them down.

'He didn't,' she said, big-eyed and scared, and I promised her, 'Yes, he did.' And her shock spurred me on, and I said how it hurt at the start. I said there was blood. I said it was in the back seat of his Alfa Romeo, in a cul-de-sac near the golf club, and he'd spread his jacket out first and afterwards he'd smoked a cigarette.

Once I'd told Tanya, I had to tell Donna, and Lisa, and when Lisa looked at me with slitted eyes and said I was lying, I got out the condom and showed them: as proof, I said, he'd given it me for next time.

I hadn't counted on Tanya blubbering it all to her mother – all of it, including the time we went to his house. We got in such trouble for that, but the trouble he was in was worse.

Even though I cracked as soon as my mum asked me, told her that I'd made it all up, she didn't believe me, couldn't understand why I'd make it up or how I'd even know what to make up in the first place. In a series of anguished phone calls, she and Tanya's mother decided Mr Knox had an unhealthy hold over me, over all of us.

There's no smoke, they agreed, without fire.

They contacted the headmistress, and that was that: Mr Knox was called before the governors and forced to resign, and I was sent to a counsellor who tried to make me talk about my parents' divorce. And then, in the autumn, we heard that Davina had left Mr Knox, had taken her babies and gone back to her mother's. It must have been her worst nightmare come true, the merest suggestion that her husband, the father of her two children, would do it again. She, more than anyone else, would have known there was no such thing as innocence.

I think she was right.

I don't believe it was a one-off.

What happened that day is that he drove me five minutes up the road, then pulled a U-turn at the garage and drove back down the other side and made me get out not far from where he'd picked me up and said, 'Now this was a one-off, you know,' and laughed. But I can still see his expression as he dropped me off: the half-smile, the eyebrow raised even as he said it wasn't to happen again.

It had happened before. And there's a certain intensity that only a fourteen- or fifteen-year-old girl can possess: I would have redoubled my efforts at snaring him. If only I hadn't told Tanya.

*

I lifted my glass of wine and took a sip, and then another. Mr Knox and Melissa were still giggling over the cocktail menu, flicking back and forth through the pages. 'Excuse me,' I said, turning to the bar and addressing the nearest barman. He didn't hear me, carried on carving twists of orange peel. 'Excuse me,' I said again, louder. He raised his finger: one moment. But I carried on. 'You see the couple over there? By the window? The man with the black hair and the blonde girl?' He frowned and put the orange down, looked at them, then back at me. 'Can I pay for their drinks?' I blurted.

'You'd like to buy them a drink?'

'Yes, whatever they're having. All of it. I want to pay for all of it.'

'I'll just get the bar manager for you. One moment, please.'

My heart was pounding. It was impulsive, and utterly stupid. My friends hadn't even arrived yet, we'd still be sitting here when Mr Knox asked for his bill in a drink or so's time, and how would I explain it to them, or to him, because the barman would point me out as the one who'd paid for it. Even if I asked them not to let on, not to give me away, my name would be on the credit-card slip, so he'd know. Or would my name mean anything to him, all these years later? Surely it would. Surely it must.

I swivelled on my stool to look at them again. Melissa, with her blonde hair and pouting glossy lips and blue eyes, didn't look very much like him. She didn't look much like Davina either, come to that. They were mock-arguing about something now. She flicked her hair and cocked her head and put her hands on her waist, a pantomime of indignation, and he took her bare upper arms and squeezed them, shaking her lightly, and she squealed, then threw her head back in laughter as he leant in to murmur something in her ear.

She had to be his daughter. She had to be.

'Ma'am, excuse me?' The bar manager was leaning across the bar, attempting to get my attention. 'Excuse me?'

'Sorry,' I said. 'I was miles away.'

She had to be his daughter.

'I understand you'd like to buy a drink for the couple by the window?'

'No,' I said. 'I'm sorry, I was mistaken. I mean, I thought they were someone else.'

'No problem,' he said, smooth, professional. 'Is there anything else I can do for you?'

I looked at him. He waited, head politely inclined. I almost asked, 'Can you find out their names?' Then I realized that, either way, I didn't want to know.

ROSE TREMAIN

The Closing Door

The children assembled at the station barrier.

Their trunks had been sent on ahead of them, so what they had with them were small suitcases, as though they might have been going away for the weekend. But the youngest of the children was ten years old, and it was from the violent weeping of this one girl that it was possible to imagine the long stretch of boarding school time to which the waiting train would carry them.

She was a stumpy little person, optimistically named Patience. The elastic of her grey school hat dug into her dimpled chin. Her mother, Marjorie, held her close and the hat was knocked to the back of her head, revealing a disorderly festoon of brown curls. Marjorie pressed her mouth to these curls, kissing them and trying at the same time to whisper words of courage, but it was very difficult for her. She felt herself to be embarking on a furiously misguided enterprise. It was the early autumn of 1954. She had surely not nurtured and fed her War Baby and single-handedly kept her from all harm and depredation in order to surrender her to this expensive school . . .

'Why do I have to go? *Why?*' wailed Patience.

'Darling,' said the mother, 'I hate it, too. Hate it as much as you do. What am I going to do when I get home and you're not there?'

But this was the wrong thing to say, absolutely wrong. It was what she felt, but should never have said, for it only brought on a new Niagara of tears in Patience. For now, not only was the child going to suffer the loss of her mother; she was also going to have to imagine this mother in distress, crying probably, sitting by the gas fire with a cup of tea and weeping, forgetting to make herself any supper, forgetting everything but this awful separation . . .

What Marjorie should have said, but could not say, was that her parents-in-law had insisted upon Patience going to what they called a 'reputable school'. They had not thought any of the London day schools were reputable enough. Children only learned to become responsible adults, they believed, if you sent them away from home. No matter if these children suffered a bit. Who in the world had not suffered? And who, indeed, more than they, who had lost their only son, Timothy, in the last week of the war?

'Tim would have wanted it,' they'd told Marjorie kindly but firmly. 'Tim despised mollycoddling. Tim would have insisted upon it. He would have wanted us to pay the fees, and we will. And you know, Marjorie dear, Tim was a very wise young man. He was almost always right.'

But she couldn't lay the responsibility for the separation on them, couldn't alienate Patience from her grandparents, because it wasn't fair on them. She was all that remained to them of Timothy. She even resembled him, with the same chunky body and disobedient hair. Marjorie saw how much they loved to stroke Patience's curls, remembering their son. They yearned to be as proud of Patience as they had been of him, and they believed, somehow, that boarding school was the key to bringing this about.

In the group of children and parents who surrounded her, Marjorie now sensed a movement. The ticket barrier had been opened and the moment was coming when all the girls would have to get on the train.

She had paid no heed to any of these people. They were nothing to her. But now she looked round at them, to see how they were managing this moment. She saw, with a feeling of relief, that there was a little crying going on among the other children. One of them, a tall, slender girl of twelve or thirteen, carrying a new lacrosse stick, had pressed the net basket of the stick over her face and was sobbing into that, while a tall man, evidently her father, helplessly patted her shoulder.

'Come on, old thing,' she heard this father say, 'think of midnight feasts and all that malarkey. Think of being Captain of Junior Lax! And half-term will be here in a jiffy.'

'I miss Jasper!' cried the girl.

'I know you do. But we'll take good care of him. Mummy will take him for a walk every morning.'

So then, thought Marjorie, if it's hard for these two, then probably it's hard for everybody, except that for most of them there might be 'Mummy and Daddy' and not just 'Mum' as Patience called her.

Patience had never known 'Daddy'. She had often been shown a black-and-white photograph of him, wearing his Irish Guards uniform, holding her in his arms in 1944: tiny Patience, swaddled in a white lace shawl, clasped in Daddy's broad-fingered hands. He had been smiling for the camera – the anxious smile of the proud father, proud soldier – but that was the last picture ever taken of him.

Since then, for Patience, there had only been Mum: Mum alone in her small flat with her part-time job in a bridal shop, Mum who had never seen anything of the world, Mum who saved string and borrowed her books from Boots' Library, Mum who loved her daughter more than life.

And it was coming nearer, nearer, the moment when Marjorie would have to unwind Patience's arms from round her waist and lead her forwards to the barrier. She tried to stand a bit more upright, but the weight of Patience clinging to her was implacable, as though she had been roped to the ground. And she thought, I am bent like an old person, bent down by the gravity of love.

'Come on, angel,' she said, as firmly as she could. 'I'm going to come with you as far as the ticket man. But then you're going to have to be brave and get on the train. Everybody else is going now. See? You can't be left behind.'

'I want to be left behind!' screamed Patience. And now she raised one of her determined little fists and hit Marjorie on the shoulder. 'I hate you for making me go!' she cried out. 'I hate you. I hate you!'

Marjorie knew that this now risked to become what Tim would have called 'a scene', and that the other parents would pity her, or even despise her, for not crushing it the minute it started, so, with surprising strength, she grabbed Patience by the fist that had struck her and turned the sobbing child round to face the trains and the great vaulted station roof above them, still black from the years of war.

'Patience,' she said, 'nothing you do or say is going to change the fact that you are going away to school. You are going to learn Latin and Greek and do chemistry experiments and act in plays and read Shakespeare and run round a huge park in the sunshine. You are going to be happy there. I'm going to write to you every day. *Every day*. But now you're going to say goodbye to me. Here's your train ticket. You are going to say goodbye to me now.'

Patience's crying ceased quite suddenly. She looked shocked, as though Marjorie had slapped her. She stood still and let her face be wiped with a handkerchief. She was shuddering and pale, with eyes puffy and red, but Marjorie knew that now she would find the courage to board the train.

Marjorie kissed her on both cheeks, set her hat gently back on her curls, mortified to notice how the wretched elastic cut into the flesh of her chin, and trying to ease it with her finger, but with her heart beating in relief that, at last, the child was attempting to master her grief.

'Well done,' she said. 'Well done, Patience.'

Then she watched her go, joining the cluster of grey-uniformed children walking to this new piece of their lives and trying not to look back, but looking back all the same and waving and then suddenly running on. She saw that the ticket puncher at the barrier was trying to laugh and joke with the boarding school girls, and she thought, Acts of kindness are not rare. We still live in austere times, but people have not exhausted their reserves of compassion.

She stood quite still until she could no longer see Patience.

In fact she hadn't been able to catch sight of her for a long moment because two women, two mothers of departing girls, their arms linked together, had barged in front of her and were waving and calling out to their girls: 'Bye, darlings! Bye! Bysey-bye!'

Something about these women – their expensive suits, perhaps, their gloves and small velvet hats, their ridiculous *Bysey-byes*, or was it their seeming gladness of heart? – awoke in Marjorie a feeling of instant dislike. She wanted to push by them, elbow them out of her way, trample on their feet, even, so that she might catch a last glimpse of Patience climbing onto the train or straining out of a window. But they somehow prevented her. They had taken up a position and would not be moved from it. Marjorie was forced to stand where she was, unable to see anything. Then a whistle was blown and the train's great engine hissed into life and it was gone, and Patience was gone.

When the train could no longer be seen, the women hugged each other, laughing delightedly.

'Right,' said one, 'now we can get on with life!'

'What a blessed relief!' said the other.

They turned and walked past Marjorie. She saw that one of them was dazzlingly pretty, with great blue eyes like Bette Davis. The other looked plain by comparison, but had a beautiful slim figure like Wallis Simpson, and you got from them the idea that they complemented each other, and knew it, and now, freed from their children, they were going to walk together back into lives they believed to be wonderful.

They went out of the station and walked towards the Number 11 bus stop. Marjorie followed. To get home to North London, she would have taken the tube, but the thought of going home – to sit alone and imagine Patience arriving in a cold dormitory and unpacking her trunk and putting her new tartan rug on some hard, iron bed – dismayed her. She preferred to shadow these strangers. She wanted to observe what life it was they were going to get on with.

They sat on the top deck of the bus, at the very front, looking down in fascination on the scurry of the suited City men. They took off their little velvet hats and shook out their shiny hair.

Marjorie sat near the back, pretending to gaze out of the window, but in fact barely letting her eyes stray from the women, who were now smoking cigarettes jammed into long black cigarette holders. She couldn't hear what they were saying to each other, but they reminded Marjorie of people at a party, laughing, waving their cigarettes about, having a good time.

Marjorie began to wonder if their children, freed from them and now being carried through the Hertfordshire countryside, were also laughing. She tried to imagine them: 'Little Bette', 'Little Wallis'. Laughing as they sped back towards their dormitory nights, their cold classrooms, their thin food.

Or was the lost and scented presence of these mothers already making them sad? Did they suspect, or even *know*, that, as soon as the train had gone, they would rush back to the grown-up world with such terrible alacrity?

On crawled the bus, going towards Victoria and the river. These were not parts of London Marjorie often visited. Nothing much ever seemed to lead her south or west. All she'd known for ten years was staying in one place and caring for Patience and working in the bridal shop. On work days, Patience would come to the shop after school and sit quietly in one of the fitting cubicles, reading her book, or else help with pinning and measuring, while the brides stood on little stools, staring at themselves, trying on veils, their eyes brimming with tears of hope.

She wondered how much further the women would travel. And when they got off at last, what would she do? She was miles from Muswell Hill. The September afternoon was already shading to evening. Perhaps she should get off at Victoria Station and begin her long tube ride home? For what right did she have to sit on a bus, passing judgement on strangers?

But she did not get off. She thought, If I see where they live, then, perhaps, I will know. Then, I will get some picture of the life their children prevent them from living. I will understand what it is – by loving Patience so desperately – I've missed and might one day have.

As the bus approached Sloane Square, the women stubbed out their cigarettes and got up and came swaying along towards her, smelling of expensive perfume and of all the smoke they had inhaled. The great blue eyes of Bette stared at her for a moment, and she imagined her whispering to Wallis, 'Wasn't that the woman with the caterwauling child at the station? What's she doing on our bus?' But they went down the stairs and walked away. They did not look up.

Marjorie jumped off the bus just as it was pulling away. She stumbled, but didn't fall. Keeping her distance, dreading to be seen for the busybody she was, Marjorie followed Bette and Wallis to a square of tall red-brick houses, arranged around private gardens. Bette had a key to one of the houses and the two women went in and the black front door was shut.

Marjorie stood some distance away, in the shadow of a lilac tree that hung over the railings of the gardens. She stared at the closed door.

After ten or fifteen minutes, a taxi stopped, not in front of Bette's house, but just opposite to where Marjorie was standing. A man wearing a City suit got out. He didn't pay the cab driver, but just walked hastily away. Marjorie pressed herself deeper into the shade of the lilac tree. The taxi drove on, and as it passed her, Marjorie could just glimpse the silhouette of a young woman, visible in the rear window.

Now, she saw the man ring the bell of Bette's house. He looked anxiously behind him, as though to make sure that the taxi had gone. Then the door was opened and Marjorie saw Wallis, whose husband this man must be, throw her arms round his neck and draw him inside the house.

'Darling!' she heard her say. 'Darling, come in!'

Then the door closed once more.

Marjorie stared at the door until the darkness shrouded it. Lights came on in the house and she looked up at these, but could see no one at any of the windows. So here, she thought, is where this has to end – with the closing of a door. How much more did I imagine I was ever going to know?

Yet she felt that she had seen something important, something that might end in ruin.

She imagined Wallis, ten or eleven years ago, wearing her bridal gown, standing on a little plinth, while seamstresses crawled on the floor, tucking and pinning. She imagined her trying on different veils and, as she laid them over her shiny hair, dreaming of her marvellous future with this man, this man in his City suit, with a safe job and a beautiful income.

But now, it was all beginning to slip away. She wasn't pretty enough for him, not as pretty as her friend Bette, not as young and pretty as the girl in the taxi. Today, freed from her child or children, she had imagined she was moving back into the selfish, grown-up life she loved, but, unknown to her, that life had turned its back and was moving away from her.

It was late now. Marjorie left the square and walked until she found a telephone box. She counted out some money and fed it into the slot – almost all the coins she had in her purse – hoping it would be enough.

She had the number of the school scribbled down on a piece of paper. She dialled it and pressed Button A when a voice answered. She asked to speak to Patience. But it was the school secretary who had picked up the telephone and this severe woman informed Marjorie curtly that calls from parents were not allowed, except in emergencies.

'This is an emergency,' said Marjorie. 'I'm ringing from a coin box and I have only limited money. My daughter was very, very upset when she got on the train. I need to know that she is all right. So please go and find her as quickly as you can.'

She was told to wait. Time passed and it got very dark in the box, dark and cold. Marjorie emptied her purse and found one more shilling in it.

At last, a subdued voice said: 'Mum? Why are you ringing from a phone box? Where are you?'

Hearing this little voice, far away, and with only a shilling of time left to her, Marjorie felt exhausted, on the very edge of collapse. She wanted to say, 'I don't know where I am. I'm miles from anywhere familiar to me. I don't know what I'm meant to do now.'

Instead, she said brightly: 'I'm fine. I just went on a little walk, to clear my head. I wanted to know you're all right. Are you all right?'

'Yes. I put my new rug on my bed, like you told me to.'

'Good girl,' said Marjorie. 'Is the dorm OK?'

'Yes.'

'Good. That's what I wanted to know. Oh, and one more thing I wanted to say: I love you very much.'

'I love you, too, Mum,' said Patience. 'But I'm trying not to think about you. It's better if I don't.'

'I understand, darling,' said Marjorie. 'I completely understand. That's very sensible of you. What matters now is getting on with your life.'

HELEN OYEYEMI

if a book is locked there's probably a good reason for that, don't you think

Every time someone comes out of the lift in the building where you work you wish lift doors were made of glass. That way you'd be able to see who's arriving a little before they actually arrive and there'd be just enough time to prepare the correct facial expression. Your new colleague steps out of the lift dressed just a tad more casually than is really appropriate for the workplace and because you weren't ready you say, 'Hi!' with altogether too much force. She has: a heart-shaped face with subtly rouged cheeks, short, straight, neatly cut hair, and eyes that are long rather than wide. She's black, but not local, this new colleague who wears her boots and jeans and scarf with a bohemian aplomb that causes the others to ask her where she shops. 'Oh, you know, thrift stores,' she says with a chuckle. George at the desk next to yours says, 'Charity shops?' and the newcomer says, 'Yeah, thrift stores . . .'

Her accent is New York plus some other part of America, somewhere Midwest. And her name's Eva. She's not quite standoffish, not quite . . . but she doesn't ask any questions that aren't related to her work. Her own answers are brief and don't invite further conversation. In the women's toilets you find a row of your colleagues examining themselves critically in the mirror and then, one by one, they each apply a touch of rouge. Their make-up usually goes on at the end of the workday, but now your co-workers are demonstrating that Eva's not the only one who can glow. When it's your turn at the mirror you fiddle with your shirt. Sleeves rolled up so you're nonchalantly showing skin, or is that too marked a change?

Eva takes no notice of any of this preening. She works through her lunch break, tapping away at the keyboard with her right hand, holding her sandwich with her left. You eat lunch at your desk too, just as you have ever since you started working here, and having watched her turn down her fourth invitation to lunch, you say to her: 'Just tell people you're a loner. That's what I did, anyway.'

Eva doesn't look away from her computer screen and for a moment it seems as if she's going to ignore you but eventually she says: 'Oh . . . I'm not a loner.'

Fair enough. You return to your own work, the interpretation of data. You make a few phone calls to chase up some missing paperwork. Your company exists to assist other companies with streamlining their workforce for optimum productivity; the part people like you and Eva play in this is attaching cold hard monetary value to the efforts of individual employees and passing those figures on to someone higher up the chain so that person can decide who should be made redundant. Your seniors' evaluations are more nuanced. They often get to go into offices to observe the employees under consideration, and in their final recommendations they're permitted to allow for some mysterious quality termed 'potential'. You aim to be promoted to a more senior position soon, because ranking people based purely on yearly income fluctuations is starting to get to you. You'd like a bit more context to the numbers. What happened in employee QM76932's life between February and May four years ago – why do the figures fall so drastically? The figures improve again and remain steady to date, but is QM76932 really a reliable employee? Whatever calamity befell them, it could recur in a five-year cycle, making them less of a safe bet than somebody else with moderate but more consistent results. But it's like Susie says: the reason why so many bosses prefer to outsource these evaluations is because context and familiarity cultivate indecision. When Susie gets promoted she's not going to bother talking about potential. 'We hold more power than the consultants who go into the office,' she says. That sounds accurate to you: the portrait you hammer out at your desk is the one that either affirms or refutes profitability. But your seniors get to stretch their legs more and get asked for their opinion, and that's why you and Susie work so diligently towards promotion.

But lately . . . lately you've been tempted to influence the recommendations that get made. Lately you've chosen someone whose figures tell you they'll almost certainly get sacked and you've decided to try to save them, manipulating figures with your heart in your mouth, terrified that the figures will be checked. And they are, but only cursorily; you have a reputation for thoroughness and besides, it would be hard for your boss to think of a reason why you'd do such a thing for a random string of letters and numbers that could signify anybody, anybody at all, probably somebody you'd clash with if you met them. You never find out what happens to the people you assess, so you're all the more puzzled by what you're doing. Why can't you choose some other goal, a goal that at least includes the possibility of knowing whether you reached it or not? Face it; you're a bit of a weirdo. But whenever you feel you've gone too far with your tampering, you think of your grandmother and you press on. Grandma is your dark inspiration. Your mother's mother made it out of a fallen communist state with an unseemly heap of valuables and a strangely blank-slate of a memory when it comes to recalling those hair-raising years. But she has such a sharp memory for so many other things – price changes, for instance. Your grandmother is vehement on the topic of survival and sceptical of all claims that it's possible to choose anything else when the chips are down. The official story is that it was Grandma's dentistry skills that kept her in funds. But her personality makes it seem more likely that she was a backstabber of monumental proportions. You take great pains to keep your suspicions from her, and she seems to get a kick out of that.

But how terrible you and your family are going to feel if, having thought of her as actively colluding with one of history's most murderous regimes, some proof emerges that Grandma was an ordinary dentist just like she said? A dentist subject to the kind of windfall that has been known to materialize for honest, well-regarded folk, in this case a scared but determined woman who held onto that windfall with both hands, scared and determined and just a dentist, truly. But she won't talk about any of it, that's the thing. *Cannot* you could all understand, or at least have sincere reverence for. But *will* not?

Your grandmother's Catholicism seems rooted in her approval of two saints whose reticence shines through the ages: St John of Nepomuk, who was famously executed for his insistence on keeping the secrets of the confessional, and St John Ogilvie, who went to his death after refusing to name those of his acquaintance who shared his faith. In lieu of a crucifix your grandmother wears a locket around her neck, and in that locket is a miniature reproduction of a painting featuring St John of Nepomuk, some tall-helmeted soldiers, a few horrified bystanders, four angels and a horse. In the painting the soldiers are pushing St J of N off the Charles Bridge, but St J of N isn't all that bothered, is looking up as if already hearing future confessions and interceding for his tormentors in advance. *Boys will be boys, Father*, St J of N's expression seems to say. The lone horse seems to agree. It's the sixteenth century, and the angels are there to carry St John of Nepomuk down to sleep on the river bed, where his halo of five stars awaits him. This is a scene your grandmother doesn't often reveal, but sometimes you see her fold a hand around the closed locket and it looks like she's toying with the idea of tearing it off the chain.

Suspect me if that's what you want to do.

What's the point of me saying any more than I've said . . . is it eloquence that makes you people believe things?

You are all morons.

These are the declarations your grandmother makes, and then you and your siblings all say: 'No, no, Grandma, what are you talking about, what do you mean, where did you get this idea?' without daring to so much as glance at each other.

You were in nursery school when your grandmother unexpectedly singled you out from your siblings and declared you her protégée. At first all that seemed to mean was that she paid for your education. That was good news for your parents, and for your siblings too, since there was more to go around. And your gratitude is real but so is your eternal obligation. Having paid for most of what's gone into your head during your formative years, there's a sense in which Grandma now owns you. She phones you when entertainment is required and you have to put on formal wear, take your fiddle over to her house and play peasant dances for her and her chess-club friends. When you displease her she takes it out on your mother, and the assumption within the family is that if at any point it becomes impossible for Grandma to live on her own, you'll be her live-in companion. (Was your education really that great?) So when you think of her, you think that you might as well do what you can while you can still do it.

Eva's popularity grows even as her speech becomes ever more monosyllabic. Susie, normally so focussed on her work, spends a lot of time trying to get Eva to talk. Kathleen takes up shopping during her lunch break;

she tries to keep her purchases concealed but occasionally you glimpse what she's stashing away in her locker – expensive-looking replicas of Eva's charity-shop chic. The interested singletons give Eva unprompted information about their private lives to see what she does with it, but she just chuckles and doesn't reciprocate. You want to ask her if she's sure she isn't a loner but you haven't spoken to her since she rejected your advice. Then Eva's office fortunes change. On a Monday morning Susie runs in breathless from having taken the stairs and says: 'Eva, there's someone here to see you! She's coming up in the lift and she's . . . crying?'

Another instance in which glass lift doors would be beneficial. Not to Eva, who already seems to know who the visitor is and looks around for somewhere to hide, but glass doors would have come in handy for everybody else in the office, since nobody knows what to do or say or think when the lift doors open to reveal a woman in tears and a boy of about five or so, not yet in tears but rapidly approaching them – there's that lip wobble, oh no. The woman looks quite a lot like Eva might look in a decade's time, maybe a decade and a half. As soon as this woman sees Eva, she starts saying things like, 'Please, please, I'm not even angry, I'm just saying please leave my husband alone, we're a family, can't you see?'

Eva backs away, knocking her handbag off her desk as she does so. Various items spill out but she doesn't have time to gather them up – the woman and child advance until they have her pinned up against the stationery-cupboard door. The woman falls to her knees and the boy stands beside her, his face scrunched up; he's crying so hard he can't see. 'You could so easily find someone else but I can't, not now . . . do you think this won't happen to you too one day? Please just stop seeing him, let him go . . .'

Eva waves her hands and speaks, but whatever excuse or explanation she's trying to make can't be heard above the begging. You say that someone should call security and people say they agree but nobody does anything. You're seeing a lot of folded arms and pursed lips. Kathleen mutters something about 'letting the woman have her say'. You call security yourself and the woman and child are led away. You pick Eva's things up from the floor and throw them into her bag. One item is notable: a leather-bound diary with a brass lock on it. A quiet woman with a locked book. Eva's beginning to intrigue you. She returns to her desk and continues working. Everybody else returns to their desks to send each other emails about Eva . . . at least that's what you presume is happening. You're not copied into any of those emails but everybody except you and Eva seems to be receiving a higher volume of messages than normal. You look at Eva from time to time and the whites of her eyes have turned pink but she doesn't look back at you or stop working. Fax, fax, photocopy. She answers a few phone calls and her tone is on the pleasant side of professional.

An anti-Eva movement emerges. Its members are no longer fooled by her glamour; Eva's a personification of all that's put on earth solely to break bonds, scrap commitments, prevent the course of true love from running smooth. You wouldn't call yourself pro-Eva, but bringing a small and distressed child to the office to confront your husband's mistress does strike you as more than a little manipulative. Maybe you're the only person who thinks so: that side of things certainly isn't discussed. Kathleen quickly distances herself from her attempts to imitate Eva. Those who still feel drawn to Eva become indignant when faced with her continued disinterest in making friends. Who does she think she is? Can't she see how nice they are?

'Yes, she should be grateful that people are still asking her out,' you say, and most of the people you say this to nod, pleased that you get where they're coming from, though Susie, Paul and a couple of the others eye you suspiciously. Susie takes to standing behind you while you're working sometimes, and given your clandestine meddling, this watchful presence puts you on edge. It's best not to mess with Susie.

One lunchtime, Eva brings her sandwich over to your desk and you eat together; this is sudden but after that you can no longer mock others by talking shit about Eva; she might overhear you and misunderstand. You ask Eva about her diary and she says she started writing it the year she turned thirteen. She'd just read *The Diary of Anne Frank* and was shaken by a voice like that falling silent, and then further shaken by the thought of all the voices who fell silent before we could ever have heard from them.

'And, you know – fuck everyone and everything that takes all these articulations of moodiness and tenderness and cleverness away. Not that I thought that's how I was,' Eva says. 'I was trying to figure out how to be a better friend, though, just like she was. I just thought I should keep a record of that time. Like she did. And I wrote it from thirteen to fifteen, like she did.'

You ask Eva if she felt like something was going to happen to her, too. 'Happen to me?'

You give her an example. 'I grew up in a city where people fell out of windows a lot,' you say. 'So I used to practise falling out of them myself. But after a few broken bones, I decided it's better just to not stand too close to windows.'

Eva gives you a piercing look. 'No, I didn't think anything was going to happen to me. It's all pretty ordinary teen stuff in there. Your city, though . . . is "falling out of windows" a euphemism? And when you say "fell", or even "window", are you talking about something else?'

'No! What made you think that?'

'Your whole manner is really indirect. Sorry if that's rude.'

'It's not rude,' you say. You've already been told all about your indirect-ness, mostly by despairing ex-girlfriends.

'Can I ask one more question about the diary?'

Eva gives a cautious nod.

'Why do you still carry it around with you if you stopped writing in it years ago?'

'So I always know where it is,' she says.

Susie gets restless.

'Ask Miss Hoity-Toity if she's still seeing her married boyfriend,' she says to you.

You tell her you won't be doing that.

'The atmosphere in this office is so *stagnant*,' Susie says, and decides to try and make Miss Hoity-Toity resign. You don't see or hear anyone openly agreeing to help Susie achieve this objective, but then they wouldn't do that in your presence, given that you now eat lunch with Eva every day. So when Eva momentarily turns her back on some food she's just bought and looks round to find the salad knocked over so that her desk is coated with dressing; when Eva's locker key is stolen and she subsequently finds her locker full of condoms; when Eva's sent a legitimate-looking file attachment that crashes her computer for a few hours and nobody else can spare the use of theirs for even a minute, you just look straight at Susie even though you know she isn't acting alone. Susie's power trip has come so far along that she goes around the office snickering with her eyes half-closed. Is it the job that's doing this to you all? Or do these games get played no matter what the circumstances? A new girl has to be friendly and morally upright; she should open up, just pick someone and open up to them, make her choices relatable. 'I didn't know he was married' would've been well received, no matter how wooden the delivery of those words. Just give us *something* to start with, Miss Hoity-Toity.

Someone goes through Eva's bag and takes her diary; when Eva discovers this she stands up at her desk and asks for her diary back. She offers money for it: 'Whatever you want,' she says. 'I know you guys don't like me, and I don't like you either, but come on. That's two years of a life. Two years of a life.'

Everyone seems completely mystified by her words. Kathleen advises Eva to 'maybe check the toilets' and Eva runs off to do just that, comes back empty-handed and grimacing. She keeps working, and the next time she goes to the printer there's another print-out waiting for her on top of her document: RESIGN & GET THE DIARY BACK.

Eva demonstrates her seriousness regarding the diary by submitting her letter of resignation the very same day. She says goodbye to you but you don't answer. In time she could have beaten Susie and Co., could have forced them to accept that she was just there to work, but she let them win. Over what? Some book? Pathetic.

The next day, George 'finds' Eva's diary next to the coffee machine, and when you see his ungloved hands you notice what you failed to notice the day before – he and everybody except you and Eva wore gloves indoors all day. To avoid leaving fingerprints on the diary, you suppose. Nice; this can only mean that your co-workers have more issues than you do.

You volunteer to be the one to give Eva her diary back. The only problem is you don't have her address, or her phone number – you never saw her outside work. HR can't release Eva's contact details; the woman isn't in the phone book and has no online presence. You turn to the diary because you don't see any other option. You try to pick the lock yourself and fail, and your elder sister whispers: 'Try Grandma . . .'

'Oh, diary locks are easy,' your grandmother says reproachfully (what's the point of a protégée who can't pick an easy-peasy diary lock?). She has the book open in no time. She doesn't ask to read it; she doubts there's anything worthwhile in there. She tells you that the diary looks cheap; that what you thought was leather is actually imitation leather. Cheap or not, the diary has appeal for you. Squares of floral-print linen dot the front and back covers, and the pages are feather-light. The diarist wrote in violet ink.

Why I don't like to talk any more, you read, and then avert your eyes and turn to the page that touches the back cover. There's an address there, and there's a good chance this address is current, since it's written on a scrap of paper that's been taped over other scraps of paper with other addresses written on them. You copy the address down onto a different piece of paper and then stare, wondering how it can be that letters and numbers you've written with a black pen have come out violet-coloured. Also – also, while you were looking for pen and paper the diary has been unfolding. Not growing, exactly, but it's sitting upright on your tabletop and seems to fill or absorb the air around it so that the air turns this way and that, like pages. In fact, the book is like a hand and you, your living room and everything in it are pages being turned this way and that. You go towards the book, slowly and reluctantly – if only you could close this book remotely – but the closer you get to the book the greater the waning of the light in the room, and it becomes more difficult to actually move; in fact it is like walking through a paper tunnel that is folding you in, and there's chatter all about you: *Speak up, Eva*, and *Eva, you talk so fast, slow down* and *So you like to talk a lot, huh?* You hear: *You do know what you're saying, don't you?* and *Excuse me, missy, isn't there something you ought to be saying right now?* and *You just say that one more time!* You hear: *Shhh* and *So . . . do any of you guys know what she's talking about?* and *OK, but what's that got to do with anything?* and *Did you hear what she just said?*

It's mostly men you're hearing, or at least they sound male. But not all of them. Among the women Eva can be heard shushing herself. You chant and shout and cuckoo call. You recite verse, whatever's good, whatever comes to mind. This is how you pass through the building of Eva's quietness, and as you make that racket of yours you get close enough to the book to seize both covers (though you can no longer see them) and slam the book shut. Then you sit on it for a while, laughing hysterically, and after that you slide along the floor with the book beneath you until you find a roll of masking tape and wind it around the closed diary. Close shave, kiddo, close shave.

At the weekend you go to the address you found in the diary and a grey-haired, Levantine-looking man answers the door. Eva's lover? First he tells you Eva's out, then he says: 'Hang on, tell me again who you're looking for?'

You repeat Eva's name and he says that Eva doesn't actually live in that house. You ask since when, and he says she never lived there. But when you tell him you've got Eva's diary he lets you in: 'I think I saw her on the roof once.' His reluctance to commit to any statement of fact feels vaguely political. You go up onto the rooftop with no clear idea of whether Eva will be there or not. She's not. You look out over tiny gardens, big parking lots and satellite dishes. A glacial wind slices at the tops of your ears. If you were a character in a film this would be a good rooftop on which to battle and defeat some urban representative of the forces of darkness. You place the diary on the roof ledge and turn to go, but then you hear someone shout: 'Hey! Hey – is that mine?'

It's Eva. She's on the neighbouring rooftop. She must have emerged when you were taking in the view. The neighbouring rooftop has a swing set up on it, two seats side by side, and you watch as Eva launches herself out into the horizon with perfectly pointed toes, falls back, pushes forward again. She doesn't seem to remember you even though she only left a few days ago; this says as much about you as it does about her. You tell Eva that even though it looks as if her diary has been vigorously thumbed through, you're sure the contents remain secret. 'I didn't read it, anyway,' you say. The swing creaks as Eva sails up into the night sky, so high it almost seems as if she has no intention of coming back. But she does. And when she does, she says: 'So you still think that's why I locked it?'

LEONE ROSS

The Woman Who Lived in a Restaurant

One high day in February, a woman walks into a two-tier restaurant on a corner of her busy neighbourhood, sits down at the worst table – the one with the blind spot, a few feet too close to the kitchen's swinging door – and stays there.

She stays there forever.

She wears a crisp cotton white shirt with a good collar and cuffs and a soft black skirt that can be hiked up easy. She has careful dreadlocks strung with silver beads – the best hairstyle to take into forever. There is no more jewellery; her skin is naked and moist. She keeps a tiny pair of white socks in her handbag and, in the cold months, she slips them onto her bare feet.

She watches the waiters, puppeting to and fro, the muscles in their asses tightening and relaxing, thumbing coin and paper tips, tumbling up and down the stairs and past her to the kitchen, careful not to touch. The maître d' has a big belly and so does the chef, who is also the owner of the restaurant. Nobody holds it against them; they work very long hours and the chef's food is extremely fine; this is not fat, it is gravitas.

'Smile, smile,' the maître d' says to everybody, staff and customers alike; he has been here the longest and she never hears him say much more in front of house, although you would have thought he might.

She goes to the restroom in the mornings and evenings, to wash her skin and to put elegant slivers of fresh oatmeal soap to her throat and armpits. She nods at the diners, who bring children and lovers and have arguments and complain and compliment the food – and some get drunk, and then there's the sound of vomiting from the bathroom that makes her wince. So many come to propose marriage she can spot them on sight:

the men lick their lips and brandish their moustaches and crunch their balls in their hands. They all flourish the ring in the same way, like waiters setting down the *pièce de résistance* – fresh steak tartare or twisted sugar confections that attract the light. Their women – provided they are pleased – do identical neck rolls and shoulder raises and matching squeals. Like a set of jewellery she thinks, all shining eyes, although one year a woman became very angry and crushed her good glass into the table top.

'I told you not to kill it with this lovey-dovey shit!' she yelled at the mustachioed man, and stalked out. The man sat with the napkin under his chin, making a soft, white beard. The napkins are of very good quality.

'Hush,' said the restaurant woman, like she was rocking the small pieces of the leftover man. The people around them ate on, and tried to ignore the embarrassed, shattered glass.

'What shall I do?' he asked, rubbing his mouth with the napkin.

'Love is what it is.' She stretched one finger skyward, as if offering an architectural suggestion.

He hurried out, his shoes making scuffling noises, like mice.

These days she must rock from cheek to cheek to prevent sores. But mostly she sits and waits and smiles to herself and her lips remind the male waiters of the entrails of a plum, so juicy and broken open. They see that she is not young, although she has good breasts and healthy breath. Watch how she taps her fingers on the table and handles the glass stem, they whisper. This is a woman of authority. She has been somebody. Some of the waitresses weep, but most of them hiss that she is a fool.

'Mind the chef kill you,' the line cook whispers.

One waitress deliberately spills fragrant, scalding Jamaican coffee onto the woman's wrist. The woman rubs her burned flesh and smiles. The waitress shudders at her happy brown eyes.

'Stupid bitch,' the waitress hisses. 'Why are you *here*?'

She is fired the next day, as are all waitresses who hate the woman.

A young male waiter fills the vacancy – three years and thirteen hours after the woman arrived to live in the restaurant. She sees him come in for the interview, nervous with his thick curly hair and handsome bow legs.

On his first day, the waiter comes running to the pass to say that he has seen a woman bathing in the restroom sink, and that her body was long and honeyed and gleaming in the early light coming through the back window. He didn't mean to see her, really, he says. He was dying for a piss and opened the wrong door.

What he does not say is this. That when he opened the door, the woman was sitting naked, with her shoulder blades propped up against the wall between the cubicles. Her legs were spread so far apart that the muscles inside her thighs were jumping. She had the prettiest pussy he's ever seen, so perpendicular and soft that he had to shade his eyes and take a breath, and then, without knowing he was capable of such a thing, he stopped and stared.

'Put simply,' he says to his closest friend, that night, while drinking good beer and wine, 'she was too far gone to stop.'

They sigh, together.

The woman, who had been rolling her nipples between her fingers before he came in, put a hand between her legs. At first he thought she was covering herself, but then he saw the expression on her face and realized that this was a lust he'd never seen before. The woman took her second and third fingers and rubbed between her legs so fast and hard that the waiter, who thought he'd seen a woman orgasm before this, suddenly doubted himself and kept watching to make sure. In the dawn, the woman's locks could have been on fire and even the shining tiles on the bathroom floor seemed to ululate to help her.

'Ah,' said the woman. 'Oh.'

The smallest sound, so quiet. It was like a mouthful of truffle or a perfect pomegranate seed on the tongue: of an unmistakeable quality.

Weeks pass, and the new waiter is miserable, not least because he knows now that he has never made a woman orgasm.

'What is she doing here, hardly ever moving from her seat? Does she not have a home?'

'Mind the chef kill you,' they whisper around him.

Despite their warnings he rages on, making the soup too peppery and the napkins rough.

Finally, the maître d' tells him the story, in between cold glasses of water, changing tarnished forks and cutting children's potato cakes into four pieces each. All through it, the waiter tries not to look at the woman under his eyelashes, although when he does, she still glows and when the chef sends her an edible flower salad for her luncheon, he can still smell the salt on her second and third fingers when he puts it down in front of her.

The maître d' explains that the story is in the menus, if you read them closely enough.

The chef is the kind of man who is in love with his work. He has owned the restaurant for twenty-two years and it is everything. He creates ever more beautiful and tasty dishes; he admires the beams and wall fixtures and runs loving fingers over the icy water jugs and bunches of fresh beans in the kitchen. The mushrooms are cleaned with a specially crafted brush. Hours must be spent on the streets and in markets talking with butchers and local fishermen so that the restaurant has the freshest, most rare ingredients. Each tile in the floor has been hand-painted. Each window-sash handmade. He has been known to stroke the carpet on the stairs, and he knows the name and taste buds of every regular customer.

He is a happy and most successful man.

But then he met the gleaming, honeyed woman in a farmers' market. She was buying a creamy goat's cheese and several wild mangoes, and he wasn't ever able to say why, but he stopped to talk and point out the various colours of the dying sun above the market. The gathering day drew purple shadows over the woman, like bruises, and he liked her very much indeed. He thought there was something missing from his life, and that he could get it from her.

At first the chef did not worry, says the maître d' to the young waiter. He knew that he could love, because he loved the restaurant, and though some might say one cannot love a restaurant the way one loves a woman, both take time and attention, so there we are.

'There we are, where?' snaps the waiter. 'We are not anywhere. Why is that woman sitting there for years?'

'You understand nothing,' says the maître d'. 'You should wait for the rest of the story.'

The chef, says the maître d', prepared for change. He would do so-and-so at a different time, so he would be able to kiss the woman. And this or that ingredient – well, after he and the woman became lovers, he would not be able to rise quite so early to collect it, so they would have to make do with another version of the dish. And so on. The chef brought the woman to see the restaurant and she sat on its couches and chairs, and admired its warm stoves and brightly coloured walls. She brought several good and mildly expensive paintings, as obeisance, and very good flowers – bird of paradise and cross-breed orchids – and lovingly arranged them in bowls. But even then, it seemed, she knew something. She stayed out of the kitchen when the chef was busy, even when he smiled and called her in.

'The steam will play havoc with my hair, darling,' she said, for these were the days when she hot-comb straightened it.

'We all knew it was coming, of course,' says the maître d', signalling for the boys to peel the potatoes louder and to bang the pots, so that the chef cannot hear his gossiping. 'We all knew, for after all, which sensible man introduces his girlfriend to his wife?'

Three months after meeting, the sweethearts decided to consummate their affair. On that fated night of intention, the woman arrived for dinner and stayed until one a.m., which was as early as the chef would close. The staff waited to be dismissed, glad for a break and glad for the lovers. The chef tried to stop looking like a cat with several litres of fresh cream – and tried to stop sweating. The woman, ah, so sweet she was, nervous and happy. They were transformed in their anticipation of the lovemaking, like young things, though neither of them young.

They were leaving through the front door when the restaurant moved two inches to the right.

'That's correct. We all felt it, standing there,' says the maître d'. 'It is hard to explain, even today, and the architect who came to see the torn window frames and the shattered tiles said it was an earthquake, albeit a very localized and small one. Electrics twisted, stove mashed, water from burst pipes running down the coral dining room walls. They opened the crooked fridges and out belched rotted fish and fowl, blackened, sweet with ruin, filling the air, making them all choke. So much money lost! Smile, smile, I told them all, but the sound! The plumbers said it was the pipes, and the electrician, she said it was the wiring, but no one knew, except us. The restaurant would not be left on its own, so it was crying.'

'Will you not kiss me,' said the woman, tugging at the chef, but no, he was unable.

'We could go far away from here,' she begged, but he looked at her as if she was mad.

'I would not hurt her,' he said, almost stern.

'A restaurant?' she said, and she tried to fit all her pain into those two words.

'It is a good restaurant,' he said. And turned back to work.

The newly hired waiter interrupted the maître d'. He was almost stuttering in his outrage.

'So-so-so – ?'

The maître d' pulled a pig haunch close to him and began to burn the bristles on the hot stove. It was not his job, but he liked doing it.

'So, the woman came to live here,' he continued. 'She stays here so that she can see the chef, and the restaurant keeps watch.'

'But-but . . .'

'They sit together, between service, and talk. They do not touch.' The maître d' smiled, almost sadly, tossing the hot pig from palm to palm. He shrugged towards the restroom. 'We have seen her too, my friend. It must be terribly frustrating.'

The woman becomes aware that something has changed. Truly, she has seen staff appalled before this. Seen them lounging around her, trying to get her attention. But this young waiter seems more determined, in the way of youth, and he keeps touching her.

'Will you not come to the front door with me?' he says, over her porridge breakfast, sent out strictly at 9.31 a.m. 'There are pink blooms all over the front of the restaurant, and ivy, and it is so very good.'

'You can describe it for me,' she says, smiling and ripping her languid eyes away. There is lavender, sprinkled in an intricate pattern, on top of her porridge.

The next day: 'Come for a walk with me upstairs,' he says. 'To the balcony. It will be good for you to have the air. The chef' – she moves her shoulders in delight at the sound of his name and slices into the waiter's heart – 'the chef, he has gone out to buy vegetables.'

'I know,' she says. 'He tells me everything that he does. But I'll stay here. It will be better.'

'Better than what?'

She laughs, shifts, pats his shoulder.

'Better than missing his return,' she says, as if he is a stupid child. She gestures to the front door, which is clear because it is too early for the madness of diners. 'I will see him with the sun against his back, and he assures me that from that distance, he can see the purple shadows on me. It will give us much pleasure.'

One afternoon, the waiter can control himself no longer. He pulls the woman to her feet, feeling her burning skin beneath his fingers. He is surprised to find the chef suddenly there, standing between them, belly glaring, his best knife tucked behind him. The waiter need say nothing more; his job, perhaps his life, is in jeopardy.

But still he thinks of her. At night, he pulls himself raw. He thinks of her over and above him, and in time the fantasies become vile and violent things. In his desperation he can think of nothing but defiling her, mashing her lips against the wall of his bedroom. He becomes a whisperer, appals himself by hissing at her, like others before him. At first she cannot hear him when he mutters under his breath.

'Stupid bitch,' he says. 'Stupid fucking bitch.' But soon he cares less, and says it when he passes her as he's sweeping, and as he puts filo pastry, with fresh bananas, passion fruit sauce and black pepper ice cream in front of her. 'Stupid bitch, I hope it makes you fat and ugly.'

She looks away, smiling into the distance.

A diner complains.

'Each time I come here, that woman is served something exquisite, off menu. Last week it was out-of-season cherries with kirsch. Last month it was an upside down tomato tart with olive sugar. Why does the chef show such favouritism?'

The young waiter rushes over. 'Madame, that is because she is a stupid bitch, and he is a cruel bastard.'

'Oh my,' says the disgruntled diner.

That evening, the waiter is fired. Before he leaves, he pisses in the fish stew on the stove, throws out a batch of very expensive hybrid vodka and flashes his cock at the calm and waiting woman sitting at the table. She is circling her wrists and pointing her pretty toes under the tablecloth. Her backbone makes a crackling noise.

'What are you waiting for?' he screams at her, as sous chef and maître d' wrestle him out. 'What are you waiting for him to *give* you?'

She answers him, but there is a noise in the walls of the restaurant and so he cannot hear what she says.

In the lateness of the night, she rises from the table. After these many years, she has become attuned to the restaurant, and to her beloved. She can hear the eaves sigh in the wind, feel the dining room chairs sag with relief as the frenetic energy of the day finally draws to a close.

She pushes open the door to the kitchen and steps in, light.

The chef is slumped over a stained steel surface, tired, a good wine at his head. He looks up and smiles at her. It is the best part of his day. The love of the restaurant around him, and now, this sweet woman. She leans on the work surface and faces him, smiling back.

He remembers her complaining, wailing friends. One tried to get the restaurant shut down. Another threatened arson. Her brother, he was the worst. He came to the chef's home, and begged.

'If she does this, my friend, she will give up everything. Home. Job. The chance of children. And worst of all, she will be second best. You make her second best.'

'I know,' the chef said. 'But she is stubborn.'

He has learned to live with guilt. Some days, he thinks it is harder for him. So many of the staff become angry, especially the women. To love them both is tiring. But he has come to respect the woman's choice.

He groans, content, as she steps behind him, puts her arms around him, nestles into the sensitive skin of his neck.

'Hello, my love,' she says.

He reaches behind him, hooks his hands at the small of her back. They look up, towards the ceiling, as if making architectural decisions.

'Has anything changed?' she asks, as she has every night, for years.

They listen to the restaurant, creaking and warm.

'No,' he sighs.

'Ah then,' she says. 'Perhaps, tomorrow.'

They kiss.

It is the same as it always is, except it seems to them both that the kiss deepens and ripens, year on year. First he kisses her eyelids, brushing his lips over lashes and the small wrinkles beginning to sprout nearby. He swallows her breath, and she his. They lick each other like small animals at their mother's hide, nipping, careful, so they do not hurt, or encourage fire. They are slow and careful and respectful, listening to the room around them. He can taste her smile on his lips. She can feel the change in his body, the way his skin thickens when she touches him, the shrug of his shoulders as he controls himself, again. She thinks that if there is one single night when his wanting is gone, she will leave this place – if there is one night when his shoulders flatten and the kiss is the kiss of a brother.

He makes a small, grunting noise against her lips.

'Ah.'

So quiet.

She can feel the kick of his penis against his belly, and the love in his fingertips, as he pulls his face away and kisses her fingers.

She is happy.

Few, she finds, understand.

The woman who lives in the restaurant stays there until her hair turns grey and her muscles soften. The chef dies at home, in his bed, thinking of her and of his restaurant. A week later, the maître d' finds her still and cooling body, her head on the soft white cloth of the table, and thinks again, as he often has done, about slicing off her still-juicy lips and sautéing them in butter to make a pie. He tries to move her body, but finds that her atrophied feet are welded to the floor. He yanks and tugs, calls for help, and several men pull and push, saying, 'Well now, be careful, respect to the lady dead', and all that, but there is no success. Eventually they stop when the restaurant begins to creak and to roll dangerously, like a ship listing on a bad sea.

By the time the maître d' returns with an undertaker and a pickaxe, the woman's feet have become tile like the floor; her body is no longer flesh but velvet, and her eyes are glass beads. In fact, as the maître d' looks on, he sees that the woman has become nothing more than an expensive dining chair, pulled up to the table, and perfect for it.

'Love,' grunts the maître d'. He is very old. He taps the restaurant walls and leaves them to it.

HELEN SIMPSON

Every Third Thought

It happened very fast, without warning. One day everybody started dying. First it was Janey Glazebrook, she woke on a Tuesday in a flood of blood before the school run: bowel cancer. She simply couldn't believe it, she'd had no inkling before except for feeling tired, which, as we all said, let's face it, everybody does. This news, so shocking, was met by talk of Philippa Meekin, Jasmine's mother, who had that very week had an operation to remove a brain tumour. Then Oliver Kitchen was diagnosed with a primary liver tumour and Sadie went to pieces at the school gates, they'd got three under nine and they'd just had the roof taken off for a loft conversion they really couldn't afford so it was utter chaos there. It's like a plague, we all said, an epidemic, a horrible sticky contagion.

'Coincidence,' said my husband Harry when I told him the latest over dinner. 'These things come in waves, you know, like buses, none for ages then three at the same time.' He's some ten years older than me – well, fifteen – so I tried to believe him, as if being older made him more of an expert. I think he married me on the Picasso principle – however old and ugly I get, with any luck I'll still be less old and ugly than him. He's very good at what he does though I couldn't tell you what that is. What I do know is, it takes a lot out of him.

But after all Harry was protected from the bad news by office life. I couldn't even go to Waitrose without bumping into some fresh horror. I'd never had any interest in the subject before, no interest whatsoever. I tend not to dwell on things. Doom and gloom were never my cup of tea, but now they seemed to lurk round every corner.

'Have you heard about Karen Pocock?' said a voice from the other side of the freezer cabinet as I reached in for a packet of organic peas.

'Don't tell me,' I blurted, but there was no stopping this bearer of bad news. Stephanie was to be in the thick of it for some reason. She was always the first to know.

Anyway, this time it was Karen Pocock. 'Karen Pocock? You *must* know Karen Pocock! She was on the PTA the year they raised enough for a climbing frame, she goes round with that funny expression on her face like there's a bad smell.' Karen Pocock, it emerged, had just found out she'd got breast cancer. Six months' chemotherapy ahead of her, no secondaries but two lymph glands involved.

'Yes,' said Stephanie, nodding vigorously. 'And you'll never believe this but that makes five cases of breast cancer now in Heatherside Avenue.'

'*Five?*'

'Five,' nodded Stephanie. 'Including Karen's next door neighbour, can you imagine, she went for tests last week, nothing in her bones but the liver scan seems to show something.'

'Five is a lot,' I marvelled. 'Do you think it might be something environmental?'

'What, ley lines?' said Stephanie. 'I think not. Myself, I put it down to dairy. And the Pill. Cut out cheese and change to condoms, that's what I say! She had a miscarriage too, and they say that ups your –'

'Must dash,' I said, moving away as fast as I could. 'See you at the book club. I've got to get Tillie from tae kwon do in a minute.'

Harry and I have three girls: Chloe, fourteen – she's a worker, she's started revising for her GCSEs already, a year in advance; Anna, she's eleven, nothing worries her, typical middle child, my little couch potato; and Tillie, who's seven. Tillie was crazed on the Narnia books about then, I associate that time with Mr Tumnus and Aslan the lion. I remember reading aloud the chapter where Lucy and Susan watch over Aslan's dead body, and there was a bit where it said, You know that feeling when you've cried yourself to sleep? I can still see Tillie's puzzled round face on the pillow, the way she said, 'No, Mum, I don't know that feeling.' How I beamed with satisfaction at this – smugness, you might call it. Ah well, pride goes before a fall.

It's an odd thing but when someone's been talking to you about breast cancer your own breasts start to fizz and tingle. I wanted to cup mine in my hands right there at the checkout till, and I thought of my girls again.

There's a lot of talk now about how it makes sense to go for pre-emptive surgery if you've got a history of breast cancer in the family. You can have both breasts cut off in case and the wounds covered with skin grafts from the back. 'That would be jumping the gun a bit,' Harry said when I mentioned this to him. Still, his grandmother and one of his cousins died of breast cancer. And his aunt.

Adrenalin was in the air. The usual worry, the good old money worry, the mortgage and so on, was pushed to the back in favour of this fertile new health worry. My next door neighbour told me she now cut out and filed all newspaper columns and magazine articles on cancer – and there are an awful lot of *them* – just in case. 'It doesn't do to dwell on things,' I said to her. 'You could be run over by a bus tomorrow.' But my heart wasn't in it; privately I found myself thinking, that filing business sounds rather a good idea.

'How's Oliver?' I asked Sadie Kitchen the next time I saw her. We were crouched on little wooden chairs waiting in a queue at a parents' evening. It was somewhere in the autumn term, the start of the new school year.

'Not good news,' said Sadie with an unhappy grin. 'We took him into UCH last night. They said. They said, he probably won't last till November.' Her eyes filled. She clenched her face in a horrible helpless smile. I grimaced back and our brimming eyes swam at each other, uselessly.

'They said his tumour's the size of an orange,' she said, blowing her nose. 'I'd just bought a net of oranges for juicing and they went straight in the bin. I'm not touching oranges again, ever.'

I do wish doctors would keep away from food when they're making their comparisons. A prostate gland is the size of a walnut, that sort of thing. Funny what can put you off your food. Tillie wouldn't touch spaghetti after Anna told her it was really dead worms. I used to be crazed on Topic, that chocolate bar with the hazelnuts, I had one on the way back from school every afternoon for years; until there was a court case where a woman bit into one and found a mouse's skull. That completely took the pleasure out of hazelnuts as far as I was concerned.

Somewhere around this time I had to go for a smear. The practice nurse did it, and once she'd finished digging around and had withdrawn those metal salad servers, I realized how jittery I'd been feeling.

'That didn't hurt a bit,' I said as I got dressed. 'Thank you.' Then I told her about the last few weeks, Death abroad with its scythe, and the state of mind this produced in my circle. If I was looking for reassurance, I was knocking at the wrong door.

'Don't tell me,' she said with feeling. She glanced again at my notes. 'Ah, you're just the age that starts to happen. I've been there. It was after a party, two in the morning, I found a lump. I was banging on the door first thing in the morning demanding surgery. Nurses are the worst because they see it all the time.'

'Yes,' I said. 'Of course.'

'Then suddenly it was happening to so many people. All at once. It's quite a shock. I took out a really good life insurance policy. It makes you decide to enjoy things.'

We both looked glum, faced with deserts of vast eternity and the wailing of children left behind.

'The only thing you can do is put your affairs in order,' she said, washing her hands vigorously under the tap. 'Don't leave too much of a mess.'

'But I'm only thirty-six,' I said.

She shrugged.

After that, for some reason everything I watched on television, every conversation I had with anyone seemed to zoom in on you-know-what. Even the children were interested.

'How old do you want to be when you die?' asked Anna over dinner one night.

'A hundred,' said Chloe. 'And I want it to happen when I'm asleep.'

'A hundred and ten!' said Tillie. 'But I want to be awake to see what it's like. As long as it doesn't hurt.'

It must have been some time in October, I'd made a recipe from the paper for pumpkin soup but – like so many pumpkin recipes – it was disappointing, I could tell that from Harry's face. He's very keen on healthy food and no animal fats because of a man at his office having had a heart attack, though I sometimes sneak in a bit of butter for the flavour.

'And would you want to be cremated or buried?' continued Anna.

'That's not very cheerful, darling,' I said.

'What's cremated?' asked Tillie.

'Burnt in a fire,' said Anna, 'so there's nothing left except your ashes.

Then they put them in a box and give it to your husband to keep under the bed.'

'No, your husband scatters the ashes, retard,' said Chloe. 'Over the sea or from a private jet.'

'I don't want to be in the ground if it's like the garden,' said Tillie. 'I hate worms. But I'm scared of fire.'

'Let's change the subject,' I said.

'There's this cool new company,' said Chloe, looking at me from under her eyelashes. She has beautiful green eyes. She knew she was winding me up. '– this company, which packs your ashes into a giant firework and then you go up into the sky and give a lot of people pleasure at the same time.'

'Nang!' said Anna. 'I'm choosing that one.'

'That's *enough*,' said Harry, putting the paper down at last. 'Didn't you hear your mother?'

The book group was no better. There was one meeting at Stephanie's house, I remember, which started with her description of Cheyne-Stokes respiration as she poured the wine.

'It comes on just before the end,' she cried. 'Long gasps of not breathing at all then snorting back in there for a while.'

'None for me thanks,' I said. 'I've put on weight over summer.'

'Ah but is it *good* fat or *bad* fat,' asked the woman who was holding out the bowl of nuts to me.

'I don't know,' I said. 'It's about half a stone.'

'Susan's married to an actuary,' said Stephanie proudly. 'We were saying the group needed new blood and she's it!'

This introduction was met with a buzz of welcome and interest.

'I used to think actuarial work sounded really boring,' said Susan modestly.

Not at all, we assured her; it was *fascinating*. She came under a barrage of excited questions. All I can remember is that it pays to eat sunflower seeds, and that the riskiest decade for tumours starts at the age of forty-five.

'Alan always says that once you reach your fifty-sixth birthday you can breathe again,' she laughed, flowering in the sun of our interest.

'Well it certainly starts earlier than that round here,' cried Stephanie, filling her glass. 'Have you heard the news about Polly Tulloch, girls? She went along to the doctor a bit embarrassed because her wee was looking like beer, very dark, and her pooh had gone white.' She paused. We waited. 'Turns out she has pancreatic cancer,' she concluded, turning down the corners of her mouth like a Greek tragedy mask.

'Who's Polly Tulloch?' I murmured to Juliet, sitting on the sofa beside me.

'I think she does a yoga class with Stephanie,' she whispered back, and I was overtaken by a terrible urge to giggle. I pretended to be coughing on some crisps.

'Is it true what my doctor told me?' Juliet pestered the actuary's wife. 'That three out of four get it?'

'I heard two in three,' added Stephanie.

'Well, but lots of those are over ninety, surely?' said Sally. 'A hundred. Then it's just a case of Anno Domino.'

'Did anyone read the book?' asked Tricia. 'Not to change the subject or anything.'

'*Wuthering Heights*,' said Stephanie witheringly. 'Didn't do a thing for me.'

'Oh no!' cried Tricia. 'Didn't you like Heathcliff? I thought Heathcliff was *amazing*.'

'I don't agree,' said Stephanie. 'Anyway, he dies, for no good reason I could see. What sort of hero's *that*? More wine, anyone?'

But since she'd already told us earlier that our risk of breast cancer rose by 6% for every glass we drank, we all said no.

'No they couldn't get it all out,' said Philippa. Her face was steroid-puffy and she'd just been showing me the scar on her part-shaven scalp. She'd kept the staples from her head and held them out to me in a little Murano glass dish.

'It's very aggressive, apparently,' she said. 'I'm trying to get Greg to see what's happening but he's finding it really hard to, um, take it on board.'

I sipped my coffee. I didn't say anything.

'It's difficult for him,' said Philippa.

'But it's even more difficult for *you*,' I blurted.

Helen Simpson

'Oh I don't know,' she said casually. 'I'm fed up with it. There's been a flood of people I haven't seen for years wanting all the gory details. Stephanie popped by for coffee twice last week, which is as good as having the plague cross painted on your door. I really don't feel up to them.'

'I was wondering whether Jasmine and the twins would like an overnight on Friday,' I said. 'That way they can come trick-or-treating with Tillie.'

'Hallowe'en,' she shuddered, and flashed me a ghastly grin.

'All Saints,' I said feebly.

'I was in Mexico once for the Day of the Dead,' she said, closing her eyes. 'November the first. The family I was staying with took me for a picnic to the graveyard where their relatives were buried and we sat around on tombstones eating little iced sponge cakes baked in the shape of skulls. Keeping them company. Everybody does it there, it had a real party atmosphere.'

'You look tired,' I said. 'Why don't you have a nap? Agnieska's got them till one, hasn't she? How's she working out?'

'I don't know,' said Philippa. 'There seems to be a lot of screaming and shouting but I can't . . . We've not been an au pair family before. I don't know how to do it. Still, I'm sure I'll learn.'

The doorbell rang. It was her next door neighbour with a batch of flapjacks and a request to cut down some overhanging branches from Philippa's cherry tree.

'Absolutely,' said Philippa. 'Blocks the light to your kitchen window as it is.'

'I must dash,' I said. 'Got to collect Tillie from her violin lesson.'

'I can't think what I want to be most,' said Tillie on the way home. 'A skellington. Or a witch. No I don't want to be a witch, all the girls are being witches.'

'Jasmine and the twins are coming trick-or-treating with us,' I said. 'That'll be nice, won't it. I bet they're witches, if they wear the same costumes as last year.'

'I might go as a grim reaper,' said Tillie.

'Not *a* grim reaper, darling,' I corrected her, turning into our road. '*The* grim reaper.'

*

278

After this, bad news flew in like iron filings to a magnet. One of Anna's teachers went off on compassionate leave when her beautiful student daughter was killed in a car accident. The teenage son of Harry's secretary Paula dropped dead of a heart attack during a Sunday morning football match. The woman in the dry cleaner's told me about her husband's seventy-year-old mother who had hanged herself from the banisters after her daughter's slow death from cancer.

It was unbearable. I felt wild with fury when I heard such awful things. I thought, that's just not on. It's one thing if you've had a good innings but Philippa *hadn't* had a good innings or anything like it, and neither had most of these people. We'd been led up the garden path. We'd been living in a fool's paradise. I wanted to make a complaint, write a letter to the manager in no uncertain terms.

Stephanie rang to let me know what she'd chosen for the next book club meeting. It was about a man who had been left paralysed by a stroke but had managed to write his life story by blinking at an amanuensis.

'What a survivor!' said Stephanie admiringly. 'Though of course he died. Now, are you going to Oliver Kitchen's funeral on Saturday?'

'I think we might be away,' I lied. Harry would be working at the weekend and I didn't want to take Tillie and Anna to a funeral. 'Anyway, I don't like it when they say they've just gone into the room next door,' I added. 'Or that they're having a nice cup of tea with their loved ones in heaven. Sorry, are you religious, Stephanie?'

'I wouldn't say I was *overtly* religious. I mean, I don't feel the need to go to church every Sunday or anything like that.' There was a pause; then, 'I believe in something to rely on,' she said, rather stiffly.

'Yes, that would be nice,' I said.

I suppose I could have gone to the doctor for antidepressants or something to cheer me up, but, well, it struck me that it wasn't *me* that things were the matter with. It was all the rest of it, all these dreadful things happening all over the place. It was the whole set-up. *That* was what was the matter. But I did go to the doctor about something else, round about that time.

'When I wake in the night,' I told her, 'I lie there and I can sometimes feel my heart miss a beat. Quite often.'

'Can you describe it a bit more?' she asked, rubbing her eyes and glancing at my notes up on the screen beside her.

'It's like being in a lift and suddenly it plunges down. It's like falling down a lift shaft,' I mumbled. I almost added that it felt like a premonition, but stopped myself.

'That sounds perfectly normal,' she smiled. 'Nothing to worry about, it won't do any harm at all. It's called an extra systole but really it's nothing to worry about.'

'Oh good,' I said. 'I thought I might need a triple bypass or something.'

'There's about as much chance of you needing a triple bypass as of your being run over by a bus,' she scoffed. 'You could try cutting out coffee, see if that helps. Now, anything else?'

I considered asking about my hot knees, a mysterious new ailment which, according to the medical encyclopedia meant either Lyme Disease (though I'd been nowhere near deer) or chlamydia (which would be unlikely at this stage) or – my personal favourite – rheumatoid arthritis. But I decided against.

'No, I'm fine,' I said. 'Now that I know it's only an extra systole and I'm not just slowly dying.'

'Oh we're all doing *that*,' she laughed; and so we parted, on a gust of mutual hilarity.

Extra systole or not, I was still having trouble sleeping. That night I gave up and went downstairs, turning on late-night television only to see real-life surgery and the grey-pink gleam of entrails. When I flicked channels the latest brutal massacre leaped onto the screen, as if there wasn't enough carnage around already from natural causes. So I went up to bed again and lay there, full of chewed food, a great useless carcass, a lump of flesh full of lumps of flesh. At five in the morning I woke up shouting, 'It's a charnel house!'

'What?' said Harry blearily.

'I'm so *sorry* for everybody,' I moaned.

'Worse things happen at sea,' grumbled Harry.

'At sea?'

'Go back to *sleep*.'

Good cheer and spirits and a smiling face turned to the sun all looked simply foolish, I decided the next day, sitting at the front of the bus upstairs looking down over a crowded pavement. Childish. Like believing in fairies. Look at all those people. Why weren't they more worried? Particularly the old ones. Why weren't the old ones all tearing round in a panic? Instead they stood there fussing over three pence change.

I was on my way to visit Harry's mother in the Hawthorn Nursing Home, which is on a dual carriageway, making it impossible to park. Hence the bus. When I got there she was sitting feeding peanuts into her cup of tea, traffic whizzing past the window, her wizened silvery arms like birch bark.

'Hello, Eunice,' I said. 'I've brought you some African violets.'

'Do you like beards on men?' she replied.

'No,' I said. 'I think they hide double chins.'

There was a pause and a cold old blue-eyed stare.

'You know it all, don't you?' she said, and smiled in some version of triumph.

Then she started feeding peanuts into her tea again.

'What's the matter?' she said when she saw me staring. 'Haven't you seen this done before?'

'Old people,' I said to Harry in bed that night. 'How do they do it? They just go on and on. Your mother's eighty-seven. And there's Sadie's husband, forty-one, he went running every morning before work and now he's dead.'

'It's just the roll of the dice,' said Harry, rolling over. 'Go to sleep.'

'But . . .' I protested.

'You could be run over by a bus,' he grunted. 'Why not worry about *that*.'

Then, about a week later, I *was* run over by a bus. I'd just dropped Tillie off at school and I was on my way back home. I'm glad she wasn't in the car when it happened, it was quite enough of a shock for the girls as it was. Anyway, I was pottering along at about twenty-five thinking about how I ought to stop off at the garden centre for some hyacinth bulbs when there was an almighty bang and the next thing I knew I was looking up into a nurse's face and wondering why.

The bus driver had fallen asleep at the wheel; rather extraordinary, that, at nine in the morning. It made the front page of the local paper. The bus had been going downhill, picked up speed, shot a red light and hit my car broadside on. He'd had a big night out, the driver, and he hadn't bothered going to bed before starting his early morning shift.

The interesting thing is that, though it was rather awful losing a leg like that, I was back to my old self otherwise. Some sort of cloud lifted and I was out of the woods. Amazing, really. No more doom and gloom! I mean, of *course* there were times when I felt sorry for myself, very sorry for myself, hobbling round in rehab being one of them, but I was always able to snap out of it. It could have been worse. As Harry says, all the important bits are still there.

I've recovered my natural reluctance to dwell on things, thank goodness. You hear people say, 'I think about death every day,' as if that's something to be proud of, but I can't help thinking, so what? We're none of us going to get any further on that subject until it's our turn. I try not to dwell on how my friend Philippa died, because that still makes me cry. It wasn't easy. It was no fun at all. But Karen Pocock got better; I recognized her name when she joined my mosaic class, and now we get on like a house on fire.

WAR &
POLITICS

ZADIE SMITH

Moonlit Landscape with Bridge

The Minister of the Interior stood in the middle of the room, assessing three suits laid over a chair. One was a pale morning-sky blue; the next tan, of light material, intended for these terrible summers; the last a heavy worsted English three-piece, grey, for state visits. They were slung across one another every which way, three corpses in a pile. The rest of the marbled room – his wife had liked to call it the 'salon' – was in boxes, labelled, optimistically, with a forwarding address. Within the hour, efficient young Ari would drive the Minister to the airport, and from there – all being well – he would leave to join his wife and children in Paris. The car would not be a minute out of the driveway, he knew, before the household staff fell on these boxes like wild beasts upon carrion. The Minister of the Interior rubbed the trouser leg of the grey between his fingers. He was at least fortunate that the most significant painting in the house happened also to be the smallest: a van der Neer miniature, which, in its mix of light and water, reminded him oddly of his own ancestral village. It fit easily into his suit bag, wrapped in a pillowcase. Everything else one must resign oneself to losing: pictures, clothes, statues, the piano – even the books.

'So it goes,' the philosophical Minister said out loud, surprising himself – it was a sentence from a previous existence. 'So it goes.' Without furniture, without curtains, his voice rose unimpeded to the ceiling, as in a church.

'You call me, sir?'

Elena stood in the doorway, more bent over than he'd ever seen her.

'Call? No . . . no.'

She seemed not to hear him. Her eyes had taken on an uncomprehending glaze, open yet unseeing. It was the same look the Minister had noted in all those portraits of heroic peasants presently stacked against the wall.

'Difficult days, Lele,' the Minister said, picking up the light blue, trying not to be discouraged by its creases. 'Difficult days.'

Elena twisted her apron in her hands. Her children, he knew, lived by the sea with their children. All along the coast the mobile-phone network had been obliterated.

'God is powerful,' she said, and bowed her head. Then: 'God sent this wind.'

The Minister sighed but did not correct her. They were from the same village originally, distant cousins – she had a great-uncle with his mother's surname. He appreciated her simplicity. She had done much for his children over the years, and for him, always with this same pious sincerity, which was, to the Minister, as much a memento of his village as the woven reed baskets and brightly coloured shawls of his childhood. But why bend so deeply, as if she were the only one suffering?

'If it were only the wind!' the Minister said, tilting his head to look through the missing skylight. 'We had measures in place for wind. It's not true that we were unprepared. That is a wicked lie of the foreign press.' He pointed at a lemon tree, horizontal and broken outside the window. 'The combination of the wind and the water. In the end, this is what proved so difficult. As I understand it, most of the deaths in the south were drownings, in fact.'

He frowned at her puffy face, made puffier by tears, and at her apron strings, cutting into a wad of encircling fat. Why was her hair so sparse? There was only a year or two between them. But, of course, he had never felt old and, consequently, had never looked it. A clear case, in the Minister's view, of the importance of mind over matter.

'God is so powerful,' Elena said, and wept into her hands.

Out of habit, the Minister thought now of Elena's suffering and multiplied it by the population. (By inquiring after her gut feelings he had been able to correctly predict three elections, the death penalties of several notorious criminals, and the winners of half a dozen television singing contests.) He put a light hand on her shoulder.

'Unfortunately, these weather events are democratic. Big countries, little countries. We are all caught by surprise. It's not possible to fully prepare for them.'

'God help the children!' Elena said. She swayed into his hand like a cow nudging a barn door. Gently, the Minister righted her.

'Well, when we're settled in Paris, Lele, we'll send for you.'

'Yes, Minister,' Elena said, but continued to weep freely, just as if he'd said, 'When we're settled in Paris, you will never hear from us again.'

'Minister,' Ari said, appearing in the doorway.

The Minister stepped forward and pressed the housekeeper to his chest. The girl of faint erotic memory had vanished, and in his arms he held an old woman, easily mistaken for his mother. Hard to believe that she had once been his sweet relief from the shock and boredom of his wife's first pregnancy, the months and months of it, in this unforgiving climate, and with such a difficult, pampered woman. Now the Minister's youngest daughter was turning seventeen, and his wife hoped to present the child as a débutante in a grand hotel in Paris, making some kind of opportunity out of a crisis. Thinking on this peculiar fact, the Minister got stuck on a sentence: *I am further from my village now than I have ever been*. Italicized just like that, in his mind. Unsettled, he drew back, pressing an inch and a half's worth of currency into Elena's hands, which, for the first time in their history, she made no pretence of declining, grabbing it from him like any beggar in the street, folding it, crying some more.

'The time, Minister,' Ari said, tapping his wrist.

The Minister had not ventured outside in three days. Yet the scrolling devastation held few surprises, maybe because the foreign news crews filmed in just this way, from the window of a moving vehicle. For the first mile or so, the magnitude of what had happened was not obvious. Up here, the storm had knocked down only every third tree, blown out a few windows, and driven a stone general and his horse nose first into the ground. By the time they reached the valley, however, any hope one had that the television exaggerated was destroyed. The water had retreated, leaving behind a shredded world of plastic, timber and wire. Under the wall that had once circled the parade ground, the Minister spotted several pairs of feet, purple and bloated, liberated of their shoes. If Ari slowed or hesitated even for a moment, the sound of hands banging on the trunk came, but mostly he did not slow, and the SUV rolled over everything in its path. The Minister thought of his children making this same journey forty-eight hours earlier. He looked through tinted windows at his people scavenging from mountains of rubble. He groaned and wept discreetly into a handkerchief.

'Oh, I'm not listening to that.'

The Minister – who had not thought that he could be seen or heard – experienced a surge of humiliation and rage, pressing him against his seat, inflaming the tips of his ears.

'It wasn't much use before' – Ari tapped the satellite navigation unit suctioned to the windscreen. 'It's totally pointless now. If a road looks OK, I'll take it. Otherwise I'll detour. Sound OK to you, Minister?'

'Yes, yes, whatever you think.' The blood that had rushed to his extremities returned to where it belonged. His tongue relaxed; his face lost its awful contortion. He wiped the wetness from his cheeks, folded the handkerchief into a sharp-tipped diamond, and replaced it in the top pocket of the grey suit.

'Of course, the whole system is linked to an American military satellite,' the Minister said, leaning forward to peer at the delusional technology as it recommended impassable roads and pointed out a bridge no longer in existence. 'If the Americans ever chose to switch it off, we would all be plunged into darkness. Metaphorically speaking.'

Ari shook his head: 'What a mess.'

Through the windscreen they could see a large gathering of people, waiting outside an empty municipal office. As the car approached, heads began to turn, followed by hands lifted to throats, patting the skin there, over and over, like some mass mating call. The Minister took a pen and pad from his inside pocket and made a note of the location. For whom, for what purpose, he no longer knew.

Ari wiped his forehead with his sleeve. 'We can't get through this.'

'We are not going to *get through*,' the Minister corrected. 'We're going to stop. There are three crates of water in the trunk.'

Ari made an incredulous face in the rearview mirror.

'They'll be just as thirsty by nightfall. Meanwhile, you miss your plane!'

The Minister retrieved his handkerchief and worked at the sweat on his own forehead.

'Your generation is so cynical. You should try to help every individual person you meet, Ari, as a reflex, without thinking.'

Ari put his head on the steering wheel. 'Here we find a fundamental weakness of the Christ doctrine,' the Minister declared, making that wise and relatable face that had always been such a success in his television lectures. 'It troubles itself too much with conscience, rationale, and so on. Now, I myself am a student of human nature. I observe all faiths, and draw my own conclusions. For example, a Christian sees a tramp in the street, he begins agonizing. Should I give him the money in my pocket? What if he uses it for drink? What if he wastes it? What if there's someone else who needs it more? What if I need it more? And so on. The Jews, the Muslims – they see a tramp, they give him money, they walk on. The action is its own justification.'

'I'm not cynical,' Ari objected. 'How can I be cynical? The fact is, I'm a Buddhist.' He examined his hair in the wing mirror and pressed the button for the back window. Fetid air – which the Minister had earlier made clear he did not want to breathe – invaded the vehicle.

'Pull over just there. Look, I don't mean to insult you – anyway, I'm nothing at all, as I said, only a student of human nature, so there's no need to be insulted. Let's get this water distributed, eh? Then we can move on.'

With a great sigh, Ari drove forward until they were ten feet shy of the crowd. Here he stopped, leaving the engine running. The Minister, who was not a tall man, swung his little feet to the right, tried the handle twice, asked Ari to release the child lock, opened the door, and slipped down into ankle-deep sludge. His left shoe came off and was submerged. Catching the eye of a handsome peasant woman with a large child in her arms – seven or eight years old – he thought he saw in her anxious face the group's dilemma. Hold your ground in this line? Or risk losing your place for a dubious little man who still cared about his shoes?

'WATER!' the Minister cried – this broke the stalemate. He had reclaimed his shoe, and now, without planning to, found that he was opening his arms wide. Had he come to embrace them all?

'We have water! Women and children first!'

The people ran towards him, ignoring his instruction. He turned from them, walking thickly through the sludge to the trunk. The first to put a hand on him was a middle-aged man with a head wound that needed attention. For a moment, he seemed to recognize the Minister. Yet if recognition was there it was also perfectly useless. There were things that had mattered before the storm and things that mattered now, and the Minister fully understood that he belonged to the former category. Who cared, today, about the Long-Haired Bloc? The Minister's offices, like much of the government, had been flattened; seeing this chaos on the news, even the Minister had not been able to rid himself of the childish notion that it had been stomped into the ground. And what was a Minister without a ministry?

'Please, I beg of you – help my family.' So said the man with the wound. At the same moment, Ari stuck his head out the window. This left the Minister little choice but to reach for his wallet, take out the remaining paper currency, and press it into the hands of the man, who immediately had a portion of it snatched from him by a little girl, who in turn had her share taken from her by someone else, at which point the beleaguered Minister lost track, rolled up his sleeves, and turned back to bend over the trunk. He struck it twice with an imperious fist; it opened, as if by magic. The first thing was to rip the plastic covering off the crates while making a swift, imprecise count of how many bottles were in each layer. But the plastic was not so easily removed, and before he had finished ripping even one corner he felt many hands reaching around him, pushing him aside, knocking him to the ground. By the time he had struggled to his knees, fallen again, grabbed onto the bumper, and dragged himself up, the crates were gone, the people were running back to the municipal building, and several small fights had broken out. The Minister hung on to the side of the vehicle and edged his way around to the back door, one shoe forever lost to the mud. He heaved himself up into his seat. Without comment, Ari passed a tub of wet wipes over his shoulder. Without comment, the Minister took it.

Before the storm, it would have taken the Minister perhaps an hour to get to the airport. Now the sun fell in one part of the sky, while the moon rose in another. He dared to look at his watch. Five hours had passed since he promised Ari that he would make no further attempts to leave the vehicle.

'But I can't hold on any longer. I'm afraid it's unavoidable, Ari.'

'Minister, everything is avoidable.'

'Do you want me to piss myself? Is that it?'

'You should not make promises your bladder can't keep,' Ari said, caus-ing the Minister to reflect that one never really knew a person until one was caught in a situation of extremity with that person.

'I tell you it's unavoidable!'

'Well, I don't know where you think I can stop. All these people are trying to get to the airport. If we stop they'll slit my throat!'

'You are becoming hysterical,' the Minister said. He pointed at a brick church whose four sides were still attached, providing the only shade for miles.

Ari parked right at its door, like a chauffeur delivering a bride. People were everywhere, along with cars and vans and news trucks. The arrival of a small well-dressed man with one shoe did not attract much attention. The Minister struggled through an inert mass of people until he reached the yard behind the church, where he relieved himself against a sliver of dusty blue wall, watching with interest as it turned as vivid as the Virgin's cloak. Somewhere off to his right, a German film crew lent a boom mike to an American film crew. 'There's a woman in there lighting candles, praying, etcetera,' an American voice said. 'Her English is pretty good.' To which a German replied, 'I sink we have enough church.' The Minister zipped up and walked with as much dignity as could be managed back through the milling crowd, accepting the sweat of many strangers. People without direction or focus, swatting halfheartedly at the flies, standing around with no purpose other than to be among one another.

He caught a flash of Ari, smoking louchely out the car window – before a tall man blocked his view. More and more people gathered, and the Minister could get no further. Then a sudden shouting and crushing; everyone turned to face the murderous sunbeams in the west, and the dark shadow of an open truck, from which two figures, silhouetted, hurled sacks into the crowd. Cornmeal? Rice? Why not demand an orderly queue? Why cause the maximum amount of chaos? Next to the Minister, a hysterical woman held her baby above her head and wailed. A nice spectacle for the foreign press! Towards them both a sack sailed; the gallant Minister moved to push the woman out of its path. He was rewarded by somebody's powerful fist connecting with his left temple. Once again he found himself in the dirt, contemplating the bare feet of his countrymen. In pain, he called out for Ari; Ari heard, Ari replied – but from this nothing followed. The crowd was too thick to penetrate. The Minister decided instead to crawl forward on his hands and knees, and in this way made progress. He was within a yard of the car when he found himself being roughly lifted to his feet and brushed down by a pair of oversized, hairy hands.

'On your feet, on your feet – we need everybody standing, if they can stand! Red Cross! Red Cross!'

The man doing the shouting was broad and dark, with a boxer's broken nose, thin, silky black hair cut in a Caesar style, and a chin with a huge, inelegant cleft. He was in uniform, though even at this confusing moment something in the Minister registered the wrongness of this, in terms both of this man's particular body in a uniform and the uniform itself.

'Please take your hands off me – I am going to my car.'

The big man smiled foolishly and gripped the Minister by the elbow. A bolt of clarifying pain arrived: broken, in the fall. At the thought of spending any time in a local hospital, the Minister's legs went weak. In response, the man took almost all of his companion's weight and began pushing his own giant body through the last two layers of people until he had hold of the car's door handle.

'Red Cross! Back this up. I'll open when you're clear.'

'Do no such thing!' the Minister croaked. But he had lost Ari's vote. The car reversed, moving just fast enough that the man and the Minister were forced to jog along beside it. Once they were relatively free of the crowd, the man jumped into the car, pulled the Minister in beside him, and shut the door.

The Minister backed away until he was pressed against the car window.

'You've made a grave error. I am the Minister of the Interior – I advise you to get out of this vehicle at once.'

The man chuckled and patted the Minister's delicate knee.

'I know who you are, Minister. I saw you arrive. I just want to go to the airport, that's all. No trouble.'

'Ari, this man is not Red Cross – that is not a Red Cross uniform. Stop this car immediately.'

The man leaned forward and placed the flat edge of a knife against the back of Ari's neck.

'Keep driving,' he said.

Ari screamed, a woman's scream. The man laughed again: the genial, warm laugh of someone who finds the world delightful.

'Put that knife down,' the Minister said, in a very small voice.

'Fine,' the man said, without any rancour, and slipped the weapon back into a pocket in his uniform. 'You'll see that it doesn't change anything.'

Considering Ari, driving and weeping, and himself – a slight gentleman in his mid-sixties with a broken elbow who did not, after all, weigh much more than sixty kilos – the Minister of the Interior understood that the man was entirely correct.

They passed the old reservoir. The Minister was nudged gently in the ribs and offered that dim-witted smile.

'Nothing to say?'

The Minister lifted his chin and looked out the window. The reservoir was a decades-old failed public-works project, presided over by the Minister, and it was always unpleasant to pass it on the way to the airport.

'You're angry. Of course, I know very well you're a proud man who doesn't like to be tricked. I suppose I *have* tricked you, Minister. But think of me! I'm disappointed!'

The sun was setting, pink, over the rancid water, and the cracked concrete walls of the overflowing reservoir made it look like the basin of some ancient ruined amphitheatre. It had a strange beauty. The Minister had never noticed any beauty in it before. He wished he did not have to notice it now, while stuck in a car with a lunatic and a coward, on the way to his own execution.

'I may not be very educated, Minister, but I have my thoughts and feelings. You shouldn't judge a book by its cover.'

The Minister, lost in a fatalist haze, turned to his captor with a mournful face and said, matter-of-factly, 'But of course you're going to kill us.'

The man frowned and bit his lip.

'So you really don't recognize me at all. Truly you don't. Ah, it's disappointing!'

From Ari, another whimper.

'I should know you?'

'Well, we went through a lot together. Though my hair's shorter now. But then so is yours. And the Prime Minister – he's bald as a coot! And he was the longest-haired boy of all! Ha! Ha! What kids we all were!'

'Please don't kill me please don't kill me please don't kill me,' Ari pleaded, and, despite the sunset half blinding them all, and the large, menacing hand presently encasing the Minister's knee, the precise and vengeful Minister took note of Ari's use of the singular pronoun.

'Who said a thing about killing anybody? No, no, no. We gave that up a long time ago. A long time ago. Some of us served our time for it, some didn't – and I say well done to those who didn't! But now you know me for sure, Minister. Marlboro! The Marlboro Man. Nobody believes me when I say the Prime Minister himself named me. But it's true! My aunt used to send me the red ones from America – you must remember that – and he loved to smoke them. One day, we were making camp, way up in the hills this was, and he said, "Hey, you, Marlboro Man" – and it stuck. Forty years later, it's still sticking.'

If a bell rang for the Minister, it was a faint one indeed. He made his hands into a steeple and pressed them, upside down, between his knees.

'You must understand, there is no way I can get you onto a plane. When we arrive, you will be arrested. It will be out of my hands. There is no other outcome.'

The Marlboro Man gave the Minister's knee a jovial squeeze.

'But I don't want to get on a plane, Minister. I wish only to go the airport. That's where we hear all the action is – and I always want to be where the action is. Money, food, girls! Besides, I helped build it – I'd like to see it again.'

It was surely a mark of the pain and distraction in the Minister's mind that only Ari grasped the significance of this revelation. The name of the infamous prison escaped the young man's open mouth like an involuntary burp. The Marlboro Man clapped Ari on the back, congratulating him for solving such a jolly riddle.

'Thirty years we've been trying to get out of that place – and then the Lord himself goes and does it for us. Down went the walls – flat as a pancake! What a thing! Anyone still on his feet simply walked out into the sunshine and looked up at the clear blue sky . . . Ah!'

He stretched his arms across the back seat. The Minister was put in mind of a holiday-maker settling into a sand dune.

'All criminal fugitives will be executed,' the Minister said, reduced to repeating what he had heard on the news. 'Their only chance is to hand themselves over to the authorities.'

'The way I see it,' the Marlboro Man said, 'this is a moment of opportunity – for both of us.' He winked, then picked up the Minister's left hand and pressed it down on the Minister's knee until he yelped in pain. 'It's all a question of timing. The thing I've always admired about you, Minister, is your timing. You've always known when to move. Always known when a reckoning is coming. And you see it, don't you? You see that the people have begun to smell your shit – and it's not so sweet! Ha-ha! Finally, they can smell it. I mean, they've *always* smelled it, but back then they were children – *we* were children! – and now they are grown and not afraid to say it to your face. Any day now. Next year, they'd have had the lot of you in cuffs, off to The Hague! So it's lucky: the wind came, just in the nick of time! Eh? The Lord is my shepherd; I shall not want! It's an opportunity, and you're taking it. Listen, I admire it! I am a student of history – now, don't laugh. I tell you, a man gets a lot of time to read in that little cell. I've been trying to educate myself. I want to be one step ahead of history – that's the game, isn't it? Maybe I don't play it as well as you. But I'm learning. Oh, yes, I've become quite the student of history.'

It was madness, of course, and the Minister did not imagine that Ari would make much sense of it, but, at the same time, it was unfortunate that within this man's madness he should have hit upon that particular phrase, so like the Minister's own, and keep repeating it, with that idiotic, implicating grin, which necessitated, the Minister now felt, a restatement of his own position, lest Ari should hear echoes where none existed.

'I, meanwhile, am a student of human nature.' With his free hand, the Minister tried to hold his crushed elbow together. 'And students of human nature understand that ungrateful children always revert to their parents' wisdom, in the end.'

'Ah . . .'

Under the Caesar hairline, the man's granite forehead wrinkled, and the tip of his tongue poked out from between his lips, like a schoolboy engaged in a fearful piece of calculation. Observing this effort, a village thought now came to the Minister – a memory, really, of the Devil as a young man. Tales concerning the childhood of the Devil were a specialty of his people; Elena had a wonderful way with them, turning them into bedtime stories for the Minister's children – a rather low-class habit of which the Minister was supposed to disapprove. Unlike his colleagues, however, and unlike his difficult wife, the Minister of the Interior was essentially a pragmatist: if it were up to him, political men would never cross the thresholds of either bedrooms or shrines. He believed in leaving people to their private fantasies. When his children were small, he liked to open the door to his study at night, slicing through envelopes with a pearl-handled knife, while listening to Elena's Devil-talk. In these tales the Devil was never quite an idiot, no, not quite. He was like this fellow to the Minister's left. A good student, very attentive, eager to get on, who nevertheless always learned the wrong lesson.

'Weren't we children?' the man cried suddenly, bringing his fist down heavily on the upholstery. 'And weren't we ungrateful? Then we became the fathers in our turn. That's the truth of it. Yes, we were young – we were heroes! But we're not long-haired any more, my brother. Yet we survived. Most people didn't. So that's to be celebrated. That's a sign. Do you see? You must see that. You and I! Survivors!'

The thud on the seat continued to radiate through the Minister's elbow.

'I do not see,' he whispered. 'I do not see, because there is no analogy at all between us. I am the Minister of the Interior. You are insane. Perhaps once you were one of us – or worked for us. I don't know. You say you did. Now you are only a criminal. A fugitive and a criminal.'

Through his agony, the Minister was able to feel some satisfaction at having hit the mark. For an abashed expression passed over the Marlboro Man's face. To hide it, he turned from the Minister to face the window.

'Oh, I meant no offence, Minister, none at all. All I mean to say is – excuse me if I'm not speaking in an elegant way – you were smart and we were stupid. That's all. And let me tell you, you were really admired in there, truly. Much more than the Prime Minister. Because we remembered that you were once one of us! Smarter than us, maybe, but one of us all the same. But him? Never, not really. For he never really got his hands dirty. Not like we did. And now they call us "mercenaries" and put us in prison and pretend they never knew us. But without men like us where was the victory? Answer me that. That boy took the glory, but it was others who did the work. He was just a pretty face. Like this one here.' He reached forward, horribly animated, and grabbed Ari's cheek between thumb and forefinger. The car lurched towards a deep gully at the side of the road – the Minister's turn to scream – before the Marlboro Man leaned all the way forward to seize the wheel briefly with his free hand, steering them true.

'Don't panic, don't panic,' their captor said, fondly. He patted the top of frantic Ari's head, sighed, and sank his great buttocks back into the upholstery.

'But you! That's a lot of blood to wash off, brother. Oh, we never forgot. Hell of a lot of blood. A river of blood. I saw it, I was there. Up to the knees! Up to the knees!'

The Minister, just now emerging from the brace position, looked up to find Ari eying him strangely in the mirror. Never mind that it was a grotesque exaggeration: a river, stained red with blood, is not the same as a river of blood. But the Minister had not forgotten, no, not the difficult things, nor did he, as so many did, exaggerate or obscure. He remembered perfectly well how the Prime Minister had looked at nineteen, marking out an ambush on a field map. He remembered how they had recruited from the villages, handing out guns to young thugs who could not even spell their own names. He remembered the two halves of a girl's head, rolling down a riverbank through reeds into water. Divided, perhaps, by this very man's machete. All their boys had fought like animals, at one point or another. But the Minister had never forgotten, either, the beauty and quiet triumph of the nights that had followed those bloody days. A different life. Sharing simple food in the moonlight, not only with the village thugs but with bold, intelligent young men, committed to the future of their nation and willing to risk anything for it – including the eternal pollution of their own skulls.

'A sissy. Always with some sissy book in his back pocket. It should have been you, brother. Up to the knees!'

So it goes. Together the Minister of the Interior and the thoughtful boy who would later give him that title had read a thrilling book by an American with a German name – Vonnegut! A tale of war. It had so electrified them at the time, and yet, forty years later, the Minister found that he retained only one sentence of it and could not even retrieve its title. But he remembered two young men bent over one battered paperback, under a tree in the cleared centre of a village. Books had been important back then – they were always quoting from them. Long-haired boys, big ideas. These days, all the Prime Minister read was his bank statements. Yet, in essence, he was the same good and simple man, in the Minister's view – naïve, almost, doglike in his loyalties and his hatreds. If you were on the right side of the Prime Minister, you stayed there. So, at least, it had been for the Minister. Whatever he had needed had always been granted, up to and including this evening's flight. He had been lucky, always.

'That's lucky!' the man cried, and the Minister, yanked from his memories, began to fear that some form of voodoo was at work. 'The water's gone down! Look at that fat beautiful moon! We can take the bridge!'

Over the last bridge they went. The small tent city that had sprung up around the airport lay before them. The knife re-emerged, this time held low, at Ari's waist. At a makeshift checkpoint, Ari stuck the green government badge in the windscreen with a shaking hand, and they were waved through, instructed to follow a police car past the camp and its abject inhabitants.

'Leave me anywhere here,' the Marlboro Man said. 'Next to one with her legs open. "Let's lift some skirts and make it hurt!" Remember that old chant? And they'd all go running with their mothers into the bushes! Ha-ha! Now, don't begrudge me that, Minister, please. You probably had some yesterday – but for me it's been a little longer.'

For a big man, he moved nimbly, passing himself over the Minister, opening the car door, and stepping down onto gravel, smiling all the while. The Minister closed the door behind him.

'What the – What are you doing? Minister? Minister? He's just walking away!'

The Minister's phone was cold in his hand. He watched the man stride into the crowd. He felt as if he were releasing the spirit of chaos into the world. But wasn't it already here?

All commercial flights had ceased. The tiny half-destroyed airport had become a base for aid workers, stranded journalists, sleeping soldiers. Only the runway still functioned. The few planes available had been chartered by the government, and passengers approached them by driving to a gate in the perimeter fence and having their documentation checked by yet more officials. When the Minister's turn came, several young men approached the car, in uniform, or else in the dark-blue suits of the faithful. 'This way, Minister, this way,' they said, hustling him out of the car. He was crossing the floodlit tarmac before he realized that he'd said no goodbyes to Ari, but when he turned to look back he could no longer even see the vehicle. Hundreds of people pressed against the chain-link fence, waving pieces of paper in the air, shouting and begging. Just outside the painted yellow line, along which the Minister had once liked to walk in his neat, upright way, wheeling a discreetly luxurious brown-and-gold suitcase behind him – just on the other side of this yellow line, instead of the usual bustle of baggage handlers and suitcases, there lay a young man in a yellow neon safety vest and ragged trousers, sleeping on the tarmac, his head resting on a boulder.

'This plane, Minister. Keep to your left, Minister. Keep moving, Minister. Minister?'

But someone was screaming his name, his given name, which he heard so rarely these days it stopped him now in his tracks. He swivelled to locate the source and soon found it, a clear head and shoulders above the majority of his diminutive countrymen. He was grinning the same stupid devilish grin and making the old gesture of solidarity, wildly above his head, with the crossed fists they had all once used to signify 'You, too, are my brother.'

'Arrest that man,' the Minister said, quietly, to the young aide beside him, who, either not hearing or not understanding, nodded twice and said, 'This way, if you please, Minister.'

Across the lake of tarmac, the Minister and the Marlboro Man locked eyes.

'Bon Voi Yah Gee! Bon Voi Yah Gee!'

Bon voyage. A phrase he'd probably only ever seen written down. Screaming it at the top of his lungs. And making that gesture, over and over, a gesture that, the Minister was painfully aware, had fallen out of fashion in recent times – in truth, had come to be reviled; the Minister himself had not performed it in many years. He could see people on either side of the lunatic hanging off his giant arms, cursing and abusing him.

The Minister tried to remind himself that nothing horrifying was happening – he was merely being wished well on his trip by an idiot. Bon Voi Yah Gee! Bon Voi Yah Gee! He turned back to his handlers and once more attempted to give his instruction, but the jet's engines started up, and all was lost in this fresh wall of noise, all except those ridiculous words, attending the Minister's footsteps like an incantation of some kind, or the rungs of a ladder, ascending and descending both, depending. Bon Voi Yah Gee! Up to the knees!

'This way, Minister. This way.' So many people seemed to be touching the Minister, guiding him, advising him, that he felt as if he were not so much walking as being carried. He stopped trying to speak. What point was there in words? Actions, only actions. A few feet from the stairs to the plane, he became aware of a sudden change in the light: an impudent grey cloud between the Minister of the Interior and that fat beautiful moon. Large warm raindrops big as acorns fell on his nose, on his single shoe, on his lapel, on the world. Rain fell off the curve of the plane in torrential sheets, rain rioted on the cheap tin roof of the airport, soaking the Minister to the skin, making it even harder to hear instructions, and then, just as abruptly, stopped. The cloud moved on, the moon returned. The Minister held his elbow together. He pressed his suit bag to his chest. 'This way, Minister, this way.' The Minister shut his mouth and followed.

WILL SELF

The Rock of Crack as Big as the Ritz

A building, solid and imposing. Along its thick base are tall arches, forming a colonnade let into its hard hide. At the centre are high, transparent doors flanked by columns. There's a pediment halfway up the façade, and ranged along it at twenty-foot intervals are the impassive faces of ancient gods and goddesses. Rising up above this is row upon row of windows, each one a luxuriant eye. The whole edifice is dense, boxy, four-square and white, that milky, translucent white.

Over the central doors is a sign, the lettering picked out in individual white bulbs. The sign reads: THE RITZ. Tembe looks at the luxury hotel, looks at it and then crosses Piccadilly, dodging the traffic, squealing cabs, hooting vans, honking buses. He goes up to the entrance. A doorman stands motionless by his slowly revolving charge. He too is white, milky, translucent white. His face, white; his hands, white; his heavy coat falls almost to his feet in petrified folds of milky, translucent white.

Tembe stretches out a black hand. He places its palm against the column flanking the door. He admires the colour contrast: the black fading into the yellow finger flanges and then into the white, the milky, translucent white. He picks at the column, picks at it the way that a schoolboy distresses a plaster surface. He picks away a crumb of the wall. The doorman looks past him with sightless, milky, translucent eyes.

Tembe takes a glass crack pipe from the pocket of his windcheater and fumbles the crumb into the broken end of Pyrex piping that serves as a bowl. Setting the pipe down on the pavement, at the base of the white wall, from his other pocket he removes a blowtorch. He lights the blowtorch with a non-safety match, which he strikes on the leg of his jeans. The blowtorch flares yellow; Tembe tames it to a hissing blue tongue. He picks up the crack pipe and, placing the stem between his dry lips, begins to stroke the bowl with the blue tongue of flame.

The fragments of crack in the pipe deliquesce into a miniature Angel Falls of fluid smoke that drops down into the globular body of the pipe, where it roils and boils. Tembe draws and draws and draws, feeling the rush rise up in him, rise up outside of him, cancelling the distinction. He draws and draws until he is just the drawing, just the action: a windsock with a gale of crack smoke blowing through it.

'I'm smoking it,' he thinks, or perhaps only feels. 'I'm smoking a rock of crack as big as the Ritz.'

When Danny got out of the army after Desert Storm he went back to Harlesden in north-west London. It wasn't so much that he liked the area – who could? – but that his posse was there, the lads he'd grown up with. And also there was his uncle, Darcus; the old man had no one to care for him now Hattie had died.

Danny didn't like to think of himself as being overly responsible for Darcus. He didn't even know if the old man was his uncle, his great-uncle, or even his great-great-uncle. Hattie had never been big on the formal properties of family – precisely what relation adults and children stood in to one another – so much as the practical side, who fed who, who slept with who, who made sure who didn't play truant. For all Danny knew, Darcus might have been his father or no blood relation at all.

Danny's mother, Coral, who he'd never really known, had given him another name, Bantu. Danny was Bantu and his little brother was called Tembe. Coral had told Aunt Hattie that the boys' father was an African, hence the names, but it wasn't something he'd believed for a minute.

'Woss inna name anyways?' said the newly dubbed Danny to Tembe, as they sat on the bench outside Harlesden tube station, drinking Dunn's River and watching the Job Seekers tussle and ponce money for VP or cooking sherry. 'Our 'riginal names are stupid to begin wiv. Bantu! Tembe! Our mother thought they was kind of cool and African, but she knew nothing, man, bugger all. The Bantu were a fucking *tribe*, man, and as for Tembe, thass jus' a style of fucking *music.*'

'I don' care,' Tembe replied. 'I like my name. Now I'm big –' he pushed his chest forward, trying to fill the body of his windcheater '– I tell everyone to call me Tembe, so leastways they ain't dissin' me nor nuffin'.'

Tembe was nineteen, a tall, gangly youth, with yellow-black skin and flattish features.

'Tcheu!' Danny sucked the inside of his cheek contemptuously. 'You're a fucking dead-head, Tembe, an' ain't that the fucking troof. Lucky I'm back from doing the man stuff to sort you, innit?'

And the two brothers sat passing the Dunn's River between them. Danny was twenty-five, and Tembe had to confess he looked good. Tough, certainly, no one would doubt that. He'd always been tough, and lairy to boot, running up his mouth whenever, to whoever.

Danny, many years above him, had been something of a hero to Tembe at school. He was hard, but he also did well in class. Trouble was, he wouldn't concentrate or, as the teachers said, apply himself. 'Woss the point?' he used to say to Tembe. 'Get the fucking 'O' levels, then the 'A' levels, whadjergonna do then, eh? Go down the Job Centre like every other fucking nigger? You know the joke: what d'jew say to a black man wiv a job? "I'll have a Big Mac an' fries . . ." Well, I'm not going to take that guff. Remember what the man Mutabaruka say, it no good to stay inna white man's country too long. And ain't that the troof.'

So Bantu, as he was then, somehow got it together to go back to Jamaica. He claimed it was 'back', but he didn't exactly know, Aunt Hattie being kind of vague about origins, just as she was about blood ties. But he persuaded Stan, who ran the Montego Bay chippie in Manor Park Road, to get him a job with a cousin in Kingston. Roots-wise the whole thing was a shot in the dark, but in terms of getting a career Bantu was on course.

In Kingston Stan's cousin turned out to be dead, or missing, or never to have existed. Bantu got all versions before he gave up looking. Some time in the next six months he dropped the 'Bantu' and became 'London', on account of what – as far as the Jamaicans were concerned – was his true provenance. And at about the same time this happened he fetched up in the regular employ of a man called Skank, whose interests included buying powder off the boat and cooking it down for crack to be sold on the streets of Trenchtown.

Skank gave London regular pep talks, work-incentive lectures: 'You tek a man an' he all hardened, y'know. He have no flex-i-bil-ity so he have no poss-i-bil-ity. But you tek de youth, an' dem can learn, dem can 'pre-ci-ate wa' you tell for dem . . . You hearing me, boy?' London thought most of what Skank said was a load of bullshit, but he didn't think the well-oiled M16s under the floorboards of Skank's house were bullshit, and clearly the mean little Glock the big dread kept stuck under his arm was as far from being bullshit as it was possible to be.

London did well in Skank's employ. He cut corners on some things, but by and large he followed his boss's orders to the letter. And in one particular regard he proved himself to be a very serious young man indeed: he never touched the product. Sure, a spliff now and then just to wind down. But no rock, no stones, no *crack* – and not even any powder.

London saw the punters, he also saw his fellow runners and dealers. Saw them all getting wired out of their boxes. Wired so they saw things that weren't there: the filaments of wire protruding from their flesh which proved that the aliens had put transmitters in their brains. And hearing things as well, like non-existent DEA surveillance helicopters buzzing around their bedrooms. So London didn't fuck with the stuff – he didn't even *want* to fuck with it.

A year muscling rock in Trenchtown was about as full an apprentice-ship as anyone could serve. This was a business where you moved straight from work experience to retirement, with not much of a career in between. London was getting known, so Skank sent him to Philadelphia, PA, where opportunities were burgeoning, this being the back end of a decade that was big on enterprise.

London just couldn't believe Philly. He couldn't believe what he and his Yardie crew could get away with. Once you were out of the downtown and the white districts you could more or less fire at will. London used to get his crew to wind down the windows on their work wagon and then they would just blast away, peppering the old brown buildings with 9-mm rounds.

But mostly the hardware was just for show. The Yardies had such a bad reputation in Philly that they really didn't have to do anyone much. So, it was like running any retail concern anywhere: stock control, margins, management problems. London got bored and then started to do things he shouldn't. He still didn't touch the product – he knew better than to do that – but he did worse. He started to go against Skank.

When the third key went missing, Skank grew suspicious and sent an enforcer over to speak to his errant boy. But London had headed out already: BIWI to Trinidad, and then BA on to London, to cover his tracks.

Back in London, London dropped the name, which no longer made any sense. For a while he was no-name and no-job. Floating round Harlesden, playing pool with Tembe and the other out-of-work youth. He lived on the proceeds from ripping off Skank and kept his head down way low. There were plenty of work opportunities for a fast boy who could handle a shooter, but he'd seen what happened in Trenchtown and Philly, he knew he wouldn't last. Besides, the Met had a way with black boys who went equipped. They shot them dead. He couldn't have anything to do with the Yardies either. It would get back to Skank, who had a shoot-to-kill policy of his own.

Without quite knowing why, he found himself in the recruitment office on Tottenham Court Road. 'O' levels? Sure – a couple. Experience? Cadet corps and that. He thought this would explain his familiarity with the tools, although when he got to training his RSM knew damn well it wasn't so. Regiment? Something with a reputation, fighting reputation. Infantry and that. Royal Green Jackets? Why not?

'Bantu' looked dead stupid on the form. He grinned at the sergeant: 'Ought to be "Zulu", really.'

'We don't care what you call yourself, my son. You've got a new family now, give yourself a new name if you like.' So that's how he became Danny. This was 1991 and Danny signed on for a two-year tour.

At least he had a home to go to when he got out of the army. He'd been prudent enough to put most of Skank's money into a gaff on Leopold Road. An Edwardian villa that was somewhere for Aunt Hattie, and Darcus, and Tembe, and all the other putative relatives who kept on coming around. Danny was a reluctant *paterfamilias*, he left all the running of the place to Aunt Hattie. But when he came home things were different: Hattie dead, Darcus almost senile, nodding out over his racing form, needing visits from home helps, meals on wheels. It offended Danny to see his uncle so neglected.

The house was decaying as well. If you trod too hard on the floor in the downstairs hall, or stomped on the stairs, little plumes of plaster puffed from the corners of the ceiling. The drains kept backing up and there were damp patches below all the upstairs windows. In the kitchen, lino peeled back from the base of the cooker to reveal more ancient layers of lino below, like diseased skin impacted with fat and filth.

Danny had been changed by the army. He went in a fucked-up, angry, potentially violent, coloured youth; and he came out a frustrated, efficient, angry black man. He looked different too. Gone were the fashion accessories, the chunky gold rings (finger and ear) and the bracelets. Gone too was the extravagant barnet. Instead there were a neat, sculpted flat-top and casual clothes that suggested 'military'. Danny had always been slight, but he had filled out in the army. Darker than Tembe, his features were also sharper, leaner. He now looked altogether squared-off and compact, as if someone had planed away all the excess of him.

'Whadjergonna do then?' asked Tembe, as the two brothers sat spliffing and beering in front of Saturday afternoon racing. Darcus nodded in the corner. On screen a man with mutton-chop whiskers made sheepish forecasts.

'Dunno. Nuffin' criminal tha's for sure. I'm legit from here on in. I seen enough killing now to last me, man.'

'Yeah. Killing.' Tembe pulled himself up by the vinyl arms of the chair, animated. 'Tell me 'bout it, Bantu. Tell me 'bout the killing an' stuff. Woss combat really like?'

'Danny. The name's Danny. Don' forget it, dipstick. Bantu is dead. And another fing, stop axin' me about combat. You wouldn't want to know. If I told you the half, you would shit your whack. So leave it out.'

'But . . . But . . . If you aren't gonna deal, whadjergonna do?'

'Fucking do-it-yourself. That's what I'm gonna *do*, little brother. Look at the state of this place. If you want to stay here much longer with that fat bint of yours, you better do some yersel' as well. Help me get the place sorted.'

The 'fat bint' was Brenda, a girlfriend Tembe had moved in a week after his brother went overseas. Together they slept in a disordered pile upstairs, usually sweating off the effects of drink, or rock, or both.

Danny started in the cellar. 'Damp-coursing, is it?' said Darcus, surfacing from his haze and remembering building work from four decades ago:

tote that bale, nigger; Irish laughter; mixing porridge cement; wrist ache. 'Yeah. Thass right, Uncle. I'll rip out that rotten back wall and repoint it.'

'Party wall isn't it?'

'No, no, thass the other side.'

He hired the Kango. Bought gloves, goggles, overall and mask. He sent Tembe down to the builders' merchants to order 2,000 stock bricks, 50 kilo bags of ballast, sand and cement. While he was gone Danny headed down the eroding stairs, snapped on the yellow bulb and made a start.

The drill head bit into the mortar. Danny worked it up and around, so that he could prise out a section of the retaining wall. The dust was fierce, and the noise. Danny kept at it, imagining that the wall was someone he wanted done with, some towel-head in the desert or Skank, his persecutor. He shot the heavy drill head from the hip, like an action man in a boys' comic, and felt the mortar judder, then disintegrate.

A chunk of the wall fell out. Even in the murky light of the cellar Danny could see that there wasn't earth – which he had expected – lying behind it. Instead some kind of milky-white substance. There were fragments of this stuff on the bit of the drill, and twists like coconut swarf on the uneven floor.

Danny pushed up his goggles and pulled down his mask. He squatted and brought a gloveful of the matter up to his face. It was yellowy-white, with a consistency somewhere between wax and chalk. Danny took off his glove and scrunged some of it between his nails. It flaked and crumbled. He dabbed a little bit on his bottom lip and tasted it. It tasted chemical. He looked wonderingly at the four-foot-square patch that he had exposed. The swinging bulb sent streaks of odd luminescence glissading across its uneven surface. It was crack cocaine. Danny had struck crack.

Tembe was put out when he got back and found that Danny had no use for the stock bricks. No use for the ballast, the cement and the sand either. But he did have a use for Tembe.

'You like this shit, that right?' Danny was sitting at the kitchen table. He held up a rock of crack the size of a pigeon's egg between thumb and forefinger.

'Shee-it!' Tembe sat down heavily. 'Thass a lotta griff, man. Where you get that?'

'You don' need to know. You don' need to know. You leave that to me. I found us a connection. We going into business.' He gestured at the table where a stub of pencil lay on top of a bit of paper covered with calculation. 'I'll handle the gettin', you can do the outin'. Here –' he tossed the crack egg to Tembe '– this is almost an eightf. Do it out in twenties – I want a oncer back. You should clear forty – and maybe a smoke for you.'

Tembe was looking bemusedly at the egg that nestled in his palm. 'Is it OK, this? OK, is it?'

'Top-hole! Live an' direct. Jus' cooked up. It the biz. Go give the bint a pipe, see how she like it. Then go out an' sell some.'

Tembe quit the kitchen. He didn't even clock the brand-new padlock that clamped shut the door to the cellar. He was intent on a pipe. Danny went back to totting up columns of figures.

Danny resumed his career in the crack trade with great circumspection. To begin with he tried to assess the size of his stock. He borrowed a set of plumber's rods and shoved them hard into the exposed crack-face down in the cellar. But however many rods he added and shoved in, he couldn't find an end to the crack in any direction. He hacked away more of the brickwork and even dug up the floor. Every place he excavated there was more crack. Danny concluded that the entire house must be underpinned by an enormous rock of crack.

'This house is built on a rock,' he mused aloud, 'but it ain't no hard place, that the troof.'

Even if the giant rock was only fractionally larger than the rods indicated, it was still big enough to flood the market for crack in London, perhaps even the whole of Europe. Danny was no fool. Release too much of the rock on to the streets and he would soon receive the attentions of Skank or Skankalikes. And those Yardies had no respect. They were like monkeys just down from the fucking trees – so Danny admonished Tembe – they didn't care about any law, white or black, criminal or straight.

No. And if Danny tried to make some deal with them, somehow imply that he had the wherewithal . . . No. That wouldn't work either. They'd track him down, find him out. Danny had seen what men looked like when they were awakened at dawn. Roused from drugged sleep on thin mattresses, roused with mean little Glocks tucked behind their crushed ears. Roused so that grey patches spread out from underneath brown haunches. No. Not that.

Danny added another hefty padlock to the cellar door and an alarm triggered by an infra-red beam. Through a bent quartermaster at Aldershot who owed him a favour he obtained an antipersonnel mine in exchange for an ounce of the cellar wall. This he buried in the impacted earth of the cellar floor.

At night Danny sat in the yellow wash of light from the streetlamp outside his bedroom. He sucked meditatively on his spliff and calculated his moves. Do it gradual, that was the way. Use Tembe as a runner and build up a client list nice and slow. Move on up from hustling to the black youth in Harlesden, and find some nice rich clients, pukkah clients.

The good thing about rock – which Danny knew only too well – was that demand soon began to outstrip supply. Pick up on some white gourmets who had just developed a taste for the chemical truffles, and then you could depend on their own greed to turn them into gluttons, troughing white pigs. As long as their money held out, that is.

So it was. Tembe hustled around Harlesden with the crack Danny gave him. Soon he was up to outing a quarter, or even a half, a day. Danny took the float back off Tembe with religious zeal. It wouldn't do for little brother to get too screwed up on his profit margin. He also bought Tembe a pager and a mobile. The pager for messages in, the mobile for calls out. Safer that way.

While Tembe bussed and mooched around his manor, from Kensal Green in the south to Willesden Green in the north, Danny headed into town to cultivate a new clientele. He started using some of the cash Tembe generated to rent time in recording studios. He hired session musicians to record covers of the ska numbers he loved as a child. But the covers were percussive rather than melodic, full of the attacking, hard-grinding rhythms of Ragga.

Through recording engineers and musicians Danny met whites with a taste for rock. He nurtured these contacts, sweetening them with bargains, until they introduced him to wealthier whites with a taste for rock, who introduced him to still wealthier whites with a taste for rock. Pulling himself along these sticky filaments of drug-lust, like some crack-dispensing spider, Danny soon found himself in the darkest and tackiest regions of decadence.

But, like the regal operator he was, Danny never made the mistake of carrying the product himself or smoking it. This he left to Tembe. Danny would be sipping a mai tai or a whiskey sour in some louche West End club, swapping badinage with epicene sub-aristos or superannuated models, while his little brother made the rounds, fortified by crack and the wanting of crack.

It didn't take longer than a couple of months – such is the alacrity with which drug cultures rise and fall – for Danny to hit human gold: a clique of true high-lowlife. Centred on an Iranian called Masud, who apparently had limitless funds, was a gaggle of rich kids whose inverse ratio of money-to-sense was simply staggering. They rained cash down on Danny. A hundred, two hundred, five hundred quid a day. Danny was able to withdraw from Harlesden altogether. He started doling out brown as well as rock; it kept his clients from the heebie-jeebies.

Tembe was allowed to take the occasional cab. Darcus opened an account at the betting shop.

The Iranian was playing with his wing-wang when Tembe arrived. Or at any rate it looked as if he had been playing with it. He was in his bathrobe, cross-legged on the bed, with one hand hidden in the towelling folds. The smell of sex – or something even more sexual than sex – penetrated the room. The Iranian looked at Tembe with his almond eyes from under a narrow, intelligent brow on which the thick, curled hair grew unnaturally low.

Tembe couldn't even begin to think how the Iranian was getting it up – given the amount of rock he was doing. Five, six, seven times a day the pager peeped on Tembe's hip. And when Tembe dialled the number programmed into his mobile, on the other end would be the Iranian, his voice clenched with want, but his accent still that very, very posh kind of foreign.

Supporting the sex explanation there was the girl hanging around. Tembe didn't know her name, but she was always there when he came, smarming her little body around the suite. Her arrival, a month or so ago, had coincided with a massive boost in consumption at the suite. Before, the Iranian had level-pegged at a couple of forties a day and half a gram of brown, but now he was picking up an eighth of each as soon after Tembe picked up himself as he could engineer it.

After that the Iranian would keep on paging and paging for what was left of the day. Now, at least three nights a week, Tembe would be called at one a.m. – although it was strictly against the rules – and have to go and give the two of them a get-down hit, to stop the bother.

Tembe hated coming to the hotel. He would stop at some pub and use the khazi to freshen up before taking a cab up Piccadilly. He didn't imagine that the smarmed-down hair and chauffeured arrival fooled the hotel staff for a second. There weren't that many black youths wearing dungarees, Timberland boots and soiled windcheaters in residence. But they never gave him any hassle, no matter how late or how often he trod across the wastes of red carpet to the concierge and got them to call up to the Iranian's suite.

'My dear Tembe,' Masud, the Iranian, had said to him, 'one purchases discretion along with privacy when one lives in an establishment such as this. Why, if they attempted to restrict the sumptuary or sensual proclivities of their guests, they would soon have vacant possession rather than no vacancies.' Tembe caught the drift below the Iranian's patronizing gush. And he didn't mind the dissing anyway – the Iranian had sort of paid for it.

The girl let Tembe in this time. She was in a terry-towelling robe matching the Iranian's. The dun blond hair scraped back off her pale face suggested a recent shower, suggested sex.

How could the Iranian get it up? Tembe didn't doubt that he got the horn. Tembe got the horn himself. Got it bad. But the stiffie was hardly there, just an ice-cream, melting before there was any chance of it getting gobbled. Not that Tembe didn't try it on, far gone as he was. If he had a pipe at Leopold Road he'd make his moves on Brenda – until she shoved him away with lazy contempt. If he was dropping off for one of the brasses who worked out of the house on Sixth Avenue – who he still served without Danny's knowledge – or even the classier ones at the Learmont, either they would ask, or he would offer: rock for fuck.

It was ridiculous how little they'd do it for. The bitch at the Learmont –
who, Tembe knew for a fact, regularly turned three-ton tricks – would
put out for a single stone. She stepped out of her skirt the way any other
woman took off her coat and handed him the rubber from the dispenser
in the kitchenette drawer like it was a piece of cutlery.

Usually, by the time they'd piped up together Tembe was almost past
the urge. Almost into that realm where all was lust, and lust itself was a
grim fulfilment. He'd try and push his dick into the rubber rim, but it
would shrink back. And then he'd just get her to un-pop the gusset of
her sateen body. Get her to stand there in the kitchenette, one stilettoed
foot up on a stool, while he frigged her and she scratched at his limpness
with carmine nails.

Tembe tried not to think about this as the Iranian's girl moved
about the bedroom, picking up a lacy bra from the radiator, jeans with
knickers nesting in them from the floor. The Iranian was taking a
smoke of brown from a piece of heavily stained foil a foot square. Tembe
watched the stuff bubble, black as tar dripping from a grader. The girl slid
between him and the door jamb. Wouldn't have been able to do that a
month ago, thass the troof, thought Tembe. She's that fucking gone on
it. Posh white girls don't eat any, and when they're on the pipe and the
brown they eat even less. Despite that, skinny as she was, and with those
plasticky features like a Gerry Anderson puppet, Tembe still wanted to
fuck her.

The Iranian finished off his chase by waving the lighter around ham-
mily, and said, 'Let's go into the other room.' And Tembe said, 'Sweet,'
keen to get out of the bedroom with its useless smell of other people's sex.
The Iranian moved on the bed, hitching up his knees, and for a second
Tembe saw his brown dick, linked to the sheet by a pool of shadow or
maybe a stain.

The main room of the suite featured matching Empire escritoires that
had seldom been written on, an assemblage of Empire armchairs and a
divan that had seldom been sat on. In front of the divan there was a large,
glass-topped coffee-table, poised on gold claw feet. On top of this were a
crack pipe, a blowtorch, a mirror with some smears of rock on it, cigarettes, a lighter, keys, a video remote, a couple of wine-smeared glasses
and, incongruously, a silver-framed photograph of a handsome

middle-aged woman. The woman smiled at Tembe forthrightly over the assembly of crack-smoking tools.

The room also featured heavy bookcases, lined with remaindered hardbacks, which the hotel manager had bought from the publishers by the yard. The carpet was mauve, the walls flock-papered purple with a bird-and-shrubbery motif worked into them. On the far side of the coffee-table from the divan stood an imposing armoire, the doors of which were open, revealing shelves supporting TV, video and music centre. Scattered around the base of the armoire were videos in and out of their cases, CDs the same.

Somewhere inside the armoire Seal was singing faintly: 'For we're never going to sur-vive/Un-less we go a little cra-azy . . .' 'Ain't it the troof?' said Tembe, and the Iranian replied, 'Sorry?' but not as if he meant it.

'For we're never going to sur-vive/Un-less we go a little cra-azy . . .' Tembe warbled the words, more falsetto than Seal, but with a fair approximation of the singer's rhythm and phrasing. As he neared the end of the second line he did a little jig, like a boxer's warm-up, and wiggled his outstretched fingers either side of his face, his head chicken-nodding. '. . . You know, man, like cra-azee.'

'Oh, I see. I get you. Yeah, of course, of course . . .'

The Iranian's voice trailed away. He'd put himself down in the centre of the divan and was using the flap of a matchbook to scrape up the crack crumbs on the mirror, sweeping them into a little vee-shaped pile, then going over the same surface again, creating a regular series of crack smears.

Tembe looked at the pipe and saw the thick honey sheen inside it. There was plenty of return there, enough for five or six more hits. Tembe wondered why the Iranian had called him back so soon. Surely the return alone would have lasted the pair of them another couple of hours? But now Tembe saw that the Iranian had got down on his hands and knees behind the coffee-table and was methodically combing the strip of carpet between the table and the divan with a clawed hand. The Iranian's starting eyes, hovering six inches above the carpet, were locked on in the hand's wake, crack-seeking radar.

Thass it, Tembe realized. The fucker's so fucking far gone he's carpet-cruising. Tembe had seen it enough times – and done it himself as well.

It began when you reached that point – some time after the tenth pipe – where your brain gets sort of fused with crack. Where your brain *is* crack. Then you start to see the stuff everywhere. Every crumb of bread on the carpet or grain of sugar on the kitchen lino looks like a fragment of ecstatic potential. You pick one up after the other, checking them with a touch of wavering flame, never quite believing that it isn't crack until the smell of toast assaults your nose.

The Iranian had turned in his little trench of desperation and was crawling back along it, head down, the knobbles of his spine poking up from behind the silvery rim of the coffee-table. He was like some mutant guard patrolling a perverse checkpoint. His world had shrunk to this: tiny presences and gaping, yawning absences. Like all crackheads, Masud moved slowly and silently, with a quivering precision that was painful to watch, as if he were Gulliver, called upon to perform surgery on a Lilliputian.

The girl wandered back in, tucking the bottom of a cardigan into the top of her jeans. She fastened the fly buttons and then hugged herself, palms going to clutch opposing elbows. Her little tits bulged out.

'Fuck it, Masud,' the girl said, conversationally, 'why have you got Tembe over if you're just gonna grovel on the floor?'

'Oh, yeah, right . . .' He slid his thin arse back up on to the divan. In one hand he held a lighter, in the other some carpet fluff. He sat and looked at the ball of fluff in his hand, as if it were really quite difficult to decide whether or not it might be a bit of crack, and he would have to employ his lighter to make absolutely certain.

Tembe looked at the blue hollows under the Iranian's almond eyes. He looked at the misnamed whites of those eyes as well. Masud looked up at Tembe and saw the same colour scheme. They both saw yellow for some seconds. 'What . . . ? What you . . . ?' Masud's fingers, quick curling back from exploded nails, bunched the towelling at his knee. He couldn't remember anything – clearly. Tembe helped him. 'I got the eightf anna brown.' He took his hand from the pocket of his jacket, deftly spat into it the two marbles of clingfilm concealed in his cheek and then flipped them on to the table. One rolled to a halt at the foot of the portrait photo-graph of the handsome woman, the other fetched up against the video remote.

This little act worked an effect on Masud. If Tembe was a cool black dealer, then he, Masud, was a cool brown customer. He roused himself, reached into the pocket of his bathrobe and pulled out a loose sheaf of purple twenties. He nonchalantly chucked the currency on to the glass pool of the table top, where it floated.

Masud summoned himself further and resumed the business of having his own personality with some verve, as if called upon by some cutting-edge *auteur* to improvise it for the camera. 'Excuse me,' he stood, wavering a little, but firm of purpose. He smiled graciously down at the girl, who was sitting on the floor, and gestured to Tembe, indicating that he should take a seat on the divan. 'I'll just throw some clothes on and then we must all have a big pipe?' He cocked an interrogative eyebrow at the girl, pulled the sides of the bathrobe around his bony body and quit the room.

Tembe looked at the girl and remained, rocking gently from the soles to the heels of his boots. She got up, standing in the way young girls have of gathering their feet beneath them and then vertically surging. Tembe revised his estimate of her age downwards. She sat on the divan and began to sort out the pipe. She took the larger of the two clingfilm marbles and laborious unpicked it, removing layer after layer after layer of tacky nothingness, until the milky-white lode was exposed and tumbled on to the mirror.

She touched a hand to her throat, hooked a strand of hair behind a lobeless ear, looked up and said, 'Why don't you sit here, Tembe? Have a pipe.' He grunted, shuffled, joined her, manoeuvring awkwardly in the gap between the divan and the coffee-table.

Masud came back into the room. He was wearing a shirt patterned with vertical stripes of iridescent green and mustard-yellow, sky-blue slacks in raw silk flapped around his legs, black loafers squeaked on his sockless feet, the froth of a paisley cravat foamed in the pit of his neck. What a dude. 'Right!' Masud clapped his hands, another ham's gesture. Upright and clothed, he might have been some motivator or negotiator freeing up the wheels of commerce, or so he liked to think.

The girl took a pinch of crack and crumbled it into the bowl of the pipe. 'I'm sure,' said the Iranian, his tone hedged and clipped by annoyance, 'that it would be better if you did that over the mirror, so as to be certain not to lose any –'

'I know.' She ignored him. Tembe was right inside the bowl of the pipe now, his boots cushioned by the steely resilience of the gauze. The lumps of crack were raining down on him, like boulders on Indiana Jones.

Tembe mused on what might be coming. Masud had paid for this lot, but could he be angling for credit? It was the only explanation Tembe could hit on for the welcome in, the girl's smiles, the offer of a pipe. He decided that he would give Masud two hundred pounds' credit – if he asked for it. But if he was late, or asked for any more, Tembe would have to refer it to Danny, who would have the last word. Danny always had the last word.

The girl lit the blowtorch with the lighter. It flared yellow and roared. She tamed it to a hissing blue tongue. She passed Tembe the pipe. He took the glass ball of it in the palm of his left hand. She passed him the blowtorch by the handle. 'Careful there . . .' said Masud, needlessly. Tembe took the blowtorch and looked at his host and hostess. They were both staring at him fixedly. Staring at him as if they wouldn't have minded diving down his throat, then swivelling round so they could suck on the pipe with him, suck on it from inside his lips.

Masud hunched forward on the divan. His lips and jaws worked, smacking noises fell from his mouth. Tembe exhaled to one side and placed his pursed lips around the pipe stem. He began to draw on it, while stroking the bowl of the pipe with the tongue of blue flame. Almost instantly the fragments of crack in the pipe deliquesced into a miniature Angel Falls of fluid smoke that dropped down into the globular body of the pipe, where it roiled and boiled.

Tembe continued stroking the pipe bowl with the flame and occasionally flipped a tonguelet of it over the rim, so that it seared down on to the gauzes. But he was doing it unconsciously, with application rather than technique. For the crack was on to him now, surging into his brain like a great crashing breaker of pure want. This is the hit, Tembe realized, concretely, irrefutably, for the first time. The whole hit of rock is to want *more rock*. The buzz of rock is itself the wanting of *more rock*.

The Iranian and the girl were looking at him, devouring him with their eyes, as if it was Tembe that was the crack, their gazes the blowtorch, the whole room the pipe. The hit was a big one, and the rock clean and sweet, there was never any trace of bicarb in the stuff Danny gave Tembe, it was jus' sweet, sweet, sweet. Like a young girl's gash smell sweet, sweet, sweet, when you dive down on it, and she murmurs, 'Sweet, sweet, sweet . . .'

It was the strongest hit off a pipe Tembe could ever remember taking. He felt this as the crack lifted him up and up. The drug seemed to be completing some open circuit in his brain, turning it into a humming, pulsing lattice-work of neurones. And the awareness of this fact, the giant nature of the hit, became part of the hit itself – in just the same way that the realization that crack was the desire for crack had become part of the hit as well.

Up and up. Inside and outside. Tembe felt his bowels gurgle and loosen, the sweat break out on his forehead and begin to course down his chest, drip from his armpits. And still the rocky high mounted ahead of him. Now he could sense the red-black thrumming thud of his heart, accelerating through its gearbox. The edges of his vision were fuzzing black with deathly, velvet pleasure.

Tembe set the pipe down gently on the surface of the table. He was *all*-powerful. Richer than the Iranian could ever be, more handsome, cooler. He exhaled, blowing out a great tumbling blast of smoke. The girl looked on admiringly.

After a few seconds Masud said, 'Good hit?' and Tembe replied, 'Massive. Fucking massive. Biggest hit I ever had. It was like smoking a rock as big as . . . as big as . . .' His eyes roved around the room, he laboured to complete the metaphor. 'As big as this hotel!' The Iranian cackled with laughter and fell back on the divan, slapping his bony knees.

'Oh, I like that! I like that! That's the funniest thing I've heard in days! Weeks even!' The girl looked on uncomprehendingly. 'Yeah, Tembe, my man, that has a real ring to it: the Rock of Crack as Big as the Ritz! You could make money with an idea like that!' He reached out for the pipe, still guffawing, and Tembe tried hard not to flatten his fucking face.

At home, in Harlesden, in the basement of the house on Leopold Road, Danny kept on chipping, chipping, chipping away. And he never ever touched the product.

GERARD WOODWARD

The Fall of Mr and Mrs Nicholson

On the twenty-sixth of January, at two o'clock in the afternoon, two men arrived at my house, with orders to take me to Mr and Mrs Nicholson. I had been working late the night before and had only just risen. I was still in my dressing gown and holding a tub of fish food in my hand when I opened the door. The men didn't show any sign of disapproval or even surprise. It seemed to be what they expected.

They were casually dressed. I guessed they were in their late forties. They had unshaven, baggy faces, and were both a little overweight. They were wearing sweatshirts, jeans, mushroom-grey bomber jackets, filthy trainers. I told them they would have to wait until I got dressed, and they came in, without my invitation, as if to make sure I did get dressed.

'Do I have time for a shower?' I asked. The men shook their heads. I went to my bedroom and pulled fresh clothes over my sweaty skin. I felt very uncomfortable. When I returned to my living room I found the men examining my tropical fish tank. One of them was bending down to peer at the fish through the glass, the other was playfully dipping his finger into the water and swirling it around.

'Carmen might bite,' I said, half-jokingly. Carmen could bite, but with her soft little teeth she couldn't do much damage. The man withdrew his finger more sharply than he had intended, then tried to cover the embarrassment by using the same wet finger to beckon me towards the door. 'Do I need to take anything with me?' I asked. The men shook their heads. 'They have everything you need,' the shorter one said.

I had only met Mr and Mrs Nicholson once, and that was about ten years previously. They had been presenting the prizes at an awards gala and I had been awarded the Nicholson Star for Short Stories. As was

318

usual at these occasions, it was Mrs Nicholson who did the presenting, while Mr Nicholson made the speeches and read out the nominations. It was widely believed that Mr Nicholson read very little fiction, while Mrs Nicholson was a keen reader of detective stories and symbolist poetry. At that particular ceremony she had clasped my hand and held my gaze with her blue eyes and smiled warmly as she handed me my certificate, speaking to me so quietly I could hardly hear her above the applause that filled the hall. 'Very well done,' she said, and repeated the phrase two or three times, until she had made sure I had heard it. She held on to my hand with such a firm grip I had to pull myself away from her. At one point her face was so close I could smell her breath. It smelt sweet and sugary, as though she had been eating a cake with lots of icing.

I didn't ask why Mr and Mrs Nicholson had sent for me. I knew that it would be pointless troubling the men who collected me with questions like that. They wouldn't even know, anyway. So I obediently followed them down the path to the street where their car was waiting, and where another man was at the wheel.

For most of the journey across the city there was little sign of unrest. Passing through the familiar districts we could see mothers and children playing in parks, people shopping, visiting the library, or using the swimming pool. At one of the police stations we passed there was a protest taking place, but the crowd was very small in number. None of us passed any comment on the spectacle, even though the sight was an unusual one.

Mr and Mrs Nicholson lived in a building known as the People's Palace, which had once been the city's main hospital, and overlooked the central square. A much larger hospital had been built in the Kleverdam District to replace it, and so no one minded about the change of use to which the old hospital had been put. In fact the people were rather proud of the new palace, and the term People's Palace was the informal name adopted by the general public. Its official designation was simply 1 Kleverdam Square.

Today the square itself was inaccessible due to the large crowds that had gathered there. I was quite taken by surprise by the number of people assembled, kept in place by a thick cordon of police who maintained a throughway for traffic to move between the square and the parliament building. Nevertheless, it was not possible, for safety reasons, to use the palace's main entrance, and instead we entered by one of the many back gates, which had been heavily fortified.

There had been very little information about the protest. There was nothing about it on the television or in the newspapers. And as I had been out of the house very rarely over the previous few weeks, I had heard very little by way of gossip. So much so that at first I couldn't be sure that the crowd gathered in the square was there for reasons of celebration or protest. I wondered if I had forgotten that it was Mr or Mrs Nicholson's birthday, or if there was some other important anniversary to be celebrated. But a closer look at the crowds, as much as I could see them from the darkened windows of our vehicle, showed unhappy faces, and banners bearing slogans of an anti-government flavour.

I had never been inside the People's Palace before, and I was struck by the lavishness of the interior decoration, and how this contrasted with the squared bleakness of the outside. There were chandeliers of cascading crystal, towering golden statues of working men and women, mosaics of common folk as Titans and Olympians. There were swirling carpets, exquisite tapestries filling walls as big as tennis courts. The lifts were like jewelled caskets, the floors were deep with soft woollen carpets. What had been wards were now long rooms full of opulence, but entirely empty of any sign of people or activity. One was described as the state reception room, and contained a single enormous table, but no chairs. Another was to house the Nicholsons' art collection, but so far the walls were empty. I was shocked at the general emptiness of the place, the wide unfurnished spaces, the tall empty vestibules over which Tiffany domes hung, casting their multi-coloured shadows on nothing. I had expected the bustle of ministers and civil servants conducting the business of state. I had expected a sense of urgency and energy. Instead it was as though the power had drained from the great machine of state, to leave the glamorous shell empty and devoid of function.

I was shown into a room before whose doors stood four armed guards. It was of a more plain design than the rest of the palace, being not much bigger than a respectable suburban living room, with a large desk, two sofas, a television, bookcases and conventionally patterned wallpaper.

There were several people in the room, including a military figure in full dress uniform, with a breastful of medals. There were some men in typical politician's suits, and a small group of media people, one with a small camera, another with a microphone. A large camera on a fixed stand was pointing towards the empty desk, behind which hung the national flag and a rather spindly araucaria. In the centre of all this was Mr Nicholson, wearing his overcoat, scarf and woolly hat, as though he had been out for a long walk in the cold. It was because, I later learned, that he had just come in from the balcony, where he had been speaking for an hour and a half to the crowd in the square. That crowd could be heard through the tall curtained windows that gave on to the balcony, but which had been firmly closed since Mr Nicholson came in. He was sitting on a stiff-backed chair, one elbow resting on the back of the sofa against which he was positioned, and talking with one of the men in suits. The man in the suit was by far the more animated of the two, not to say agitated; he talked in a fast, pleading voice, bending down so that he could talk directly into Mr Nicholson's face. One got the impression he would have liked to have taken hold of Mr Nicholson by the shoulders and shaken him. Mr Nicholson, on the other hand, talked with a quiet but firm voice, as though explaining the uselessness of the other's point.

The two men who'd accompanied me drifted off into different parts of the room without giving me any indication of what I was supposed to do. People carried on with their business without taking any notice of me. One of the men sauntered over to the tall curtains and tentatively parted them, to peep out into the square. Even this tiny movement was spotted by the crowds, and a cry went up, then a chant whose words were impossible to make out. The other man went up to a bookcase and casually leafed through a leather-tooled volume. There was no sign of Mrs Nicholson. I decided to sit on one of the sofas, clearing a space for myself among the heap of newspapers that were spread out on it.

Eventually the conversation between Mr Nicholson and the man in the suit came to an end, and at that point the man at the bookcase indicated my presence to the old man with a jerk of the head. Mr Nicholson turned to me and gave me a long stare, but his expression was of a sort of tired indifference, as though I was just another thing he had to deal with. He gestured with a turn of the wrist that I should come over to him. He gave the impression of a man who was too tired to even stand up. So I went over to him and sat on another stiff-backed chair that one of the men put in position.

'You are the writer?' he said.

'Yes.'

'Good. I need you to write me something.'

'OK.'

'You are one of my wife's favourite writers. She advised me to call you in. She will be here in a minute.'

'What do you want me to write?'

Mr Nicholson looked puzzled. 'A speech.'

'I see.'

'What did you think you were going to write? A detective story? No, I need a speech. A good one. The best one I have ever made. I will be speaking from that balcony in one hour. The crowd outside are hostile. Ridiculous. I would call them barbarians but they are gaining influence. I have to do something to appease them. Just half an hour ago I made a speech promising a wage rise of twenty per cent. Across the board! They laughed at me. They jeered and booed. Barbarians. These are people who laugh at a wage rise. You see, then, what I need is a speech that will get to their hearts more than money can. You understand? And I need another speech for the television broadcast I will make one hour later.'

'Mr Nicholson, I have never written a political speech before.'

'So? My previous speechwriters have written hundreds, and they were still no good. You write stories to move people. That is what I need. What's the difference?'

I couldn't answer at first.

'It's a difference of genre, I suppose.'

'That sounds like prevarication. If you are a writer, you can write anything. All that matters is that you are good with words. Don't worry, I will give you a few facts I want you to include. My wife will be here in a minute. She will be better at explaining. She is a big admirer of your tales.'

I wondered if I had the option of refusing the commission. Mr Nicholson seemed to read my mind, because he said, 'You needn't think you have any choice in this matter. Now that you are here you are trapped, along with the rest of us. The only way out of here is by cutting a path through that crowd out there, and I would much rather do that with words than bullets. To put it quite simply, the future of our great country rests on the words you can produce in the next sixty minutes.'

'Fifty-five,' said the military man, who had shuffled over and was listening to our conversation. 'And the crowd is still growing. There are coaches arriving from every corner of the country. They are bringing people in on the backs of vegetable lorries.'

'Then the city must be sealed off. How many times have I told you?'

'We have road blocks on all the main roads. But what can they do if a lorry doesn't stop?'

'They can shoot the driver.'

'I confess some of the troops are reluctant to kill their own people in cold blood.'

'Then let them kill in hot blood. It is your job to produce fighting men.'

Just then Mrs Nicholson entered the room, and the atmosphere changed abruptly. She issued a long string of oaths, the colour and tone of which I had never heard coming from the lips of a woman before, nor the volume and pitch, which was attenuated and loud. She immediately began issuing commands and commentary, at such speed I was unable to follow what was happening. She beat her fists upon the decorated breast of the military man, and sent him from the room with orders to talk some sense into the army he was, supposedly, in charge of. Having voiced her anger and frustration, she then stalked about the room muttering and drawing her stole, a fine check-patterned piece of fabric, carefully about her. I felt as though I had intruded upon a private marital dispute, because she continually hurled comments and criticisms at Mr Nicholson, as though she was complaining about him not pulling his weight in the housework. Had he had a shed to retire to, I feel he would have done so at that moment, but husband and wife were trapped in the room, along with the rest of us.

It was some time before Mrs Nicholson noticed me. By then I had moved away from the part of the room occupied by her husband, and was standing by the desk near the window. Her demeanour seemed to change immediately, a warm smile bloomed on her face and she held out both arms as she came towards me. She took me by the shoulder and delivered her face to my lips to be lightly kissed, once on each cheek, and then once more on the left cheek. Three kisses was a sign of great affection and affinity.

'I am so glad you were able to come,' she said, as I blinked away the strong smell of eau de Cologne, 'we are in such desperate need of a good wordsmith. My husband has sacked all his speechwriters, and his advisers as well. Do you mind me using the term "wordsmith"?' I had hardly time to shake my head before she went on, 'I think it is a very dignified and noble term, for someone who fashions artefacts out of words, just as a blacksmith does with iron. You may take that analogy to heart. We need words as strong as iron to come from your pen. We want words that will rain down on the ears of the great public like bullets, like hammers.'

I began to wonder if either Mr or Mrs Nicholson were familiar with my work at all. What she demanded seemed the very opposite of my usual writing practice. I had never thought of words as hammers or bullets. I thought back to my quiet little stories, with their gentle metaphors and subtle (so I liked to believe) observations, and tried to imagine their words raining down from the sky like missiles. It was impossible. Mrs Nicholson seemed to detect my doubts. 'Is something the matter?'

'I was just wondering why you chose me, among the very many excellent writers who live in this city.'

This produced a look of charming imprecision on Mrs Nicholson's face, of the type that one never sees on leaders of any nations. I felt a sudden thrill of connectedness with the woman, an entwining intimacy so unexpected that I could hardly breathe for a few seconds. It was as though a painting in an art gallery had reached out and touched me.

'But your writing is of a very different order from that of anyone else. You have a very special power – to move people, to stir their passions, to persuade them of the truth of something. In your stories the worlds you have invented come to life with such persuasiveness, you can only feel, as a reader, that you have been there.'

I was distracted, momentarily, by what sounded like a burst of rifle fire outside, but which was quickly identified and dismissed as firecrackers.

'I think there are many writers who are like that. It is a basic requisite of the job.'

'No. You are very wrong. Some writers are full of wonderful ideas, but lack the skills to bring them to life in a believable way. But you – you can bring people and places to life as much as if they really existed. And that is what is lacking in the kinds of speeches that my poor husband had to deliver to the general public earlier today and yesterday. Long strings of facts and figures, but with nothing to persuade the audience of their truth. There was not even the slightest metaphorical tinge to them. They didn't even speak of the nation as their mother. Even the most basic political thinker should understand that the nation is their mother. Then they will realize – those people outside – that in directing their impatience towards the leadership of their country they are slapping their own mother in the face.'

I thought back to the stories I had written, and in particular the one for which I had been awarded the Nicholson Star. If Mrs Nicholson had read any of my stories, that would most likely be the one. 'The Button'. It was about a city that was terrorized by a giant button. Whenever there was some calamity in the city – whenever there was a fire or a street accident or a power failure or a riot or disturbance of any kind, a giant button could be seen running away from the scene, glimpsed down a side street, or on a bridge, or scampering along a concrete walkway, or disappearing into a pedestrian underpass. The button was a typical button, an archetypical button, you might say – round, brown, four-holed, the sort you see on a sturdy overcoat. The button had a pair of legs – so people reported – but descriptions of the legs differed from eyewitness to eyewitness – some said the legs were in trousers, some that they were in tights, some that they were bare. The city was driven mad over speculation as to who the button might be. There were suggestions that he was a rogue advertising mascot for a button or clothing manufacturer, who'd stolen his costume and gone out of control. But no such manufacturer could be found to account for the rogue button. Meanwhile there was speculation about what the button could mean, that it was the insignia of a revolutionary group, or an underground movement of some sort. In the newspapers there were long editorials on the symbolism of buttons – how they represented a coming together, the joining, the fastening of two halves. How did that work politically? Could it be a symbol of fascism, or communism, or anarchism?

'The Button'. It ends badly, that story, for the city. Struck by a plague of paranoia, both for what the button portends and for speculation as to its identity, the populace eventually consume themselves in a tide of slaughter and burning, until there is nothing left but ashes and blood. And a button, watching from the mountaintop overlooking the city.

As a story it was very unlike anything I had ever written before, or have since.

'There you are,' said Mrs Nicholson, pointing to the table, 'we have everything you need. You will write a speech for my husband at this table. Or if you prefer, you can sit on one of the couches. Or on the floor. I don't know how writers work. Would you like to use the colonel's laptop? I don't think he'll be needing it. Or do you like to work on paper?'

It seemed that I had forgotten how to write, or what I needed in order to think of stories. Did I work on paper normally, at home? Or did I use a computer? Suddenly I thought of the fish. How long would I be here? Would I be back in time to give them their food? How long can a fish live without food? I once left them for a whole day without any food, and I have to say, they didn't look well.

I decided that I worked with pen and paper. A pad of paper was provided, but it was wide ruled, which I hate. And no margin. The pen was a good old-fashioned fountain pen which Mrs Nicholson fished out of Mr Nicholson's inner breast pocket, without Mr Nicholson seeming to notice.

'Astonishing isn't it, really? A pad of paper and a pen, and with that you can change the course of history. I suppose that is why you like being a writer really, isn't it? The power?'

I laughed inwardly again. Mrs Nicholson accusing me of having a hunger for power? This was a woman who had desired nothing else all of her adult life, and for a good part of that life she had wielded near-total power. No one knows how much influence she exerted over Mr Nicholson, although from what I could see in the room at this moment I felt the rumours to be confirmed, that she was the real power behind the throne, and that Mr Nicholson was nothing more than a cardboard president. She continued to work the room like a hostess at a cocktail party, though instead of idle chitchat she was dictating the orders of state and planning the future of our country, which would be determined in the next few hours. She moved from minister to minister discussing and planning, commanding and berating. I could see that everyone in the room was in awe of her, was even frightened of her. Of Mr Nicholson, there was nothing to note. He continued to sit in his chair with a glum look on his face. He rested his elbow on the chair back, just as if he was in the back room of a coffee shop discussing the racing form, having just lost a few pounds on a frisky nag. But he was passive. He had given up. He was letting everyone else do the work and the worrying, and he was going to do nothing but wait until someone had come up with a plan.

The blank paper stretched before me like a cement path. Rarely had a pen felt so heavy in my hand, or as blunt. Unused to my grip, its nib scratched and scored the paper, spluttered, juddered, nearly split. Blobs of ink fell and formed black abscesses on what few words I'd managed to write. I thought back to my story about the button and realized that I had written it without once attempting to understand or answer the questions it put into so many of my readers' minds. Who was the button? That simplest of questions. My readers thought there must have been clues as to who it was, and they searched everywhere for them. They wondered if the button was someone famous in the real world – some dared even suggest he was Mr Nicholson himself, or (given details about the slenderness of the button's legs) that he was Mrs Nicholson. Others that he was a figure from history, that he was Trotsky, or Christ, or Socrates, or Dante. Many candidates for the identity of the button were suggested, though I had never even given the matter any thought. I had not considered the question, because the identity of the button was as much a mystery to me as it was to the citizens of the little city in which he appears. And therein lay my problem with Mr Nicholson's speech. How was I, a writer of fiction, expected to bring forth facts into the world in such a way they could be believed, when my natural inclination is to pose questions?

I glanced over from my desk towards Mr and Mrs Nicholson, at the other end of the room. To my surprise they were drinking tea from delicate white china cups while perusing some documents. Mrs Nicholson noticed me and came over with a sheet of paper.

'How are you getting on?' Her face went stony when she saw the page I'd been working on, empty but for a few words and ink blots. 'Is this all you've done? Where's the rest of it? Do you realize if we don't have a speech in the next thirty minutes we will have no alternative but to order the army into the square? Here, perhaps this will help you.' She handed me a sheet on which there were lists of numbers, figures that showed how inflation had been brought down in a steady curve for the length of the Nicholsons' presidency; they showed also the figures for crime, which were as low. All the other measures – unemployment, obesity, divorce rates, all these had fallen steadily. The only things to have risen were longevity and incomes. And the projected figures were even healthier. Prosperity was rising steadily. Prices were coming down. Homes were being built all over the country. Very impressive figures. But of course they were rubbish. Had I not seen it for myself, I would never have believed it. The figures were simply plucked out of the air by Mr and Mrs Nicholson. I had seen them in the act, making up the numbers, jotting down whatever looked like a reasonable and believable number for whatever economic sector they were considering. It contradicted the evidence of one's eyes in the most striking way. I had seen the dole queues and the bread queues. I had seen the homeless people on the streets and I had seen how heartlessly they were dealt with by the authorities (high-pressure water hoses). I had seen the people driven out of their homes, which were then cleared away for some grandiose structure or other – the great stadia in which no sports are played, the empty-walled palaces of culture curated only by rats and small bears, libraries of empty shelves. And now I was being asked to write as though I had seen none of these things. I was not one to be disloyal to the Nicholsons, but I began to quaver at the thought of incorporating these spurious 'facts' into my speech.

'Can these figures be backed up?' I asked Mrs Nicholson.

'Of course they can. Why do you ask such a ridiculous question?'

'I just want to make sure.'

'But you are a writer of fiction. Why should you care?'

'I didn't think you wanted me to write a work of fiction. You wanted me to write a speech that had the power of fiction.'

'If you don't write something in the next twenty minutes you will lose the power to live, I can tell you that. Now just incorporate these facts without making the speech boring, and I think you will now need to work very fast, we want an hour's worth of words from you. Would you like an incentive?'

She glared at me in such away that I felt my heart withdraw into a shell. When she left me I began writing, but I wrote as if I was writing the first draft of a piece of fiction – spontaneously and with little thought about what I was writing or where it was going. I free-ranged across what areas of my imagination had not been locked down with fright. At last the pages began to fill. The words came so quickly I was tripping over my own handwriting. My imagination was freed up by the fact that I began to sense that the speech I was writing would never be delivered. The crowd outside was now reaching a new pitch of volatility. The barricades between the square and the palace were beginning to crumble. The protesters spilled out beyond the square to fill the streets as far as could be seen. The whole city, it seemed, was becoming a site of protest. Mr Nicholson did nothing but sit with his head in his hands. The feeling was that it would be too dangerous for him to make a personal appearance on the balcony. Mrs Nicholson, who had been absent from the room for a few minutes, appeared with blood sprinkled across her face.

'On learning that the army is no longer taking orders from him, I have just personally executed the commander-in-chief of our armed forces.'

At this, Mr Nicholson lifted his head from his hands, but only in order that he could look at the ceiling in despair. Mrs Nicholson took a tissue out of her handbag and, using the glass over an eighteenth-century portrait that hung on one of the walls, dabbed at the blood on her face, having dampened the tissue with spit. From then on what little control I had over my life receded beyond reach. I was at the mercy of Mr and Mrs Nicholson and the small world that was left to them. Did they mean to utilize some sort of evacuation plan, and if so, would I be part of it? Or would I be left in the palace when the mob finally broke through – and what must I do then, hide in a cupboard, or pretend to be an innocent orderly, a cleaner or janitor or odd-job man? I was at the mercy of this late-middle-aged, childless, married couple. And it was against all reason that I felt a certain affection for them, even as Mrs Nicholson wiped the blood from her cheek. I realized I was watching a rare moment in history, the evaporation of the aura of power from a couple who had possessed it for most of their lives. The panic and despair and depression that the couple were exhibiting only served to render them more human. I heard Mr Nicholson suddenly blurt out – 'Forty per cent. If we cut defence, foreign aid, bureaucracy, sack the civil service except for the vital functions, we could make wage rises across the board of forty per cent. Tell your writer friend to tell them that.'

'You're dreaming,' Mrs Nicholson said. 'They don't care about their wages any more. They have been fed so many lies by our enemies they no longer believe anything we say to them. You, you –' she pointed to the two men who had brought me – 'get everything ready, we need to go now.' The men looked troubled, doubtful, unsure of procedure. 'Well? Are you just going to stand there?'

The people in the room began getting ready. The film crew had begun filming the events as they were happening. Having removed the camera from its tripod where it had been carefully set up to film the broadcast that would now never be made, they pointed it at whoever was talking, and no one in the room seemed to mind, or notice. Gradually we began moving towards the main doors, shuffling together without any clear sense of purpose or where we were going. Once out of the doors and into the large concourse that led back towards the dome, two of the men in politicians' suits suddenly began to run off in the opposite direction, without a word. 'Let them go,' said Mrs Nicholson, not that anyone was trying to stop them. Mr Nicholson didn't even seem to notice. 'And you,' she pointed to the camera crew, 'you can follow them. We don't want you.' The camera crew were slow to respond, and just pointed their camera at Mrs Nicholson. She signalled to the bodyguards and they immediately pounced on the film crew, taking their camera and knocking the people to the ground, and giving them a severe beating. One of the men fiddled with the innards of the camera, and pulled its memory out, which he then bent in his teeth. Mrs Nicholson laughed. The crew were semi-conscious on the floor, their faces rapidly swelling with bruises, and coagulating blood. My bowels were chilled, as I wondered if I would be next in line for such treatment, but to my surprise I was ushered along with the dwindling party, along a narrow corridor to a service lift.

Then up several levels, the five of us, and out through cluttered corridors, up a narrow staircase and through some heavy doors, suddenly we were out in the open, among the house-sized air-conditioning vents and lift-shaft winding houses. Rounding a block we saw the helicopter, its rotors spinning at a steady rhythm. It looked pitifully small, hardly bigger than a model, I thought at first. The pilot was wearing headphones and reading a map. His face seemed to drop as he saw us approach. He shook his head and held up a hand, fingers spread, meaning there were too many of us. In the noise and the light breeze of the rotor blades I could not hear anything that was being said, but I got the gist of the conversation. The pilot was saying he didn't have enough fuel to take us very far, and that the fewer passengers he had to carry, the further the fuel would take them. The bodyguards suddenly ran off, and the pilot took off his headphones, as if he was about to join them, but Mr and Mrs Nicholson were already climbing into the helicopter. Mrs Nicholson physically restrained the pilot, by placing a firm hand on his shoulder. The pilot continued to shrug and shake his head. He was now saying that the flight would be too dangerous. If the Nicholsons had lost control of the army, it was likely the helicopter would get shot down by surface-to-air missiles. I don't know how it happened but suddenly I was in the helicopter as well. Mrs Nicholson had urged me in to join them, when I had had half a mind to join the bodyguards and take my chances with the crowds. But an unaccountable loyalty had sprung up in my feelings, and I felt duty-bound to stick with the Nicholsons, and see them safely out of the city. And perhaps it was my writer's curiosity that persuaded me to stay with them, to see where they had it in mind to go, to find out what sanctuary awaited them, to see what power looked like when it had lost all the instruments for the exercise of that power.

We lifted off, toppling sideways almost instantly, then lunging forward, clear of the rooftop. Suddenly the ground filled our forward vision, the streets which seemed like gorges cut through cement plains, flowing with rivers of people. It was true, a fact, that the whole city centre was now awash with protestors, the grievances of the people had become a viscous fluid filling every cranny of the capital, had not my heart already fallen through my body thanks to the clumsy aerobatics of our pilot I felt sure it would have lifted to see such a pure expression of popular will. The people had become an architectural phenomenon, filling the space between buildings. I glanced at Mrs Nicholson, who was sitting squashed up against me, and once the helicopter had achieved a more level flight position, I could see, reflected in the window (for she was turned away from me), a look of horror on her face – or was it wonder, awe, terror, as she contemplated the new physical form the city was taking. Mr Nicholson was sitting in the front seat, alongside the pilot, and I could not see any reflection of his face, though I could see his head shake despairingly from side to side, just as it had done for most of the afternoon. Otherwise he was frequently in close conversation with the pilot, who had repeatedly to shout things in his ear to be heard. He claimed, so I could only just make out, to be taking such a swinging, erratic course in order to dodge any possible strikes from the ground. We swooped low, then swung left and right. We felt almost as if he was trying to throw us out of the vehicle. Now Mrs Nicholson was shouting at him. There were arguments over the flight plan and our final destination. Mrs Nicholson had found a map and was pointing out to the pilot where we should be going, and that we needed to swing round in a different direction. By now we were clear of the city and below us were ploughed fields and quadrilaterals of pine forest. So far the whole journey had been at less than a thousand feet and, most of the time, much lower. Our speed was slowing as well. Mrs Nicholson continually berated the pilot but he kept pointing to his fuel gauge, saying he was running low. They would not be able to get to the destination over the border into our neighbouring state.

In the end the helicopter was brought to land in a field of potatoes, about twenty miles from the city. By now Mrs Nicholson was screaming at the pilot, slapping him on the back of his head, while the pilot protested that it was not his fault that the helicopter didn't have enough fuel. 'I'll get you a car,' he said, 'I just need to get to the phone box. There's one in that layby. That's why I landed here, if you'll just let me.'

'We don't have time to stand in a potato field waiting for a driver, you fool. The army has been following us on the ground. They'll be upon us in five minutes. We have to commandeer a vehicle.'

By now all four of us were out of the helicopter and stumbling through the potatoes towards the nearby road, on which there was little traffic. While the pilot went over to the phone, one of those emergency phones for people whose vehicles have broken down, Mrs Nicholson stepped out into the road to flag down the solitary car that was heading towards us. She stood there, still in her well-to-do housewife's coat with her handbag dangling from her elbow, waving both arms frantically at the approaching car, an expensive-looking sedan, which, for a moment, seemed about to swerve around Mrs Nicholson, but screeched to a halt when she stepped sideways to counter the move. She signalled to us to follow her out into the road, for one of us to take her place while she talked to the driver. The driver, I could see, was a respectable, professional-looking man in his late fifties or sixties, in casual clothes. He looked severely panicked as we climbed into the car. I figured that he had had just been listening to the radio, and had heard about the helicopter on the roof of the palace, and now couldn't quite believe that this outlandish narration had come to life before his eyes. He had probably seen the helicopter itself as it came down.

'I am very sorry,' he said, 'but I cannot drive you anywhere.' His tone was deeply sincere. He may even have once been an ardent supporter of the Nicholsons. But now that they had been ousted, anyone seen to be helping them could find themselves in serious trouble. I too was beginning to realize this, and was spending all my time wondering when would be the right moment to make my escape.

We began moving, the driver, who turned out to be a doctor, hunched and petrified at the wheel, because Mrs Nicholson had produced, from her dainty white handbag, a dirty great revolver, and was pointing it shakily at the back of the doctor's head.

The helicopter pilot was nowhere to be seen when we drove off, so it was just me and the country doctor who formed the Nicholsons' entourage. Once we were going steadily Mrs Nicholson put down the gun and began consulting a road atlas that was on the parcel shelf. We were about a hundred and fifty miles from the sanctuary that had been set up for the Nicholsons, and we were all taking turns to try and read the map and figure out where we were and which way to go, when the doctor saw his chance, slammed the brakes on and fled from the car and into a wood by the side of the road. We were too thrown and confused by the sudden halt to make any attempt to chase the terrified doctor, whose departing cry was, 'I have a family! I have a family!' He had left the keys in the car. Mrs Nicholson turned to me and said, 'You drive.'

I wondered what would happen if I refused. Would Mrs Nicholson take her place at the wheel? Perhaps she couldn't drive. As for Mr Nicholson, he looked in no fit state to drive anything. She didn't point the gun at me when she asked me to drive, and I took a certain pride in that fact. I had won the Nicholsons' trust. They had no one else in the world. Everyone had abandoned them. This made them both heartbreakingly vulnerable and frighteningly dangerous. They could not be left alone, for they seemed to be people with no practical skills. They had been driven everywhere for most of their adult lives. They had lived like well-attended monarchs with every need met by their retinues. The only thing they possessed was the authority of command, the ability to compel and instil obedience, but now this was lost on everyone in the nation but me. As such, I felt an enormous responsibility to remain obedient, even though I would far sooner be among the revolutionaries who were presumably, at this very moment, dismantling the vestiges of the Nicholsons' regime, room by room. And so without a moment's hesitation I stepped around the car and took my place in the driver's seat. The doctor had left the keys in the ignition, though I could see there was very little fuel left. To avoid the military vehicles and road blocks we turned off onto country lanes that led into the mountains. We thought there might be a way of using very small roads to reach the border, avoiding the main centres of population and the freeways altogether – but the problem was the lack of fuel. After an hour or so in the mountains, we realized we would have to risk turning back towards the main road to find a petrol station.

And it was at such a petrol station that my journey with the Nicholsons ended. We had taken the precautions of concealment as we rejoined the freeway. Mrs Nicholson lay down on the back seat and covered herself with a blanket while Mr Nicholson decided to seclude himself in the boot, while I pulled into a garage and began to fill up. I don't know how it was that the military vehicles were so quickly upon us. Perhaps the doctor had got word to the army that his car had been taken by the Nicholsons, or perhaps the garage owner had thought there was something odd about the car, but while I was in the shop paying for my fuel the forecourt was suddenly alive with the roar of military engines, and an armoured car, a truck and two jeeps pulled in, soldiers in full armour poured out, and the car was surrounded. I watched from inside the shop as all this was happening. Mrs Nicholson was pulled from the car as if she was a hold-all, and thrown to the ground. She screamed with indignation. Mr Nicholson was quickly found in the boot, and likewise pulled out without any thought to his dignity or comfort. The two were then lifted to their feet and marched around the side of the petrol station, where there was a car wash. I cautiously began to leave the shop, anxious to see what would be done to the Nicholsons. I could not believe that they would be dealt with summarily, without trial or right of appeal, but I heard the shots even before I left the shop, a volley of bullets from several automatic weapons. I was frozen with fear and halted by the flower stand, just next to the night-service window. An acrid fog wafted from behind the building, and I made the corner just in time to see what had been done. Mr and Mrs Nicholson's bodies were lying on the cement at the entrance to the car wash. Mrs Nicholson was lying on her front, her arms spread, her handbag still round her forearm, and her coat spread open like a cape. Mr Nicholson was in an odd position, having first fallen to his knees, and then backwards, so that his lower legs were tucked beneath his body, and his abdomen was pushed up higher than his head. I could see his face had the same fed-up expression it had had all day, though the eyes were firmly closed. Both bodies were oozing little red rivulets. I heard a soldier making a joke about how they should put the bodies through the car wash. Another was carefully recording the scene on a video camera. There was debate about what to do with the bodies. Eventually they were lifted by their arms and legs, two soldiers at each end, and put in the back of a truck. Then the whole squad of vehicles roared into angry life, and with a multiple spewing of blue exhaust, was gone.

The soldiers had taken no interest in the car they had found the Nicholsons in, or who had been driving it. Perhaps they were just so thrilled at having found the pair that they had forgotten about it, or perhaps they thought it was irrelevant. I was no one to be bothered with. Who was I, after all? A writer of whimsical tales that had happened to attract the attention of the first lady of our great country. That had been awarded the Nicholson Star for the short story 'The Button'. I had thought about asking Mrs Nicholson why she had liked that story so much, but I had never got the opportunity. I had wondered if she had any thoughts on who the button was, or what he represented. And now I had lost that chance. One critic had thought the button represented a fascist organization, that it stood for the binding together of the people, just as the bundles of sticks had to the original fascisti. But now I believed that the button represented anarchy, chaos, undirected, unrestrained energy. How can a button, a thing that fastens and contains, represent such an idea? Well, because a button can be undone. A button can liberate as easily as it constrains. It can keep the world in check, or it can release the world to run unchecked.

Odd, how the same thing can be seen so differently. I took myself back to the car, after a little contemplation, in silence, of the bloodstains by the car wash. Perhaps it would be good to drive on to wherever the Nicholsons had been heading, over the border into the sanctuary of our neighbouring state. I could claim asylum, if need be.

And then I thought of the fish, unfed for a whole day, and I drove back to the city.

JAMES KELMAN

justice for one

They were marching already when I fought my way to the meeting point up the hill. Now there were voices all around, and of every kind. I was blundering about not understanding what I was to do. How did they know and I did not?

Somebody tried to sell me something or give me something I was unsure which. Somebody else asked me a question. I was not sure about that either. I could not decipher what they wanted to know or even understand what they said. Was it even myself they were talking to? I heard someone saying: Shit he's drunk out his skull.

Me? I was not drunk, not drunk out my skull. Shit man I was not drunk at all. What the hell were they on about? I asked them but they paid no attention. They had made up their mind.

This is what people do, especially in this part of the world. A woman said, We're going this way.

What way? I said but the woman had gone, whoever she was.

A typical life experience. Woman go away: it could be the title of a Spanish movie. Probably it is already.

On all sides folk were walking past. They moved quickly. Some were coming so close I felt a draught from their body, going to bang into me. Somebody said, The army are there and they are waiting for us.

I shouted, I beg your pardon!

Take your hand off my arm, cried a man.

Sorry mate, it is so damn dark and all that smelling smelly shit; what is that smell? said another man, somebody with a hoarse voice. He had quite a kindly voice, and he added, Better get out of here . . . And then he grasped my wrist.

Hey, I said, dont do that. Whereabouts are they anyway?

Down the hill.

Are there many?

I dont know friend, somebody said there were hundreds.

For God sake!

I know. And coming in our direction! Then the hoarse man smiled. He actually smiled.

Did you say our direction? I said.

He only smiled at me. He was no longer holding my wrist, and I had that sense he was about to vanish from in front of my eyes. I wanted to keep him here, just like hold him back, not let him escape, he was escaping. How come I couldnt escape but he can! That was me, that is what I was thinking. Jesus, our direction, how come?

Instead of answering he glanced at another marcher, another woman; this one had a band wrapped round her forehead and some hair falling over its sides; her cheeks were smudged and the blood was there. He jerked his thumb in my direction, shaking his head in a gesture to her, about me, as if I was somebody to avoid. But I was only wanting to know why they were marching from that direction. I shouted: How come? Surely that's the question.

What do you mean? muttered the woman. I dont like the way you are saying that.

But if they're marching from that direction! I said. Then I stopped and shrugged. She did not care.

I could see another couple of people looking at me; they too were suspicious. I shook my head at them, as if I was just seeing them for the first time.

It was dreadful. But what could I do except walk on. This is what I did, yes, I kept walking. Of course I did. So that was it. Much was explained, even to predictability. One of the folk watching stopped directly in front of me. Another woman. There were many women, yet I could not pass her without making a nonsensical comment. I stopped walking to do it. The earth is good. I said it into myself though perhaps my lips moved. I wondered about myself. It was a surprise I had any self-respect at all. I asked the woman what was wrong, if something was wrong and she replied. You will not get far.

Sure I will.

Not the way we're going. She put her hands onto my wrists and tugged me forwards.

What the hell are you doing? I said.

She smiled. My attention was attracted to her shoulders. It was not a time for physical attraction. Her shoulders were beautiful. At the point where the machine gun opens up on you, on you, your attention is drawn to the curve of a woman, a woman's shoulders. My God, almost I was crying.

Saddened by something. I saw it in her. This was a thought she had had, and in connection with myself. But not sex, it could never have been sex, to have been with me, lying with me, it could never have been that. Shit man. No. Never. She was pointing in the same direction the crowd had marched. Okay. That is the way ahead, she said, that is a proper march.

Yes but that is also how the crowd is advancing. Do you wish me to follow the crowd. Is that an elitist thing to say?

She was gazing at me.

Do you think it is?

She thought I was mad. You do, I said, I can see you do. It is a terribly elitist thing to say.

Now she avoided eye-contact. Just keep walking straight, she said, and stay to the rear.

I shall miss the action.

Is that not what you want? The difference is you will not go wrong.

Oh.

Yes.

So that is the difference?

Yes.

I said, But how do you know what I want?

But I looked at her shoulders when I said it, and I did that so she would notice. It was almost disgusting. I think it was disgusting.

She shook her head. Perhaps she was ashamed of me.

I smiled. You think you know me but you dont. You dont even know when I am being sarcastic.

She turned her back to me, and resumed walking. I managed not to go after her, nor to call after her. There are times for being funny, this was not one of them. I saw a man spit on the road. It was in regard to me! He was spitting against me!

Shit. What had I done to deserve that. Talking to the woman with the beautiful shoulders. Perhaps he thought it demeaning, that it demeaned us all. He also walked away. Then the chanting began:

Justice for one justice for all.

I looked for the woman but she too had gone.

So many people, they just started chanting, and these slogans. There was nothing wrong with these slogans. I tried to say the words aloud and succeeded. I was pleased. I said the words again. I was laughing, just how I could say them, just as good as anyone.

We all were marching. Armed forces march and so do people. We marched over the brow of the hill. I knew the terrain.

I listened to the slogans and knew them as fair. These were good words, except the way I said them they sounded different, they sounded as though different, as if in some way singular, they became words to actually decipher, as opposed to a slogan, the sort that one marches to. I tried to pick up that latter rhythm, the way everyone else had it. Justice for one justice for all. Great rhythms, great slogans but could I do it? Or was I only emulating the passion of these other people? As a boy I missed the beat – I always missed the beat. Now here it was again, half a line behind, I was half a line behind, behind everyone else.

Justice for one justice for all. Nothing wrong in that. I walked briskly on, one foot in front of the other. A peculiar sensation overtook me. I could no longer see things clearly. People and objects blurred, was that a building or was it a jumbo aircraft? Where the hell was I was this a city street or was it a country lane? Was that a herd of animals or what, what was it? Over now some yards distant somebody was – her, it was her again, it was that woman, one of the women, it was one of the women, which one was she? She was watching me. Hey! I waved to her but she ignored the wave; she was still watching me, and then not.

Beyond here were things. And what things! Things that were guaranteed to scare me. Some folk were heroes. This woman was one of them. Obviously she was. And the man who seemed her companion. I saw him too. Both were heroes. It could not be denied. Their actions were heroic.

Mine were not. The very idea! I smiled. Beyond the current conglomer-
ation I could not perceive one entity, not one single entity, not one, not
that.

It was where they were walking, it was down a hill, it is where they
were going. And everybody shouting different things, slogans and laughter, somebody, trying to start a new chant, people were. And now the
army were into view. Everybody knew it, there was a shiver now and some
folk threw down cigarettes and trampled them and others again opened
their packets and got out another and snatched at them with their
lighters.

If it was for men was it for women! I asked the first person next to me,
a middle-aged woman in her forties or maybe fifties.

I beg your pardon?

Is it for men, or is it meant to be women as well? I'm not keen on
women being here.

I dont know what you are talking about.

But what does it all mean? I said, I never ever work it out, I was never
able to.

What did you say? The woman seemed irritated.

Dont take it too seriously, I said.

A couple of younger fellows rushed past now, arms laden with stones.
That meant the army right enough, there would be a pitched battle. That
was how it went. History showed us this. It did not require demonstration
upon demonstration and does not entail actual changes in how we live
our life. I had to go with them, I shouted and ran ahead.

CATASTROPHIC WORLDS

LUCY WOOD

Flotsam, Jetsam, Lagan, Derelict

Mary and Vincent Layton lived in a small house that overlooked an empty beach. The beach was wide and rocky – there were rocks the size of doors that had been thrown up by the tide, and smaller stones that banked up in drifts. Rows of low, dark rocks radiated out across the beach like the hands of a clock. These were the worn-down layers where the cliff used to be, before it had been whittled down to its bones.

Their house was painted white, with a porch at the side and a garage at the back. There was a road behind it. In front there was the cliff – still being worn down, still being whittled – but they'd been assured it would not affect them in their lifetime.

They'd moved in over the summer. Finally everything was sorted and in order: their work had reached its natural end point; finances were tied up; their children were married and settled. There were no loose ends. They'd been together for a very long time – they could hardly believe how long really – but now, finally, there were no loose ends.

Vincent had found a job to fill his weekday mornings, doing gardening work for people around the town. Sometimes Mary would go and help but more often she would walk along the cliffs or the beach, or just sit looking out. It was quiet and everything else seemed very far away. There was no TV, no mobile signal. They didn't have to think about anything at all.

One morning Mary was out walking when she saw something glinting further down the beach. She made her way towards it. Clouds hung low in the sky – they were pale, almost yellow, like eyes that were old or tired. The rocks were slippery and she walked carefully – if she fell and broke something then that could be it, and all the work, all the years of planning, would be for nothing. She avoided the places with wet mossy weed, and stepped instead on the fat brown ribbons, which creaked softly under her shoes. It was still early. She'd always woken early but now, instead of lying awake in bed, she got up and came down to the beach.

She crossed the rocks and stepped down onto the sand, which was coarse and flecked with colours. Sometimes it looked bronze. Sometimes it looked silver. It always felt cold, even in the sun, and she often wondered how deep it was.

The glinting thing was half-buried. It was a plastic bottle; one of those small water bottles with ridges all around it. The plastic was tinged blue and the top was sticking up among all the stones and shells. It didn't look right. It didn't look like it was supposed to be there. She crouched down, scraped up a handful of sand and pressed it over the top of the bottle. Then she dug up another handful and did the same, until it was completely covered. She stood back and looked. There. She couldn't even tell where it was any more. And later, the tide would take it away for good.

The next morning there were five bottles strewn across the rocks below the house.

Mary stood on the path looking down at them. It was mizzling. The beach seemed flatter and washed of colour, except for the blue of the bottles. She went down the path and over the rocks. They were rectangular five-litre bottles and the plastic was thick and shiny. She collected them one at a time and put them in a pile, then turned and looked back at the cliffs, across the sand, and out at the sea. There was nowhere for the bottles to go. They were too big to bury, and there were too many of them. The tide wouldn't reach that far for hours. She thought about putting them behind one of the big rocks, but she would probably still be able to see them from the house. And, even if she couldn't see them, she would know they were there.

She picked the bottles up awkwardly, holding one under each arm and the rest against her chest, and carried them over the rocks. There was a car park at the other end of the beach which had a bin in it. She crossed the beach and went over to the bin. It was overflowing and there were extra bags stuffed with rubbish on the ground underneath it. She put the bottles down by the bags and turned to leave. The wind knocked one of the bottles over and it fell with a hollow thud. Another one blew back towards the sand. Mary watched it moving. It made a scraping sound as it skidded against the gravel. She picked the bottles up again and carried them back across the beach. She walked up the path towards the house and unlocked the garage. There was a shelf against the back wall and she put them on there, lining them up neatly in a row.

She locked the garage and went inside. Vincent was in the kitchen, making lunch. She went up behind him and put her arms around his waist. He smelled of bonfires and paint. His waist had thickened over the years. So had hers. Sometimes their bones clicked. She leaned into his warm back. He reached his arm around and rubbed her hip.

'Our daughter phoned,' he said. He took four slices of bread out of the bag and put them on plates. The kitchen was small and white and clean. There were white plates in the cupboard, a few white mugs, two bowls and two glasses. They had got rid of almost everything.

'I didn't think we'd given her this number yet,' Mary said.

Vincent put cheese in the bread and cut each sandwich in half. He wiped the crumbs up carefully. 'Something's happening with Jack again.'

Mary watched as Vincent got up the last crumbs with the tip of his finger. He passed Mary her plate and picked up his own.

'Let's eat these in bed,' Mary said. They could do things like that now. They could close all the curtains and afterwards they could sleep until dinner if they wanted to. There was nothing to stop them.

The next morning she took her usual route out of the house and along the path down to the rocks. Before she opened the gate she stopped and scanned the beach. For a moment she thought she saw something glinting and her heart began to beat faster than usual. But it was nothing. The beach was clear and empty. She undid her hair and let it stream out. She started humming. There were shallow pools among the rocks and they rippled in the wind.

She took the long way round, past her favourite rock, which was covered in a dark sheet of mussels.

Her boots crunched on the stones. She passed heaps of seaweed that must have been pushed in by the tide. Some of it was orange, and some was blue, and there were hundreds, maybe thousands, of tiny blue and white shells.

She reached down and picked up some of the seaweed. She liked the way it popped under her hands. But it wasn't seaweed. This was stiff and tough and fraying at the edges. She dropped it and looked at the other piles. They weren't seaweed, none of them were – they were heaps of twisted nylon rope. She crouched down and picked up one of the shells. The edge of it dug into her finger. It was a fragment of plastic. All along the tide line, as far as she could see, the beach was covered in small, sharp fragments.

She turned quickly and went back to the house. The wind knotted her hair into clumps and she tied it up tightly away from her face. She looked through the cupboards for the bin bags. There weren't any left. She went into the garage and found the bucket, which they used to clean the car and the windows. She took the bucket down to the beach with her, knelt in the damp sand, and started picking everything up – rope, plastic, translucent strips of polythene. After a while she stopped doing it piece by piece and scraped up entire handfuls. When the bucket was full she stood up and stretched her legs. Her back was stiff and there was a faint, dull ache in the joints of her hands. She carried the bucket back to the house, opened the garage and emptied it onto the floor. Everything spread in a tangled heap. She locked the garage and went inside.

Vincent was pouring drinks. 'Where've you been?' he asked. He kissed the soft skin on the side of her neck.

'Just my usual walk,' Mary said. She took off her coat.

'You missed lunch,' he told her. He emptied crisps into a bowl and passed them to her.

Mary looked at the clock. Her stomach was empty. When she reached into the bowl the salt stung her fingers.

There was a letter on the table. The envelope was thick and cream-coloured and headed with Vincent's old company's logo. It was still sealed.

Vincent saw her looking and went over to the table, but neither of them opened the letter.

'Why are they writing to you?' Mary said.

'I don't know.'

'I didn't think they needed to write to you any more.'

Vincent took the letter and put it in the drawer underneath the phone. The white kitchen and the white lights made his skin look almost grey. It was Mary who'd first persuaded him to take that job, even though he hadn't wanted to. There were other things he'd wanted to do. She held his hand. Their fingers laced between each other's. Vincent reached over and picked something out of her hair – it was tangled in and it took him a moment to loosen it. It was a strip of blue plastic. That night, when she was getting undressed, she found another strip caught in the cuff of her shirt.

The next day she got up early, took the bucket and went straight to work on the beach. She picked and sifted until her knees throbbed and her hands felt like they were about to seize up. The more she picked up, the more she saw – there were ring pulls, tin lids, bottle caps, tags, rusty springs coiled under stones, watch batteries, translucent beads that she could only see if she squinted, hidden among the grains like clutches of eggs. There were bits of Styrofoam that were exactly the same colour as the sand, and bright specks of glass.

The sun slipped down lower. The tide came in. Finally she stopped and stood up. She'd only covered a few square metres.

When she went to bed there were bits stuck to her feet. When she brushed them off they scattered across the floor and fell down between the boards. She got up and tried to pick them out without waking Vincent. He murmured and reached for her. She got back into bed. Bits of plastic blew in on a draught under the door.

On the day before the rubbish collection Mary took their bin bag from the kitchen and put it by the side of the road. She'd bought a new roll of black bags, and she took them down to the garage, unlocked it, and went in. The room was full. A fetid smell rose up, like something in a ditch that hadn't drained away. The floor was a teeming mass of boxes and crates, ropes, plastic bottles, wet shoes, chipped and broken toys. There were reams of greasy netting with tins and plastic beads and pen lids caught in them; and a heap of oil cans and rubber gloves and mouldy bits of fabric. In the far corner there was a pile of sand and a sieve. Some-times things looked like sand, but they weren't sand, really.

She stood in the middle of the garage and looked around. There was so much of it – it was piled halfway up the walls. She gripped the roll of bags. What she needed to do was fill each one and then leave them out for the collection. Then, by tomorrow, it would all be gone. She went over to the edge of the pile and started filling the first bag. She filled it quickly, tied the top and started on another, breaking up the boxes and crates, not stopping until everything in the garage was cleared. It took a long time. When she'd finished she dragged the bags outside one by one and put them by the road. A car drove past and slowed down, looking at the vast, toppling pile. Her cheeks burned. But they would be gone by the morning.

Vincent was waiting in the hall. 'We'd better go,' he said. He was buttoning his coat.

'Go?'

'To the Gleesons'. They invited us, remember?'

'I don't remember,' Mary said.

'They said we should go over.'

'Why?'

'I suppose to have a drink. Talk.'

'Talk,' Mary said. 'About what?'

Vincent leaned down and tied his shoes. 'I guess they want to get to know us. Where we lived before, what we're like, what we did.'

Mary leaned back against the wall. 'Before?' she said. She could still smell the rank saltiness on her hands. It was probably on her clothes. She took off her coat and her shoes. She slipped her hand up the back of Vincent's shirt. 'Let's stay in,' she said. His skin was creased and soft. She knew each bone of his spine.

Vincent phoned in for them and they spent the evening listening to music and eating leftovers from the fridge, with the radiators turned up high.

The wind picked up and surged all night. The tiles clattered like bits of stone falling off the cliff. Hail chipped at the windows. Mary lay awake listening to the waves hitting against the beach. She thought about the bags out on the road. The palm tree scratched against the wall. She sat up suddenly. Where would it all go, after it had been collected? It wouldn't really be gone, would it? It would just be somewhere else. It would be somewhere else, instead of here. Maybe, eventually, some of it would end up back on the beach. Her heart beat hard, almost painfully. She couldn't think about that. She'd done what she could. Eventually she lay back down and closed her eyes.

She slipped out early the next morning, while Vincent was still asleep.

There were two messages from their daughter on the answer phone. The red light flashed slowly.

When she opened the front door it hit against something. She pushed harder but it still wouldn't open more than a few inches. There was something on the other side – she could almost see it through the letter box. She shoved harder and the door finally opened. There was a pile of wet netting slumped against it. She pushed it away with her foot and went out. The grass was strewn with rope and shoes and tins. Some of the bin bags had ripped open, some had tipped over and come untied, some had rolled down the path and burst. Plastic had been flung across the road. There were bottles and strips of cardboard caught in the hedge; packets flapped on the ground like injured birds. There was a rubber glove pressing against the downstairs window.

Mary stood in the middle of the garden for a long time. Then she turned, picked up her bucket, and walked slowly down to the beach.

The sand was churned; stones had been flung around into new trenches and drifts. Water trickled off the cliff in thin streams, as if a cloth were being wrung out. Mary looked across the rocks, deciding which way to go first. There was something bright further ahead, on the other side of the beach – a row of something that she couldn't quite make out. The rocks on that side were taller, more jagged. She didn't normally go that way. The early-morning sun flashed on whatever it was. They looked like discs. Mary closed her eyes but still saw the shapes on the backs of her eyelids.

There were no flat places to rest her feet so she just kept going – stepping quickly from rock to rock without giving herself time to lose balance. Finally she could see what they were – it was a mass of hub-caps, piles of them, like a stranding. Some had been thrown up on top of the rocks. Others were cracked in half. Her heart beat hard again. There were so many of them. More were washing in and rolling at the edge of the tide.

She left the bucket and picked up as many as she could, tucking them under her arms and holding a stack in both hands. Then she turned and made her way across the rocks. She would leave them by the path, then go back for more.

She was almost on the sand when she slipped. She reached out with her foot but found nothing. The hub-caps clattered down. She stretched out her arm but still there was nothing, then her wrist twisted against the ground and something rough grated against her cheek. The stones and the sand were very cold.

When Vincent found her she'd managed to drag herself so that she was almost on the path. He leaned her against him, taking her weight, and walked her slowly back to the house, lifting her with each step.

'What have you been doing?' he asked. He gently prised the hub-cap out of her hands.

She couldn't get out of bed. Vincent brought her breakfast on a tray in the morning, then, when he got back from work, he made lunch and they ate together, sitting propped up on the pillows. He brought in the radio and rubbed her swollen ankle while they listened.

The room was small and bare and white. Once, a piece of plastic, or maybe a wrapper, caught on the window and flapped in the wind. Mary closed her eyes. When she opened them again it had gone. The walls smelled like fresh paint and she lay there, breathing it in. This was how it was meant to be: the quiet, the sea somewhere outside the window. She slept deeply and for a long time.

One lunchtime she woke up from a nap and Vincent wasn't there. 'Vincent?' she called. 'Are you back?' She was hungry. She tried getting out of bed but as soon as she put any weight on her foot it wrenched and gave way. She sat back down. It grew slowly dark. Finally she heard the front door open and a few moments later Vincent came in. His hands were cold but the tops of his cheeks looked very hot.

'It's late,' Mary said.

'It was work,' he told her. 'I overran doing the Millers' garden.' He brought her tea and a sandwich and straightened the covers. He sat next to her and switched on the radio. He turned the volume up high.

After a while he said, 'Do you ever think about it?'

'What?' Mary asked.

'It was your parents' and I . . .'

Mary must have moved suddenly because a shot of pain went through her foot. 'Why are you talking about that?' she said.

'I just thought about it today.'

'We said we wouldn't,' she told him.

Vincent nodded. He turned and patted her pillow so that it was more comfortable. 'I should have checked it all out,' he said. 'I don't know why I didn't check.'

'We said we wouldn't go over it any more,' Mary said. All that was done with now. She hadn't thought about it for a long time.

Vincent was late back again the next day, and the day after that. He fell asleep straight after dinner but woke up through the night, his legs and arms moving restlessly.

The following morning he was gone before she was awake. Mary's breakfast was on the bedside table. She drank cold tea and ate cold toast. The phone rang. She got up and put her foot carefully on the floor. There was a dull ache but she could stand. She walked slowly through the house. The phone stopped ringing. The message light was flashing red. The kitchen was clean and quiet. There was another unopened letter from Vincent's company on the table.

She went out and turned towards the living room. The door was closed. It was never closed. The phone rang again and she went back into the kitchen. She watched it ringing for a moment, then picked it up. 'Hello?' she said. She nodded slowly, said a few words, then put the phone down. Vincent hadn't been showing up for work.

She opened the living-room door. The room was full. Every shelf, every inch of floor space, every chair, was covered with things from the beach. The hub-caps were stacked in tall piles, like coins. There were fruit crates, balls of rope, a bag over flowing with what looked like computer parts. There were fishing buoys – some orange, some green, some bleached to no colour at all. Sheets of plastic leaned against the window, casting a warped light. The room smelled stale, but also humid. Water droplets collected and rolled down the walls.

She went over to the window and looked out. Vincent was standing near the edge of the water, on the far side of the beach, staring at something. She closed the living-room door, put on her shoes, tied them carefully over her ankle, and went outside. The wind was picking up again. The tiles clacked. The palm tree was frayed. There were bin bags stuffed full in the porch and more along the side of the path.

She went down to Vincent and slipped her arms around his waist. He put his hand on her hip.

'It was just there,' he said. 'I came down and it was just there.'

Mary followed where he was looking, past the rocks, and over towards the water. At first she thought it was another rock. It towered up next to the cliff. Then she saw dark red metal. There was some kind of writing painted on the side. It was a shipping container, almost the size of the house, draped in seaweed and barnacles. It was padlocked. The metal was thick and corrugated. One side was bent inwards, like a chest when someone is holding their breath.

'I thought it was going to be different,' Mary said. She held Vincent tighter and leaned into his back.

'Maybe by the morning . . .' Vincent said.

But they both knew it would still be there in the morning. It was, perhaps, unmovable.

They stood there, together, watching it.

HILARY MANTEL

The Clean Slate

About eleven o'clock this morning – after the nurses had 'tidied her up' as they put it, and she'd fixed her eye make-up – I sat down by my mother's bed and coaxed her to do the family tree with me. Considering how self-centred she is, it worked out surprisingly well. She would like to write 'VERONICA' in the centre of the paper and strike lines of force running outwards from herself. But (although she thinks this would give you an accurate picture of the world) she does have a grasp on how these things are done. She has seen the genealogy of the Kings and Queens of England, their spurious portraits glowing by their names, stamp-sized and in stained-glass colours; their plaits of flaxen hair, their crude medieval crowns with gems like sucked sweets.

She has seen these, in the books she pretends to read. So she understands that you can also do a family tree for us, the poor bloody infantry.

The pictures by the names will be equally spurious. A woman once told me that there was no family so poor, when the last century ended, that they didn't have their photographs taken. It might be true. In that case, somebody burned ours.

I began this enterprise because I wanted to find out something about my ancestors who lived in the drowned village. I thought it might provide a reason for my fear of water – one I could use to make people feel bad, when they advise me that swimming is good exercise for a person of my age. Then again, I thought it might be a topic I could turn into cash. I could go to Dunwich, I thought, and write about a village that slipped into the sea. Or to Norfolk, to talk to people who have mortgaged houses on the edge of cliffs. I could work it up into a feature for the Sunday press. They could send a photographer, and we could balance on the cliff edge at Overstrand, just one rusting wire between us and infinite blue light.

But Veronica was not interested in the submerged. She twitched at the ribbons at her bosom – still firm, by the way – and eased herself irritably against the pillows. The veins in her hands stood out, as if she had sapphires and wore them beneath the skin. She hardly listened to my questions, and said in a huffy way, 'I really can't tell you much about all that, I'm afraid.'

The people from the drowned village were on her father's side of the family, and were English. Veronica was interested in matriarchies, in Irish matriarchies, and in reliving great moments in the life of matriarchies by repeating the same old stories: the jokes that have lost their punchlines, the retorts and witty snubs that have come unfastened from their origins. Perhaps I shouldn't blame her, but I do. I distrust anecdote. I like to understand history through figures and percentages of these figures, through knowing the price of coal and the price of corn, and the price of a loaf in Paris on the day the Bastille fell. I like to be free, so far as I can, from the tyranny of interpretation.

The village of Derwent began to sink beneath the water in the winter of 1943. This was years before I was born. The young Veronica was no doubt forming up thoughts of what children she would have, and how she would make them turn out. She had white skin and green eyes and dyed her hair red with patent formulations. It didn't really matter what man she married, he was only a vehicle for her dynastic ambitions.

Veronica's mother – my maternal grandmother – was called Agnes. She came from a family of twelve. Don't worry, I won't give you a run-down on each one of them. I couldn't, if I wanted to. When I ask Veronica to help me fill in the gaps, she obliges with some story that relates to herself, and then hints – if I try to bring her back to the subject – that there are some things best left unsaid. 'There was more to that episode than was ever divulged,' she would say. I did find out a few facts about the previous generation: none of them cheerful. That one brother went to prison (willingly) for a theft committed by another. That one sister had a child who died unchristened within minutes of birth. She was a daughter whose existence flickered briefly somewhere between the wars; she has no name, and her younger brother to this very day does not know of her existence. Not really a person: more like a negative that was never developed.

The village of Derwent didn't die of an accident, but of a policy. Water was needed by the urban populations of Manchester, Sheffield, Nottingham and Leicester. And so in 1935 they began to build a dam across the River Derwent. Ladybower was the dam's name.

When Derwent was flooded it was already flattened, already deserted. But when I was a child I didn't know this. I understood that the people themselves had left before the flood, but I imagined them going about their daily work till the last possible moment: listening out for a warning, something like an air-raid siren, and then immediately dropping whatever it was they were doing. I saw them shrugging into their stout woollen coats – buttoning in the children, tickling smiling chins – and picking up small suitcases and brown paper parcels, trudging with resigned Derbyshire faces to meeting points on the corner. I saw them laying down their knitting in mid-stitch, throwing a pea-pod half shelled into the colander: folding away the morning paper with a phrase half read, an ellipsis that would last their lifetimes.

'Leicester, did you say?' Veronica beamed at me. 'Your Uncle Finbar was last seen in Leicester. He had a market stall.'

I shuffled my hospital armchair forward, across the BUPA contract carpet. 'Your uncle,' I said. 'That's my great-uncle.'

'Yes.' She can't think why I quibble: what's hers is mine.

'What was he selling?'

'Old clothes.' Veronica chuckled knowingly. 'So it was said.'

I didn't rise to her bait. All I want from her is some dates. She likes to make mysteries and imply she has secret knowledge. She won't say which year she was born and has told a blatant lie about her age to the admissions people, which could of course jeopardize her insurance claim. Also, I am conjoined to the same insurance scheme, and they might begin to wonder about me if they ever compare files and see that by their records my mother is only ten years older than me.

A man once told me that you can date women by looking at the backs of their knees. That delta of soft flesh and broken veins, he swore, it is the only thing that cannot lie.

'They were a wild lot,' Veronica said. 'Your uncles. They were,' she said, 'you must remember, Irishmen.'

No, they weren't. Irish, yes, I concede. But not wild, not nearly wild enough. They drank when they had money and prayed when they had none. They worked in the steamy heat of mills and when they knocked off shift and stepped outside, the cold gnawed through their clothes and cracked their bones like crazed china. You would have thought they would have bred, but they didn't. Some had no children at all, others had just one. These only children were precious, wouldn't you think? But one failed to marry, and another spent much of his life in an asylum.

So far, so good: what sort of family do you expect me to come from? All-singing, all-dancing? You'd just know they'd be tubercular, probably syphilitic, certifiably insane, dyslexic, paralytic, circumcised, circum-scribed, victims of bad pickers in identity parades, mangled in industrial machinery, decapitated by forklift trucks, dental cripples, sodomites, sent blind by measles, riddled with asbestosis and domiciled downwind of Chernobyl. I assume you've read my new novel, *The Clean Slate*. I was working on the first draft at the time I decided to tackle Veronica. I had the theory that our family was bent on erasing itself, through divorce, elective celibacy and a series of gynaecological catastrophes. 'But I had children,' Veronica said, bewildered. 'I had you, didn't I?' Yes, Miss Bedjacket, you bet you did.

Probably the one thing you couldn't guess would be that I come from the drowned village. As a child I could hardly realize it myself. There is such a thing as portent-overload. Of course, I had the whole thing wrong. I misunderstood, and was prone to believe any rubbish people put my way.

Suppose that in Pompeii they had been given an alert: time, but not much of it. They would have left – what – their oil jars, their weaving shuttles, their vessels of wine, dashed and dripping? I can't really picture it. I have never been to Italy. Suppose they had taken the warning and cleared out. That was how I thought Derwent would be: a Pompeii, a *Marie Celeste*.

I thought that the waters would rise, at first inch by inch, and creep under each closed door. And then swill about, aimless for a while, contained by linoleum. The first thing to go would be the little striped mats that people dotted about in those days. They were cheap things that would go sodden quickly. Beneath the lino would be stone flags. They would hold the water, like some denying stepmother, in a chilly embrace: it would be the work of a generation, to wear them down ...

And so, thwarted, the water rises, like daughters or peasants denied, and plunges hungry fingers into the cupboards where the sugar and the flour is kept. The colander, resting on the stone sink, goes floating, the water recirculating through its holes. The half-shelled pea-pods bob, and eggcups, pans and chamber pots join the flotilla, as the water rises to the window sills. A street's worth of tea brews itself. Cakes of soap twirl twelve feet in the air, as if God were taking His Saturday soak. Gabbling like gossips on a picnic, the water surges, each hour higher by a foot, riser by riser creeping up the stairs and washing about the private items of Derbyshire persons, about their crisply ironed bloomers floating free of lavender presses: the lapping of wavelets hemming their plain knee-bands with lace. The flannel bedsheets are soaked, and the woollen blankets press on the mattresses like the weight of sodden sin: till the mad gaiety of the waters takes them over, and buoys them up in the finest easy style. The beds go sailing, tub chairs are coracles; the yellowed long johns with their attached vests wave arms and legs, cut free from conjugal arrangements, and swim like Captain Webb for liberty and France.

This was what I imagined. I thought some upriver valve was eased, and the flood began.

But in fact, the Ladybower dam was downvalley from Derwent village. There was no flood. Derwent died by drips. The rain fell and was bottled. The streams flowed and were contained. Ladybower closed her downstream valves and gradually the valley filled, in the course of nature, from the hillside streams and the precipitation of Pennine cloud bursts. It filled slowly: as tears, if you cried enough, would fill a bowl.

Veronica is old now. She does and does not understand this. She could always entertain what they call 'discontinuities'. That is to say, slippages in time or sense, breaches between cause and effect. She can also entertain big fat sweating lies, usually told either to mystify people or to make her look good. I cannot tell you how many times she has misled me. I take the map of the Derwent valley to the light. I look back at her in the bed. I am sorry to say it – I wish I could say something else – but the plan of the reservoirs looks very like a diagrammatic representation of the female reproductive tract. Not a detailed one: just the kind you might give to medical students in their first year, or children who persist in enquiring. One ovary is the Derwent reservoir, the other is Hogg Farm. This second branch descends by Underbank to Cocksbridge. The other branch descends by Derwent Hall, past the school and the church, through the drowned village of Ashopton to the neck of the womb itself, at Ladybower House and Ladybower Wood: from there, to the Yorkshire Bridge weir, and the great world beyond.

What I know now is this: they demolished the village before they flooded it. Stone by stone it was smashed. They waited till the vicar had died before they knocked down the vicarage. I think of Derwent Hall and the shallow river that ran beside it, the packhorse bridge and the bridle path. They knocked down the hall and sold what they could. The drawing-room floor – oak boards – went for £40. The oak panelling was sold at 2s and 6d per square foot.

The village of Derwent had a church, St James & St John. There was a silver patten and an ancient font which the heathens at the hall had once used as a flowerpot. There was a sundial, and four bells, and 284 bodies buried in the churchyard. Nowhere could be found to take in these home-less bones, and the Water Board decided to bury them on land of its own. But the owner of the single house in the neighbourhood raised such objections that the project was called off. It seemed they would have to go under the water, the dead men of Derwent.

But the churchyard at Bamford offered to house them, at the last push. They were exhumed one by one and their condition recorded – 'complete skeleton', together with the nature of the subsoil, the state of the coffin and the depth at which they were found. The Water Board paid £500 and it was all settled up. A bishop said prayers.

Through 1944, the water rose steadily. By June 1945, only a pair of stone gateposts and the spire of the church could be seen.

When I was a child, people would tell me AS A FACT that in hot summers, the church spire would rise above the waters, eerie and desolate under the burning sun.

This is also untrue.

The church tower was blown up, in 1947. I have a photograph of it, blasted, crumbling, in the very act of joining the ruins below. But even if I showed this to Veronica, she wouldn't believe me. She'd only say I was persecuting her. She doesn't care for evidence, she seems to say. She has her own versions of the past, and her own way of protecting them.

Sometimes, to pass her time, Veronica knits something. I say 'something' because I'm not sure if it has a future as a garment, or if she'll be wearing it anywhere out of here. She has a way of working her elbows that points her needles straight at me. When the nurse comes in she drops her weapons in the fold of the sheets and smiles, nicey-nice.

Every Saturday night, in the village where Veronica grew up, the English fought the Irish, at a specified street, called Waterside. As a child I used to play on this desolate spot. Bullrushes, reeds, swamps. (Be home for half past seven, Veronica always said.) I expect they were not serious fights. More like minuets with broken bottles. After all, next Saturday night they would have to do it all over again.

No; it was the Derbyshire people who were the wild bunch, in my opinion. Two brothers used to go around the pubs and advertise each other: my brother here will fight, run, leap, play cricket or sing, against any man in this county. The cricketer destroyed his career by felling the umpire with a blow in his only first-class match. Another brother, making his way home by moonlight, manslaughtered a person, tossed him over a wall and took ship for America. Another walked the bridle path from Glossop to Derwent in the company of a man who described himself as a doctor, but was later discovered to be an escaped and homicidal lunatic.

I like to imagine cross-connections. Perhaps this 'doctor' was my psychotic Irish relative who was committed to a madhouse. I tried to run my theory past Veronica, and see if the dates fitted at all. She said she knew nothing about the bridle path, nothing about a lunatic. I was about to take her up on it when a nurse put her head around the door and said, 'The doctor's here.' I had to stand in the corridor. 'Coffee?' some moron said, gesturing to two inches of sludge on a warm-plate. I just ignored the question. I put my head on the clear, clean plaster of the wall, which was painted in a neutral shade, like thought.

After a time, a doctor came out and stood by my elbow. He did a big act of ahem to attract my attention and when I continued to rest my head on the restful plaster he percussed my shoulder till I looked around. He was a short, irate, grey-haired man. He was smaller than me, in fact, and trying to impart news of some sort, almost certainly bad. As I write, the average height of an Englishwoman is a hair's breadth below 5'5". I barely scrape 5'3", and yet I tower over Veronica. A tear stings my eye. *So small.* Within the space of a breath, I witness myself: tear is processed, ticked, and shed.

The Ladybower Reservoir has a surface area of 504 acres. Its perimeter is thirteen miles approximately. Its maximum depth is 135 feet. One hundred thousand tons of concrete were used in its building, and one million tons of earth. I am suspicious of these round figures, as I am sure you are. But can I offer them to you, as a basis for discussion? When people talk of 'burying the past', and 'all water under the bridge', these are the kind of figures they are trading in.

ELEY WILLIAMS

Fears and Confessions of an Ortolan Chef

In many ways my workplace is the loveliest in the whole country. They are still songbirds, after all, even when they are screaming in the pot.

You once told me that nobody could ever fall in love with a person whose job involved boiling birds in liquor. I did the usual thing and attempted to romanticize the delicacy of the dish and its traditions. I described the birds as ingredients – the word *gourmand* was used until, in horror at my pretension, you set about tickling it from my vocabulary. You had wanted to move in with someone who made excellent sandwiches and the occasionally impressive dessert but I began to wonder whether I was in danger of becoming something far more sinister in your eyes, all bloodlust and dirty tricks beneath a cloche.

Fear of this made me switch tactic and I began talking about the specific dish in terms of the brandied birds as being like insects trapped in amber or tapped syrup on a tree trunk. You asked whether I ever thought about the words *eau de vie* on the brandy bottle's label and moved to the colder side of the bed. Hungrier and sadder and fatter with love than I have ever been before, I stopped explaining the method by which the meal is cooked and the rituals involved in its consumption and tried to push it from my mind.

The next day I came home stinking of illegal food to find a handwritten list on the kitchen counter. I picked up the piece of paper and read it while you explained we should attempt an experiment or regimen for our first month living together. Grease from work smudged the margins of the piece of paper in my hands and turned its corners translucent. You had compiled a syllabus for us – for a month we only read books that had been banned after publication, we ate unethically and often in bed, and we ignored the DVDs that lay taped-up in our packing crates and instead sought out films that had at some point been censored or outlawed upon release. The content of these films ranged from cannibals to mad doctors to Lloyd George. They were bad for our newly veal-bulky stomachs and *Areopagitica*-bleary eyes.

The kitchen where I work blinds the ortolans and keeps them alive in lightless boxes beneath the sink. According to custom, the birds are then fed on figs every day until they double over at which time it is my job to drown them individually in Armagnac. There is also a tradition required of those who demand to eat ortolan which involves a certain amount of pomp and prop-cupboards. It is a complete irritation for our waiters and the restaurant's laundry bill. According to the rite each diner should cover his or her head with a large embroidered napkin. Beneath this hood one can bite off the head of the bird and eat its body, bones and all. I sometimes catch glimpses of the customers during the meal through the kitchen doors and they look like they are attending a séance or waiting for their hangmen.

If you are in the know, ours is the restaurant to contact for this banned meal. My friend who works on Reception tells me that most of our bookings are made over the telephone in such hushed whispers that the clients-I-mean-customers-I-mean-guests regularly have to be told to speak up. The orders come flooding in. Our assiduous staff are trained in discretion and how best to evade eye contact when pulling out chairs for our diners and taking their coats. Our restaurant caters for whole groups who seek illicit songbirds. We have a back room that is reserved precisely for parties who order this dish, the only one fitted with a dimmer switch.

The more I think about it, I suppose the meal is not really like a séance or like gallows at all. Although an ortolan is generally eaten in silence, or with a performance of silence that is maintained in order to imply gravitas, you can hear the smacking of lips and groans of enjoyment beneath the napkins. There is a general feel of boardroom shoulder-slapping and people talking about golf over dessert.

As our first month living together drew to an end, I found a spreadsheet on your laptop. You are researching titles of more banned books to read in your own time. I start to think that stealing looks at you while you sleep is like being in a kitchen and knowing where the knives are kept.

I grow sick of metaphor and sick of the idea of the bird. I am certainly sick of having pride in any talent I might possess in terms of the birds' preparation – they are just claws and fluff and hard mouthparts on a plate. I told you once about the day the dishwasher had flooded because some leftovers had worked their way into the machine's filter and clogged the drains. I was nominated to sort out the problem and I spent the night elbow-deep behind the dishwasher, twirling a length of wire along the pipe until I felt something snag. The open-mouthed little head did not meet my eye as I pulled it from the grey water and slough of the sink. As I mopped up and washed my hands I could hear the ortolans beneath the sink sing a little louder as they sensed that I was close.

'I don't capture the birds,' I told you in our early days in our new house as I helped you unpack. 'We pay people to do that.' This clarification seemed important.

'Do you ever think where they come from?'

'I just know ortolan pays the big bucks.'

'Not *ortolan*. Ortolans. The birds sitting in hedgerows and trees. Being a nuisance under café tables.'

'We serve goose, not geese. We serve beef, not cows.'

'They're poached,' you say.

'In Armagnac,' I said.

You let me deliver the line and we listened to the sounds of the traffic outside, and when you asked me to leave the room I made my way to the kitchen to make you coffee. When I returned the door was closed. I left the cup outside on the landing, cleaned my hands, went back to the kitchen and unpacked three of your favourite plates from their bubble-wrap and broke them one by one against the kitchen counter.

We certainly make our elite tent-headed diners pay through the nose for the privilege of forbidden food. We buy them from a boy who wears a big silver watch and bright white sneakers. He charges over €150 for each ortolan bunting and brings them to an alley around the back of the kitchen every month, his bag pulsing with birds still fluttering and hop-angry. Before bedding down on our sofa for the night, I checked that there was no dinner grease from the day left glazed against my skin.

*

As far as I can remember you have only ever appeared in one of my dreams. In the dream I am preparing a fantastic breakfast for you. It was definitely you although I did not recognize the kitchen nor the bedroom to which I brought the plates on a tray. There were ironed napkins on the tray with my initials on them. As you sat up and ate the dish – delicately, fastidiously, gnawing around the bones of the bird with cat-like enjoyment – you did not stop smiling. You kept smiling and kept my gaze even as you licked your plate clean. Your waking diet would never allow this, neither the food nor the gusto, and I remember as you pushed the tray away you ignored the napkins, moved forward beneath the bedclothes and wiped your face clean on my face. The rest is all a little hazy but I do remember that the dream-us then read the paper together for dream-hours under an embroidered coverlet. I remember that I breathed on your feet when you told me that they were cold. You thanked me, and then you looked in my eyes and told me in a strange, high voice that you could not see. You told me that your breath felt on fire. Then you smiled again and passed me the magazine supplements, and I woke up covered in a cold scorching sweat.

When I tell you about this dream you say that you have had a recurring nightmare since we moved in where I come through the door with feathers in my hair and my thumbs stinking of brandy. I then beg you to lead me through what I insist on calling the most important doors of the house. In the dream, I beg you to help me pull all our bed linen, towels and curtains up over my body and hide my face.

I used to think that a beak must be the most brittle part of any face until I caught sight of my eyes in the bathroom mirror. You have started coming home at night with lipstick on your sleeves and catkins in your hair but I do not want to ask. In between your breaths at night I think I can hear the sound of tooth on bone from the day's kitchen. It is louder than any chopping board or dinner gong. Each evening I watch the diners' heads emerge sleek with sweat when they finally remove their napkins. I had forgotten what it was like to feel fine with showing that kind of desire.

This week when the boy with the big silver watch and the sneakers arrives at the arranged time, I will grab his bag from him and rip it apart right there in the alley. The birds that he brings have their wings clipped so will not be able to take to the sky as I would like. As I give the boy a kicking and he gives me a kicking and we grapple together on the ground, fighting tooth and nail by the bins outside the kitchen, the birds will have to scatter along in the gutter of the street.

I'll talk to you about wings tonight rather than hands. I'll mute the radio, take the heat off, put some bottles down and whatever they're marching for or against on the news tonight I will make sure that I'll hold you and sing from dawn until dawn for both our sakes, and for all the little songs I've stopped.

SARAH HALL

Later, His Ghost

The wind was coming from the east when he woke. The windows on that side of the house boxed and clattered in their frames, even behind the stormboards, and the corrugated-iron sheet over the coop in the garden was hawing and creaking, as though it might rip out of its rivets and fly off. The bellowing had come into his sleep, like a man's voice. December 23rd. The morning was dark, or it was still night, the clock was dead. He lay unmoving beneath the blankets, his feet cold in his boots, chest sore from breathing unheated air. The fire had gone out; the wood had burned too high again with the pull up the chimney. It was hard keeping it in overnight. Coal was much better; it burned longer, but was hard to find and too heavy to carry.

He pulled the blankets over his face. *Get up*, he thought. If he didn't get up it would be the beginning of the end. People who stayed inside got into trouble. No one helped them. Part of him understood – who wanted to die outside, tossed about like a piece of litter, stripped of clothing by the wind and lodged somewhere, dirt blowing dunes over your corpse? Crawling into a calm little shelter was preferable. He understood.

Something hard clattered along the roof, scuttled over the slates, and was borne away. There was a great *ooming* sound above, almost oceanic, like the top of the sky was heaving and breaking. Whatever had been kept in check by the gulfstream was now able to push back and lash around. People had once created aerial gods, he knew, fiends of the air or the mountaintops. He took it personally, sometimes – yelling uselessly up the chimney, or even into the wind's face, his voice tiny and whipped away. Not often though, because it didn't really help, and the chances of getting hit were worse.

When it came from the east a lot of the remaining house roofs went, and whole walls could topple – another reason not to stay inside too much, you had to be alert to the collapses. But this house was good; it had survived. He turned on his side and shivered as the cold crept down his neck. The sofa he was lying on always felt damp. The cushion he was using as a pillow smelled of wet mortar. He didn't usually sleep in this room, but Helene was now in his. He would have liked them to sleep together, to be warmer.

Another object crashed past the house, splintering against the gable, and flying off in separate clattering pieces. He couldn't remember the last still day, the trees standing upright and placid. Stillness seemed like a childhood myth, like August hay-timing, or Father Christmas. Last night, he'd slept restlessly; his dreams were turbulent – wars, animals stampeding, and Craig, always Craig. After a night like that it was hard to get going.

Get up, he thought. And then, because it was too difficult today, he thought, *Buffalo*. He pictured a buffalo. It was enormous and black-brown. It had a giant head and the shoulders of a weightlifter, a tapered back end, small, upturned horns. The image came from a picture he'd kept in a box in the bunker, one of the things Craig had taken. The buffalo looked permanently, structurally braced.

He sat up, moved the blankets away, and stood. He found the torch next to the sofa and switched it on. The cold made him feel old and stiff. He moved around and lifted his legs gymnastically to get his blood moving. He did some lunges, like warming up for football. There was a portable gas stove in the corner of the room and he set the torch next to it, ignited the ring, boiled a cup of water and made tea. He drank the tea black. He missed milk most of all. There weren't even any smuts in the grate. Perhaps he'd leave the fire a day to save fuel – the temperature was about four or five degrees, he guessed, manageable. So long as Helene was warm enough.

He took the torch and moved through the building to the room where she slept. It was warmish. Her fire was still glowing orange. She slept with the little Tilley lamp on. She didn't like the dark. She was sound asleep, lying on her side, her belly vast under her jumper. He picked up one of the blankets from the floor and put it back over her. She didn't move. She seemed peaceful, though her eyes were moving rapidly behind her eyelids. The wind was quieter this side of the house, leeside. It whistled and whined and slipstreamed away. Little skitters of soot came down the chimney and sparks rose from the cradle. He looked at Helene sleeping. Her hair was cut short, like his, but hers curled and was black. When they were open her eyes were extremely pretty. A lot of the boys in school had fancied her. He imagined climbing onto the bed and putting his arm over her shoulder. Sometimes when he was checking on her she woke up and looked at him. Mostly she knew he was just checking, bringing her tea, or some food, or more wood for the fire. But sometimes she panicked. And he knew she was worried about the baby coming; that frightened him too. He'd found a medical book on one of his explorations, but still.

She'd done well, he thought, lasting it out, but she was very quiet, mostly. He thought probably she hadn't developed any methods to help, like picturing the buffalo. She was probably thirty, or thirty-five. She'd been an English teacher, though not his; she hadn't recognized him when he'd found her. She liked sardines in tomato sauce, which was good because he had lots of tins. She always thanked him for the food. *That's all right*, he'd say, and sometimes he'd almost add, *Miss McDowell*. She never said anything about what had happened to her, or the baby, but he could guess. No one would choose that now. He'd found her in the Catholic cathedral, what was left of it. There were two dead bodies nearby, both men; they looked freshly dead, with a lot of blood. She was looking up at the circular hole where the rose window had been. She wasn't praying or crying. He thought she'd done well.

He left tea for her in a metal cup with a lid, and some sardines, and went back to his room. He did a stock check. He did this every day, unnecessarily, but it made him feel calmer. Calor gas bottles, food, clothes, batteries (one less for the dead clock), duct tape, painkillers, knives, rope. The cans were piled in such a way that he could count them by tens. This house still had water, a slow trickling stream that was often tinted and tasted earthy. He still hadn't worked out if the property had its own well, lots of the garden was buried. But it made life easier – he didn't have to rig up a rainwater funnel. He'd been collecting packets of baby formula too, but when he'd showed Helene she'd looked confused, then sad. There was a box with more delicate things inside, frivolous things, photographs – of his mother, and his little brother in school uniform – his passport, though that was useless now other than to prove who he was, and the pages he'd been collecting for Helene. There wasn't much to read in the house. He'd been hunting for the play for a month or two and it was a very difficult task, most books had been destroyed, the wind was an expert at that. Once buildings were breached, nothing paper lasted; it warped and pulped, the ink smudged. Sometimes he found just a paragraph, or a line, on an otherwise unreadable page.

So dear the love my people bore me, nor set a mark so bloody on the business: but with fairer colours painted their foul ends. In few, they hurried us aboard a bark, bore us some leagues to sea, where they'd prepared a rotten carcass of a boat, not rigg'd . . .

The town's library had been demolished in the first big storms. No wonder: it had been built in the sixties, as part of the civic centre. The older the building, the longer it lasted, generally: people had gotten very bad at construction, he thought, or lazy. He was very good at salvaging now. He was good at it because he was good at moving around outside. He wasn't timid, but he never took anything for granted either. He wore the rucksack strapped tight to his body, like a parachute. He taped up his arms and legs so they wouldn't billow, he tested the ropes, and he always looked in every direction for airborne debris. He never, never assumed it was safe. He'd seen too many bodies with blunted heads.

After the stock check, he took a tin of salmon out of the stack, opened it and ate it cold. He was hungry and he ate too fast. His mouth hurt. Ulcers starred his tongue. He probably needed some fruit, but he'd rather give the fruit to Helene. In winter having two meals was important – breakfast and dinner – even if they were small. Otherwise he'd get sick. This was the fourth winter. Last Christmas he hadn't really celebrated because he was by himself, but having Helene made things nicer. He scraped the last flakes out of the tin with his nail and ate them, then drank the oil, which made him gag. He saved the tin – while they were still greasy they were good for making flour-and-water dumplings over the fire, though the dumplings tasted fishy. As well as the surprise gift, he'd been planning their Christmas meal. He'd had a tin of smoked pheasant pâté for two years, it was too special to eat by himself. There was a jar of redcurrant. A jar of boiled potatoes. And a tin of actual Christmas pudding. They would have it all warmed up. Two courses! He even had a miniature whisky, with which to set fire to the pudding. It was important to try to celebrate.

He went to the back of the house, peered through a gap in the storm-boards and watched the dawn struggling to arrive. Daylight usually meant the wind eased slightly, but not today. The clouds were fast and the light pulsed, murky yellow aurorae. The usual items sped past on the current – rags, bits of tree, transmuted unknowable things. Sometimes he was amazed there were enough objects left to loosen and scatter. Sometimes he wondered whether these things were just the same million shoes and bottles and cartons, circling the globe endlessly. The clouds passed fat and fast overhead, and were sucked into a vortex on the horizon, disappearing into nothing. There was sleetish rain, travelling horizontally, almost too quickly to see.

It was probably a bad idea to go out today. His rule was nothing more than a ninety, what he gauged to be a ninety. This was worse. But he had two days left and he wanted to find more pages.

He went back to his room and got ready. He put on waterproof trousers and a jacket. He cleaned and put on the goggles. He pulled the hood of the jacket up, yanked the toggles and tied them tightly, a double knot. He taped the neck. He taped his cuffs and his ankles, his knees and his elbows. He put on gloves but left them untaped so he could take them off if he found any more books; he would need his fingers to be nimble, to flick through and tear out. It might mean he would lose a glove, or both, but he'd risk it. When he was done he felt airtight, like some kind of diver, *a storm-diver*, he thought. But it was better not to get heroic. For a while when he'd gone out he'd worn a helmet, but it'd made him feel too bulky, too heavy, not adapted. He weighted the rucksack down with the red stone – he didn't like to think of it as his lucky stone, because he wasn't superstitious, but secretly he did think it was lucky. It was egg-shaped, banded with pink and white – some kind of polished gneiss. He'd found it looking through the wreckage of the geology lab at school. It sat in the bottom of the rucksack, as a ballast, leaving enough room for anything he discovered on his excursions, but preventing the bag's flapping. He had plastic wrapping for anything delicate. He was good at discerning what was useful and what was not; he hadn't brought back many useless things, though the temptation was to save beautiful items, or money. His mother had always joked his birthdays were easy – as a kid he didn't need many toys or field comforts or gadgets. His mother had died of sickness. So had his little brother. So had thousands of other people. It wasn't just the conditions, it was what the conditions led to, Craig had told him. In some ways Craig had been clever.

There were two doors to the house – one on the north side and one on the west. He stood by the west door and thought, *Buffalo.* He opened the door and felt the draw of air, then opened it wider and moved into the alcove behind the storm door. The storm door opened inwards and could be locked either side. He moved the bolt, forced himself out into the buffeting air, planted his feet and fastened the door behind him. Either side of the house, the wind tore past, conveying junk, going about its daily demolition. Behind him, the house felt solid. It was a squat, single-storey longbarn in the low-lying outskirts of town, with shutters and big outer doors. He'd modified it a bit, with nails and planks, building break-walls. This was his fifteenth house. The first – his mother's, a white 1930s semi – had gone down as easily as straw, along with the rest of the row. They'd gone to the gymnasium as part of the reorganization, then to a shared terrace. The brick terraces had proved more durable, he'd lived in two, but they were high-ceilinged; once the big windows and roofs gave out they were easy for the wind to dismantle. Before the barn, he'd been in the bunker near the market with Craig, a sort of utility storage. It was a horrible, rat-like existence – dark, desperate, scavenging. Craig was much older than him. He'd wanted things and had taken things. There had been three big fights, and the last one made such a mess. But he wasn't sorry. Maybe he should have stayed in the bunker alone but he didn't want to. A lighthouse would have been best, round, aerodynamic, deep-sunk into rock, made to withstand batterings. But the coast was impossible. Before everything had gone down he'd seen news footage; he couldn't quite believe the towering swells, the surges. He had nightmares about those waves reaching this far inland.

He inched along the barn wall, towards the open. He'd planned a new route through town. He would keep to the west side of streets wherever he could, for protection, but that meant being in the path of anything collapsing. In the past he'd outrun avalanching walls, he'd been picked up and flung against hard surfaces and rubble heaps, his collarbone and his wrist had been fractured. There were only so many near misses. He would need to judge the soundness of structures, only venture inside a building if the risks seemed low. He would go into the Golden Triangle – some of the big Victorian houses there were still holding and they were more likely to have what he was looking for. At the corner of the barn he knelt, tensed his neck and shoulder muscles and put his head out into the rushing wind. The force was immense. He checked for large oncoming objects, then began to crawl along the ground. What had once been the longbarn's garden was now stripped bald of grass and the walls were in heaps. Clods of earth tumbled past him. The wind shunted his backside and slid him forward. He flattened out and moved like a lizard towards the farm buildings and the first rope. He had different techniques, depending on the situation. Sometimes he crawled miles and came back bruised black underneath. Sometimes he crouched like an ape and lumbered. Other times he made dashes, if there were intermittent blasts, cannonballing the lulls, but he could get caught out doing that. Sometimes it was better to walk into the wind head on, sometimes leaning back against it and digging your heels in worked.

It'd been a while since he'd been out in anything this strong. It was terrifying and exhilarating. The wind bent him over when he tried to stand, so he stayed low, a creature of stealth and avoidance. He clung to the cord that ran between the buildings. He'd rigged it himself and had tested the binding only a few days ago, but still he gave a good yank to make sure it hadn't begun to untether. A lot of the ones in town he'd redone too. He traversed slowly while the wind bore between the buildings. After the farm, there was a dangerous open stretch. The Huff, he called it, because the weather always seemed in a filthy temper there. It had been a racecourse, quite famous. Beyond it, the town started properly: its suburbs, its alleys and piles of stone. Once it had been a town of magnificent trees. Plane trees, beeches, oaks: the big avenues had been lined by them, their leaves on fire in autumn, raining blossom in spring. Now they were mostly gone – uprooted and dying. There was a lot of firewood to haul away. He hardly ever saw anyone else taking it. He could probably count on one hand the number of people he saw in a month. Occasionally, a big armoured vehicle passed through, military – its windows covered in metal grilles. The soldiers never got out. A lot of people had gone to towns in the west because it was supposed to be milder, there was supposed to be more protection. He didn't believe that really.

When he got to the Huff he almost changed his mind and went back. The air above was thick with dirt, a great sweeping cloud of it. There was a constant howling. Every few moments something rattled, fluttered or spun past, bounced off the ground and was lobbed upwards. On tamer days he'd sledged across the stretch on a big metal tray, for fun, putting his heels down to slow the contraption and flinging himself sideways to get off. Today, no larks, he'd be lucky not to break his neck. It was too wide a tract of land to rope; he had to go without moorings. Crossing would mean surrendering to the wind, becoming one of many hurled items, colliding with others, abraded, like a pellet in a shaker.

He gave himself a moment or two to prepare and then he let go of the farm walls and began to crawl across. He tried to move quickly to keep up with the thrust of the current, but it was too strong. Within moments the wind had taken him, lifting his back end and tossing him over. He felt the red stone slam into his spine. He started tobogganing, feet first. He tucked his head in, rolled on his side, brought his knees up. The ground was hard and bumpy and pounded his bones. He put his hands down and felt debris filling his cuffs. Something sharp caught his ankle bone and stung. *Shit*, he thought, *shitshitshit*. But he went with it, there was nothing he could do, and after a second or two he managed to regain some control. He hoofed his boots down and tried to brake. He was nearly at the edge of the racecourse, where the old, flint wall of the town began. The wind shoved him hard again and he went tumbling forward. He presented his back and hit the pointed stones and stopped.

He lay for a moment, dazed, brunted against the structure, with dirt pattering around him. It was hard to breathe. The air tasted of soil. He turned his head, and spat. When he opened his eyes one pane of the goggles was cracked, splitting his view. His ankle throbbed. Other than that he was all right, but he had to get moving. He pushed himself up and crawled along the boundary wall, around trolleys and piles of swept rubbish. At the first gap he went through. He sat up, leant against the flints and caught his breath while the wind roared the other side.

He bent and flexed his leg, cleaned his goggles, emptied his gloves.

Moron, he thought. He did want to live, moments like this reminded him. He sat for a time, tried to relax. The boundary wall was twelve feet thick and sturdy. Whoever had built it had meant business. Probably the Romans. Sections along the river had been restored when he was a kid, as part of the 'fan-Tas-tic flood defence initiative'.

He looked at the town. Roofs and upper floors were gone; cars were parked on their backs, their windscreens smashed. The big storms had left domino rubble in every direction, scattered fans of bricks and tiles, bouquets of splintered wood. Old maps meant nothing, new streets had been made, buildings rearranged. He had to keep relearning its form as its composition shifted.

He got up, crouched low, surveyed the route and limped off. It was a mile to the Golden Triangle, through Tombland and the market. He saw no one. He kept to the safer routes and used the secure ropes when he had to, hauling himself along. He squinted through the broken goggles, seeing an odd spider-like creature everywhere in front of him, but he didn't take them off – the last thing he needed was to be blinded. The ruins were depressing, but he occasionally saw miraculous things in them. An animal, though they were rare. There were no birds, not even dis-tressed gulls; nothing could cope in the torrent. The rats had done OK, anything living below ground level. Cats and dogs were few, always ema-ciated and wretched. There was no food, nothing growing, and not much to kill. People's survival instincts were far worse, he often thought, but they could at least use can openers. Two years ago, on the edge of the Huff, he'd seen a stag, a fantastic thing. It was reddish, six points on each antler, standing perfectly still, like something from the middle of a forest, as if it had always stood there, as if tree after tree had been stripped away, until the forest was gone and there was nothing left to shield it. He'd seen awful things too. A man sliced in half by a flying glass pane, his entrails worming from his stomach. Craig's broken skull, the soft, foul matter inside. Who you became afterwards was who you told yourself you were. Good things had to be held onto, and remembered, and celebrated. That was why he had to get the pages for Helene and why they would try to have a nice Christmas.

He made his way slowly through the town, forcing his body against the blast, starting to favour one leg as his ankle stiffened. He kept leeside wherever he could and watched for flying timber and rockslides. He crossed the little park at the edge of the Golden Triangle. There were stumps where the central pavilion had stood. The trees lying on the ground were scoured bare. Sleet had begun to gather along their trunks. He hoped it wouldn't turn to snow; it was hard enough keeping his footing.

When he got to the district he was surprised to see smoke leaking from one of the heaps. He made his way over, cautiously, but it was just a random fire burning along a beam, some stray electrical spark perhaps, or friction. Two rows away the houses were in better shape, some only had holes in the roofs and lopped-off chimneys. The windows were mostly gone. He could hop through the bays if the lintels were safe. He always called out to make sure they were empty first. He'd been in some of the houses before, checking for food, batteries, essentials. They'd been lovely places once, owned by doctors and lawyers, he imagined – his mum had always wanted to live there. There were remnants of cast-iron fireplaces, painted tiles; even some crescents of stained glass hanging on above the doorframes. He tried a couple, searching through the downstairs rooms – he never went upstairs if he could help it, it was too dangerous. The wind moaned through the rooms, shifting wet curtains and making the peeling wallpaper flicker. Damp and lichen speckled the walls and fungus grew from the skirting boards. There were pulpy masses on the shelves, rotting covers, the sour smell of macerating paper. He stepped among the detritus, broken glass and broken furniture, digging through piles, tossing collapsed volumes aside like wet mushrooms. He'd been dreaming about finding a complete works since he'd found Helene – that would really be something special – bound in plastic perhaps, unviolated. But, like Bibles, they were the first to go, their pages wafer thin, like ghosts' breath. He'd studied the play in school, not with any particular enjoyment, he'd been better at science. He could remember bits of it, the parts he'd had to read out. *As wicked dew as e'er my mother brush'd with raven's feather from unwholesome fen drop on you both! A south-west blow on ye . . .* He was sure Helene had taught it; certainly she'd have read it. Reading it again might help her. She could begin to think differently. She could read it while she fed the baby. So far she'd said nothing about the baby, not even any names she liked. Sometimes she put her hand on her stomach, when the baby was moving. He'd found some sections of the play, dried the pages, sorted the scenes and put them in order, as best he could. He'd glued and glued things in between. It wasn't an attractive-looking gift; he'd never been very artistic.

After ten or eleven houses he was starting to lose hope and was worried about the daylight. The wind was not letting up: if anything it was gaining power. There'd been a couple of worryingly big bangs nearby, something shattering, a frenzied thudding. He went back out onto the street. There was a big house further along, free-standing, walled. It had upper bays as well as lower. A vicarage, maybe. Part of the roof was gone. The gate was padlocked but the frame had come away from the post and he forced his way through the gap. In the garden the plant pots and urns were smashed apart but a small fruit tree was still standing, defiantly, petrified black globes hanging in its branches. He checked round the periphery of the house. Then he went through a lower window and down a hallway. His ankle felt sore, but that was OK, injuries you couldn't feel were far worse.

He knew, even before he got to the big room at the back of the house, that he was going to find what he was looking for. Some things you knew, like echoes, good and bad things that were about to happen. He forced a swollen door into a parlour. It was quite quiet inside, not too much damage or decay. It would have been a nice place to sit and watch TV or read. The walls had once been red but were now darker, browny, like dried blood. There was a fireplace, heaped full of charred wood, pieces of chimney brick and sleeving. There was a man in a chair, a corpse. His eyelids were shrinking upwards over the empty sockets; some wisps of hair left on his head. The skin was yellow and tight and shedding off the cheekbones. A blanket was wrapped around his shoulders, as if he was cold. There was no bad smell in the room, it had happened a long time ago. Probably he had done it himself, a lot of people had. He didn't look too closely at the man. He went over to the shelves. There were rows and rows of hardbacks. He could even read the titles on some of the spines. *Encyclopaedia Britannica. Audubon.* And there was a collection of Shakespeares, mottled, green mould blooming along them, but readable. He found it in the middle. He took off his gloves and opened it carefully; the edges of the paper were moist, stuck, and they tore slightly when moved, but the book held together. He turned gently to the end. *I'll deliver all; and promise you calm seas, auspicious gales and sail so expeditious that shall catch your royal fleet far off.*

He took off his rucksack, wrapped the book in plastic and put it inside one of the small compartments. He put the rucksack back on, clicked the straps across his chest, drew them tight, and put on his gloves. It would be a good house to go through for other things, but he didn't want to get caught out and not be able to get across town and over the Huff to the longbarn. He didn't want to leave Helene alone longer than he had to. He would come back, after Christmas, and search properly. He closed the door on the dead man.

On the way out he saw his own reflection in the dusty, cracked hall mirror. Like books, not many mirrors were left either, the wind loved killing them. Probably a good thing. His coat hood was drawn tightly around his head; he was earless and bug-eyed, and one eye lens was shattered. The metallic tape around his neck shone like scales. He looked like some kind of demon. Maybe that's what he was, maybe that's what he'd become. But he felt human; he remembered feeling human. His ankle hurt, which was good. He could use a can opener. And he liked Christmas. He turned away from the mirror and climbed back out of the window. Snow was flying past.

MARK HADDON

The Pier Falls

23 July 1970, the end of the afternoon. A cool breeze off the Channel, a mackerel sky overhead and, far out, a column of sunlight falling onto a trawler as if God had picked it out for some kind of blessing. The upper storeys of the Regency buildings along the front sit above a gaudy rank of coffee houses and fish bars and knickknack shops with striped awnings selling 99s and dried seahorses in cellophane envelopes. The names of the hotels are writ large in neon and weatherproof paint. The Excelsior, the Camden, the Royal. The word Royal is missing an o.

Gulls wheel and cry. Two thousand people saunter along the prom, some carrying towels and Tizer to the beach, others pausing to put a shilling in the telescope or to lean against a balustrade whose pistachio-green paint has blistered and popped in a hundred years of salt air. A gull picks up a wafer from a dropped ice cream and lifts into the wind.

On the beach a portly woman hammers a windbreak into the sand with the heel of a shoe while a pair of freckled twins build a fort from sand and lolly sticks. The deckchair man is collecting rentals, doling out change from a leather pouch at his hip. 'No deeper than your waist,' shouts a father. 'Susan? No deeper than your waist.'

The air on the pier is thick with the smell of engine grease and fried onions spooned onto hot dogs. The boys from the ticket booth ride shotgun on the rubber rims of the bumper cars, the contacts scraping and sparking on the live chicken wire nailed to the roof above their heads. A barrel organ plays Strauss waltzes on repeat.

Nine minutes to five. Ozone and sea-sparkle and carnival licence.

This is how it begins.

A rivet fails, one of eight which should clamp the joint between two weight-bearing girders on the western side of the pier. Five have sheared already in heavy January seas earlier this year. There is a faint tremor underfoot as if a suitcase or a stepladder has been dropped somewhere nearby. No one takes any notice. There are now two rivets holding the tonnage previously supported by eight.

In the aquarium by the marina the dolphins turn in their blue prison.

Twelve and a half minutes later another rivet snaps and a section of the pier drops by half an inch with a soft thump. People turn to look at one another. The same momentary reduction in weight you feel when a lift starts descending. But the pier is always moving in the wind and the tide, so everyone returns to eating their pineapple fritters and rolling coins into the fruit machines.

The noise, when it comes, is like the noise of a redwood being felled, wood and metal bending and splitting under pressure. Everyone looks at their feet, feeling the hum and judder of the struts. The noise stops and there is a moment of silence, as if the sea itself were holding its breath. Then, with a peal of biblical thunder, a wide semicircle of walkway is hauled seaward by the weight of the broken girders underneath. A woman and three children standing at the rail drop instantly. Six more people are poured, scrabbling, down the half-crater of shattered wood into the sea. If you look through the black haystack of planks and beams you can see three figures thrashing in the dark water, a fourth floating face down and a fifth folded over a weed-covered beam. The rest are trapped underwater somewhere. Up on the pier a man hurls five lifebelts one after the other into the sea. Other holidaymakers drop their possessions as they flee so that the walkway is littered with bottles and sunglasses and cardboard cones of chips. A cocker spaniel runs in circles trailing a blue lead.

Two men are helping an elderly lady to her feet when yet more decking gives way beneath them. The shorter, bearded man grabs the claw foot of an iron bench and hangs onto the woman till a teenage boy is able to lean down and help them both up, but the taller man with the braces and the rolled-up shirtsleeves slides down the buckled planking till he is brought to a halt by a spike of broken rail which enters the small of his back. He wriggles like a fish. No one will go down to help him. The slope is too steep, the structure too untrustworthy. A father turns his daughter's face away.

The men running the big wheel are trying to empty each gondola in turn, but those stuck at the top of the ride are screaming and those lower down are unwilling to wait their turn and jump out, some twisting ankles, one breaking a wrist.

On the beach everyone stands and stares at the hole punched into the familiar view. The coloured lights still flash. Faintly they can hear the 'Emperor Waltz'. Five men tear off shoes and shirts and trousers and run into the surf.

A line of seven ornamental belvederes runs down the centre of the pier. The western side of this spine is now impassable, so everyone seaward of the fall is squeezing through the bottleneck on the eastern side to reach the turnstiles, the promenade and safety. At the narrowest point people are starting to lose their footing and tumble so that those still upright must either walk on top of them or fall and be trampled in their turn.

Sixty seconds gone, seven people dead, three survivors in the water. The man with the braces and the rolled-up sleeves is still alive but will not be for long. Eight people, three of them children, are being crushed by the crowd pouring over them.

One of the belvederes is listing now, the metal structure being twisted so hard that the twenty-two glass windows explode one after the other.

The pier manager has opened the service gate beside the turnstiles and escapees are fanning onto the pavement, dishevelled, bloody, wide-eyed. A small boy is being carried in the arms of his father. A teenage girl with a shattered femur sticking through the skin of her right leg is suspended between the shoulders of two men.

The traffic along the promenade comes to a halt and a crowd lines the rails. The whole front is so quiet that everyone hears the noise this time.

Two minutes and twenty seconds. The belvedere falls first, dragging the metal framework and the decking after it. Forty-seven people drop into a threshing machine of spars and beams. Only six of these people will survive, one of them a boy of six whose parents wrap themselves around him as they fall.

The rubberized wires carrying power along the pier spark like fireworks as they are torn apart. All the lights go out on the end of the pier. The barrel organ wheezes to a halt.

The men swimming out to help are lifted on the small tsunami generated by the mass of broken pier entering the water. It passes under them and heads towards the beach where it sends everyone scurrying above the high-water mark as if it were infected by the event which caused it.

The arcade manager sits in his tiny office at the end of the pier, the dead receiver pressed to his ear. He is twenty-five. He has never even been to London. He has no idea what to do.

The pilot of a twin-engined Cessna 76-D looks down. He can't believe what he is seeing. He banks and circles the pier to double-check before radioing Shoreham tower.

The pier is now in two separate sections, the ragged end of one facing the ragged end of the other, forty-five tons of wood and metal knotted in the water between them. Some of those stranded on the seaward section stand at the edge desperate to be seen and heard by anyone who might rescue them. Others hang back, trying to gauge the most dependable part of the structure. Three couples are trapped in the ghost train listening to the noises outside, fearful that if they manage to get out they will find themselves watching the end of the world.

On the landward section two people lie motionless on the decking and three others are too badly injured to move. A woman is shaking the body of her unconscious husband as if he has overslept and is late for work, while a man with tattooed forearms chases the petrified cocker spaniel in a large figure of eight. An elderly lady has had a fatal heart attack and remains seated on a bench, head tilted to one side as if she has dozed off and missed all the excitement.

Faint sirens can be heard from the maze of the town.

Two of the swimming men turn back, frightened that they will be struck by yet more of the pier collapsing, but the other three swim on into the archipelago of bodies and broken wood. The pier looms overhead, so much bigger than it has ever seemed from the beach or up there on the walkway, so much darker, more malign. The men can hear the groan and crunch of girders still settling beneath them in the water.

They find a terrified woman, two girls who turn out to be sisters and a man still wearing his spectacles who floats upright in the swell like a seal, only vaguely aware of his surroundings. The woman is hyperventilating and lashing out so wildly that the men wonder initially if she is caught on something under the surface. Only the sisters seem wholly compos mentis, so one of the rescuers escorts them back to the shore. The man wearing the spectacles asks what has happened then asks for the explanation to be repeated. The panicking woman won't let anyone come near her, so they have to tread water and let her expend all her energy and come perilously close to drowning before she is tractable.

Just beyond the end of the pier five empty lifebelts are making their way out to sea.

A young man on the promenade lifts his Leica and takes three photographs. Only when he reads the paper the following morning will he realize what is happening in these pictures. Immediately he will open the camera and yank the film out of its drum so that the images are burned away by the light.

The air-sea rescue helicopter rises from its painted yellow circle on the runway at Shoreham, tilts into the prevailing wind and swings off the airfield.

Five minutes. Fifty-eight dead.

On the promenade a number of those who ran to safety have failed to find wives or husbands or children or parents. The manager has closed the gate but these people are weeping and shouting, trying to get back onto the pier. There are no police in attendance yet and he can see that keeping them here against their will may be as dangerous as letting them through and he doesn't want this responsibility, so he reopens the gate and twelve of them pour past as if he has opened the doors to a January sale. The last of these is a girl of no more than eight years old. He grabs her collar. She fights and weeps at the end of his arm.

The lifeboat is scrambled.

On the eastern side of the pier a farmer from Bicester is trying to prise the six-year-old boy from between his parents. The boy can surely see that they are dead. Half his father's head is missing. Or perhaps he can't see this. He won't let go of them and his grip is so tight that the man is afraid he will break the boy's arm if he pulls any harder. He asks the boy what his name is but the boy won't answer. The boy is in some private hell which he will never entirely leave. The farmer has no choice but to turn and swim, towing the three of them ashore. Only when he tries to stand will he realize that his ankle is broken.

The tattooed man comes running down the pier clasping the cocker spaniel to his chest and when he runs through the gate onto the promenade the two of them are greeted by cheers and whoops from a crowd eager to celebrate some small good thing.

Eight minutes. Fifty-nine dead.

The helicopter appears in the sun-glare from the west. Everyone on the promenade hears the growing pulse of the rotors and turns to watch.

None of the eleven people running onto the pier find their missing relatives among the injured and unconscious so they stand near the ragged chasm and shout to the people on the other side. Have they seen an old lady in a green windcheater? A little girl with long red hair? But the people on the far side are not interested in the lady in the windcheater and the girl with red hair because they are missing relatives of their own and they are terrified that the rest of the pier will collapse and the only thing they want to know is when they are going to be rescued.

Two ambulances reach the seafront but the traffic is jammed so tight that the crews have to run carrying stretchers and emergency bags. Five stay with the injured on the front, three continue onto the pier itself.

Three policemen are trying to push the spectators back, some of whom resent being evicted from ringside seats. Nobody realizes how many people have died. Everyone is thinking how they will tell the story to friends and family and workmates.

On the pier a woman is slid sideways onto a spinal board. An elderly man with a broken collarbone is given morphine.

Fourteen minutes. Sixty dead.

On the promenade people are wondering if it was an IRA bomb. No one wants to believe that time and weather can be this dangerous, and it is exciting to think of oneself as a potential target.

As the helicopter hovers over the end of the pier the people below fight to be the first to grab the winchman as he descends, but the downdraught batters them away from its epicentre and he alights in a circle of empty decking. He scoops a little girl from her mother's arms and the sight of her being clipped into a harness shames them. As she is hoisted aloft they start gathering the other children, lining them up in order of age ready for the next lift.

The swimmers come ashore – the sisters, the confused man, the struggling woman, their three rescuers. People rush forward with towels. It looks like a competition to see whose will be chosen. The struggling woman drops to her knees and digs her hands into the sand as if nothing and no one is going to separate her from solid ground ever again.

The body of the old woman who had a heart attack is carried through the service gate under a white sheet into a sudden hush. There are still people on the front who think she is the only person who has died.

The farmer towing the little boy and his dead parents hauls them into the shallows and feels one end of his broken fibula grinding against the other. It should hurt but he can feel no pain. He needs very badly to lie down. He rolls over into the water and looks at the clouds. People rush into the surf, then see his cargo and come to a halt. A young woman steps between them, a nurse from Southampton where she works in the accident and emergency department. She has seen much worse. She is the only black person on the entire beach. She puts her hands flat on the boy's shoulders and some of those watching wonder if she is using voodoo, but it is the steadiness of her voice which enables him to let go of his parents' bodies and turn and be held by someone who is not frightened. The colour of her skin helps too, the fact that she is so different from all these other people among whom he no longer belongs. Her name is Renée. They will stay in touch with one another for the next thirty years.

The fourth child is lifted into the helicopter, then the fifth.

The arcade manager emerges from his tiny office. He realizes that if he is the last person winched to safety he will be able to say, 'I stayed at my post.'

The last couple escape from the ghost train, the husband kicking his way through Frankenstein's Monster painted on the plywood sheeting of the facade.

Twenty-five minutes. Sixty-one dead.

The lifeboat arrives and the crew begin hauling people from the water. Some cannot stop talking. Some slither into the bottom of the boat like netted fish, sodden, glassy-eyed, oblivious. A boy of thirteen floats in a dark recess between two fallen girders. He refuses to come out and will not respond to their calls. A crew member jumps into the water but the boy retreats into the flooded forest of wreckage and they are forced to abandon him.

The winch is stowed and the helicopter swings away with all the children on board. Many of them have left parents on the pier. Several don't know if their parents are alive. For all of them the hammering roar is a comfort, filling their heads so completely that they are unable to entertain the terrifying thoughts that will return only when they are helped down onto the tarmac and run through the wind from the rotors towards the women from the St John's Ambulance waiting for them outside the little terminal building.

On the promenade a man in a dirty white apron squeezes through the crowd bearing hot dogs and sweet tea from the stand he runs beside the crazy golf. He returns with a second tray.

Other boats are being drawn towards the pier, a Bristol motor cruiser, an aluminium launch with a Mercury outboard, two fibreglass Hornets. They idle just beyond the moraine of bodies and debris, unable either to help or to turn away.

The boy of thirteen will not come out from the flooded forest because he knows that his sister is in there somewhere. He cannot find her. After thirty minutes he is hypothermic and feels desperately cold. Then, quite suddenly, he doesn't feel cold at all. This doesn't seem strange. Nothing seems strange any more. He wants to take his clothes off but hardly has the energy to stay afloat. Out there, only yards away, the world continues – sunshine, boats, a helicopter. But he feels safe in here. He is not thinking about his sister any more. He cannot remember having a sister. Only this deep need to be in the dark, to be contained, unseen, some primal circuit still alight on the dimming circuit board of the brainstem. He sinks into the water five times, coughs and forces himself back to the surface, but with less effort each time and with a less distinct sense of what he has just avoided. The sixth time there is so little left of his mind that he lets it go as easily as if it were a book falling from his sleeping hand.

A journalist from the *Argus* stands in a phone box reading the shorthand he has scribbled onto four pages of a ring-bound notebook. 'Shortly before five in the afternoon . . .'

One of the men trapped on the far end of the pier is terrified of flying. He is wearing a Leeds United T-shirt. The prospect of being lifted into the helicopter is many times worse than that of the structure collapsing beneath him. He knows that his only other choice is to jump from the pier. He is a strong swimmer but the drop to the water is sixty feet. The two possibilities toggle at increasing speeds in his mind – fly, jump, fly, jump. He feels sick. His wife is airlifted in the second batch and in her absence his thoughts race at increasing speeds until he realizes that he will lose his mind and that this possibility is worse than flying or jumping. At which point he sees himself turn away from the crowd and run towards the railing. The sensation of watching himself from a distance is so strong that he wants to cry out to this foolish man to remove his shoes and trousers first. He remembers nothing of the leap itself, only the terrible surprise of waking underwater with no memory of where he is or why. He fights his way to the surface, refills his lungs several times and forces off his double-knotted shoes. He can see now that he is at the seaside and that he is floating in the shadow of some vast object. He turns and the wrecked pier looms over him. He remembers what has happened and turns again and swims hard. After a hundred yards he stops and turns for a third time and finds that the distance has turned the pier into a part of the view. He looks towards the town, the crowds, the blue flashing lights, the Camden, the Royal. He is unaware that people saw him jump and that he is now starring in his own brief episode in the afternoon's greater drama. He feels victorious, unburdened. He swims steadily towards the beach where he is cheered ashore, wrapped in a red blanket and led to an ambulance. His wife will spend three hours thinking he is dead and will not forgive him for a long time.

There is now no one left on the far end of the pier.

The final person dies, deep inside the tangle of planks and girders. He is fifteen years old. He helped his father on the helter-skelter, collecting the mats and going up the ladder at the back when kids got scared or started a fight inside. He has been unconscious since he fell.

The lifeboat returns and the crew retrieve fifteen bodies from the water.

An hour and a half. Sixty-four dead.

A Baptist minister offers the use of his church hall. Survivors are escorted by policemen and firemen over the road, up Hope Street, through a door beside Whelan's Marine Stores and into a large warm room with fluorescent lighting and a parquet floor. The lid of a tea urn is rattling and two ladies are making sandwiches in the kitchenette. People slump onto chairs and onto the floor. They are no longer being observed. They are among people who understand. Some weep openly, some sit and stare. Three children are unaccompanied, two boys and a girl. The parents of the younger boy have been airlifted to Shoreham. The other two children are now orphans. The girl saw her parents die and is inconsolable. The boy has concocted a story in which his parents fell into the sea and were picked up by a fishing boat, a story so detailed and told with such earnestness that the elderly woman to whom he is telling it doesn't realize anything is wrong until he explains that they are now living in France.

A policewoman moves quietly round the room, squatting beside each group in turn. 'Are you missing anyone?'

Outside, the lifeboat returns for a third time with a cargo of rope and orange buoys to keep away the curious and the ghoulish.

Three hours and twenty minutes.

Six men from the council works department erect shuttering around the pier entrance, big frames of two-by-four covered with sheets of chipboard.

In the hospital most of the broken bones have been set and the girl with the shattered femur is having it pinned in surgery. A woman has had a splinter the size of a carving knife pulled from her chest.

Evening comes. The front is unnaturally empty. No one wants to look at the pier any more. They are elsewhere eating scampi and baked Alaska, watching *The Railway Children* at the Coronet, or driving to neighbouring resorts for evening walks against a view that can be comfortably ignored. In spite of which the conversation keeps circling back, because at sometime this week everyone has stood in a spot which is now empty air. Everyone can feel the thrilling shiver of the Reaper passing close, dampened rapidly by the thought of those poor people. But was it a bomb? Was there a man on the front with a radio control and a trip switch? Had they perhaps sat next to him?

Nine people remain buried under wreckage. The authorities know about eight of these. The ninth is a girl of fifteen who ran away from her home in Stockport six months ago. Her parents will never connect her to the event in the newspaper and will spend the rest of their lives waiting for her to come home.

The orphaned boy and the girl are driven to the house of a couple who foster for the local social services until their grandparents arrive tomorrow. The boy still believes his parents are living in France.

The reunited families have gone. The hall is almost empty now. The only people who remain are those waiting for family members who will never come.

None of the survivors sleep well. They wake from dreams in which the floor beneath them vanishes. They wake from dreams of being trapped inside a cat's cradle of iron and wood as the tide rises.

2 a.m. Clear skies. The whole town so precise and blue that you could lean down and pick up that moored yacht between your thumb and forefinger. Only the surf moving and a single drunk shouting at the sea. The gaudy lights along the front have been turned off as a mark of respect, leaving a scattering of yellow windows and the hotel names in green and red neon. Excelsior, Camden, Royal.

3 a.m. Mars just visible above the Downs and a choppy stripe of moon across the sea. There is a dull boom as the far end of the pier's landward half drops and twists like a monster shifting in its sleep.

The TV crews arrive at 5 a.m. They set up camp on the prom and outside the police station, smoking and telling jokes and drinking sugary coffee from Thermos flasks.

Dawn comes and for a brief period the wrecked pier is beautiful, but the epicentre of the town is already moving eastwards, down the prom towards the dolphinarium and the saltwater swimming pool. The pier is already becoming something you walk past.

People get their holiday snaps back from the chemist's. Some of the pictures contain the final images of family members who are now dead. They smile, they shade their eyes, they eat chips and hold outsize teddy bears. They have only minutes to live. In one freakish photograph a teenage boy is already falling downwards, his mouth wide open as if he were singing.

Funerals are held and the legal wrangle begins.

Paint peels, metal rusts. Gulls gather on the roundabouts and the belvederes. Bulbs shatter, colours fade. Cormorants nest on the rotten decking. In high winds the gondolas on the big wheel sway and creak. The ghost train becomes a roost for pipistrelles and greater horseshoe bats; the tangled beams and girders underwater become a home for conger eels and octopus.

Three years later a man walking his dog along the beach will find a sea-bleached skull washed up by a winter storm. It will be laid to rest with full funeral rites in a corner of the graveyard of St Bartholomew's Church under a stone inscribed with the words, 'The kingdom of heaven is like unto a net, that was cast into the sea, and gathered of every kind.'

Ten years after the disaster the pier is brought down in a series of controlled explosions and over many months the remnants are lifted laboriously by a floating crane and towed to a marine breakers in Southampton. No other human remains are found.

ENVOI

HELEN DUNMORE

North Sea Crossing

Carl wakes at six. There are shadows on the ceiling, bright sloppings of sea. Or do you call it a ceiling, when it's a boat? He lies tight under the quilt and watches the room heave. His throat aches, but he knows it's not seasickness.

'You can't be seasick. I've never known it so calm.'

The boat gives a lunge like a selfish sleeper turning over in bed, dragging the quilt with it. His father is buried in the opposite bunk. He never twitches or snores. Once Carl talked about a dream he'd had, and his father said, 'I never dream.' The second his father wakes he starts doing things.

On one elbow, leaning, twisting, Carl watches the water. It's navy, like school uniform, with foam frisking about on top of the slabs of sea. Even through the oblong misted window the sea is much bigger than the boat. He'll get up. He'll go and explore. He'll walk right round the decks and come back knowing more about the boat than his father.

'Hey Dad,' he'll say, 'guess what I saw up on deck!' and then his father's waking face will crease into a smile of approval.

No. Much better to go out, come back, say nothing. Later, maybe, if his father asks, he could say, 'Oh, I thought I'd have a look up on deck.' That way it won't be like running to him saying, 'Look at me! Look what I've been doing.' His father doesn't like that.

'Just do it, Carl. Don't tell the world about it.'

Remember when he'd thought it was a good idea to go out and chop logs. He'd haul in a basket of clean-cut logs, all the same size, enough to keep the fire going for two days. *'Did you do those, Carl?'* 'Yes, Dad. Thought we were getting low.' *'Good. Well done.'* But the wood was damp and

395

slippery. When Carl brought down the axe it skidded on the bark and the lump of wood bounced away off the chopping block. And then his father was suddenly there, watching.

'What the hell are you supposed to be doing?'

'I'm chopping some logs, Dad – I just thought –'

'That wood's green. It won't be ready to burn for another year.'

Carl saw his father looking at the mangled wood. 'Next time, ask,' he said.

A small thought wriggles across the ceiling where the sea patterns had played. Why won't his father have central heating like everyone else? Like Mum? No, it has to be a real fire. *Warm soup swilling round metal pipes – who wants that when they could have a real fire.'* The quilt has slipped off his feet. They're long and bony and they look as if they belong to someone else. The feet Carl used to have don't exist any more. Someone has taken away their firm, compact shape. Now he trips over things and stubs his toes. Last night he hit his big toe so hard against the step to the cabin bathroom that he thought it was broken. He sat on the bunk, nursing it. His toe was red and there was a lump on it that hadn't been there before. The kind of lump a broken bone makes, poking out. If he sucked it . . . He leaned forward, screwed his face round and hoisted up his knee, but he couldn't get his foot in his mouth any more. And it used to be so nice doing that, sending little shivers up the sole of his foot into his spine as he sucked and licked. What if he twisted round a bit more and braced his back against the end of the bunk . . . And there he was, knotted, when Dad came back to the cabin. He didn't say anything, just looked while Carl untangled himself like a badly tied shoelace.

There's no more sun on the ceiling. Everything has turned grey, and the sea is quieter, but as close at the window as a bully calling round after school. Its folds look greasy. It's settling down just like Dad said it would. Carl swings his legs and feels for the floor, which thrusts up at his feet like someone pretending to punch you and then pulling back: *'You really thought I was going to hit you, didn't you? You were scared!'*

Anyway, he'll be first washed and dressed. The shower is quite nice, then its trickle of water suddenly burns and makes Carl yelp. But it's all right. Dad can't have heard through the door. Carl comes out, hair slicked back, teeth immaculate. Dad can't stand mossy teeth. Now a thick whiteness is flattening the water. Fog. A second later the boat gives a long scared *Mooo*. 'Fog,' says Carl to himself. 'Fog at sea.' He looks round at the neatness of the cabin. Everything is stacked and folded; even his father is folded away under the quilt, sleeping so well you wouldn't guess he was breathing. 'It's just like being in a ship's cabin,' thinks Carl, delighted. He loves things to be exactly as they should be, no more and no less. But his father has woken up. It wasn't me, it was the foghorn, thinks Carl. He finds he is saying it aloud.

'I know a foghorn when I hear one,' says his father. Then he is out of bed, standing naked at the window. He always sleeps naked. Carl watches the shadow of his father's genitals as he stands there, legs braced, staring knowledgeably into the fog. He reaches round a hand to scratch his buttock. His arms are long. In a minute he'll turn round. Carl looks down. He fusses with the pillow, buffing it up, but as he does so he catches the snake of his father's backward glance.

'What are you doing that for? Can't you leave things alone?' This time his father doesn't say it, but by now the words say themselves anyway, inside Carl's head.

His father wears a watch on his naked body. Now he looks at it.

'They start serving breakfast in quarter of an hour. Stoke up and it'll keep you going. You can eat as much as you want – it's all in the price.'

Carl has read the breakfast list outside the restaurant. Eggs, cheese, ham, bacon, cereals, toast, rolls, jams, marmalade, as many refills of coffee and tea as you want. 'It's a real bargain,' said the woman reading it beside him. 'But only worth it if you eat a big breakfast.' Then she smiled at him. 'I'm sure that won't be a problem.' Why can't they go to the cafeteria? There you can buy a mini box of cornflakes and a giant Coke. In the restaurant he'll have to eat and eat until he feels sick to make it worth the money.

'What's the matter? Feeling queasy?'

There are tufts of hair coming out of his father's belly. Carl doesn't want to have to look at his father's penis, but he can't help it. He just can't look anywhere else. His father's penis is so big and dark and it's the same colour as a bruise. And it stirs. Perhaps it's the movement of the boat.

'No,' says Carl, 'I'm not seasick at all.' But he says it wrong. It comes out as a boast.

'I should bloody well hope not. That sea's as flat as a cow's backside. But visibility's going down,' his father adds critically, professionally, glancing back over his shoulder at the sea as if he owns it.

They walk up the staircase to the restaurant. All that is left of the boat's rocking is a long oily sway from side to side. Carl feels tired inside his head. There are plenty of people about, playing video games and slotting coins into snack machines, but nobody talks much. The fog presses down on them all. In the restaurant his father pays for two breakfasts and it costs nearly ten pounds. Carl starts to work out how much breakfast they must eat to justify the ten pounds. As they go past a table a baby is suddenly, silently sick, pumping out a current of red jam and wet wads of bread. Both parents lean forward at once and drop tissues over the vomit. The father takes another tissue and wipes strings of vomit from round the baby's mouth. The baby cries weakly and the father says something, stands, scoops him out of his high-chair and carries him off, held close against his chest.

'Have bacon and eggs,' says Carl's father as Carl puts rice krispies, an orange and an apple on his tray.

'I'm going to come back again,' says Carl quickly. He pours orange juice in a long stream from the dispenser into a half-litre glass.

'You don't need all that,' says his father.

They take seats by the window, looking out at nothing. The noise of the engines is swollen by the fog, as if the boat is sailing inside a box. Carl pours the milk over his rice krispies and raises his spoon to his mouth. His father loads a fork with strips of bacon and cut-up egg. Carl's stomach clenches. His spoon hangs in mid-air, doing nothing. His father stabs the forkful of bacon and egg towards Carl, but at that moment there is a soft 'thuck', a slight, infinitely dangerous noise which silences the restaurant. Its echo is louder than the echo of the huge engines. People look at one another, then quickly away. Carl notices a shiver run down the pale orange curtains. His spoon hangs, his father's fork stays poised in its stab. The boat swings forward like a man gathering himself on a high diving-board. Carl feels his heart tip inside him, a huge tip which will overbalance him and leave him helpless on the floor at his father's feet. Or is it the boat tipping? Someone is putting on the brakes, much too hard. Carl's orange juice glass goes *hop hip hop* along the table, reaches the edge where there is a ridge to stop things sliding, and then falls on to the floor.

'It's all right,' says Carl to himself, 'it doesn't matter. You can go back and have as much as you want once you've paid.'

But his father isn't even looking at the orange juice. He is staring out of the window, listening.

'They've put the engines into reverse,' he says, but not to Carl. A man looks over from the next table. Carl's father is a man people turn to. He always knows what's going on. A small flush of pride warms Carl. 'Into reverse,' he thinks, 'into reverse.' The boat pushes against itself, back-pedalling. Long lumpy shivers run through it, bump bump bump as if it is riding over a cattle-grid.

'Let's get up on deck,' says his father. But there's all this breakfast on the table. Eggs, bacon, rolls, little sealed packets of cheese. His father's coffee has slopped right over the top of his cup and run away in a thin brown stream over the table. Often Carl has thought that his father could pee black pee out of his big bruised penis.

'Carl,' says his father, not angrily. He is right by the boy, standing over the chair where Carl just sits and watches the stream of coffee. He puts his hands on Carl's upper arms. He could easily lift him but he doesn't. His hands tell Carl what he has to do, and Carl rises and leaves the table without giving the breakfast another thought. Everybody else remains at their tables, their eyes following Carl and his father, and at that moment the ship's loud-speaker system begins to honk in a language Carl doesn't understand.

'We've had a collision,' says his father.

Carl looks up at him without speaking.

'It's all right. We'll find out what's happening.'

Behind them people are beginning to struggle up, fumbling for bags and children. There is a lady with baby twins. Carl was watching her last night. Now she staggers as she tucks one twin under her arm and wrestles the second out of his car seat.

'Dad –' begins Carl, but suddenly they're moving fast, out of the restaurant and nearly at the second staircase which leads up to the deck. People are crowding up the steps. They're not really pushing but Carl thinks that if he stopped they would keep walking over him. But his father is ahead of him and his body is wider than Carl's making way.

'Hold on to my jacket,' says his father, and Carl gets hold of it with both hands. People dig into him on both sides but he keeps moving, carried up the narrow stairs holding on to his father's jacket. No one would be able to walk over his father. The heavy doors to the deck have been wedged back and they squeeze through, grabbing at the white space beyond.

They are up on deck. An edgy mass of people flows to the rails, but there is nothing to be seen. Only fog, licking right up to the edge of the boat. None of the people round him are speaking English. More sound spurts out of the speakers, but it is twisted up like bad handwriting and Carl can't understand a word.

'It's OK,' says Carl's father. 'We ran down a yacht in the fog. They've put a boat out from the other side.'

The crowd ripples as the news passes over it. It's all right. No danger to passengers. We've stopped to pick up the crew, that's all. And the hot panicky feeling rolls away into the fog. The lady with her twins is up on deck, and now people are eager to help her. Another lady holds out her hands to take one of the babies, hoists him into her arms and joggles him to make him smile. People find they have still got bits of breakfast in their hands, and those who have picked up life-jackets let them dangle as if they're of no importance at all.

'Run down a yacht,' thinks Carl. 'Splintered to matchwood.'

The big ferry thrums and rocks on its own weight.

'How will they find them in the fog?' he asks his father.

'They'll have flares. Let's go to the other side.'

Is the fog clearing? It is whiter than ever, and it hurts Carl's eyes. Maybe that's the sun behind it, trying to break out. There is a sharp smell of sea and oil. Announcements come jerkily, in the same voice they used to announce breakfast and the bingo session last night. It's very cold, and to Carl's amazement quite a few people are going down below, rubbing their arms, making way for one another.

'You first.'

'No, please, after you.'

A man comes up with his camcorder. Its blunt nose butts around in the fog and finds nothing.

His father leans on the rail, looking down. The rail is wet with spray or fog, and it makes a dark bar on his father's jacket. He's looking down-ward and backward, behind the ship. The speakers sound again.

'They've picked up the dinghy,' says Carl's father.

It all takes so long. Carl is cold and shivering and he can't see much because a wall of adults has crowded to the rail. Suddenly his father says sharply, 'There they are!' He is leaning out over the rail, grasped by two men. A pair of binoculars is handed to him over the heads of the crowd. People shove against Carl from all sides. He can't see anything at all.

'They're bringing the boat alongside,' he hears his father say. 'There's the dinghy.'

His father is the leader. Everyone is asking questions.

'Are they all right?'

'How many are there – can you see?'

And a woman beside him says, 'At least they had time to launch the dinghy. Must've been terrifying. Imagine being hit by this thing.'

Then his father's voice. 'There's two of them. A man and a boy.' Carl hears the charge in his voice. A man and a boy. What sort of boy?

'They're alongside. They'll be bringing them up. Can't see any more from this angle.'

The pressure of the crowd relaxes. Carl wriggles through to his father, who is down from the rail and talking to another Englishman.

'– any more of them?'

'– sailing alone with the boy . . .'

'– bloody awful thing to lose your boat like that –'

Carl stands and watches and listens. A man and a boy, sailing alone in the North Sea. The big ferry like a clumsy cliff bulging out of the fog to sink their boat. He tries to catch his father's eye. He tries a joke. 'Well, at least it wasn't the bow doors! We were lucky.' But his father looks at him.

'*We* weren't in any danger,' he points out coldly.

Not like that other boy. His father's criticism hangs in the air. His father had the binoculars. He'd have seen the boy's face. And the man's, too.

The fog is clearing now. Suddenly, when Carl looks, holes open in it and he can see right along the grey water. It's very calm. He can't help saying, 'It wasn't rough, anyway,' but his father has an answer for that, too.

'That's why it happened. If there'd been a wind it would have blown the fog away. They'd have seen our lights.'

But by lunchtime the whole thing might as well never have happened. They'll be in port in three hours' time. The cafeteria and restaurant are crowded and there is a pub quiz in the Marco Polo bar. Carl has been playing the video games at the bottom of the second staircase. He's done really well on *Rally Rider*. But it's so expensive and there's no one to turn to and say, 'Hey, did you see that? Level fourteen!' His father can't stand video games.

'I might have known you'd be here,' says his father's voice just as Carl gets farther than he has ever got before. 'Come on, we're going to eat.'

They find a table. 'Wait here while I pay for our tickets,' says his father. You have to buy a ticket and then you can eat as much as you want from the buffet. People go past with their trays loaded. There are two empty chairs opposite, and he must keep that one for his father. His father has touched it, indicating that it is his. But then a man puts his hand on Carl's father's chair. He is a big, stooping man with a worried face. Carl blushes and says, 'I'm sorry. My father is sitting there,' but the man just smiles and pulls out the chair, then beckons to someone else. Carl looks. It's a boy, a thin, fair-haired boy about his age. His hair is so pale it's nearly the colour of the salt spilt on the table. The man smiles again at Carl as he sits down, while the boy pushes his way politely down the rows of other people's chairs, and squeezes into his place. The father pats the boy's arm as he sits down. They both have meal tickets but they don't seem to know what to do with them. They talk briefly, seriously, heads close together.

Suddenly, Carl sees that the boy is crying, without sound, pushing big tears away from his eyes with his fingers. His father talks to him all the time in a murmuring, up and down voice, as if he doesn't mind, as if the tears are something he had expected. They're sitting close together anyway, but then the father puts his arm around the boy. Carl ducks his head down and flushes. What if his father sees? What if his father says something in that voice of his that can cut worse than a knife? Even if the boy doesn't understand he'll recognize the tone of voice. And his father is coming back, weaving his way across the room with a full tray in his hand, not holding on to anything because he's got a perfect sense of balance and the sea is as flat as a cow's backside. Carl darts a miserably apologetic smile at his father.

'I'm sorry,' he says, as soon as his father is close enough to hear, 'I couldn't keep your place –'

'No, of course not,' says his father. Carl stares, but can't hear any sarcasm, can't see any cold disgust on his father's face. 'Come on, there are some more seats over here,' continues his father, and leads the way to a nearby table where a family has just got up from its meal. There's rubbish all over the table. Normally his father would hate it, but he doesn't seem to mind.

'Did you talk to them?' he asks Carl, with a little backward nod of his head towards the table Carl has just left.

'No, I – they weren't speaking English.'

'Norwegians,' says his father confidently. 'But I don't suppose they were in the mood for conversation.'

Carl stares at his father, bewildered. Then there is a click in his mind like something loading on to a computer screen.

'Oh,' he breathes, 'it's *them*.'

'Yes, of course. What did you think?'

'I don't know, I –'

'I just hope the ferry company's given them a free lunch, that's all,' says his father.

'But it might not have been – I mean, we don't know whose fault it was,' says Carl.

'Sail takes priority over steam,' says his father, stubbing Carl out. But something's got into Carl. He opens his mouth again.

'That boy,' he says, 'that boy was crying.'

He follows his father's glance at the man, the boy. They are sitting still, close together, weary, their meal tickets crumpled on the table in front of them. Then the man reaches forward and touches, very lightly, his son's hand.

'Reaction,' says Carl's father, 'a perfectly natural reaction once danger's over. They were sailing back from England – managing perfectly well till our bloody ferry went across their bows.'

Across their bows, thinks Carl. What does it mean? He feels his shoulders bow down too, crushed by the phrase, by the cliff of what his father knows and he does not. The engine of his father's scorn churns and cuts into him. Then a small, treacherous thought slips into Carl's mind. He looks across at the father and son at the other table. He's seen something his father hasn't seen. The boy's sliding tears, the father's face bent down to his. That language the man was murmuring. Carl's father speaks a bit of Norwegian, like he speaks a bit of everything. But does he really know what it means, that language the Norwegian father spoke to his son?

Author Biographies

A. L. Kennedy was born in Dundee in 1965. She is the author of seventeen books, including *Indelible Acts*, *Day* and *Serious Sweet*.

Tessa Hadley was born in Bristol in 1956. She is the author of eight books, including *Accidents in the Home*, *Married Love* and *Bad Dreams and Other Stories*.

Kazuo Ishiguro was born in Nagasaki, Japan in 1954. He is the author of eight books, including *The Remains of the Day*, *Never Let Me Go* and *An Artist of the Floating World*.

Jackie Kay was born in Edinburgh in 1961. She is the author of thirteen books, including *The Adoption Papers*, *Trumpet* and *Red Dust Road*.

Graham Swift was born in London in 1949. He is the author of thirteen books, including *Shuttlecock*, *Last Orders* and *Wish You Were Here*.

Jane Gardam was born in Coatham, North Yorkshire, in 1928. She is the author of fifteen books, including *God on the Rocks*, *Going Into a Dark House* and *Last Friends*.

Ali Smith was born in Inverness in 1962. She is the author of fourteen books, including *The Accidental*, *How to Be Both* and *Autumn*.

Neil Gaiman was born in Hampshire in 1960. He is the author of forty-one books, including *American Gods*, *Coraline* and *Norse Mythology*.

Martin Amis was born in Oxford in 1949. He is the author of twenty-five books, including *London Fields*, *Time's Arrow* and *Yellow Dog*.

China Miéville was born in Norwich in 1972. He is the author of fifteen books, including *King Rat*, the *Bas-Lag* series and *Looking for Jake and Other Stories*.

Peter Hobbs was born in 1973 and grew up in Cornwall and Yorkshire. He is the author of three books, *The Short Day Dying*, *I Could Ride All Day in My Cool Blue Train* and *In the Orchard, the Swallows*.

Thomas Morris was born in Caerphilly in 1985. He is the author of *We Don't Know What We're Doing*.

David Rose was born in 1949. He is the author of two books, *Vault* and *Posthumous Stories*.

David Szalay was born in Montreal, Quebec, in 1974. He is the author of four books, including *London and the South East*, *Spring* and *All That Man Is*.

Irvine Welsh was born in Edinburgh in 1957. He is the author of fifteen books, including *Trainspotting*, *Filth* and *Porno*.

Lucy Caldwell was born in Belfast in 1981. She is the author of four books, including *Multitudes*.

Rose Tremain was born in London in 1943. She is the author of several books, including *Restoration*, *The Road Home* and *Trespass*.

Helen Oyeyemi was born in Nigeria in 1984. She is the author of several books, including *The Icarus Girl* and *Boy, Snow, Bird*.

Leone Ross was born in Coventry in 1969. She is the author of three books, *All The Blood Is Red*, *Orange Laughter* and *Come Let Us Sing Anyway*.

Helen Simpson was born in Bristol in 1957. She is the author of six books, including *Four Bare Legs in a Bed and Other Stories*, *Constitutional* and *Cockfosters*.

Zadie Smith was born in London in 1975. She is the author of several books, including *White Teeth*, *NW* and *Swing Time*.

Will Self was born in London in 1961. He is the author of twenty-three books, including *The Book of Dave*, *Umbrella* and *Phone*.

Gerard Woodward was born in London in 1961. He is the author of several books, including *August*, *I'll Go to Bed at Noon* and *Nourishment*.

James Kelman was born in Glasgow in 1946. He is the author of several books, including *A Disaffection*, *How Late It Was, How Late* and *Kieron Smith, Boy*.

Lucy Wood was born in Cornwall in 1986. She is the author of *Diving Belles*, *Weathering* and *The Sing of the Shore*.

Hilary Mantel was born in Glossop, Derbyshire, in 1952. She is the author of thirteen books, including *A Place of Greater Safety*, *Wolf Hall* and *Bring Up the Bodies*.

Eley Williams is an author and lecturer. She is the author of *Attrib. and Other Stories*.

Sarah Hall was born in Carlisle in 1974. She is the author of seven books, including *How to Paint a Dead Man, The Beautiful Indifference* and *Madame Zero.*

Mark Haddon was born in Northampton in 1962. He is the author of several books, including *The Curious Incident of the Dog in the Night-Time, A Spot of Bother* and *The Pier Falls and Other Stories.*

Helen Dunmore was born in Beverley, Yorkshire, in 1952 and died in 2017. She was the author of twelve novels, three short story collections, eleven collections of poetry and numerous books for young adults and children, including *A Spell of Winter, Bestiary* and *The Betrayal.*

Acknowledgements

'Spared' from *Indelible Acts* by A. L. Kennedy. Published by Jonathan Cape, 2002. Copyright © A. L. Kennedy. Reproduced by permission of Antony Harwood Ltd Literary Agency, 103 Walton Street, Oxford OX2 6EB.

'Funny Little Snake' by Tessa Hadley. Published by *The New Yorker*, 2017. Copyright © Tessa Hadley. Reproduced by permission of the author c/o United Agents.

'Come Rain or Come Shine' from *Nocturnes* by Kazuo Ishiguro. Published by Faber, 2009. Copyright © Kazuo Ishiguro. Reproduced by permission of the author c/o Rogers, Coleridge & White Ltd, 20 Powis Mews, London W11 1JN.

'Physics and Chemistry' from *Why Don't You Stop Talking* by Jackie Kay. Published by Pan Macmillan, 2002. Copyright © Jackie Kay. Reproduced with permission of Pan Macmillan through PLSclear.

'Remember This' from *England and Other Stories* by Graham Swift. Published by Simon & Schuster, 2014. Copyright © Graham Swift. Reproduced by permission of Simon & Schuster.

'Dangers' from *The People on Privilege Hill* by Jane Gardam. Published by Abacus, 2007. Copyright © Jane Gardam. Reproduced by permission of David Higham Associates, Waverley House, 7–12 Noel St, London W1F 8GQ.

'The Universal Story' from *The Whole Story and Other Stories* by Ali Smith. Published by Anchor Books, 2003. Copyright © Ali Smith. Reproduced by permission of Wylie Agency.

'Troll Bridge' copyright © 1993 by Neil Gaiman. Reprinted by permission of Writers House LLC acting as agent for the author.

'The Unknown Known' by Martin Amis from *Granta 100*. Published by *Granta* magazine, 2007. Copyright © Martin Amis. Reproduced by permission of Wylie Agency.

'Entry Taken from a Medical Encyclopaedia' from *Looking for Jake and*

Acknowledgements

Other Stories by China Miéville. Published by Pan Macmillan, 2005. Reproduced with permission of Pan Macmillan through PLSclear.

'Winter Luxury Pie' from *I Could Ride All Day in My Cool Blue Train* by Peter Hobbs. Published by Faber, 2008. Copyright © Peter Hobbs. Reproduced by permission of the author c/o Rogers, Coleridge & White Ltd, 20 Powis Mews, London w11 1jn.

'All the Boys' from *We Don't Know What We're Doing* by Thomas Morris © 2015. Published by Faber and Faber Ltd. Reproduced by permission of Faber and Faber Ltd.

'A Nice Bucket' from *Posthumous Stories* by David Rose. Published by Salt Publishing, 2013. Copyright © David Rose. Reproduced with permission of Salt Publishing through PLSclear.

Chapter 2 from *All That Man Is* by David Szalay © 2016. Published by Jonathan Cape. Reprinted by permission of The Random House Group Limited.

'Catholic Guilt (You Know You Love It)' from *Reheated Cabbage* by Irvine Welsh © 2009. Published by Jonathan Cape. Reprinted with permission of The Random House Group Limited.

'Poison' from *Multitudes* by Lucy Caldwell © 2016. Published by Faber and Faber Ltd. Reproduced by permission of Faber and Faber Ltd.

'The Closing Door' from *The American Lover and Other Stories* by Rose Tremain © 2011. Reprinted with permission of The Random House Group Limited.

'if a book is locked there's probably a good reason for that, don't you think' from *What Is Not Yours Is Not Yours* by Helen Oyeyemi. Published by Pan Macmillan, 2016. Copyright © Helen Oyeyemi. Reproduced with permission of Pan Macmillan through PLSclear.

'The Woman Who Lived in a Restaurant' from *Come Let Us Sing Anyway* by Leone Ross. Published by Jonathan Cape, 2005. Copyright © Leone Ross. Reproduced with permission of the author c/o Curtis Brown.

'Every Third Thought' from *Constitutional* by Helen Simpson © 2005. Published by Jonathan Cape. Reprinted by permission of The Random House Group Limited.

'Moonlit Landscape with Bridge' by Zadie Smith. Published by *The New Yorker*, 2014. Copyright © Zadie Smith. Reproduced by permission of the author c/o Rogers, Coleridge & White Ltd, 20 Powis Mews, London w11 1jn.

Acknowledgements

'The Rock of Crack as Big as the Ritz' from *Tough, Tough Toys for Tough, Tough Boys* by Will Self. Published by Bloomsbury Publishing Plc, 1998. Copyright © Will Self. Reproduced by permission of Bloomsbury Publishing Plc, 31 Bedford Avenune, London WC1B 3AT.

'The Fall of Mr and Mrs Nicholson' from *Legoland* by Gerard Woodward. Published by Picador, Pan Macmillan, 2016. Copyright © Gerard Woodward. Reproduced by permission of the author c/o Rogers, Coleridge & White Ltd, 20 Powis Mews, London W11 1JN.

'justice for one' from *If it is your life* by James Kelman. Published by Hamish Hamilton, 2010. Copyright © James Kelman. Reproduced by permission of the author c/o Rogers, Coleridge & White Ltd, 20 Powis Mews, London W11 1JN.

'Flotsam, Jetsam, Lagan, Derelict' from *The Sing of the Shore* by Lucy Wood. Published by Fourth Estate, 2018. Reprinted by permission of HarperCollins Publishers Ltd © 2018 Lucy Wood.

'The Clean Slate' from *Learning to Talk* by Hilary Mantel. Published by Fourth Estate, 2003. Reprinted by permission of HarperCollins Publishers Ltd © 2003 Hilary Mantel.

'Fears and Confessions of an Ortolan Chef' from *Attrib. and Other Stories* by Eley Williams. Published by Influx Press, 2017. Copyright © Eley Williams. Reproduced by permission of the author c/o C+W, 5th Floor, Haymarket House, 28–29 Haymarket, London, SW1Y 4SP.

'Later, His Ghost' from *Madame Zero* by Sarah Hall. Published by Faber, 2017. Copyright © Sarah Hall. Reproduced by permission of Faber and Faber Ltd.

'The Pier Falls' From *The Pier Falls and Other Stories* by Mark Haddon © 2016. Published by Jonathan Cape. Reprinted by permission of The Random House Group Limited.

'North Sea Crossing' from *Love of Fat Men* by Helen Dunmore. Published by Viking, 1997. Reprinted by permission of the Helen Dunmore Estate and The Random House Group Limited.